To Sue
Aug 2006
— with love + best wishes
Michael Knell

CW01432169

Publish and be damned
www.pabd.com

The Elephant's Nest

Michael Knell

Publish and be damned
www.pabd.com

© Michael Knell
This book is sold subject to the condition that it shall not, by way of trade
or otherwise, be lent, resold, hired out, or otherwise circulated without the
publisher's prior consent in any form of binding or cover other than that in
which it was published and without a similar condition including this condition
being imposed on the subsequent publisher.

First published in Canada 2006 by Michael Knell.
The moral right of Michael Knell to be identified as the author of this work has
been asserted.

Designed in Toronto, Canada by Adlibbed.
Printed and bound by Lightningsource in the US or the UK.

This novel is a work of fiction and the characters and events in it exist only in
its pages and in the imagination of the author.

ISBN:1-897312-17-2

Publish and be Damned helps writers publish their books.
Ourservice uses a series of automated tools to design and print
your book on-demand, eliminating the need for large print runs and
inventory costs. Now, there's nothing stopping you getting your book
into print quickly and easily.

**For more information or to visit our book store please visit us at
www.pabd.com**

CHAPTER 1

At number forty-seven Bridlington Street the age-riddled Emma Robson was tearfully worried. The long-time widow of a local mariner tragically lost at sea, she was one of the few people left in Seathorpe who knew the true history of the town - one of the few who had stayed behind when all the others had left in those terrible poverty stricken days. Many times during that hot June night of ninety-five memories of those days gone by flooded back into her mind, and she wept.

It wasn't that the memories were terrible – no, time had healed all that – they were fond memories now. They were of times when she was younger, when she knew people, knew everybody, and when despite all she was happy. Then, she wasn't alone.

Unable to sleep, torn with worry, she sat anxiously with the light off leaning forwards in the old-fashioned rickety cottage chair by the bedroom window, peering out into the darkness. Waiting.

She was desperately waiting for daybreak to arrive. Wishing and praying for those first dagger-like fingers of the morning-light to steal over the hills and probe into the darkness. For those pointing, welcome tentacles to slash great chasms of a new life, of a new day born, into that wicked black void and make the evil darkness quickly retreat, as it knew it always had to – but only to return the following evening to yet again challenge the tiring daylight.

Emma waited impatiently for that first light to come, for the time when she could safely venture outside to search for Bobby, her nineteen-year-old tom cat who hadn't returned home that night. It was sad, but Bobby was all she had left in the world now. To her he was much more than a cat. He had become her life, her only reason for being, for existing at all, and tonight, for the first time in memory, he was missing – not there. It was not like Bobby to stay out all night. He never stayed out at night. He was far too old for the kind of thing that kept toms out all night. Besides, he didn't have the bits – hadn't for years!

However all the bits were present, and in good working order, only two doors away in the small back bedroom of number fifty-one. There the hormone-explosive fourteen-year-old lad, Steven Topps, whose parents had gone away for a whole week and left him alone to look after the house, had just scored for the first time in his life. So, it wasn't with the girl of his dreams, he was forced to concede. It was with Glory-hole Gloria, one of the town's bikes - but hey, that didn't matter. It was mind-blowing. It was everything that he had ever thought and hoped it would be - and more. Much more.

Hardly pausing to catch his breath, ignoring the pleas of the straining bedsprings and the repetitive banging produced by the headboard that was laboriously digging a hole in the plaster wall, Steven was going for number two, and he wondered just how many more times he could manage it that night. A lot more, he was sure of that! Breaking his drunken concentration momentarily as his eyes fell on the two empty bottles strewn on the floor next to the bed, he giggled stupidly and lost his momentum – but not to worry, he thought, giggling some more as he looked back into the brown saucer eyes of his equally drunk but grateful receptor - he could catch up. Lunging hard into her again, she squealed, as she had so many times that night - and as only a professional well-oiled bike knows how. But Steven enjoyed it – to him it was like an accelerator.

Gloria giggled back up at him. It was just a giggle - he didn't have to know what it was for, she thought, remembering how earlier, by going straight to the cupboard where the drink was hidden, she had nearly given the game away. She had secretly been in that house many times before, but not without good reward, and she knew Steven wouldn't be happy were he to ever discover her sordid little secret. She giggled again, but this time it was more in appreciation of him. Even with all his rugged inexperience, she considered, Steven was far better in bed than his father, and already he was certainly much more of a man. She wished she could tell him that – but no, she knew she couldn't. But one day, perhaps, one day.

Like Emma, Steven too held a wish that night, and his too was a desperate one - most desperate. He wished that morning would never come - that this memorable night for him, this night for which he had waited so long, and had ached for so many times, would never end. Oh, how he dearly wished that it could last forever and that this could be his eternity.

'Oh, God! Oh, yes!' Gloria screamed, her fingernails frantically digging into the back of his neck; clawing at him.

'Oh, I'm coming, I'm coming!' Steven shouted wildly at her, with his hands frantically clenching her buttocks as he attempted to pull his whole body up inside her.

She squealed and pulled his head down hard towards hers, her mouth enveloping his as she pulled him in tighter and tighter against her, squashing his face into hers until he couldn't breath; her tongue madly exploring his mouth, feeling his teeth, dancing with his tongue until she felt him explode inside her, and then tremble as the orgasm ripped throughout his entire body.

Now, in between these two domains of obtuse emotions and desperate wishes, way down in the drab cellar of number forty-nine, the middle-aged man who was securely tied to an old-fashioned wooden dining chair in the centre of the room, Mark Patterson, was not wishing for anything. He knew there was little point in him wishing. He was already aware that morning would not be coming, and nothing would be going on much longer – well, not for him, anyway!

'You bastard! You utter fucking bastard!' bellowed the mean-looking, hook-nosed man as he launched once more into Mark's bloody, already well-pummelled nose.

'Please, Phil! Oh, come on, please!' Mark pleaded back, looking out at his aggressor through a growing red mist. 'I tell you, I haven't been cheating you! I promise you I haven't. I wouldn't rip you off. You ought to know I wouldn't. Do you think I'm that stupid? I'm not that stupid - you ought to know that by now, Phil. You must know I wouldn't do something like that to you. Come on now, we need to talk this over sensibly. It's all a big mistake. It's nothing more than a misunderstanding. It is, really it is – I promise you. Please Phil, let's see if we can work this out.'

The man was frantically and unashamedly pleading for his life, even though deep down inside of him an acceptance that his efforts were being wasted on Phil was already well-rooted. He knew; he was totally convinced that it was hopeless - but pleading was all he had left. It was all he could think of doing. What else was there? Nothing short of a miracle could save him now, he was sure of that. And he was equally as sure that miracles didn't happen that often in Seathorpe - there had certainly been none that he could remember.

Mark had seen Phil like this before, many, many times. He was fully acquainted with all the villain's evil ways, so there was no doubt in his mind, none at all, as to what was going to happen to him that night. Maybe he didn't yet know the exact means of dispatch that would be employed - but he knew what the end result would be, and he tried hard not to think of it.

Summoning up all the force he could muster, Phil answered the man's pitiful pleas with yet another resounding swipe to the bloodied face. 'Don't you Phil me, you bastard! It's Mister Blunt to you from now on, arsehole,' he shouted down at him, 'If it wasn't you, then who the fuck was it then? Who? There ain't no other fucker it could've been! There ain't, is there?'

Mark's head fell forward onto his chest as consciousness drifted away from him. Two front teeth slowly emerged from his half-open mouth, at first sliding slowly down the red mucous covering his chin, and then falling to land amidst the mass of bloody saliva that had already drooled down forming an ever-expanding pool of red from his chest to his stomach, forever desecrating the grey Savile Row suit and ruining the hundred pound shirt purchased only the previous day. But any such fine detail was of little consequence to the doomed man. He would have no use for either of them again.

With no further pleasure to be gained from beating the unconscious man, Phil turned and grabbed the nearly full bottle of whiskey from off the crowded, large, old fashioned desk beside him. Only later, when his temper had subsided, would he realise that it was one of his more expensive ones – a Knappogue Castle 1951 Vintage bottle from the now dearly missed B. Daly distillery where Tullamore Dew was once produced. It was certainly not the kind of stuff he would knowingly waste on an impending corpse. But, at that time, Phil was not in a knowing state. Thrusting the bottle towards the man who had eagerly rushed forward to lift Mark's blood-splattered head up once more, to have it lined up ready to receive the next devastating punch, Phil first looked him in the eye, and then nodded - signalling towards the unknowing captive.

Don took the bottle of whiskey from his boss and studied it strangely for a moment, apparently wondering if, or more perhaps why he was being offered a drink at such a time. Bemused, he looked back vacantly at Phil. Vacant looks were common with Don – he rarely grasped much the first time.

'Do I really have to bloody spell it out for you? Fool! Fucking idiot! Pour the bleeding stuff down his throat! My God! I'm surrounded by bloody idiots! Nothing but bloody idiots!' Phil screamed at the man, angrily stamping his foot at the same time, whilst his face turned a shade of crimson with the exasperation. The prominent dark wriggly blue veins on either side of his brow started to swell up and were visibly throbbing, threatening to burst with each beat of his heavy pulse, and his eyes were seemingly in danger of popping clean out of their sockets. 'All of it! Jeeesus!' he yelled, with his face turning yet another two shades more colourful. 'Get it all down him! And when that lot's gone, you can shove this fucking lot in his arm! That'll sort him out! The bastard!'

Phil scowled bolts of thunder at the slumped form in the chair, spitting venomously into the unconscious man's gory face before turning back towards the desk to carefully fill a syringe with the liquid that had been slowly warming in the saucer perched above the flickering flame of a nightlight.

'Yes, Boss. All of it, Boss,' Don, responded nervously, all the time watching Phil out of the corner of his eye. Yanking the oblivious man's head fully backwards so his mouth pointed upwards, he rammed the bottle of golden nectar into the unresisting blood-filled orifice, and then waited for the gurgling of the emptying bottle to stop before daring to ask, 'What now, Boss?'

'You dance a fucking tango with him, don't you? My God! Christ Almighty! Idiot! What the fuck do you think? Stick this fucking lot in him! Find a fucking vein, and make sure it's a good one! Give him all of it!' Phil spat, handing over the full syringe. 'Then you and your brother can take the arsehole out for a drive. Take him up to the cliff top and throw the fucker off Jumper's Point! Give the bastard a flying lesson he won't forget! Huh! Won't remember, more like! Get rid of the shit, once and for all!'

'He'll certainly be flying all right with that lot inside him!' Patrick joked, looking up from the easy chair in the corner of the room where for the past thirty minutes he had been quietly engrossed in the totally unnecessary task of cleaning his M1911 Colt 45. It didn't need cleaning. It hadn't been used recently. It was spotless. But cleaning it was an excuse to hold it. An excuse to feel good.

Phil responded to the gunman's quip with an icy glare. It was enough, more than enough, to convince Patrick to shut up and to return to his maintenance task.

Don's younger brother, Paul, who of the two of them was noticeably brighter, didn't wait to be asked. He swiftly left the room by the French windows. Hurrying through the backyard, he crossed the alleyway to fetch the car that was parked directly opposite in the Inferno nightclub's car park.

Until then, all the way through Phil's smouldering anger right up to his Vesuvius-like eruptions, Paul had succeeded in looking busy by laboriously counting small cellophane packages of white powder and placing them in neat piles of ten on the coffee table beside Patrick. The young man had long since discovered his now well-worn and trusted method of avoiding the boss' wrath: always appear to be busy doing something. It didn't really matter what, so long as you *appeared* to be busy. Studying a blank sheet of paper, seemingly engrossed with some great problem it fictitiously held had previously worked for him, and on more than one occasion.

Quickly, before Phil lost his temper again, Don frantically pulled Mark's limp arm up and out of his jacket sleeve in order to search for a vein into which he could inject the dream liquid. At last finding one with a suitable prominence he slapped it hard several times, and then stabbed the needle into it forcefully. With one long slow push, he completely discharged the syringe's lethal contents into the victim's bloodstream. Suddenly, the never-to-know-consciousness-again man's head involuntarily lifted slightly, its mouth opening wide as a loud gaseous belch escaped before the shoulders below hunched forward and his back started to arch.

'Handkerchief!' Phil screamed with no undue urgency on seeing the movement. 'Oh, no! Oh, God! His handkerchief, you blithering idiot, not yours! Use the one in his top pocket, for God's sake! If he fucking brings that drink up you'll have to start all over again! And you'll clean up the bloody mess! Now, shove it in his mouth, you fucking ignoramus! Oh, Jeeesus! Talk about thick!

'Of course, you won't forget to remove it before you push him over will you, you bloody idiot? No fucker accidentally falls off a cliff with a pissin' hanky stuck in their gob, do they? So, you just make fucking sure you remember to take it out!

'Right, that sounds like your brother with the car now. Go on, get this bastard out of my sight, and hurry – it'll be getting light soon! Get rid of the shit once and for all! No one, but no one, crosses me and gets away with it, and that's something every fucker 'ad better start remembering!'

The black Volvo 850 Estate purred softly, waiting like some obedient pet in the gravel yard outside the double doors whilst Don and Paul untied the bulky limp body. Awkwardly they struggled the near-lifeless form out of the room and into the back of the vehicle where they covered it over with a tartan blanket. From his chair in the corner Patrick looked up enquiringly at Phil, as if anticipating a need.

'Yes, I suppose you'd better go along with them to make sure they get it right. Knowing those two daft buggers, they'll throw the bloody car over and come back on the fucking body,' Phil quipped, with as much sarcasm as he could manage at that time.

'Right, Boss,' the gunman acknowledged, with a look of satisfaction momentarily shooting across his face. A look that Phil would have undoubtedly questioned, had he not failed to notice it.

Packing the now meticulously clean gun securely into its shoulder holster, Patrick strode out of the room after the brothers, informing Phil over his shoulder, 'We should be back in about ten minutes or so, all being well.'

Phil grunted, and then walked over to stand at the open doors waiting to watch the car drive away. His nostrils flared wide, appreciating the clean salt-laden air of the night that was gently breezing inland through the gaps between the front-line buildings. His brow savoured the cool freshness of every waft. It was a brief, but welcome relief from the cigarette-smoke-ridden cellar where the tobacco stained ceiling, the turned ochre paintwork, and the yellowed wallpaper screamed out a deadly warning. One that went un-heeded.

He waited, watching the men patiently with a feeling of self-satisfaction

13

as they bundled into the car. Glowing with this sense of fulfilment, this feeling of having effectively solved a major problem once and for all, he considered he could now relax for a few moments. He could enjoy all the peace and tranquillity of night. He had earned it.

Paul skilfully slid the car out of the yard. First turning left to speed to the end of the alleyway before turning right towards the sea-front, the sleek vehicle headed off along the promenade and into the night to follow the coastal road - the road which, further along, would take it on up to the southern cliff tops and on to the precarious over-hang known locally as Jumper's Point.

Taking pleasure from the few stolen precious moments, a deeply satisfied man, Phil leaned backwards to rest his shoulders squarely against the doorpost. Studying the dark, barely discernable shapes of the large buildings along the front silhouetted in the moonlight, he recalled how much Seathorpe had changed in the short time he had been there.

He knew, had been told, the basic history of the place - of the fishermen who were forced to leave; departing long before he arrived. The unfortunate victims of an imposed quotas system as the result of the cod wars, some told him. Sold out by the government the fishermen themselves had actually said, despairingly packing their modest chattels and leaving their homes in search of a new life.

Deserted by its workforce, Seathorpe became run down, neglected, and almost a ghost town for a time. Only years later, with the help of a regeneration grant from the government, did it struggle to become a bit of a tourist attraction. Trying for the cream teas crowd, it did manage to tempt some of the coach companies doing the nearby Wookey Hole and Cheddar Caves trips to add it to their itineraries, and it also became a destination for a few Mystery Tours offered by several not too far away coach companies, but not many.

Mainly catering for the bored middle-aged and the elderly, the town started to enjoy some late afternoon and early evening life. However they soon found out that this type of visitor, whilst being a great viewer, was not a great spender. The townspeople discovered they could not survive on them alone, and so in nothing short of sheer desperation the local business people borrowed heavily and they updated, opening up penny-arcades and cafeterias as they went all-out to become a popular bucket and spade family type of resort.

The town spent its money and it waited. But, despite all the costly changes and the massive advertising campaigns, few people came. The entertainment venues, bars, discotheques, cafés, ice cream parlours, amusement arcades, and the seriously big fun fair were, to be kind, only sparsely populated even at the very height of the season. That is, until Phil and his henchmen arrived on the scene.

Since that momentous day, just a few short years earlier, the resort had almost miraculously changed. Now the place was packed to bursting point each season, with all the venues straining under the load. The silted-up old harbour, since being dredged and fully restored, had evolved into becoming an enviable modern marina that each year accommodated many hundreds of rich visitors' yachts and motor launches - the toys of those people who have money to spend. Real money.

Along with the rich, from early spring until late autumn youthful fun-seekers would arrive there too - in their countless tens of thousands. They came on motorcycles, in cars, lorries, vans, and campers. In fact, they came by anything that would move, anything that was likely to get them there, with all of them eager to pour copious amounts of their hard-earned cash into the resort in exchange for just a few days of unhindered happiness - a few days of what they called 'freedom'. The freedom to have fun, to party, to dance, to get drunk, to take drugs, and to enjoy lots of wild sex.

The rich visitors, and there were many of them, were happy paying over the odds to stay in one of the many guest houses or small hotels that had grown out of the rows of once neglected terraced houses hiding behind the front line, thereby giving these buildings a prosperous new lease of life. Others less fortunate, or perhaps telling you they enjoyed the lifestyle, were content to stay at the cheaper camping or caravan sites littered across the top of the steep cliffs that rose up like protecting walls on either side of the bay, or in the ones sprinkled on the woody slopes of the more gentle hills that encircled the town behind.

Phil laughed out aloud as he considered that the resort's motto, should it ever be forced to adopt one, would unquestionably need to include those immortal words: 'Sex, Drugs and Rock & Roll', although the last part of that title might need to be superseded each year by the name of the latest dance craze.

Convinced that getting rid of Mark had been the right thing to do, Phil sighed once more, a long deep sigh of satisfaction, before sauntering back into the room they affectionately called the cellar. In truth it was not a cellar at all - not in the correct sense. It was merely the lowest floor of the terraced house that boasted three stories at the rear but only two at the front where, like all the houses at that end of the resort, it had been built into the side of the hill climbing away from the coastline.

Sitting down behind the desk, Phil glanced at his watch to find it was almost three-thirty. There was still time to ring Ian - still time to tell him the good news. Picking up the handset, he quickly punched in the number for the nightclub.

'Elephant's Nest. Ian Bell, the House Manager speaking. How can I help you?' the polite answer came back straight away.

'You alone?'

'Oh, it's you, Phil. Yes, I'm alone. Why?'

'Has Bob been paid yet?'

'Yes. It's been quiet tonight so I did some of the cashing up early. I'm afraid your cut on the takings wasn't very good, Phil. A little less than £400 in fact, and I suspect Bob might only have made about the same on the drugs side - perhaps a little more if he was lucky, though I doubt it. But yes, he's been paid – he left a few minutes ago, so I guess he should be down there with you anytime soon.

'Mark hasn't arrived back yet, though. Not that he was needed. We only had about four hundred through the door all night, and then the sods weren't drinking much either! What's it been like your end tonight? How was it at the Inferno?'

'Piss poor there as well!' Phil complained. 'Only about eight hundred, I guess. We had to keep both the top bars closed off 'til gone midnight, else the bleedin' place would've looked empty. Never mind, I suppose it's not all doom and gloom. I was talking to that silly old fucker Ron from the campsite earlier today. His bookings have been down drastically this week, but judging by what he's got coming in the next few weeks we should have a bumper time to look forward to, thank God! Think I'm gonna have to get some extra stuff in by the sound of it - and perhaps put another lad down there with you to give Bob a hand.'

'No probs, Phil. Subject to Mark's approval, of course.'

16

'Oh, you don't have to worry about Mark,' Phil laughed. 'He's not in any position to disapprove.'

'No, I suppose not really, but you know what he's like if he's not consulted. He insists on being kept fully informed about everything that's going on – you know him!'

'No, Ian, you misunderstood me. That arsehole really is in no position to disapprove. Not ever again!'

'Oh.' Ian went silent for a moment. 'If you're saying what I think you're saying, won't that create a few problems?'

'No, why should it? You're the one who holds all the bleedin' licenses for the joint, aren't you? We all know Mark couldn't because of all his past form. Not a "fit and proper person" as the magistrates love to call it, so that's worked out quite well for us. Just bloody carry on as normal for the time being. We all know the silly fucker never got around to making a Will, so with no wife, family, or anybody to inherit anything the bleedin' club will have to be sold off, won't it? It'll probably be auctioned, I reckon - the money going to the pissin' State.

'But that's where you come in, don't you? You have to deter any silly fucker from buying it. I'm bloody sure you can manage to do that, can't you? When the arse'oles come round to view the place, you tell them a few hairy stories and show them a false set of poor accounts. That should be more than enough to do the trick. Then when the initial interest falls off, if there is any, which I doubt, I'll put in some fucking ridiculous offer and snap the bleedin' place up for peanuts!'

'Yes, of course I could manage to do all that quite easily, that would work, but . . .' Ian paused, wondering if he should continue. Plucking up courage, he dropped the bombshell. 'Where on earth did you get the idea that Mark had no family?' he asked.

'Didn't he always say he had no family? Least that's what he told me. He was fucking emphatic about it. Why?' Phil started to feel uneasy. His senses, and a sudden empty feeling in his stomach told him he would not want to hear what was coming next.

'Well, it's just that I happen to know there is family. There's a Will too. I've seen it, although I don't know exactly what's in it. It's with his solicitor. Yes, he has family all right, there's a younger brother living somewhere down in Kent - got a corner grocer's shop in a place called,

Brisham, I believe it is. Somewhere down there on the coast, anyway. He's a happily married man with a grown-up kid, by all accounts. Oh dear, now, what the hell is his name? I should know it. Is it John? Yes, that's right, it is. I remember the brother's name is John. It's John and his wife is Mary. Anyway, the youngster is definitely called Tommy. That much I do know for certain. Mark always sent him Christmas and Birthday presents - expensive ones at that! For some reason he thought the world of the boy. Idolised him, he did.

'No, Phil. I think when Mark told you that he had no family, he must have meant he had no family in the terms that they'd sort of disowned him. Apparently, they are proper little goody-goodies – the real-life Brady Bunch. They didn't go along with Mark's kind of lifestyle, and not wanting their lad corrupted they'd asked him to make himself scarce many years ago. No Phil, he didn't mean he really had no family.'

'Oh, shit!'

Bob walked in through the double doors, annoyingly whistling something out of tune as he often did. Heaving his tatty-looking green canvas shoulder bag on to the coffee table, and in doing so scattering Paul's neatly piled white packets, he was in time to witness Phil slamming the desk phone down in anger. Phil glared up at the man, his eyes like lightning bolts, thunder rolling all across his face. Saying nothing he looked back down again to check his watch. It was now all but three-forty, he observed. Too late, too late by far to stop the flying lesson. Anyway, he realised, with that much heroin pumped in him . . . No one could survive that much.

'Bad night, Boss,' Bob informed him.

'You'd better fucking believe it!' Phil roared back at the man. Standing up, and then wondering why he had stood up, he collapsed back down heavily on to the chair again, burying his head in his hands.

Bob went over to the desk and started counting out the night's haul in front of his tormented boss. 'Only eight hundred and twenty quid,' he stated, putting the last pile of twenties down. 'That's both lots. I've brought nearly all the stuff back with me. No one was buying anything.

'Oh, and by the way, Mark wasn't there at all tonight. I didn't see him once. I kept my eyes peeled too. I'm absolutely positive nobody else was dealing. Are you a hundred per cent sure he's been crossing us?

I'm not. I think the punters just ain't buying much at the moment. They probably got enough of it cheap at that bloody pop thing in Glastonbury. Apparently, what with all the good weather, the world and its partner turned up there to see some last minute stand-in – a bloke by the name of Jarvis Cocker, and a group called Pulp. It's all anyone talks about now.'

'Shit! Shit! Shit! Of course, Glastonbury!' Rapidly, it was beginning to dawn on Phil that he could have been wrong. He could have been so very wrong. Maybe Mark hadn't been cheating on him after all. Maybe he hadn't been selling his own stuff.

'All done, Boss,' Patrick was beaming his competence, as the three men noisily burst in through the back doors having successfully completed the foul deed at the cliff top. 'Reckon he'll wash up in the bay some time tomorrow night.'

'Shit! Shit! Shit!' Phil smashed his fist down hard on the desktop once more, spilling the neat piles of money that Bob had so carefully counted out. 'Lock up here. I want every fucker over the Inferno in five minutes. Every fucker!'

The incensed boss-man stormed out through the double doors, slamming them hard behind him. Scurrying through the back yard, across the alley and around the car park perimeter to the back door of the Inferno Club, he rang the bell, three long rings. It was only moments before he was let in.

'Leave the door,' he snapped at the bouncer, 'the others will be over in a few minutes. Where's Dave?'

'In the office,' sixteen stone of prime meat in a red blazer replied.

'Haven't none of these bastards got fuckin' homes to go to?' Phil spat at him, waving his hand at the sprinkling of club-goers still hanging back nursing the last few dregs in their glasses. 'It's nearly four o'fucking clock. Fuck 'em all off out of it! Now!'

The bouncer signalled to his colleagues. Immediately more red blazers closed in, determined to remove the last of the protesting punters. The staff could see the gang boss was in an evil mood. They knew better than to upset him any further.

Crossing the dance floor at speed, in his hurry Phil attempted to take the steep private stairs up behind the deejay box two at a time. Erupting extreme profanities into the air when he slipped, painfully grazing his shin, he was forced to revert to his normal one at a time method. Fuming even more now, one puff short of exploding, he barged into the office at the top of the steps in time to see Dave locking the giant Waterman safe in the corner.

'Poor night again,' Phil's business partner said glumly, looking around at him.

'Christ Almighty! Even you! Why is it every fucker likes to tell me bad news? Everywhere I fucking go it's fucking bad news, bad news, bad news! Fuck! Fuck! Fuck! When am I gonna hear some bloody good news?'

'I wish you didn't swear so much,' Dave stated disapprovingly. 'I'm sure it's not necessary. I manage to get by quite well without all those obscenities.'

'Bollocks!'

Patrick appeared at the door behind the exasperated Phil only moments later. 'The boys are all downstairs waiting, Boss,' he reported. 'All the punters and staff have gone now - that is except for Sid and Denise, of course.'

'Right, we'll be straight down,' Phil told him. Then turning back to face Dave, 'Seems like we've got a problem. One hell of a fucking problem! You'd better come down, too. See if your brain can come up with any fucking bright ideas! Christ knows - we fucking need 'em!'

Dave could tell by the look on Phil's face that the man had encountered more than the usual run-of-the-mill hitch. The evidence was written all over it. Eager to learn more, he followed his business partner down the steps to the bar area - the one that overlooked the lower dance floor. There, seated on barstools in a neat line along the front of the long shiny, black marble and chrome counter, the gang were waiting for them.

Bob was sitting at the end nearest to them as they entered. He was by far the scruffiest-looking one there. B.O. Bob, he was called behind his back, and not unjustly. The man shunned any type of deodorant, preferring to smell as nature intended. Wearing his dark green baggy suit, the same one he wore every day and the one that would probably live out its entire life without ever knowing a dry cleaner, the man was about twenty-eight years of age, or perhaps thirty-something but not admitting it. He was a rugged-looking man with a square, stubble chin and unkempt greasy hair - the unwashed type of greasy. Two spells in Borstal as a youth, and an eighteen-month prison sentence a few years later for grievous bodily harm had achieved little, apart for keeping him out of circulation for a while.

Next along the line were the two brothers, Don and Paul. They were twenty-six and twenty-four respectively, and thought to be of Italian descent. Smartly dressed in their loud blue suits, they were both enviably good looking. The fact that neither of them had form was purely because they had never been caught; certainly not because they were angels. Although more than a bit stupid at times, Don was much the harder man of the two. He was the stereotypical thug, the true ruffian, whereas his younger brother came across as a far more genteel kind of person. Paul was a man who could easily charm anyone - only later would they realise their wallet was empty.

Fourth, sitting in the rogue's line up, was Patrick. A man who was always casually dressed, but never scruffily. Today he wore black jeans and a black bomber jacket. He was a proud Irishman, thirty-two and twice divorced, with a slim, jockey-type physique. The house in Bridlington Road, directly behind the nightclub where the gang used the downstairs back room as an office, the cellar, belonged to him, although it was not his choice of abode - it had been a present from Phil for some services past rendered.

Patrick was the gunman of the gang. He was into firearms in a big way. Explosives, too. It was more than a fascination this man had with them. Far more. Amongst his sizeable collection he boasted three modern Colt 45s, a Walther P99 – that of James Bond fame, although Patrick's had the larger magazine - and an impressive •44 Magnum Special. An Uzi sub-machine gun was his prize possession, one which, annoyingly, he had never had occasion to use.

Always a worry to people was Patrick. What this man lacked in stature, he more than made up for with his firearm abilities. Phil often wondered if he would live - or maybe die! - to regret having such a man in the gang. Nevertheless keeping a gunman as a back up was an unfortunate but a necessary evil.

Most forms of brutality, even with knives, were pretty much okay with the boss-man - he just got a little nervous when it came to firearms. They could be so instant, and so final. But then, Patrick could always be relied on when the chips were down. He was one of those men who would prefer to make a stand and to die fighting, rather than run from trouble.

Sam, Graham and Mike, the three lads aged eighteen, nineteen and twenty respectively, were at the end of the line-up. Casually dressed in the very latest, most expensive top designer wear, they were the junior members of the gang. The ones who did many of the more mundane jobs like cutting, splitting, weighing, and distributing the drugs to their relevant destinations, as well as being general skivvies for the more senior members.

Behind the counter, Sid the bars manager, whose main task these days was being in over-all charge of the three large bars, one on each floor at the Inferno, was dressed in his black and whites. Though looking extremely smart, he still retained a foreboding element that made any unruly punters quickly come to their senses. Sid was a nasty piece of work. Now in his late thirties, the man had served several spells inside for an assortment of crimes, all of which had included varying degrees of violence, and all of which had incurred extra time for violently resisting arrest. Towering at least six foot-four in height, a big built man, and sporting a square heavily pockmarked face with a large bent-to-the-left nose, he was someone not to mess with. Few did.

Away from the bar at a small table in the distant corner, the last of those present, Denise, sat patiently waiting. One of the many bar girls at the Inferno, she was eighteen, pretty, and everybody knew her as Phil's bit of stuff. But that was not through choice - she simply had to go along with it or lose her job. With no father around to support her sick mother, losing her job was an eventuality she wasn't prepared to contemplate. So, she would suffer the man's advances. Phil, after all, was very generous towards his women.

As they approached the small gathering Dave nodded across to Sid to signal that a free drink all round was in order. If the Devil should cast his net now, he thought, quickly side-stepping so that Phil would be the one sitting the closest to stinky Bob. Five years, he regretted, as they took their places at the end of the bar where they could see all along the line, five years of being mixed up with this crazy lot. If only he had not spent so much money modernising the club. And for what reason had he spent it? Just to be the biggest, and the best? What a fool! What an idiot! If only he had sold up when this bunch of rogues arrived on the scene demanding their protection money – sold up instead of stupidly taking Phil on as a partner, an equal one at that, just to save his precious pride; his stupid ego. If only it had been someone else, someone decent instead of Phil, then things might have been different. If only . . .

'Pay attention,' Phil ordered, his steely eyes picking out each member of his crew in turn before he continued. 'We've landed up with a fucking problem. A fucking big problem! It appears I've been misinformed, ain't I? And by you fucking lot! Every fucker here let me go on believing that Mark had no family, didn't they? Well, it turns out he fucking 'ad! He had got relatives. There's only a bleedin' brother somewhere that no fucker here told me about! Some arsehole who will no doubt land up inheriting the bleedin' Ellie. That's fucking great, ain't it? Ain't that put a fucking great spanner in our works, eh? It may only be half the size of this bleeding place, but we sure as shit sticks can't afford to lose it! Not unless you fuckers 'ere are prepared to take a lot less.'

The expressions on the men's faces suggested they were not.

'Now you all know how much I was hoping we could've got a bleedin' partnership at the Ellie,' Phil continued, 'instead of just doing a squeeze on the place, but that never worked out - Mark wouldn't have none of it. Well, tonight, what with his little accident, I was expecting to do even better. I was expecting to have been able to buy the shit-'ole. Have it all, lock, stock and pissing barrel, for some stupid fucking knock down price - but that ain't likely to happen now, is it? Not with a fucking family around. Those plans have gone down the bloody swanny, ain't they?

'What will happen when they find Mark's body, Christ only knows. I, sure as fuck, don't! No doubt there will have to be some kind of a fucking inquest. There always is - that's fucking normal these days. And no doubt the authorities will soon trace his bleeding solicitor. He was a well-known businessman after all, so it is gonna make the fucking news, ain't it? That fucker, whoever he is, will soon pop his head up to get his bloody two-pennyworth, you can bet on it! So, I suppose what happens to the place now all depends on what that stupid arse does, and the bloody executors of the Will - whoever the fuck they are!

'That's something else I knew fuck-all about - his last bleeding Willy and fucking Testicle! No one here told me fuck-all about that either!

'Anyway, as I was saying, I suppose it's up to all that as to whether the club will even stay fucking open while everything's being sorted out legal like. Now, I don't need to tell you how much we stand to lose if they decide to shut the bloody place! Anything up to ten or eleven grand a week in peak season - and that's without the pissin' drugs! It's our second biggest take, for fuck's sake!'

He swilled his beer noisily, studying them all, wiping his mouth on the back of his hand and belching loudly before continuing, 'Providing these arsehole authorities are satisfied that Mark fell off that fucking cliff accidentally while on some mad fucking drug-crazed trip, pissed out of his tiny little mind, everything should be done quickly. I mean, it's not fucking unheard of 'ere, is it? Crack-heads are always falling off the fucking cliffs! But if there are any bleeding suspicions about the cause of death, if for some reason it ain't put down as accidental or mis-a-fuckin'-venture, then the damn club could be shut for some time. And that won't be good fuckin' news!

'Of course, there's always a chance that when they find this shit'ouse of a brother who no doubt will get everything, he won't want anything to do with the bleeding place. He may put it straight on the bleeding market, for all we know. Sell the fucking place. If that's the case, then maybe there's still hope of us buying it sensible-like - especially if poncey Ian is kept on to look after it. But if not, we may be in for some fucking trouble, because whoever does fucking take it on, or buy it, will have to be persuaded to pay their bloody insurance and give us sole drug dealing rights, won't they?

'Now that should all be okay, no fucking problem if it's some bleeding first-timer - no fucking problem at all. But if a sodding brewery was to take it on, or some wide boys come down from the smoke, just like we did, we could suddenly find ourselves in deep shit! Deep fuckin' shit! We might not only lose that fucking income, it could become the thin end of the bleeding wedge. A crack in our little empire that could spread like fucking wildfire! We could lose the whole fucking lot in no time!'

He paused, producing another long drawn out belch before continuing, 'So, has any fucker 'ere got any thoughts, any bleedin' bright ideas, on the matter? And is there any fucking more that I should know about? That no fucker 'ere has bothered his arse to tell me? I fucking hope not!'

Phil picked up his glass again and looking over it, along the line of men, he glared at them again, each in turn.

It was Bob, the nearest to him, who spoke first. 'Well, Phil. Most of us came here with you, let me see, it must be some five years ago now, when things got too hot for us in Soho. If you remember, it didn't take us too long to get a foot in all the major concerns then, did it? So surely, no matter who takes the club on, we wouldn't have any more of a problem than when we first came here, would we? We sold our protection to every concession on the front within the first few weeks, didn't we? And they weren't all mugs then, but we still managed it. We took them on, and we won. In fact, come to think of it, we won quite easily. And look how well things have gone since then. The place has more than doubled in size - nearly trebled, I reckon. Loads of new places have opened up, all of them happily paying their share. Everybody's pretty much okay with how it is. You get the odd moan now and then, but so what? Don't you think you're perhaps getting a little too worried, a little too soon?'

'Ha! Maybe I am, maybe I'm not. But haven't you forgotten about Teddy, Big John, Piffer, Blacky, and all the others we had with us then? They've all bleeding gone now - all moved on, ain't they? Some have even started their own bleeding operations elsewhere, 'cept for dear old Teddy, of course, rest in peace. We were nearly twenty sodding strong in those days, now we're less than fucking ten at times. Fuckin' slim-line and efficient that may be, and it's worked bloody well while everything's run smooth, ain't it? But now? Now we just ain't geared up for any serious hassle - that much I do know! Remember, none of our bloody clients know we've slimmed down - not that fucking much, anyway. They still think the others are only a phone call away. If they were to fucking find out, a few of the bastards might get stroppy and refuse to pay up. That's the crux of our bleeding problem, you see. If we take on some heavy bastard and we fucking lose out, we would lose the whole pissing lot! But, if we didn't fuckin' take them on, then the other shittin' clients might become suspicious about our capabilities. We could still lose every-fucking-thing!'

'Seems to me it was a bit stupid getting rid of Mark in the first place, just because you thought he was selling a few E's of his own,' the youngster Sam casually offered, between yawns of boredom, from the far end of the bar.

Sid's left hand flew out with the speed of lightning. It was back on the bar caressing his pint again before Dave fully realised what had happened. Sam, however, didn't realise until a full two minutes later. That was about the time he regained consciousness and began wondering how it was he came to be lying on the floor, and why his jaw should be hurting.

Phil ignored the incident. He was used to Sid's way of dealing with things. 'Well, that's how things fucking stand at the moment. So, I suppose nobody's got any bright ideas then?' He waited for a moment. 'No. I didn't fucking think so. Well, the way I see it is we're going to have to get some bleedin' help in. And bloody fast. But we gotta be real careful. We can't ask anyone who's half fuckin' organised – that would be too damn risky. Fuckers might get greedy. Might see us as an easy fuckin' pushover and take the whole pissin' lot off us! Everything! No, what we really fucking need are a few independent heavies. The brawn with no bleedin' brain types. The sort that will do anything just to get the money for the next round of pissin' drinks. So, what I need from you load of shite'oles now is a bit of effort. A recruitment drive is called for. I want you to find us at least half a dozen reliable blokes, some real fuckin' heavies that we could use. And I don't want no ponces. They need to be proper rough diamonds, the type of arse'oles who know how to look after them-bleedin'-selves if we do have to put the bloody pressure on.

'We ain't gonna lose that club without a fuckin' fight. No fuckin' way! And if it does come to a fight, I'm telling you now, we had better fucking win it, or some of you bastards'll be sorry!'

CHAPTER 2

The tattered old blue and cream electric milk float shuddered, noisily chinking to a halt outside Patterson's, the little convenience store on the corner of Ashford Road in Brisham. The one where someone had whitewashed over the shop windows and half-heartedly painted out the name on the sign above. Arthur, the deliveryman, jumped out of the vehicle and grabbing two fully skimmed pints from a crate on the back he swiftly delivered them to the shop doorway. Sighing heavily as he walked back with the empties on his fingers, he remembered how once he would have off-loaded three whole crates there, sometimes more, every morning. But that was back in the good old days. The days before the shop had been forced to close. The days before the massive supermarket had opened up in the nearby High Street and stolen all their customers.

Realising that he too was feeling the pinch now, he sighed again. More and more of his customers were deserting him and buying their milk from the supermarket. There they could buy it much cheaper than the dairy could afford to sell it. And there too, at the supermarket, they had the added advantage the milk came in those lightweight plastic containers that didn't have to be washed out and returned.

Yes, he considered, his round was getting smaller and smaller almost as each week passed. There was never any commission to be earned these days either - there hadn't been for a long time. It was depressing, and he wondered just how long it would be before his round became so small that the dairy would merge it with another one - how long before his job would disappear? He sighed yet again. It was almost a groan. Such was progress; such was the modern age, he resented, as he jumped back into the wagon and made it chink a few more yards along the road.

It was six o'clock - the town hall clock confirmed it from a distance. Above the empty shop the family were beginning to stir, though for what reason they had no idea. They had nothing to get up for these days, certainly not that early, it was only habit that forced them to do so. A habit based on years of having to be up to receive the day's deliveries of milk, newspapers and fresh produce.

More than a year had passed since the small grocery shop closed its doors for the last time. The business never was a gold mine, but it had provided an adequate source of revenue for the family, and for many years they were able to maintain a reasonably decent standard of living from the long hours and hard work it demanded of them. Those hours and all that hard work involved meant little to them. It was their shop. Their business. And that was all that really mattered. They were proud of it. Anyway, they considered it not so much a job as a way of life - one they had grown to love. The little store was a centre for the local community, a place where friends came to shop, where gossip was exchanged, and a place where everyone was happy, even if their style of happiness was to have a moan about everything and anything. Whatever it was, Patterson's was the centre for it. The place where it all happened - or it did until the supermarket opened.

Once the new supermarket opened up only two streets away with its massive promotions aimed at killing off all the competition, the shop fell on hard times and began to lose money more heavily as each week passed. One by one their friends and neighbours, the people who used to shop there, started to avoid them. They would guiltily sneak home by different routes, heavily laden with carrier bags stuffed to the brim with supermarket bargains. It took only a few short months for the shop's debts to pile up beyond any hope of salvation, until finally, when it became obvious that they were having difficulty repaying a loan, the bank refused them any further financial backing. Reluctantly, they were forced to close the business.

Of course, the Pattersons had not been the only ones to suffer because of the new sell everything, stack it high and sell it low, supermarket. Several other local businesses had failed. The cobblers on the next corner, which had been a family business for generations, passed down from father to son more times than anyone could remember, that too had to close. Nobody wanted their shoes repaired anymore - not when they could buy a brand new pair next to the potatoes for the price of a sole and heel job.

It was only now, little more than a year later, that some of their old customers were beginning to realise the supermarket's bargains were actually few and far between, and that they didn't bear close inspection. The quality of their merchandise was not as good. Nowhere near. The cheap shoes didn't last more than a few months, the vegetables had no taste, and the fruit, badly stored at wrong temperatures, went off overnight.

But now that realisation was too late - far too late. Now, with no opposition to contend with, the supermarket giant was able to, and blatantly did, hold its customers to ransom. They knew that none of the small corner shops could ever realistically afford to re-open. They were also fully aware that should one of them miraculously find the heart or the money to try, it would only take a few major promotions to wipe them out again - customers were that fickle!

No, it had to be accepted that, as with most towns, the days of the small corner shop that sold quality goods with a friendly personal touch had passed. They had left Brisham forever.

Unemployment in the area was nearly twice the national average so there was very little hope of John, who had recently celebrated his fortieth birthday quietly with just a few cards and a bottle of his favourite wine, gaining meaningful employment. He had tried, tried continuously for many months, even travelling as far as Brighton over twenty miles away looking for work, but nobody wanted to employ a forty-year-old failed grocer.

Mary, John's wife who was two years younger than him, had managed to secure some part-time work for a short while as a packer in the nearby raincoat factory, the one on the corner of Bury Road, but within three months that too had closed, adding further to the local unemployment situation. At her age there was no other work available. The few jobs that did arise from time to time always appeared to be filled by someone much younger than her, or else she found they required modern skills - ones she didn't possess.

Tommy, their son, who for some reason known only to him and never divulged hated that name and insisted on simply being called Tom, had turned eighteen the previous week. It should have been a time of great celebration for him, for all of them, of a boy reaching the modern times accepted age of adulthood - but it was not. There had been no celebration. There had been no money with which to do any celebrating.

He too was unemployed. He had never managed to find a job since leaving school, but that too was not for the lack of trying. With little or no money at any one time he could rarely afford to go out, and to do all the things that youths normally do. Consequently he had very few friends with whom he could have celebrated the special day, had that been possible. So, the big day came and went like any other, passing almost un-noticed.

Tom was a tall, symmetrically fresh-faced lad with short tousled fair hair, bright blue eyes, and a perfectly well-formed, unblemished athletic physique. Handsome, one would have to consider to be a major understatement when describing him. He was stunning in the way that top models, film stars and pop idols are, with the added extra that nobody knows what it is, but they know when it's there. Were he to have been one of the lads about town he would never have gone short of anything - but with no money, a lad about town was something he could never be.

Most days Tom would spend a few hours on his one luxury: a computer bought in better times. He kept a diary of his uneventful life on there, somehow making it appear interesting, and he would write short stories. Hundreds of them. Incredible works of fiction would roll off his fingers onto the keyboard. But no-one wanted them. He'd tried to have some published, but without success, so his top drawer was now full of rejection letters. Kind, but fruitless, and kept only as a reference so he didn't submit the same story twice to a publisher.

Apart from his writing, as much as Tom did find to do with himself most days was to take Ben, the family's five-year-old pet Alsatian, out for his walks. Sometimes, on a cold winter's day, he would sit under a tree in the park sheltering from the elements and letting the dog roam at will. In the summer, on hot days, he might go down to the nearby beach and lie on the sand with his top off, gazing up at his piece of the sky, and daydreaming while Ben tried to eat the waves. And just occasionally he would go into the town on his own to window shop, and to spend hours looking at all the things he would love to be able to buy – but all the time knew he never could. However, with his admirable temperament, he never became bitter or resentful. He was a lad who easily accepted his lot in life, and one who always managed to remain cheerful. There were few things that ever wiped the cheeky grin from Tom's face - it lived there.

Tom was first up, as he invariably was, that bright sunny July morning. Collecting the milk from the doorstep, dressed only in his revealing underpants, he was greeted by an amused postman who handed him two official looking envelopes, both of them addressed to his father. One he could see was obviously local - another Bank reminder, he guessed. It was the familiar looking brown envelope, the sort they had received too many of lately. The other one, looking equally as official, was postmarked Seathorpe. An inquisitive frown crept across the boy's forehead.

'Tea up,' he shouted some twenty minutes later, kicking open his parent's bedroom door. Making the tea was a task he happily performed every morning, and as usual he had already showered and dressed before delivering the early morning cuppas to their room. 'And there's some mail. Looks like more bills,' he added.

'What else?' his mother joked, sitting up and modestly adjusting her rose flowered nightdress that appeared to match the wallpaper, the duvet cover, and the curtains, but on closer examination didn't really. She had merely been careful in choosing similar patterns – the matching ones would have been unaffordable. Leaning over she took the tray of tea and letters from him.

Ben could be heard barking downstairs by the front door, insisting it was time for him to be taken out for his morning constitutional, so Tom crossed the room and pulled back the bedroom curtains allowing the cruel bright morning light to spill in, before disappearing downstairs to oblige him.

Turning over, Mary prodded her husband several times. It was a well-worn morning routine. The expected grunt was the only response until, with sheer desperation, she pulled the duvet off him to expose his well-preserved naked body to the harsh light of day.

The desperate action produced the long awaited, and ritualistic, 'Mmm . . . Morning, love. What time is it?'

'Nearly Six-thirty. Postman's been - there's a couple of letters for you on the side by your tea. Tom's already up and out. He's taking Ben for his early morning walk, so I suppose I should make the effort too and have his breakfast waiting for him for when he gets back. You stay there another half hour, love. You'll only be under my feet if you get up now.'

Mary gave him the customary kiss, more the peck that comes with the familiarity of nearly twenty years, and then slid out of the bed into her slippers. Pulling on her dressing gown she headed for the bathroom.

Her husband groaned as soon as she was gone. Life was such a bore, these days. Everything was so mundane. Why did they bother to get up at all? What on earth for?

Reluctantly pulling himself up into a sitting position, fluffing up the pillows behind him and re-arranging the duvet, John reached across for his reading glasses before sipping his tea. Fool! Wrong order, he cursed inwardly but still loudly as the glasses immediately steamed up. How many times had he done that now, and still not learned? Putting the tea back carefully to wipe his glasses on the pillowcase, he then opened the first letter.

He had already guessed what it was. Yes, he was correct. It was another one from the Bank. Another reminder that he still owed them more than twenty thousand pounds, only this letter was the strongest one so far. This one was real nasty. It stated in no minced words that it was the formal notice that the Bank were going to repossess, and then sell by auction, the property he had placed as surety for the loan they had taken out to pay off some of their debts. Plus, of course, they ever so politely reminded him, he would be liable for all the costs incurred in the repossession of the property.

Property? That was not property, he considered. It was their home! The truth rattled painfully through his head. Their home was going to be sold from under them. They had just twenty-eight days in which to vacate the premises. Twenty-eight days to find somewhere else to live. Twenty-eight days? With no money, and a mountain of debt, how the hell were they going to do that?

'Not another one from the Bank?' Mary enquired, coming back into the bedroom still drying her hair - her skin healthily glowing from the hot shower. 'Don't they ever give up?'

John didn't answer her - he couldn't. He simply handed her the open letter. Sensing by his action it must be serious, very serious, she sat on the side of the bed before reading it, slowly. Twice. Leaning across, he put his arm around her to comfort her as she began to cry.

'They can't do that! They can't! We must have some rights,' she sobbed. 'They can't just put us out on the streets. They can't, can they?'

'I'm afraid they can, pet. We had to put the bricks and mortar up as surety. It was all we had. They have every legal right to sell the property to recoup their losses. You see, it was not a mortgage, but a business loan that we took out. It was an arrangement where if we didn't pay the money back on time we agreed to surrender all rights of tenancy. At the time it was the only way we could get hold of any money. Little did we know then how impossible it would become to pay it back.'

Mary sniffed, and wiped her red eyes. She forced a smile at him, saying, 'I'd better go and do that breakfast. Perhaps it might be better if you did get up after all. We're going to have to do a lot of thinking today. I mean, we're going to have to work something out, aren't we?'

Her eyes started to water again as she bolted out of the room. John noticed it and felt gutted. He knew he was responsible; that all this was entirely his fault. It was he, after all, who had arranged for the loan and, much against his better judgement, had not told her about all the fine details, or the risks involved, simply because he saw no point in having her worrying as well. What good would that have done? But then, he had never expected their situation to become as bad as it did - to have gone that wrong. Now, with hindsight, he realised it would have been better, far better, for them to have let their business fail earlier - to not have attempted to save it. At least that way there would not have been so much debt around their necks now, and they probably wouldn't be losing their home.

Feeling sick about the whole affair, and he did feel quite physically sick, he dragged himself out of the bed and headed for the bathroom. There, barely splashing some cold water on his face - he felt in no mood to shave - he consciously avoided looking in the mirror knowing he would have hated what would have been in there looking back at him. This morning, of all mornings, was not the morning to challenge the beast that never forgives anything. Quickly dressing in the previous day's clothes, seeing little point in changing them, he trudged down the stairs to console his wife.

He found Mary in the empty shop sitting on the stool behind the counter; the familiar stool she used to sit on every day to rest her ankles between serving customers, in better times. She was staring at all the empty shelves, the cabinets, the display units, and the painted over windows with tears streaming down her face. The painted over shop windows they couldn't afford to have changed to normal ones, and the fittings they couldn't afford to have removed to enable them to reclaim the shop as another, much needed, room. The fact there was no space for a sitting room hadn't mattered to them once - there would never have been the time to use one. But over the last year, what with all the spare time on their hands, a sitting room would have been nice.

John stood behind her, the memories now beginning to gnaw at his brain too. His eyes found the dark green banners advertising tea, one stuck across the top of each window, and the memories flooded his mind. He recalled the time he had struggled, perilously balancing atop a stepladder, to put them up straight, and how after so many failed attempts, when he thought he had finally done the job to perfection, he had proudly called Mary out to see his magnificent achievement, fully expecting to be praised. Her words rattled through his brain again as if it was then, 'It's Indian tea, dear,' she had said, quite calmly, 'not Australian. Be a love and put them the other way up!' Wiping his moistening eyes on the back of his hands, he told himself not to be so emotional, it wouldn't help matters.

'We've had some good times in here over the years, haven't we? Memorable times,' Mary reminisced, quickly drying her eyes on her pinafore as soon as she sensed him standing behind her.

'We certainly have,' he answered softly, stepping forward, putting his arms around her neck and hugging her tightly.

'Do you remember the day when the till went wrong?' Mary asked, looking over her shoulder to force a smile at him. 'When the drawer shot right out of it, breaking all those lemonade bottles and spilling the cash everywhere? The mess those bottles made, shooting fountains of fizzy pop into the air, remember?'

'And old Mrs Fisher was in here, wasn't she? Her little Pekinese wet itself all down her front in fright, didn't it?' John added, as they both started to laugh.

'And, and,' there were different tears appearing now, tears of laughter that started to roll down Mary's face as she spluttered, 'and when Tom was little, when he leaned too far into the ice cream freezer to get a lolly and slid inside? Only his little bottom and frantically waving legs sticking up out the top!'

'Thank you,' said Tom, who had returned from his dog walking duties and was standing at the door behind them grinning, with the now satisfied and happily panting Ben sitting alongside him. 'Won't I ever live that down? I was only six at the time! Anyway, what on earth are you two doing in here?'

'Ooh, the toast!' Mary suddenly remembered it and ran out towards the kitchen, flapping her hands madly in the air in a manner only possible for a woman.

John put a comforting arm over his son's shoulder, explaining the bad news to him as they slowly followed her into the kitchen to see what, if anything, had been salvaged for their breakfast.

'And was the other letter equally bad news?' Tom asked, as they sat down at the table.

John looked at him blankly for a second, and then remembering there was another letter he rushed upstairs, returning a few moments later still reading it, with a puzzled look on his face.

'It must be Mark,' he said finally.

'What must?' Mary was trying to see over his shoulder, whilst also trying to prevent the eggs sticking to the pan.

'It's a solicitor's letter, dear. It says we should contact Sprockett, Blanckton and Pluggall, where we may learn something to our advantage. That's their usual way of telling you somebody's died and left you some money, isn't it? Oh, dear. I bet it's old Mark. I can't think of anyone else who would leave us anything. Well, there is no-one else really, is there? I'll ring them now. We'll find out what it's all about. If it is Mark who has popped his clogs, we might be in for a few thousand. That would come in handy right now, wouldn't it? You can bet your life old Mark was loaded, what with all the dubious things that he was into!'

'Well there's little point in ringing them now,' Mary said, looking up at the clock on the wall. 'You're not likely to catch them working before nine o'clock, if then.'

'This is going to be a long two hours,' Tom managed to get out, between the necessary chewing his breakfast demanded. 'Poor old uncle Mark, if it really is him. I suppose it could easily be him because he sent me nothing for my birthday last week. Not even a card, which was a bit strange. I think that's the first time he's ever forgotten, isn't it? Oh dear, what a shame. I used to like him. We never did see much of him though, did we? I wonder why he hardly ever visited us?'

John stole a cautious look at Mary. Perhaps now that Tom was grown up he should be told something of his uncle's questionable activities, and how they had told him to stay away, John thought, but this was probably not the best time to do it. No, he decided, now would certainly not be the best time to decry a perhaps deceased blood relative - especially one who may have left them some money.

Nine o'clock did finally arrive. The clock on the wall had suffered more looks in those two hours than in the previous two years. At a polite five-past-nine John phoned, and in the engineer and the oil rag tradition first got the receptionist, then the solicitor's secretary, before finally the real thing.

'Well, Mr Patterson,' the solicitor said, 'firstly, please accept our deepest sympathies for the loss of your brother, Mark, who it appears seems to have died in er, in tragic circumstances.'

'Tragic circumstances?' John queried, and then placing his hand over the mouthpiece quickly confirmed to the others that it was indeed Mark who had died.

'Yes. I don't know if you are aware of the fact, but your brother was said to be fond of having, shall we say, more than a little tipple most days? And, we are told, he also quite often indulged in the taking of, er, er, of illegal substances. It would appear from the coroner's inquest that he probably fell off one of the cliffs in a bit of a drunken state one night, apparently, we're informed, with the additional help of a considerable amount of heroin in his bloodstream.

'It seems a group of local lads found his somewhat battered body floating in the marina a week or so ago. The autopsy report, however, does conclude that his death was not actually through drowning. There was very little water found in his lungs. No, it was probably caused by falling on to the rocks. Anyway, the inquest verdict duly recorded his death as accidental rather than being by misadventure. Always better, that - accidental. Tidier. Makes things far easier to deal with!'

'Good Lord!'

Mary and Tom looked on in silence.

The solicitor continued, 'Your brother, as you are most probably aware, was a reasonably wealthy man, Mr Patterson. Now, according to his Will there is but one sole heir to his entire estate, er, the sole heir being named as his nephew, Tommy. Your son, in fact, Mr Patterson. You, and your wife Mary, have been named as the trustees of the estate until your son is twenty-one.

'This, er, this is a little unusual these days and I will have to advise your son, who I believe has now attained the age of eighteen years, that should he wish to contest waiting those three years there would be no problem. It would just be a mere formality to succeed as there is no strict stipulation of age in the Will, just one unfortunate reference to twenty-one. Eighteen is the legal age for an inheritance now, as you are no doubt aware.

'However, as I was saying, according to the Will as it stands, at present the two of you are to be responsible for the management of the estate until Tommy succeeds.

'Now, the monetary part of the estate that we are talking about amounts to a little over five hundred and fifty-five thousand pounds sterling - that is, er, after all the duties have been paid. And in addition to this sum of money there is the property. This being the nightclub known as the Elephant's Nest. It's a sizeable building situated on the promenade at Seathorpe, and it incorporates a rather spacious four bedroom flat above the nightclub where your brother used to reside. A fairly recent valuation of the whole property, last year actually, put it at somewhere around one-and-a-half million pounds.

'Then, of course, there are all your brother's personal effects. These have been kept securely locked in the flat since we were informed of the death. They, being mostly of sentimental value, have not been valued.'

John was speechless. Rigid. For a moment language left his brain - took a hike. There were no words he could find.

'Hello? Hello? Mr Patterson, are you still there? Have we been cut off? Oh, damn! Hello? Hello?'

'Yes, yes, I'm still here,' he finally managed. 'My God! Really? There's all that? That much? Oh, my God!'

Tom and his mother looked at each other wide-eyed, and then back at John.

'Yes, it is quite substantial,' the solicitor agreed. 'Now, acting purely in the interests of your brother's estate we have allowed the nightclub to remain open, under our watchful eye of course, whilst your whereabouts were being sought. Of course, decisions like that will soon become your responsibility but there are, naturally, a few formalities to go through first. Firstly, I need to have sight of all three Birth Certificates . . .'

John was in a daze. The words were back, but now passing through his head with little or no meaning. They were foreign. He was frightened to pick any, lest they were wrong. Fortunately, Mary seeing his predicament put her ear to the phone. In her methodical way she started to write everything down, listing all that had to be done.

'Once again Mr Patterson, our sincerest condolences. And we do look forward to seeing you at your earliest convenience. Goodbye for now.'

'How much did you get?' Tom asked, intrigued.

His father forced a laugh as he replaced the handset, like someone with a cold would on winning the booby prize of a box of tissues.

'Absolutely nothing, son,' he said. 'Sweet nothing. Seems like you got it all! Mark has left everything to you. How's that for a Birthday present?'

'What?'

'Yes. Five hundred and fifty-five grand, I think he said. Oh, and there's a nightclub!'

'No!' Mary exclaimed. 'Really?'

'Well, you didn't really expect him to give it to us, did you?' John replied. 'He was hardly likely to do that, not after we as good as ostracized him. Tom's got it all, but he did name us as the trustees until he's twenty-one.'

'A nightclub! I own a nightclub? Most excellent!' Tom was understandably excited. 'And, and all that money! You and mum must take as much as you need to pay off the Bank. That'll solve that problem straightaway!'

'That's such a lovely thought, son,' his father said, ruffling the lad's tousled hair. 'But unfortunately it doesn't work that way. We will only be allowed to look after it for you until you actually get it. Like the nightclub, we can run it for you - or get somebody else to run it because we wouldn't know how, but we can't sell it or misappropriate large chunks of money. It's yours, when you're twenty-one. Although he did say you could easily contest the wait as you are in law an adult now, but that, I guess, would take at least a few weeks to all go through. Too late to help us here.'

Tom looked disillusioned. He sat deep in thought for a while. Mary did what any homely woman would do at such a time - she made more tea.

'I've got it!' Tom said at last. 'In law I'm an adult now and I have a lot of money just waiting for me, presumably even earning interest and growing by the minute. Couldn't I get a loan on the strength of that? Surely that should be possible.'

His father thought for a moment about the proposal. 'Yes, I suppose that might be possible. But wouldn't that be wasting the money? I mean, if we pay off the debts we will be able to keep this house - but then what? We are all still unemployed. That wouldn't change. To re-open the shop is clearly not viable. That would simply be a waste of time and money. The bills would still keep coming in and amounting up. There's the gas, the electric, the rates, and all the other bills that we have to pay - we would soon be falling into debt again, or worse, seriously eating away at your inheritance. It could happen all over again.

'No, that is not the way to go. This place is dead. Brisham has had it. There doesn't seem to be any future for us here at all; none whatsoever. So, I am thinking, why don't we all move down to Seathorpe? Why don't we live over this nightclub, like Mark did? Perhaps we could even learn how to run it. At least we'd all be gainfully employed and doing something with our lives, wouldn't we?'

'Most excellent!' Tom exclaimed.

Mary, too, was in full agreement, 'It's an absolutely brilliant idea,' she said. 'And when the Bank auction this place off in a few weeks we should even get some money back out of that, too. It has to be worth sixty thousand, though I suppose at auction it will probably only fetch something like forty. But even that would give us another twenty grand to play with. We could replace the car, get some new clothes, and do so many things we have not been able to do for such a long time. What an absolutely marvellous idea!'

And so it was that little more than two weeks later a removal van, closely followed by a packed family car, left Brisham and headed west in search of Seathorpe.

CHAPTER 3

It was nearing two o'clock on the clear, hot, sunny late July Friday afternoon. The old blue Sierra Estate, although it had seen far better days, was still proving reliable and easily keeping up with the pantechnicon as it cautiously made its way along the precarious, winding cliff-top road, past Jumper's Point, to the brow of the steep hill that wound all the way down to the promenade.

'I say, what a fantastic view! Breathtaking!' Mary suddenly exclaimed, looking down from the top of the hill as the town with the sea-front promenade below became visible to them for the first time. 'You can see everything from up here - the whole town. It looks an absolutely lovely place to live. Just look at that golden beach at the far end, and those massive rocks at this end with all the little rock-pools between them. Oh, and look at that sea. It's so calm, there's hardly a ripple to be seen.'

Tom, sharing the back seat with Ben, fought hard, but unsuccessfully, to make the dog sit still. He wanted to experience some of this magnificent panorama he was hearing about for himself, but all he managed were a few glimpses here and there through the dog-snotted side windows, as they carefully followed the winding road. He had, however, already made his mind up that he was going to enjoy living in Seathorpe. The acres of campsites they had passed through only minutes ago, alive with scantily clad, some even completely nude, young people soaking up the sun, with pop music blaring and a happy-go-lucky attitude radiating from them, had convinced him of that. It certainly looked a lively, fun place to live.

This was the first time that any of them had seen the resort. With all the necessary arrangements being completed through their own solicitor in Brisham, and with Mark's funeral having already taken place before the solicitor managed to trace them, they had been saved the expense of making any prior visit.

To travel there today, John had been forced to sell his last remaining endowment policy, fortunately for a not too severely penalised sum. The money it raised, almost three thousand pounds, providing them with the necessary cash for their moving expenses, and paying off some of the other smaller bills they felt morally obliged to settle before leaving.

'Do you reckon that's it?' John enquired of his passengers, whilst skilfully following the removal lorry as it negotiated a particularly perilous sharp right-hand bend, and then almost immediately another one bearing to the left to expose the town to them again. 'If it is, it's positively enormous!'

'Where?' Tom and Mary asked in unison. Tom in the back still fighting hard to see.

'There! Can't you see that big elephant jumping up and down? There, on top of the first big building on the front. That has to be it. Yes, I can read it now: The Elephant's Nest. That is it. My goodness!'

With one enormous heave Tom finally managed to push Ben to one side. Thrusting his head between his parents in the front seats he could see the old, but very large, looked like three storey if you didn't include the tower, red brick building with blue and pink neon lights flashing wildly on to the promenade. On top of the tower at the end nearest to them a large cartoon of a sitting elephant, one bearing a remarkable resemblance to Dumbo, although with more modest ears, appeared to be bouncing up and down on a giant nest as strip lighting alternated.

'All that's ours?' Tom was visibly shocked. It far exceeded even his wildest dreams of what the place would look like, and he had dreamed considerably in those last painfully slow passing couple of weeks. 'Most excellent!'

Minutes later they were driving past the front of the building with its overhanging canopy packed with flashing lights changing in time to an overpoweringly loud, heavy music beat emerging somewhere from out of concealed speakers. Turning right at the end of the building, and continuing along the small service road which led around to the rear of the building, they stopped outside a back entrance. One that still had the words 'Stage Door' solidly engraved in the red brickwork above it. Bins, boxes, crates, and barrels of all shapes and sizes were littered around the large yard-come-car-park they found themselves in, with some of the obstacles needing to be man-handled aside by the removal men in order to give the lengthy lorry enough space in which to turn and back up to the door.

'It's an old theatre,' Tom proclaimed excitedly. 'Most excellent!'

The stage door opened and Ian strode towards the car. Confidently, he introduced himself to the family who were awkwardly attempting to clamber out. Ben was first to alight, as he invariably was by pushing his way through the gap between the front seats and then squeezing himself between John and the steering wheel - excitedly giving everyone swiping great mouthfuls of fur with his wagging tail in the process. Once clear he made a beeline for the nearest refuse bin so, with all due ceremony, the new place could be christened as home.

'A cup of tea, coffee, or perhaps a snack, before you start unloading?' Ian enquired of them. They were all in agreement. 'The cafeteria inside is open. Well, not open properly. We sell drinks, ice creams, sandwiches, hot dogs and burgers, and all those kind of things through the hatch on to the street during the day. The inside café only really opens for the first couple of hours in the evenings, when the club's open. Come on, I'll show you. Introduce you to Sarah. By the way, I have asked the rest of the staff to be here early tonight so that you will have a chance to meet them all before we open. You'll find it sometimes gets a bit hectic once the punters start arriving, so it might be best to get that over and done with early.'

The group followed the manager inside the building, along a wide corridor, passing a flight of red painted concrete stairs with a black wrought iron banister leading off sharply to the right.

'That's the back way up to the flat,' Ian informed them as they passed by. 'It also serves as one of the emergency exits for the upstairs bar, but don't worry, most of your stuff will probably go up on the hoist. You won't have to drag it up there. This was an old theatre at one time, as you must have gathered by now. The hoist is the way they used to get the large scenery in. Luckily for you, Mark got it working again a couple of years ago, so he could get a piano up to the flat. It comes out on what's now called the top landing up there, so it couldn't be easier - but you'll see all that for yourselves later.'

The two removal men bringing up the rear were noticeably relieved to hear about the hoist. Already doing 'a cheap job', and with only two of them on such a hot day, they were not well pleased to discover the enormity of the building. Granted there was not a lot of furniture as the small flat over the shop had but two bedrooms and a small kitchen-come-diner, but to carry everything up all those stairs, all the way to the top of the building, would have been an unenviable task.

Pushing through the two heavy swing doors at the end of the corridor, they arrived in what once had been the theatre's main auditorium, or stalls as the ground floor would have been called. Tom's head twisted in every direction possible as he looked around him in awe, marvelling at all the intricate plaster decorations picked out in gold against the deep red walls, and the scrolls of flowing ribbons, and the cherubs, some with harps, some with bows and arrows. The detail was exceptional. It couldn't possibly have looked better when the place was built, he considered, relishing how nice it was that it had all been preserved and not painted over as is often found in old buildings. Then he gasped as his eyes found the more modern additions: the futuristic lighting hanging down from large gantries angled in all directions between giant suspended speakers over the almost engulfing dance floor. Eight, he had already counted before swivelling to discover the really enormous ones stacked high on either side of the stage. It was all so amazing; so incredible.

Crossing the sprung wooden dance floor which claimed at least half of that level, the party negotiated a maze of small chrome tables, each with its own set of stools encompassing it, until they arrived at the café counter where the smell of the percolating coffee welcomed them.

'Hello, it's so nice to meet you,' Sarah greeted them with a refreshing smile. One that was obviously genuine, and not the forced one reserved for customers. 'I hope you had a pleasant journey. It was a long one, wasn't it? You must be thirsty. Hungry too, I'll bet. What would you like?'

Tom's subconscious suggested things for which he dared not ask, things that he had yet to experience for real, but things of which his imagination knew no bounds. I really am going to like it here, he told himself, mentally undressing the attractive girl behind the counter, whilst at the same time trying to secretly adjust his clothing where, in certain places, it had suddenly become too tight for comfort.

At eighteen, and still not popped a cherry, something for which he felt inwardly ashamed as all his friends had achieved that long ago whilst still at school, becoming aroused was a common problem. It seemed even the strangest of things could turn him on; some of which he felt quite ashamed about and refused to believe. But it mattered not one bit to that which these days, he was convinced, spent all its time stretching upward like some sapling in a deep forest searching for daylight. He found its habits annoying at times, and far too often embarrassing.

Ian pulled two of the tables together, and then armed with coffee and several rounds of assorted sandwiches they sat around them, leaving the removal men to sit elsewhere. Tom purposefully grabbed the stool that left him facing the counter. From there he could watch the lovely Sarah performing her duties. He loved the way that every time she served someone through the hatch to the outside world she had to lift herself up slightly, off her heels, in order to reach them. That action was playing hell with his uncomfortably trapped manhood which throbbed mercilessly begging for relief each time she did it. Their eyes met on several occasions as she turned back around, momentarily locking on to each other's, further enraging Tom's already furious prisoner, uncontrollably, until he knew that he was damp down there and prayed it wasn't showing through his jeans. She fancies me, she wants it, and she wants it desperately, he thought, noticing her enormously dilated pupils, and wondering if his were as apparent.

'This, quite obviously, is the main area,' Ian explained, indicating the vast expanse with his open arms. 'The café part is on this side, as you can see, with the licensed bar mirroring it, on the other. You'll find sometimes many of these tables have to be stacked away to get more people in, especially at weekends when we can be exceptionally busy. And, if we get really packed, the stage is opened up as well and used as an extra dancing area.

'Through the doors on the other side of the stage are the old dressing rooms. Some of them are now the fridge and food storage rooms for the café, and under the stage, with an entrance off the same passageway, there's a large storeroom-come-cellar with fridges, barrels, pumps, and all the drinks stock and essential things that service the bars. All those doors are always kept securely locked, of course, otherwise you'd have half the punters sneaking in there helping themselves. You'll soon find out, you need eyes in your jacksie in this business! There is always somebody trying to get one over on you!

'Anyway, to continue, behind us through the other double swing doors is the foyer. That's still very much the same as it would have been in the theatre days, with the cloakroom, toilets, stairs to the upper levels, and all that. Oh, and you have a front door off the foyer too, on the opposite side to the cloakroom. You'll find there's a sizeable hall as you go in, complete with your own downstairs private facilities at the bottom of the staircase to save you running all the way upstairs when we're open.' Looking across at John, he whispered, adding, 'It's not a good idea to hang out with the punters, if you get my meaning. You never know if one might be harbouring a grievance - always best to use your own.'

John nodded back his understanding. He and Mary were still trying to come to terms with the sheer enormity of the place. Words had failed them and they were both beginning to feel a little foolish at having no input to the conversation.

'Where is the deejay's box?' Tom enquired enthusiastically in an attempt to force his mind to focus on a less arousing subject.

'Upstairs,' replied the manager, 'on the first floor across the front of the old lower circle. The rest of it, behind it, is what we call the quiet bar. You're somewhat shielded from the noise of the disco in there, but it's far from quiet really. It has its own small, well-stocked bar at the back, with much plusher seating than down here, but there's only room for about a couple of hundred or so people up there comfortably because the front area, where the deejay works, is quite large and completely sealed off from the public. That's the part that houses all the technical stuff, the consoles, amps, lighting controllers, and all that kind of thing. So, of course, from the upstairs bar you can't actually see any of this auditorium at all, but the deejays being right at the front have an excellent bird's eye view of how well everything is going down on the dance floor.

'By the way, the resident deejay is called, Ronnie. A very nice guy, you're sure to like him. He'll be here this evening as usual, normally turning up around eleven o'clock, but if you're really interested in seeing how it all works up there, I expect our other deejay, Randy, will be in early to do a bit of practising. He sometimes gets here as early as half-four. Spends hours up there practising, he does. He'll show you how it all works. Randy does the early evenings, also fills in if Ronnie is away or off sick at anytime. He's good, very good in fact, but you'll find Ronnie is what they term "the tops" when it comes to mixing.'

'How is trade these days?' John asked, feeling relieved that he had at last thought of something to say.

'Quite good at the moment. We had a few quiet weeks earlier this year, but it seems to have picked up again. Tonight, being a Friday, we can expect at least seven or eight hundred in, maybe a few more if we're lucky. You'll find we normally get a couple of hundred in between eight, that's when we open, and eleven, then within the next hour or so all the rest arrive. All at once, it seems. That's when it really gets hectic in here. We have had well over a thousand in before now but, thankfully, that only happens rarely. The licence covers more than a thousand, the number is dependent on how many tables and chairs you choose to remove, but over a thousand is pushing it a bit for us – they're drinking it faster than we can re-stock it!'

Ian paused for a moment before continuing, 'I understand from the solicitor that you've not actually had any entertainment experience, is that right?'

'Yes, that's only too true. It's all completely new to us. So, what we would like to do initially, if it's okay with you, is to let you carry on with the running of things. I mean, you appear to have done so very competently since my brother's death, you ought to carry on. We will hover around you observing, and hopefully in time learn the ropes. Not that we intend getting rid of you. No, not at all. It's just that I feel that if we own the place, then we ought really to know how to run it.'

'Of course. That's all fine by me,' Ian smiled at them all in turn. 'I just hope you realise what you've let yourself in for. It gets quite rowdy in here later, and you'll find there's always one or two fights to cope with of a weekend. Something else you'll soon discover is that when it's going full swing, there's not a corner anywhere in the building, including your flat all the way up there, where you can completely escape from the noise of the music, especially the beat coming from the enormous bass bins. Don't worry though, you do get used to it - in time.

'When you've moved all your stuff in, it might pay you to get your heads down for a couple of hours. Don't forget, we're licensed until three and stay open until four tomorrow morning, so that'll be the first bit of peace you're likely to get once it all starts. Even then, believe me, you'll still be able to hear the beat of the music in your heads for an hour or so after that!'

'Most excellent!' Tom, to both his parent's annoyance, used his best-loved phrase yet again. It was becoming far too well-worn.

Moving the furniture in, even with the use of the hoist, took up most of the next two hours. They were fortunate that Mark had never furnished all of the rooms. Three had been left completely empty so allowing them to get their own furniture in without too much trouble. The main job completed, although they knew the unpacking would go on for days, if not weeks, they took Ian at his word and fell into their beds. It had already been a very long day for them and they were truly whacked.

Thump. Thump. Thump. Thump. Mary and John groaned, realising the disco had started up. Randy had arrived to practice. They buried their heads deep under their pillows, pulling them tightly in over their ears. It didn't help. Tom leapt up as soon as he heard the sound. Closely followed by Ben, he went to investigate.

Finding the quiet bar at the second attempt, he first lost his way landing up in what must have been the old upper circle, the place now appearing to serve as a junk room stacked with old tables, chairs, bits of equipment, lighting fixtures, boxes, suitcases, and even some wet clothing, Tom told Ben to wait outside as he went through the door into the deejay's box. A solid wall of sound hit him the moment he entered, almost taking his breath away with the bass beat physically jack-hammering on his rib cage, altering his heartbeat, forcing it to beat in time to the rhythm of the music, and speeding up his breathing to compensate.

Tom was impressed with all the equipment that, despite the size of the room, still looked crowded and crammed. Two record decks, a dual rack mount CD player, a projection TV system, a large format tape player, three video players, several monitors, he recognised all of them, but that still left him wondering about quite a lot of the other items in there, amps, mixers and lighting controllers he supposed, and then behind him he couldn't hesitate a guess at the number of records and other media items there must have been on shelf after shelf – from floor to ceiling, they almost filled the entire wall.

'Hello,' he shouted, coming up behind the young black guy wearing the earphones, and tapping him on the shoulder.

'Shit man!' Randy exclaimed, spinning around and noticeably jumping. Then, sliding one of the controls down to kill the noise, he said, 'You 'alf frightened me to death, man! Wow! So, you must be Tom. Ian said you might look me up. Hi, man! Great! I's Randy. Nice ter know ya! Randy's my name, being Randy's my game!'

Tom shook the hand that was offered him, and then got totally confused with the ritualistic hand movements that followed where, at one point, he supposed they should have twisted thumbs and smacked palms.

Randy found his confusion hilarious. Putting his arm around Tom's shoulders, he shook him, chummy fashion. 'Hey, man!' he said. 'So you's my new Boss man. That's cool. What kinda music you into? We's got it all here, man! You name it, I's bet you we's a got it!'

Tom had to confess he wasn't actually 'into' any kind of music. He liked most kinds, he guessed, but he'd only ever been to a proper discotheque once, and then he hadn't danced.

'Hey man, that's criminal. You mean you don't go out dancing? Criminal, man! How's you gonna pick up the chicks if you can't boogie on down to the music? You do like the chicks, don't you?'

'Of course I do!' Tom retorted. 'It's just I've never had the money to do that kind of thing. It's not that I didn't want to.'

'No grief man, no grief,' Randy replied, holding his hands up in a surrender fashion and rolling his eyes. 'We's all types come in here, man. They's all God's folk as far as I's concerned.'

Tom grinned at him. He decided he liked Randy. He liked his attitude, the way he was so open, so forthright. What you saw was what you got.

'What you reckon to this, man?' Randy slid the control up halfway, the beat pounded at Tom's body again, involuntarily his legs started to move slightly, his head nodding in time with the music.

'It's good!' Tom shouted, hardly hearing his own voice.

'Good, man? Good?' Randy turned the noise down to be heard. 'It's wicked, man! Wicked! I's will get you on that floor tonight, you'll see! We will soon have you dancing. It's a rave night later on when Ronnie takes over - be a lot of stray chicks hanging around just begging for it. By the way, what do you use?'

Tom looked bewildered. Feeling a complete fool, he nervously asked, 'Use? Use what?'

Randy stood motionless for a second or two, disbelieving, then burst into uncontrollable fits of laughter with the tears rolling, streaming, down his cheeks. 'Oh, man! What planet you's from? You's really been sheltered. Man, are you in for some shocks tonight! I's reckon you's parents will go ape tonight!'

'Why?'

'This is a hot place, man! Real hot! All the young guys 'n' dolls, they comes to Seathorpe to let their hair down. Anything goes here, man! I's mean anything! They will all be down there tonight, smoking the wacky, popping the pills. Snorters, injectors, popper queens, we gets 'em all 'ere! Some will even be bonking in the dark corners before the night's over, you wait 'n' see. This is Seathorpe. You know, you can get high on the fumes just walking along the front on a weekend night here, man!'

Tom looked visibly shocked. He was beginning to wonder how his parents would handle such a place.

'Don't get me wrong, man! I's not saying you's gotta be like that. Not everyone is. It's just that's the world man, the real world. It's all out there and it all lands up here in Seathorpe. I's don't use a lot myself. Smoke a bit of the weed now and then, of course, nearly everybody does here, but rarely anything else. Perhaps pop the occasional pill, usually an E, most people do, but nothing heavy, I's never takes the needle, man! No, definitely not into that! That's real bad shit man! Don't let nobody tell you nothing different 'bout that!'

'Doesn't anyone try to stop all these drugs? Don't the police do anything about it?' Tom asked, with a look of horror creeping over his face.

'No, you can't stop it, man! Thousands of people comes here every week, thousands, you would need an army to police it. Anyway, if you stopped it you would kill the resort. Nobody wants to do that; it's what the people come here for - a good time, man! You's gotta have a good time, ain't ya? Of course it's only here on the front of a night, or else up on them camp sites, that there's ever any trouble. The town never gets ragged. It's only the posh Hoorah-Henrys that can afford to book into the town, man, and they knows better than to spoil it. They wouldn't want to have to use them campsites; not them, man! No way, man.

'The town people, they benefits financially big style from all these others being here - so no one grieves, man. Believe me, they all does all right. Anyway, man, when you's high you don't fall out with no one, you's the happiest little bunny on earth. Mind you, you'll see the bouncers will frisk a few on the way in tonight to stop them bringing any drugs in, that's normal procedure, but that's only so they will have to buy more once they's in here. Man, drugs in Seathorpe is big, big business. The Inferno crowd, they's got it all sewn up.'

'The Inferno crowd?'

'Yeah, man, the big night-club at the other end of the prom. Twice the size of this one it is, man, and more! Run by the local Mafia. They's got a hold over everyone along the front, and most of the town too. Real nasty lot they are, man! Avoid! Man, I's shouldn't be telling you this, but I's reckon they had more than something to do with you's uncle's mysterious accident. Yes, man. I's sure do!' Randy's smile had faded.

'What?'

'It's true, man. I's been here for two years now, and I's seen a lot of the funny things old Mark got up to. I's mean, he smoked the wacky all right, man. He loved it. And he drank a lot. Yeah, and he was always poppin' the pills, impressing the chicks, man. Some nights, man, I's known him pick up as many three and take them all upstairs together for a good shagging! It was well known that he'd an insatiable sex drive - and that he had a dick like an elephant. Man, they'd go begging him for it! The chicks. They all wanted it.

'He was a fun guy, was Mark. Fun guy! The best, man! Even calling this place the Elephant's Nest was Mark's idea of a joke - bet you didn't know that, man! It used to be called the Palace once upon a time.

'Yeah, your uncle was a funny old fucker. Had a lot of strange ways. He really loved them drunken, drugged-up orgies. Always arranging them, he was. But he was a good boss, man. He was a real decent chap at heart, a person who would help anyone. I's had a lotta time for him. Man, you know, some nights I's seen him so high he's been floating on that dance floor, but I's never known him touch heroin. Never, man! He just wouldn't. He was dead set against any of the hard stuff, man. If he was high on heroin the night he died like they say he was, he didn't take it himself I's would guarantee it!'

'Why didn't you tell the police that?'

'You's joking, man! One: They wouldn't be interested. Two: I's don't want a Chinese chuckle! Man, you's got a lot to learn!'

'Like, what's a Chinese chuckle?' Tom asked, feeling naive again.

'It's when you's a smile from ear to ear. Cut throat, man! A Glasgow grin!' Randy gestured, tracing a line across Tom's throat with his finger. 'You's better stick by me for a while, man, else you ain't gonna last long in this town!'

Tom stayed with Randy for another hour, thoroughly intrigued, watching him trying out all the new releases, practising mixing them in different orders, and marking the b.p.m. on them with a fluorescent marker pen. He had never realised that so much effort was involved in getting one piece of music to smoothly follow another. It was only after Randy had suggested that he should try to change decks that he fully understood what a real mess-up sounded like, with the two bass beats chasing each other, out of sync with each other, and sounding like a herd of wild horses galloping across a prairie. Certainly, it was a noise likely to clear any dance floor.

Telling Randy he'd catch up with him again later, and then once more unsuccessfully attempting the peculiar handshake, Tom left to take the still patiently waiting outside the door Ben for a brisk walk around the block.

Deciding, on leaving the side service road, to cross the promenade and to sit on the sea wall, to look back at the nightclub, and to take it all in whilst letting the dog roam the shore line at leisure instead of having the walk, he kept thinking back to Randy. He was such a great guy, he hoped they would become close friends. Since losing track of his old school chums there had been few friends – well, none actually.

After fifteen minute's of Ben exploring the rock pools opposite the club, Tom checked his watch and was amazed to discover it was nearing six o'clock, so he decided to take the dog back and feed him. Then he would go to his room for a sleep until the place opened at eight, he thought. No, dammit, he suddenly realised it needed to be earlier, remembering his mother was having dinner ready for them at seven-something. Would he get enough sleep by then to let him see four o'clock in the morning? He needn't have wondered - he didn't get any sleep. The strange tales that

Randy had told him kept him awake by creeping back into his mind.

Seven o'clock came and Tom gave up any idea of trying to sleep, deciding instead on beating the bishop and taking a long hot shower. Finding some of his clothes after opening the third box, he dressed in a pair of black jeans and a tight white tee shirt and then went into the kitchen-come-dining room to see what there was to eat.

'Only microwave pies, peas and chips today, I'm afraid,' Mary apologised. 'It'll be next week before I'm straight enough to cook a proper meal.'

Tom told his parents, over dinner, some of the things Randy had said about the drug scene, about the 'anything goes' tone of the place, and the fact that Mark didn't take heroin. Politely he left out the bit about the elephant. No doubt some time in the future they would pick that story up for themselves.

Mary looked shocked, and John was thinking of something to say, when Ian's voice bellowed around the room, 'Opening in fifteen minutes, Mr and Mrs Patterson, if you'd like to see what happens.'

Looking up they saw the Tannoy in the corner. John went over to it, and pressing a button hopefully, he said, 'Be right with you.'

#

'The new lot's arrived at the Ellie,' Patrick informed Phil the minute he walked into the cellar. 'I saw the removal van arrive earlier, when I was on my way up to the camp.'

'I know, Ian phoned me at home,' Phil replied.

'Is it business as usual tonight, then?'

'I don't see why not. From what Ian's told me they sound like a load of bleeding idiots. All prim an' proper and ultra clean. Right wankers! I reckon at the first sign of fucking trouble they'll all be so frightened they'll piss off back to where they came from. Anyway, I've got a few bleeding ideas we might put into action tonight just to make sure.'

'Ideas?'

'Yeah. It seems they got this poncey son called Tom. He's about eighteen, clean cut and all that. Apparently he's the real owner of the Ellie, his parents are only bleedin' trustees. Anyway, it sounds like the stupid little fart has never even sniffed a wine gum, let alone got drunk.

'I'll send a couple of the lads up to give Bob a hand tonight. We'll see if they can't get friendly with him. Put a bit of drink down the stupid little fucker and maybe pop a couple of E's into him before the night's out. We should be able to tell how the fuckin' land lies then! Huh! They'll probably be so shitted up seeing their darling son blown out his pretty little mind that they'll pack their bags straightaway!'

CHAPTER 4

Feeling more than a little embarrassed, and somewhat like a royal party inspecting a guard of honour, the family slowly made their way along the line of staff assembled in the foyer with Ian introducing each one to them in turn.

'They all wear badges with their names on so you don't have to remember them straight away,' he assured them. 'This, of course, is Sarah who you met earlier. She's been home for a couple of hours, but she comes back at weekends to do an extra shift. Needs the money, she says. Incidentally, in case you wondered, Friday night is always classed as a part of the weekend in this game.'

The girl smiled at them. Tom started to melt again. Something woke up from a slumber and moved, and its owner began reciting silly things in his head as he desperately tried to ignore it - it wasn't there.

'Next is Louise, she normally works behind the bar upstairs.'

'Hello,' the dark haired, well proportioned girl breathed, giving Tom a look that undressed him and made something shout loudly: Oh, yes, I am here!

One potato, two potato, three potato, four, obviously wasn't working for the lad – perhaps the subject matter was wrong.

'And then we have Jane. She works the main bar with Sarah.'

Tom knew the sweat must be showing by now. He wiped his brow, trying to be casual with the action, trying to look cool as the blonde girl with an enormous bust that was heavily involved in losing a battle with her 'it must be two sizes too small to fit' white tee shirt greeted them. Tom's battle was already lost. Feeling foolish, he was forced to clasp his hands loosely in front of him in an attempt to hide his embarrassment before walking on. Now I not only feel like royalty, he thought, I must bloody look like one them - I've seen the Queen walk like this! Slowly, he moved along the line and, now abandoning the recitations, he began to pray to God that none of them would want to shake his hand.

'There are two more bar girls on the payroll at the moment, Donna and Debbie.' Ian told them. 'They're both part-timers who normally only work Friday and Saturday evenings. They'll be here around ten-thirty, a little before the big rush. I'll have to introduce them to you later. We also have to hire a few casuals most weekends to help us out, especially if it's exceptionally busy. You know, holidaymakers from the campsites who need to earn a few extra bob in order to stay here that bit longer. The same ones seem to come back year after year. You'll get to know them.

'This is our bars manager, Derek,' Ian continued, moving further down the line. 'Derek prefers to do all his own cellar work, so we don't actually employ a separate cellar-man.'

Derek, a distinguished looking man of about forty, coming across every bit the stereotype of an ex RAF chappie, complete with the waxed handlebar moustache, shook all their hands vigorously. Tom despaired, realising his God call hadn't connected. He tried bending forward slightly when it came to his turn to shake hands in the hope that the strain on his tight jeans didn't show as much, and he prayed again. This time in the hope that his posture didn't make him look as if he was bowing or, God forbid, about to curtsy. There were a lot of calls that didn't get through that day.

'And this is Beryl, front of house. Important job that, taking the money.'

'Pleased to meet you,' the middle-aged woman with enormous hooped earrings said sweetly, whilst successfully managing not to crack any of the many layers of makeup on her face.

'And lastly, we have the heavy mob. This is Doug.'

An oversized hand shot out to shake theirs firmly. Eighteen stone if he's an ounce Tom surmised, surveying the bouncer towering way above him. I wouldn't like to meet that on a dark night, he thought.

'Simon,' Ian continued, putting his hand on the man's shoulder. 'Simon is keen on karate. He's a black belt, by the way.'

The young man, surprisingly slenderly built for a bouncer, shook their hands warmly, wishing them well in their new venture. By now to Tom it was merely another hand and another missed call - he was beginning to feel persecuted.

'Finally, we have Chris and Jack. Obviously, I don't have to tell you they're identical twins. Gets some of the punters going at times, thinking they're seeing double,' Ian quipped.

Relieved to be at the end of the line at last, they shook hands with the twins, two very heavy blokes with greatly expanded waistlines. Tweedledum and Tweedledee amusingly sprang into Tom's mind, though he managed to stifle the threatening grin by blowing air up his face in an effort to cool himself.

'Oh, and that's Randy, the early night deejay,' the manager informed, pointing to the young Jamaican poking his head around the stairwell corner to see if everyone was ready. 'Yes, we're all okay. Blast us into orbit,' Ian told him jokingly.

A few moments later the whole place rocked to the scratchy original sixties version of 'Mighty Quinn' echoing around the building. Surely, that's a bit dated for this place, Tom thought. Even I know that!

'Oh, I should have mentioned,' Ian had to raise his voice now. 'You must remember that record. It's the signal for the staff to be in their positions for opening, but more importantly it's our emergency record. Should you hear it played during the night then you know there is a big problem. Something serious like a fire, or a bomb scare. The staff have to enact the emergency procedures to evacuate the building if that record is ever played. We carry out a fire drill and log it every Saturday, so you'll see how it all works tomorrow.'

The music soon changed into a lively modern beat, belting out as the first of the punters started to trickle in. Mary elected to go back up to the flat to clear away the dinner things, and then she planned to undertake a bit more unpacking, leaving John to follow Ian around observing how things were done. Tom considered following his father, but then thought that the two of them following Ian around would look quite daft, so instead he decided on drifting into the bar to order a coke from Sarah. He hoped she might start a conversation.

By nine-thirty, Tom had downed three large glasses of coke. Disappointingly there had been no more conversation than was absolutely necessary to obtain them, though the girl had been very efficient, quick to serve him and most polite. Feeling disillusioned, having had no experience in coming out with chat-up lines, he'd always been too shy so there never had been a girlfriend, he sat at a table in a corner away from the bar, at the stage end, to watch the cavorting on the fast-filling dance floor. The spectacular light show was mesmerising him.

Tom hardly noticed the three young lads, all about his own age, walking across from the bar to sit at the next table. That is, until squeezing between the two tables, one of them clumsily managed to knock over his drink.

'Damn! Sorry there, mate. Let me get you another,' the lad said apologetically. 'What was it?'

'That's okay. It was only a glass of coke. Don't bother, I don't have to . . .' Tom's voice trailed out. The young man who had taken his glass was already half way back to the bar.

'Don't let go of it when he comes back,' joked one of the other lads, leaning across and shouting over the music, 'he's as clumsy as hell. He'll only have it over again! We reckon he needs glasses! I'm Graham by the way. This is Mike, and the clumsy oaf is called Sam.'

'I'm Tom,' he politely introduced himself.

Moments later they were all trying hard not to laugh at Sam, who returning with the drink had again bumped into the table.

'This is Tom,' Graham told the clumsy one.

'Hi, Tom,' Sam said. 'Sorry about that, mate. I got you a large one to make amends. We haven't seen you here before, have we? Just got in? Here for the week are you?'

'No, actually we moved down here today,' Tom said, hurriedly gulping down some of the coke so he could omit telling them he owned the club, in case Sam should feel embarrassed about buying him a drink for which he obviously would not have had to pay.

'Yeah, well you've found the best club for picking up the girls on your first night,' Sam told him. 'It's not the biggest, but it's the best. You are here to find a girl, I take it?'

'If it's boys you like, you'll need to go to Dorothy's. That's only two streets away,' Mike shouted across.

Tom gulped more coke. 'Girls. I like girls,' he said, wondering whether it was the heat, or the flashing lights, that was making him feel so light-headed.

'Yeah, I reckon we'll all do alright in here tonight. You wait and see. Smoke?' Graham offered out a tobacco tin full of ready-made roll ups. Sam and Mike each took one.

'I don't,' Tom said.

'No, we don't either, not really. Not good for your health, but you do have to smoke a few wackys in a place like this, especially if you want to pull. Gotta pose a bit, haven't you? It breaks the ice, as well. The chicks like 'em, too. Gets them right rampant! Go on, have one. I mean, it ain't gonna kill you, is it?'

Tom hesitated at first, and then took one. Sam lit it for him. Mike proclaiming it was his round jumped up and took the glasses to the bar.

'Gets you a bit first time,' Sam explained, 'but just take it back. Hold it down as long as you can. You'll soon get used to it.'

Inhaling deeply Tom resisted the urge to cough, holding the smoke back for as long he could. His head started to swim, but soon he began to feel relaxed, so relaxed, and then suddenly so happy. He liked the feeling, he thought, inhaling deeply again.

Mike returned with more drinks. Putting a large one in front of Tom, he told him he'd bought him another coke, but he was welcome to have something stronger if he wished - it wouldn't be a problem to go back to get it. Tom started to giggle. His throat was irritating him, burning, so he gulped down several great mouthfuls of the coke to soothe it.

'Just look at the tits on that lot!' Sam exclaimed, nodding at the five girls who had positioned themselves around the table two along from theirs. Tom struggled to focus. He was getting hotter, feeling woozy, but his eyes finally picked out the girl in the white top, the one that had the fantastic colours dancing around on it. He knew, just knew, he would do anything to know her, to be with her, to have sex with her. Oh, God! He had to have sex with her!

'Strewth! It doesn't take much to get you excited, does it?' Sam commented, seeing Tom fighting with his jeans again, and trying hard to rearrange himself into a less noticeable position. 'Here, get that down in one, it's Graham's round. That's Karen, by the way. The one you're looking at. The one in the white top. She's a good laugh, she is. Easy with it, as well. You get on the dance floor in a minute and give her the eye and I'll bet she'll come over to dance with you. She likes meeting new people.'

Tom found he had a cigarette in his hand again. Was it his second, or third? He couldn't remember. Did it matter, anyway? No, nothing mattered. He dragged heavily on it, holding the smoke in as he gulped down the last of the coke and handed the empty glass to Graham, politely asking if he could possibly have something a little stronger this time. He was too far gone to notice the other two choking back their laughter.

Feeling so relaxed with his new found friends, so comfortable, he confided, 'I can't dance, Sam. Can't I just buy her a drink?'

'Hell, no! You can't do that, she'd be insulted. That's what you do with prossies. She'd tell you to piss off. No you have to dance around a bit having a good time first - let everyone see how well your body moves, then anything goes!'

'But I can't dance. I don't normally go to discos.'

Graham returned with the drinks. Handing them out, he placed a triple vodka and orange in front of Tom.

Sam said, 'Don't worry, Tom, I've got something that'll sort that out for you. Here, pop this in your mouth and swallow it down with a mouthful of that drink. That'll make you move to the music. One of these and anyone can dance, I promise you! Anyone at all! Go on, get it down you. Its going to take about twenty minutes to half an hour to start working anyway, so you'd better swallow it now before someone else comes along and catches her eye.'

Tom giggled, he felt great, but the thought of someone else . . . No! Popping the tablet on his tongue, he swallowed quickly, chasing it down with a large mouthful of the triple vodka.

'Here,' Tom slurred a few minutes later, fumbling in his pocket until he found the twenty pound note which he threw down on to the table, 'I gotta pay fur sumfink . . . Get some more drink . . . I gotta have a pee.'

Standing up, swaying, he tried to focus again, this time to see the way out to the toilets, to find the easiest way through the crowd that had now multiplied to many hundreds. He couldn't see a way out, not an easy one, so he sat down again, holding himself whilst giggling stupidly.

The first rave record of the night came on. Ronnie had arrived and taken over the console, but Tom would never have realised. The dancing-to-the-beat disco lights changed, superseded by intensive strobe lighting, laser pictures writing themselves on the screens and on the walls, sirens, klaxons, and periods of near complete darkness. Ecstatic screams of appreciation erupted from the now bursting dance floor.

It was pitch dark, another siren wailed, the dancers were screaming their tits off, the poppers were out, people were floating, dancing in the air and playing with the angels, when suddenly Tom felt strong arms grabbing him, picking him up bodily in the darkness, lifting him up, up, up, and carrying him away. He was unable to resist. He didn't want to resist. He giggled. Then, there was bumping, being carried, pulled, up some stairs, bump, bump, bump, footsteps echoing round and round and round mixing with the music that went round and round and round. Up, up, up. Forever and ever and ever and then suddenly falling, falling, falling, down, further and further, more and more, down and further down. Now there was a light, a blinding light. A face. Oh, what a lovely face. It was such a beautiful friendly face, so nice, so kind, so loving. Oh, everything felt so wonderful!

'Man, you's some fuckin' idiot!' Randy shouted down at him.

Tom put his arms out, he wanted to cuddle him, he needed to, he felt so loving. Giggling again, 'I want a peeeeeeee,' he sang.

'Oh, man! No! Really?'

'I want a peeeeeee.'

Randy switched off the light and, opening one of the tower's small slatted windows, he pulled the boy up, steering him towards it.

'Here, man, have this one on the town.'

Tom stood at the window relieving himself for what, to Randy who was still having to hold him up, seemed an eternity. The light went on again. Randy spun around pulling Tom with him.

'Bloody hell! Certainly runs in the family, doesn't it?' Sarah was standing in the doorway holding two large mugs of black coffee.

Tom giggled, and put his arms out. He wanted to cuddle her. Oh, how he wanted to cuddle her.

'Where's his old man?' Randy asked her as she bent down to place the mugs on the dusty wooden floor.

'Is that a trick question?' Sarah quipped, but Randy missed the connection so she carried on, 'Ian's talked him into doing the coats. One of the part-timers hasn't turned in so we're a bit short.'

'How about his mother? Where's she?'

'She's down there nattering with Beryl. You know how Beryl can natter. She could natter for England! They're getting on great guns! Randy . . . . Isn't he going to put that away?'

'Oh,' Randy spun the helpless giggling mass around so he faced away from her. Taking a deep breath, and lifting his eyes to the ceiling, he fumbled with Tom. 'Oh, man! I's done some things in me time but this . . .'

Sarah burst out laughing, 'He's cute, really. I'd go for him if he wasn't the boss. Hey, I'd better get back before I'm missed. See you later.'

'Thanks, love,' he called after her, 'I's owes you one.'

Randy turned off the light. Sitting the young lad on the floor, and propping him up by leaning him against the wall, he stayed with him until nearly half an hour later when, with a lot of encouragement, the last of the coffee was gone and Tom had drifted off into a deep sleep. Satisfied the lad had now crashed, and that he probably wouldn't wake up for at least three or four hours, Randy decided to go back downstairs to see what the three lads from the Inferno gang were up to.

The whole place was heaving when he re-entered the main area. At least eight hundred, he guessed, possibly more. Amyl nitrate fumes mixed with the unmistakable smell of marijuana induced an instant high and camouflaged the putrid smell of the stale body odour and sweat being released by the bucket load, dripping off the bodies of the writhing mass on to the floor where only the stickiness of the spilt drinks prevented it from becoming slippery to the point of being lethal. Pushing his way through the crowd, now six deep at the bar waiting to be served, he caught Sarah's eye.

'How is he?' she went over to him and asked, much to the annoyance of several others who had been waiting to be served.

'He's crashed out, he will be okay. Is the crowd he was with still here?'

'In front of stage with that stinky Bob last time I saw them. Selling it like there was no tomorrow.'

Randy pushed his way back through the heaving throng, out into the foyer again, and then made his way upstairs. Using his key, he went through the 'Staff Only' door, up another flight, along the corridor, diverting briefly to go up yet another flight to check that Tom was still sleeping peacefully in the tower, before following the alternative route down three flights of stairs to come back out into the main area through the door by the stage. The one through which he had earlier grabbed Tom.

Putting a firm hand on Sam's shoulder, he nodded that he should follow him out through the door. Hesitantly the young man obeyed.

'What's the crack, man?' Randy demanded, holding him threateningly. 'What the fuck you lot up to, getting him in that state. You knew who he was, didn't you? Now, you tell me, what the fuck's been going on, man?'

'Get your bloody hands off me!' Sam screamed at him. 'Touch me and the rest of 'em will take you out!'

'Yeah? And what will they do to you when they find out how much time you's spending at Dorothy's, eh? Phil would castrate you first, then kill you afterwards, man, if he knew what I's knows about you!'

Randy was bluffing. He knew no such thing for real but he played hunches and he had a hunch, for what reason he didn't know, it was just a feeling, but the shocked look on the lad's face suggested he was right; that he had hit a nerve.

'You wouldn't dare! Anyway, it's not what you think!'

'Oh, I's knows exactly what it is, man.' Randy decided to push his luck further, 'You's like palming off some of Phil's drugs. You's selling them there, aren't you, man? You knows Phil's homophobic. You know he won't have nothing to do with Dorothy's, so I's suppose you think you's pretty safe. I's tell you, man, if he even suspected you were going there, you would be dead!'

'What was it you wanted to know?' Sam asked, deciding it might be prudent not to call the black deejay's bluff. He wondered just how much Randy really knew. What had he been told? And by who?

'I's wants to know why you lots been spiking Tom's drinks all night. Why you's been popping him drugs. What's you, or should I's say what's Phil, hoping to achieve doing that shit, man?'

'I don't know. Honestly, I don't. Phil told us we got to do it. I don't know what he's got planned. That's the truth, believe me!'

Randy smiled at him cynically, leaving him in no doubt that he didn't believe his story. He was not satisfied.

'Look, it's true, really!' Sam spluttered. 'If it's any help we had to get him wrecked and then disappear for a while. We had to stop trading and be away from here between two and three o'clock. So, whatever he's got planned must be for after two, but before three. That's all I know, really it is.'

Glancing at his watch first, it was a little after twelve-forty-five, Randy brought his foot up until it found the pit of Sam's stomach. With a mighty shove he sent the young man reeling back crazily through the double doors into the disco, then taking the stairs several at a time, he returned to the tower to find Tom, as he had expected, still sleeping peacefully.

'Man, you's better bleedin' answer,' he said under his breath, whilst speedily pressing the buttons on the mobile phone.

'You got me,' the voice answered almost immediately.

'Ollie?'

'Ran the man! Yeah 'tis I. Me feet on the ground, me head in the sky. Where'ya at?'

'Ollie. I's need help, man. Man, does I's need help! Can you get your car outside the back fire exit at the Ellie in the next half hour?'

'You ain't blagging the place, is you boy?' Ollie shrilled down the phone in his characteristically high-pitched voice.

'Don't be stupid! No, man, I's in deep shit! Can you get here?' Randy was pleading.

'Stay alive, be there in five!'

Pushing the aerial back down, Randy once more rushed down the three long flights of stairs. Opening the emergency exit door, he waited anxiously until at last it arrived. The big old customised Thunderbird convertible cruised into the yard, slushing to a halt outside the door.

'What's this crack? Hiding round the back,' the six-foot-four black driver sang out, leaping from the car without opening the door. Randy signalled him to follow him up the stairs.

'Who dat boy, boy?' Ollie enquired, opening his eyes wide, and still being the comedian as he entered the tower room.

'Never you mind that now, man. We's gotta get him outa here, pronto!'

CHAPTER 5

'Evenin' Beryl,' the stout middle-aged man greeted her confidently as he bustled his mass through the door.

Looking up, Beryl saw Detective Inspector Summers crossing the foyer. Sporting a poorly fitting striped blue suit, with a mustard coloured tie and brown brogues, the bright red socks that he wore were undeniably clashing with everything else and mattered far more than the cardinal sin of mixing blue with brown. The man's brave, perhaps more outrageously stupid, fashion statement was all topped off by a brown trilby hat that had undoubtedly seen better days. To Beryl's easily amused mind the man before her, to all effect, resembled something like an animated over-filled hot dog, but she chose not to laugh at him. That would have been too kind. Instead, finding one of her appropriate looks, there was one for every occasion, she fired it at him. This one screamed of disrespect.

Approaching the ticket office, closely followed by his gum chewing, more casually dressed and much slimmer young colleague, the Inspector continued drawling, 'Understand the new bosses have arrived. Taken over, like. Thought we had better just pop in to see them. You know, have a word, so's to speak.'

Beryl scowled at the man. Pressing the button by the side of her she spoke into the desktop microphone, 'Ian. We have some visitors. Pinky and Perky are at front of house to see you. Do you read?'

The reference to pigs was clearly picked up by the two men who looked at her contemptuously for a moment, however they decided it would be wise not to pursue it. It would be best to let it go. Sweet and mummsie-looking Beryl might outwardly seem, but they knew her better than that. She was definitely not one they would wish to cross swords with unnecessarily.

'Be right there,' Ian's voice crackled back through the static.

They waited impatiently, fidgeting self-consciously as Beryl surveyed them with another one of her well-practised looks. One she had long perfected. It was the kind of disgusted look that a person might give to the owner of a dog that had just excreted on the pavement directly in front of them. She even dusted her nose with her handkerchief to add realism to the effect. Knowing better than to look back at her, or to challenge her eyes in any way, the two policemen wandered over to stand at the entrance, preferring to stare out through the glass doors into the night at the sporadically passing traffic. Several minutes passed.

'Ah, Detective Inspector Summers, and Detective Constable Jones,' Ian called out to them when he finally arrived in the foyer, 'how nice it is to see you both again. It has been a long time, hasn't it? Now, to what do we owe this honour? There's nothing wrong, I hope?'

'No, just passing, Ian. Just passing. Nothing wrong. Heard the new people had arrived so we thought we'd better just pop in. You know, have a word. Introduce ourselves to the new owners, so's to speak. Are they around, perchance?'

Ian steered the two policemen over to the coat check-in counter.

'Mr Patterson,' he said, flashing his eyes upwards, 'these two gentlemen are from the local constabulary. They would like a word with you and your wife. If you want to take them up to the flat for some privacy, I can get Beryl to watch the counter. She can always call one of the Security guys if someone wants their coat.'

'Ah, Mr Patterson,' Summers pulled himself up to his full stature, thumbing his lapels, and rising up and down on the balls of his feet, trying to look important as he greeted him. 'We were just passing,' he said. 'We thought we ought to have a word with you, and your good lady, of course. Ought to introduce ourselves, so's to speak. There's no time like the present, I always say. Somewhere in private, away from all that damn noise might be better methinks. And perhaps you could find your son as well. Tommy, isn't it? I understand that he is in fact the true proprietor, or he shortly will be, and that you are only technically holding the ownership in trust until he succeeds title, is that correct?'

'Yes, I suppose so, although it's only my wife and I who are legally responsible at present, not Tom. If there is anything wrong, I'm afraid it's down to us. Right, well I suppose you had better come up to the flat. Ian, I wonder, would you be kind enough to find Tom for me? Send him up to the flat?'

66

'I think he may have gone up there, already,' Ian replied. 'I've circled the whole place a couple of times in the last hour, I'm pretty sure he's not down here anywhere. Come to think of it, I haven't seen him since before midnight, but I'll certainly have another look. I'll get Security to search for him as well.'

John led the way up the stairs to the flat where Mary was still busy methodically unpacking the many boxes surrounding her. She said she had not seen Tom for hours either. He had definitely not returned to the flat all evening. She would have heard him.

Offering them a choice of tea or coffee, which they both politely declined, Mary carried on with her unpacking whilst the policemen waited patiently, though in painful silence, for Tom to appear.

'I'm afraid Tom's not in the building,' Ian's voice bellowed through the Tannoy little more than ten minutes later. 'We've done a complete search from top to bottom. One of the bar girls thinks that maybe Randy has taken him out to show him Seathorpe by night. She said she saw them together earlier.'

Mary looked up at her husband, worried. It was not like their son to go off anywhere without telling them. That was something he had never done. He would always tell them where he was going if he went out, and what time to expect him home. It was something that had never been forced on him, but something he always did naturally. It was just his polite way.

'Perhaps we'd better come back another night then, when we can catch you all together,' the Inspector suggested, forcing a smile at them which could not conceal that beneath it he looked rather uneasy. 'We won't hold you up any more now, I can see you are both very busy. Nice meeting you.'

With the gum-chewing Jones following closely on his heels, Inspector Summers politely tipped his hat at them and speedily left.

#

Ollie leapt out of the car and running up the steps of the large terraced house, he rang the doorbell. Two short rings, one long, two short, and one long. A face peered out from behind an upstairs curtain that moved slightly. Moments later, the front door swung open.

'This better be good,' Ollie's grotesquely fat, but equally as tall, older brother stated, standing in the doorway wearing only a pair of atrociously pink-spotted, white boxer shorts with his enormous gut protruding, more flopping, over the top of them. 'You know what time it is, boy? You know? This ain't no time to come a knocking, I'm busy. I'm a tellin' ya I has got a woman here tonight. I is entertainin'. Now what the hell's you a doin' ringing mah doorbell at this time a night?'

'Need to use your place for awhile, big brother. We need your help, like we need a mother.' Ollie sang out, running back down the steps.

'What? What's that you say? You serious, boy?'

Tom became vaguely aware of being lifted again. Half carried, half dragged up more steps. He could feel his toes strangely tingling as they bumped against each riser. Bump, bump, bump. It was a peculiar feeling. One that he could vaguely remember having experienced somewhere before. It was a nice feeling. Strange, but nice. He giggled, his nose started to run, so he giggled some more.

'Sorry about this, Winston,' Randy apologised as they awkwardly squeezed Tom's limp form past the enormous protruding stomach and through into the living room, letting it fall full-spread along the settee, 'sorry old mate, but we's in real deep shit, man!'

'You're sorry! You're sorry! You know what I was a doing, boy? And just who the hell is this little honky? Why has you brought him inside mah house? Why has you done that? You ain't a gonna be leaving him here! Oh, no! Don't you go a thinking you can leave 'im 'ere! No sireee!'

Ollie started to coo again: 'It's Randy's new boss at the Ellie. They call him Tom, and he's not wellie. He's okay, really, quite a guy. But Phil's lot got him, made him high,' he sang.

'Yeah, man. They's got him in this state with drink and drugs, Christ knows why,' Randy jumped in quickly to continue the story. He couldn't bear listening to Ollie's shrill poetry a moment longer. 'Problem is we's only got a couple of hours to bring him round, man. We needs to get him back to the Ellie before they closes, before he's missed, and we doesn't dare take him back in this state. Can you make some of your special mash for him, man? Please, man, please! Extra strong!'

'Jeeeesus! I don't believe it! I justus don't a believe it! Mash! You is a wanting mash at this time o' the night! And for a honky, too! I'm a tellin' ya, I is floored, boy! You has a got me, I is really floored! Truly I is! Well, I suppose you has a better take him outside into that yard, boy. You sit him out the back right now cos I ain't a havin' him throwing up in here! No way! Oh, no! No, siree!'

Begrudgingly, Winston disappeared into the kitchen, leaving them to drag Tom out through the French windows into the back yard. Sitting either side of him, propping him up on the old rickety park bench underneath the kitchen window, they could hear the tins and jars being slammed around in the kitchen as Ollie's big brother went to work preparing his special concoction; his miracle cure.

'Mash. Extra strong,' he said, emerging a little while later. Grinning, he handed Ollie the foul smelling steaming mug.

Randy tilted Tom's head all the way back and forced the boy's mouth wide open. Pulling away as far as he could to avoid the disgusting smell of the mixture, he watched while Ollie shovelled a piled high spoonful of the porridge-like substance in, forcing it deep into the back of the boy's throat, then poking it even further down with his finger. The reaction was as expected, and almost immediate. The mouth began desperately trying to spit the stuff out, while the throat was gagging violently with some of the mixture trying to go down at the same time as some other was trying to evacuate upwards. Already the stuff was beginning to work. Consciousness was slowly returning. Tom's eyes had started to open. There was an awareness. Panic was written there. Ollie shoved more of the foul smelling mixture into the boy's mouth, then holding it tightly shut he pushed some up, right up, into the lad's nostrils. Tom leapt to his feet, his eyes wide open, spluttering, snorting, coughing, choking, with his arms flaying around in all directions.

'Give him the full treatment, to make sure,' Ollie shrill-laughed as he handed over the mug. 'Only, you do it, boy. Cos that's not mah door!'

'Oh, man! No, man! Really?' Randy protested, leaning forward, grabbing hold of Tom's belt and unbuckling it. 'Man, oh, man!'

Wriggling Tom's tight-fitting jeans down to his knees, not without difficulty, Randy threw him across his lap. Forcefully, he inserted as much of the obnoxious substance as he could into the only place it could go, whilst shouting loudly into the ear of the writhing and screaming lad, 'Man, does you ever bleedin' owe me one!'

The fiery pain from everywhere the mash had entered him sent Tom's adrenaline rocketing, and his metabolic rate spun in to hyper-drive. All the drug induced, mellowed senses and confused brain cells being suddenly over-ridden, by-passed by the never before experienced, impossible to ignore, stimulation. In an instant brain chemicals were induced wiping out the saturating psuedo dopamine effects with their own brand of methylphenidate to the exact amounts.

Opening his eyes fully again, consciousness forced back with a vengeance, Tom grabbed up his jeans, looked at the two of them in horror for a split second, then in total disbelief he screamed. He needed the loo. Oh God, how he needed the loo! Urgently, he screamed! The look of panic that was living on his face only moments ago had changed to one of sheer terror. Ollie and Randy burst into fits of hysterical laughter, tears began to stream down their faces. Speedily they bundled Tom into the outside toilet and left him there. They knew what came next. It was certainly not a time to hang around.

The moans and groans, coupled with various other indescribable lavatorial noises persisted, echoing around the dimly lit yard for a full fifteen minutes before an almost convincingly sober, but terribly embarrassed, Tom nervously emerged.

'God! What the hell have you done to me? What's this muck I've got all over me? More to the point, where the hell am I?' he asked, trying hard to remember the last couple of hours.

'Oh, that's a little something we call Cabellana, man. It's an old Jamaican remedy for rum-eye, but it works well with drugs too. It's a secret formula that's been passed down through time, generation to generation, though few people seems to know about it these days. It's so potent, we reckons it could bring back the dead, man! But don't you go feeling rotten,' Randy said, putting a comforting arm around the 'feeling oh, so ashamed' youth's shoulders. 'Winston and Ollie have had to do the same thing to me on more than one occasion, man. If it's any consolation, at least you made it to the loo!'

'Thank God for that!' Tom exclaimed, beginning to feel slightly better. 'I don't seem to remember much of what happened tonight. I know I was sitting in the disco when some lads got friendly. They bought me some drinks, I can remember that. I can remember trying one of their funny cigarettes too, and then it all gets a bit hazy.

'Wow! So, that's what drugs are like, eh? Most excellent! Wild! I can remember feeling very nice, very sort of loving at one point, but . . . Oh my God! No! Tell me no! My parents didn't see me like that, did they? They didn't, did they? Oh, God, no! And how on earth did I manage to get here? Where is here? It's all so hazy. I don't remember anything that could be real. Oh, my God, I feel so foolish. I didn't do anything really stupid, did I?'

Randy winked at him, laughing, 'Not unless you call groping me, kissing me, and sticking you's tongue all the way down my throat silly, man. It don't matter though, man, I's loved it really. You got me real horny! Pity we didn't finish it, though!'

'No!' Tom roared in disbelief that he could do such a thing. His face immediately shooting from the over-indulged pasty colour he had been wearing to a bright red, with no in-betweens.

That was more than one too many for Ollie. Unable to hold it back any longer, he flew off indoors. Choking sobs, followed by wails of hysterical laughter erupted from within the kitchen as he helplessly rolled about on the floor holding his stomach muscles with his hands to try to stop the pain.

'Joking, man! Just joking!' Randy came clean, the tears of mirth uncontrollably streaming down his cheeks again. He too had to bend double now, holding his stomach tightly to stop the laughing hurting it any more. It was impossible, so impossible, but finally he did manage to continue, 'No, you were no worse than any of us has been at sometime. Don't worry about it, man. It's cool. And no, man, you's parents didn't see you. That's why we brought you here, so nobody would see you, but we will have to leave soon, man. We ought to get back before closing. I's reckon we should walk back, there's still time if we leave soon. It's a fair old way so you should be completely recovered by the time we gets there, man.

'By the way, in case you's not realised it, man, those cokes you were downing all night must have been spiked with something. At least double vodkas, I's reckon. They weren't just cokes because you were well on the way long before you had that first spliff. I's was watching you getting more and more drunk from the deejay's box. Man, you were really set up! Pity you can't see all the bar from up there, man, or I's could have told you exactly what you's been drinking. I's bet you don't even remember taking that pill either, man!'

'Pill? What pill?'

'No, I's thought not. Come on, man. It's nearly time we made a move, but you's better run upstairs and take a quick shower first. It's alright with Winston. First door top of the stairs, man.'

'Okay, I'll be as quick as I can. God! My mouth and my nose are burning They feel like they're on fire! And elsewhere! Jesus, you really don't want to know about my arse! What the hell does he make that stuff with - sulphuric acid?'

Randy grinned. He knew all about his arse.

#

'What d'ya mean he wasn't fuckin' there?' Phil spat the question at the fat Inspector. Standing up, glaring into the man's eyes, he thumped his fist on the desk, kicking the chair away behind him. 'What d'ya fuckin' mean? Ian phoned me earlier, the little fucker was as high as a bleedin' kite then! Idiots! You're nothing but bloody idiots! Stupid bastards! What the fuck do I pay you for? Didn't you have a good look round? He had to be there. He couldn't have gone bloody far in that state, could he?'

'But Phil, Ian looked himself. Everybody looked. Security, everybody! He was not there, I tell you. He must have gone out. Don't forget, we don't even know what he looks like yet,' the Inspector spluttered.

'Bloody idiots! Piss off! Now we have nothing to hold over them, no leverage at all! Fuck knows what's going to happen when Bob asks for our cut tonight, especially if the old man's there. Ian can't exactly lose thousands of fucking pounds a night now, not with him watching every move, can he? Idiots! Bloody idiots! Just fuck off! Go on, get out my bleedin' sight!'

Phil started to pace up and down, deep in thought. The two police officers didn't need telling to leave again - they eagerly beat a hasty retreat. Paul, sitting in the corner by the coffee table had finished counting out the little cellophane packets. He decided to re-count them, all over again. Now was not the time to appear unoccupied.

Picking up the phone, Phil called Ian. 'You'll just have to tell the old

1

boy it's standard bloody practise. Tell him everybody does it. It's the recognised thing. Then separate Bob's money and see what happens. Play it by ear. Tell him what's likely to fuckin' happen if he doesn't pay up. Frighten the silly old fart! If he doesn't bloody pay up, then we will have to do something for real. We'll have to hit the place tomorrow night. Shit or fuckin' bust!'

CHAPTER 6.

It was shortly after four o'clock that morning when Tom and Randy arrived back at the club. Any hopes they might have held of returning unnoticed were dashed when, on entering by the back door, they discovered Simon approaching from the inside to check the door was secure for the night.

'Your parents have been looking for you,' the security man informed Tom. 'I think your mum's more than a bit worried you'd got lost or something. They're upstairs in the office cashing up. Do you want me to call them, to tell them you're okay?'

'No, thanks. I'll go straight up there,' Tom replied, tugging on his friend's shirt for him to follow.

'I's can't go in there while they's cashing up,' Randy explained, but nevertheless still following him up the stairs. 'Only management is allowed in there when the money's being counted, man. There could be anything up to twenty grand floating around in there on a good night. People gets a bit nervous with that kinda money about, man.'

'Rubbish! Of course you can come in. Don't forget, I'm the boss, or I will be in a couple of weeks time when it's all sorted out. If I say it's all right, then it's all right, believe me. I mean, after all you've done for me tonight, if I couldn't trust you who the hell could I trust? Now come on.'

Tom rang the bell outside the door then looked up grinning directly into the lens of the closed circuit camera. The door was opened almost immediately. It was Ian who ushered them inside, before quickly scanning the passage and bolting it again.

'Tom,' his mother looked up from counting a stack of twenty-pound notes. 'I was getting worried. Where on earth have you been? It's not like you to go off out without saying something.'

'Sorry, mum,' he apologized, giving her the loving son look. 'I think it

was through being so tired after the long moving day, then what with all
the noise and smoke down there earlier, the stuffiness and that, I came
over a bit queasy. Randy noticed I didn't look too good so he took me out
for some fresh air. Cutting a long story short, we bumped into a couple
of his friends. We all got talking, like you do, and finally landed up going
for a coffee somewhere miles up the road, not realising how late it was
getting.'

Ian took a long hard look at Tom and tried not to show his surprise
that the youth, to all visible signs, was completely sober and in full
command of his faculties. 'I'll quickly go over what we've done so far,'
he told him. He then explained how each till had been totalled, checked
against the sum registered, and the money then brought upstairs for a
final counting.

'So everything's okay?' John asked. 'All the tills are within a few
pounds of being correct. I suppose we don't have to go looking for the
odd quid that's over or under, do we?'

'No, you'd never find it. You're never going to get anything exactly
right, not with the amount of money that turns over in such a short time,
especially in what amounts to being an organised chaos most of the time.
It does get hectic down there, as you will have seen. There will always be
some mistakes made. It's only if it's regularly down on a till that it is ever
worth investigating. Fortunately, that hasn't happened for years.

'Right, so if we now add these three sums together, we get the grand
total of what we should have. That's, let me see, nineteen thousand four
hundred and fifty-two. See, that is less than fifteen pounds different to
what we actually have. Quite a good night, anyway!'

'Amazing! The old corner shop took nearly a month to make that
kind of money,' John said light-heartedly, 'and here it's just one night's
takings. I find that absolutely amazing!'

'Ah! It only sounds a lot,' Ian explained. 'You mustn't lose sight of
the outgoings, they're big money as well. Real big. A great deal of what
we've taken is used up straight away to replace all the food and drink
that's gone tonight, and then don't forget there's the staffs' wages for
the night, the heating and the lighting - you'll never believe the gas and
electric bills, they're absolutely phenomenal! On top of that there's the
buildings insurance, the third party insurance we have to have, the rates,

the taxes, all the different licences, not forgetting the maintenance, the depreciation costs, and the such-like. They mount up to a hell of a lot of money at the end of the day, and that's before we start on the music side. That's before we buy all the latest records, CDs, and videos that are released each week. Some weeks Ronnie spends hundreds of pounds and perhaps only plays them a couple of times. But that's the game. You have to be up-to-date or else the punters won't come.

'Plus you have to remember, we don't take this much every day. Early and mid-week is much quieter, and through the winter months you wonder why you bother opening at all. Then of course there is the, er, you can call it the local insurance if you like. It's, um, sort of accepted to, er, to have to give up ten per cent of the gross takings each night for, shall we say, peace of mind. Someone will be calling up for that shortly, I should think.'

Tom felt Randy nudge his leg with his knee. John and Mary, as if one, stopped what they were doing and looked up at Ian in disbelief. Had he said what they thought he had said?

'Do you mean protection? We have to pay protection money? Ten per cent? A sort of Al Capone mob racket? Here, in Seathorpe? In this day and age? Surely not?' John was plainly unhappy with the idea. 'Is that what you're trying to say, Ian?'

'Yes, I'm afraid it's been accepted practise here for a long time. Well, about five years actually. All the big concessions on the front pay their ten per cent. We're all in the same boat. The expenses to just be here, to simply exist, are extremely high as I have explained. If for any reason one were unable to trade, even for a short while, they would soon be out of business. Gone bust! Remember, open or not, what this place costs a day to run. You wouldn't have to be closed for too long before you were in trouble. Serious trouble. It's far better to pay up, smile, and accept it as a way of life,' Ian advised, mustering as much charm as he could find.

'I'm damned if I will!' John said sharply. 'If they cause any trouble here, I'll have the police on to them. People ought to make a stand against thugs like that! There will be no more ten per cents from here, I can assure you! You can tell that to whoever it is who collects it. This is modern day, hi-tech, England - not Chicago in the bloody twenties!'

'Perhaps we ought to talk about it before we do anything rash, darling,'

Mary suggested, fearful of the consequences. 'I mean, if it's normal practise . . .

'What will happen if we don't pay?' Tom joined in the debate. 'What will they be likely to do?'

'They could do anything,' Ian replied. 'They're a rough lot. They could burn the place down, send a load of rowdies in to wreck the place, maybe even slash a few faces to put the frighteners on and scare all the punters away. Anything. It really is best not to cross them. Truly, it is.'

'Oh my God!' Mary exclaimed, the colour rapidly draining from her face.

The bell rang. All eyes turned to the monitor to see the man waiting outside.

'That's Bob, the collector,' Ian said. 'Shall I let him in?'

'Let him in,' John said, quickly scooping up the money he turned and put it into the safe. 'I'll tell him, all right,' he snarled. Turning the lock, he put the key in his pocket. 'I'll tell him.'

Ian pulled the bolt, and opened the door. The sickly smell of body odour preceded the man as he entered. Tom and Randy quickly moved back farther into the office to avoid being too near the putrid smelling man.

'Hello there,' he said, offering out a grubby looking hand, 'so we meet at last. You know who I am of course? Bob?'

John ignored the hand. 'Yes, I know who you are. I know what you are. And I will tell you now: I am having none of it. You can tell your boss to go take a run and a jump. Things have changed here now we are running this place. There will be no more ten per cents, not from here. You can also consider yourself barred. I don't want to see you on these premises again. Now get out of here before I call the police and have you arrested.'

'Ha! That's a laugh! That's a real gem! Perhaps you ought to put this idiot in the picture, Ian,' the collector said, turning sharply on his heels. 'You ain't heard the last of this,' he threatened, as he left, 'not by a long way. You're going to be sorry! Very sorry indeed!'

The door slammed shut.

Mary exclaimed, 'Dear God Almighty! What have we got ourselves into? What on earth did he mean? Aren't these crooks frightened of the police?'

'I'll just make sure he gets out okay,' Ian said, opening the door and quickly going after the man.

'I don't think they are frightened of the police,' Tom said, 'but I think Randy could fill us in on that score quite a bit. He knows all about them. What they are like; how dangerous they really are. Perhaps you would like to give us your views, Randy? Are we being stupid, not paying up?'

Randy looked back at Tom with a 'thanks for dropping me in it, chum' kind of expression. 'Man,' he said, 'you's probably have been a bit silly by not paying up. They's a nasty lot, man. Real bad news. You's talking of getting the police on to them. No hope, man! Ain't gonna happen. The gang are the law on the front and the police, they's happy to leave it that way. Saves them a lot of problems, man. You's sure to get a visit from Summers and Jones before long. They's just a couple of the bent coppers who work out of Phil's pocket. Phil is the gang boss man, by the way. Real bad news, man!'

'They've already been,' John interrupted, 'but they left without saying anything much because we couldn't find Tom.'

'Yeah, man. They do a lot of dirty work for Phil. That's when he's being nice, man. When he's not, he sees to it himself. For instance, I's don't know if you's been along the front yet, but six doors down there's a mini casino-come-leisure thing closed down. That was old Fred Titcombe's place. Been there for years he had, man. He tried to make out he wasn't taking as much money as he really was. Tried to pay his ten per cent on a fictitiously low figure, man. But Phil soon worked out he was being conned. Set him up a couple of times, he did. Twice Summers and his sidekick raided the place and found under age gambling going on.

'Of course, old Fred he knew it was Phil who set him up, but still he didn't give in. He kept on lying about his takings. They found his body in there two months ago, supposed to have been electrocuted through changing a light switch with the power still on. Man, that ain't right! Old Fred he wouldn't have done that! He was so lazy he would never have done it himself. He would have talked someone else into doing it for him. It was his way, man. Fred, he never did anything himself. He wouldn't even make himself a cup of tea, not lest he really had to. No, that was Phil's work all right. Phil got rid of him. I's would guarantee it, man!'

'Same with Mark . . .' Randy suddenly felt the stony silence, became uneasy, and decided he had already said too much.

'Go on,' Tom encouraged him, 'we'd rather know it all.'

'But Mark, he was your brother, you may not want to hear it,' he said looking across at John, and then turning back to Tom in an attempt to change the subject. 'By the way, this was his mobile phone, you better have it now, man. He lent it to me that, er, you know, earlier that day. I's been looking after it ever since then. Didn't want to give it to Ian because it's a sorta personal thing, man.'

Tom took the phone and studied it, checking the numbers in its memory. He didn't recognise any, but then he didn't expect to. Mary and John exchanged glances, confirming with each other that they should hear the rest of Randy's story, so it was insisted that the young deejay continue with his account.

'Well, I's already told Tom most of this, and it ain't nice, but if you's really sure you want to know how I's sees it all, man, I's tell you.

'Mark was a good boss. He was a good bloke to work for, man. A real good all round bloke. Of course everybody knew he was a bit of a rogue who liked his drink, drugs, and women, and that he would cut a few corners here and there if he could. But he would never hurt anybody, man. Never do anybody down. Always help the underdog, he would. That's why everybody loved him, man. He was a genuine kinda guy.

'As sure as God made little apples, man, it was Phil or his mob who bumped him off, I's would swear it! Old Mark, he would never have got so pissed - whoops, sorry Mrs P – I's mean he would never have got so drunk, or so high, to fall off them cliffs. He wouldn't even have walked that far anyway, especially up a hill. Not Mark. No way, man! He walked nowhere! And heroin? No way, man, definitely no way, I's knows that for sure, man! Mark, he smoked the wacky-baccy, he popped the old ecstasy tablets regularly, took them like sweets he did, but he wouldn't touch heroin, cocaine or even crack. He was dead set against any of the real hard stuff, man. And I's knows there's no way he would have injected heroin, not himself. He was like real frightened of needles. He was terrified of them, man! I's mean, a proper baby! Last year he even made me go to the clinic with him, almost holding his hand, when he went for the jabs before going on his holidays. He fainted, man! Went out like a light! I's tell you, man, if he was pumped full of heroin it was by someone else, and I's bet it was Phil or his mob that did it!'

The stony silence returned with a vengeance. Mary, who now herself felt faint, decided to sit down. John remained standing, stony-faced.

Tom once again, broke the earth-shattering quiescence. 'If you were us,' he asked his friend, 'what would you do now? I mean, should we go out now, find this Phil bloke and pay up? Say sorry? Or should we make a stand? It sounds very dangerous, making a stand, doesn't it?'

'Man, don't put this on me! All I's can say is if you don't pay up there'll be trouble, that's for sure. Big trouble. But if you do, can you really afford it? Mark, as I's already said, man, he was a bit of a rogue, a sharpster. He had a lot of irons in the fire, man, a whole lot of little fiddles, so he could afford to pay. But if you's going to run this place totally legit, all above board, as I's suspect you are, can you actually pay that much out and still survive?

'I's no business expert that's for sure, but from what I's learnt by knocking around with Mark, keeping my eyes open like, I's think you would be sailing a bit close to the wind, man! It would only take one or two major disasters, one or two large bits of expenditure, to knock you out. I's means, man, you really do not wanna know the prices of some of that sound and lighting equipment! We's talking many tens of thousands of pounds, man! And you's nothing without it! Nobody goes to a disco with no sounds, man! You can't even afford to insure the stuff either because them insurers they has so many get out clauses built into their policies, man. The insurance costs thousands and thousands of pounds, yet they rarely pays out. Mark told me that. The main lighting rig, the big scaffolding thing in the middle hanging down on chains that has about half the lights we uses on it - that, and the controller, was put in two years ago, man, just after I's got here. That alone cost Mark eighty thousand, I's knows that because he showed me the bill, man. And them prices, they keeps going up!

'Mark, he ran this place because he loved it. He loved the atmosphere of hundreds of people around him, all having a good time. He didn't run it for the money, because after all the bills have been paid there ain't a lot left. Least, that's what he's always told me. You's gotta remember, Phil's cut is on the takings, man. Not on the profit. Tonight, man, was a good night, a very good night, and I's bet you made quite a lot of profit, but you should see it in the winter! Perhaps a hundred in on a Friday if you's lucky, man. And the heating, lighting, staff for the night, and all the rest of the bills coming to a lot more than any money you made.

'I's remember last year when the gales blew a hole in the roof and broke the elephant. That cost Mark fifteen grand, even with all the contacts he knew. If anything goes wrong up there you don't just climb a ladder. Not to that height you don't, man. It's a masses of scaffolding, and lots of men, and a lots of work job. And you can't even shut down for the winter because if you did, you would find nothing worked for long when you re-opened next season. Heating pipes gets blocked. Fans seize up. Bulbs, they all blow. Amps they distort and die. Everything goes funny, man. Everything. It's been tried before, and it don't work. It'd cost you a fortune to close down for the winter, man, that's why it stays open all year round. Even when it's losing money, it's still cheaper than closing.'

'So,' Tom seemed to be taking charge, 'there's no way we're going to pay up. We can't afford to. That ten percent is probably the difference between us surviving and making a reasonable living, or going bust. And we're definitely not going down that avenue again. We shall have to think of ways to protect ourselves, and the club, from this Phil character. Let me see, tonight, and that is only one night, he would have creamed nearly two thousand pounds off us. That's some money! He must have been getting something like ten grand a week in the summer from this place!'

'I's guess that's somewhere about right for the peak season,' Randy confirmed, "but don't forget it's only a few hundred in the winter."

Tom looked Randy in the eye. 'Don't take this the wrong way,' he said, 'but you, your mate Ollie and his brother all look more than half-handy. I bet you have many other half-handy friends, too. Could we not come up with enough people who would, for a sum that we could afford, take on this mob with us and get rid of them once and for all? I mean, how many thugs does this Phil have? How many do you think we'd need to put him off, or to even run him out of town?'

'Well, man,' Randy turned, checking the door was closed before continuing, 'I's once had a similar conversation with Mark, but that's about as far as it got. Phil, he somehow found out about it - came down on us like a ton of bricks he did, explaining a few things as well. You see if we did get rid of him then no one would control the front. There would be no one to keep it all together. The drug supplies, they would dry up or at best become irregular. The police, they would have to re-take charge of the area, and that would kill the feel free and easy atmosphere – all that everyone's comes here's for would disappear overnight. In other words, man, the people would all start going elsewhere. They would stop coming and the whole place would die. That's something nobody wants, man! You would get no backing for that from the locals!

'Even Mark, a bit of a rogue that he was, he didn't want to get involved in running the drug scene. And that's what it all revolves around here, man, drugs. Take a few reccy ones himself he certainly did, but to supply them, that's different. Remember man, you has to supply the hard ones as well to keep some of the idiot punters happy. He didn't want to know anything about that side of it, man! So to wipe Phil out, we could easily wipe out the whole resort. And it was only him that really got it all going here in the first place! Most people were struggling to make ends meet before he came. Many might remember that, man, and as much as they hate paying the protection money, they may still side with him if they thought they could lose everything.'

'How on earth did Phil find out about you and Mark discussing things?' Tom was curious.

Randy looked at the door again. 'I's don't trust that Ian, man,' he said quietly. 'I's no proof, but I's got this gut feeling he's on Phil's payroll.'

'Oh!' Tom stole a glance at his parents before reminding Randy, 'You didn't say how big his mob is.'

'Well, there's only about ten that I's can think of at present, that's if you don't count the other traders, or their mates, who might just help him out, but years ago, before my time here, there were supposedly something like twenty of them. Whether or not they's still all on hand to bail him out if need be, I's don't know man, but I's doubt Phil has left too much to chance.'

Catching sight on the monitor of Ian returning, Tom touched his lips signalling to Randy to stop talking, before he opened the door.

'He's gone,' the manager informed them on entering, 'but he's not a happy bloke. I think we'll probably be hearing from Phil very soon.'

Tom decided to lay some bait and prayed that his parents wouldn't give his game away. 'I hope we do,' he said confidently, tapping the mobile phone. 'I've just been in touch with a couple of mates from back home.

We can expect something like a dozen heavy lads turning up here in the next few days, Ian. Perhaps more, if we are lucky. They're coming here first so we'll have to find some accommodation for them, but that shouldn't be too much of a problem, should it?' He smiled questioningly at the troubled manager.

Ian turned perceptibly pale. 'Er, no, I shouldn't think so,' he answered nervously. 'Um, if it's okay with you, I'll be off now. Everything's all locked up and shut down safely. I will, er . . . I will lock the front doors as I go and I'll see you about mid-day tomorrow to show you how we normally do the banking. Is that alright?'

Tom looked across to his father, who took the prompt, saying, 'Fine. Yes. Thank you. See you tomorrow - well later today, really. Thanks Ian. Goodnight. Mind how you go.'

Ian forced a smile before hurrying out.

'What was all that about?' Tom's father asked, as soon as the door closed.

'I thought we ought to play for time,' Tom replied. 'If Randy's right, Ian will be on to Phil within minutes. Now, if he thinks we know how to look after ourselves, that we have some real heavy friends, then that may be enough stop him doing something awful in the next few days.'

'And then what? What happens when he sees nobody turns up?'

'We'll think of something. We have to! God, I'm tired,' he yawned. 'How far have you got to go, Randy? Can we get you a taxi?'

'No thanks, I's will be alright, man. I's will walk home. It's not far. You has to let me out though – I's don't have keys for the front, and nobody goes out the back on their own this late at night. Not always safe, man. Goodnight Mr and Mrs P. See you tomorrow, sometime.'

The parents bade the lad a fond goodnight, thanking him for all his help. Tom followed him down to the foyer to let him out.

'Somehow I feel I know you like an old friend,' Tom said, grabbing hold of the young Jamaican and spinning him round to face him immediately before he went out through the doors into the cool of the night. 'I can almost read you like a book. You've got nowhere to go, have you?'

'Shit, man! How's you know that?'

'Never you mind! From now on, you live here. No arguments! We have a spare bed. I'll give you a hand putting it together, and then tomorrow we'll sort you out a room of your own.'

'Man, how in tarnation did you know I's had nowhere to go?'

'No great secret, really. You were not in any great hurry to go. You apparently spend all your spare time here - so much time you couldn't possibly have another job. And then there were the flashy clothes I saw drying in the old upper circle when I lost my bearings up there earlier today - they had to be yours! Plus, I saw the wages book earlier. On a tenner a night you aren't likely to be renting accommodation at a seaside resort, and if you lived with friends, or your folks, you wouldn't be washing your clothes here, would you?'

'Jeees! Sherlock Holmes, man! He would have had nothing on you! No, you's right, I's got nowhere to go. Mark used to look after me and let me's kip down in a spare room, mainly because I's used to look after him. Like when he got a bit too drunk, or too high, man, I's would have to get him to bed safely. It was a sort of arrangement we had that worked well, man. That is until he died, of course. Lately I's been hiding up in the storeroom, the old upper circle, when it's come to closing time. Nobody ever goes in there.'

'Right, well you live here now, and for as long as you want to. You can look out for us now, although I don't think any of us will be getting too drunk, or too high. At least I hope not.

'I must confess though, I did find some of tonight quite fun. Most excellent! Actually I could easily be tempted to try something again one night!' Tom grinned, giving his new friend a wink. 'And as for your wages, I think ten quid a day is disgusting for all what you do! We will have to get that changed to something decent tomorrow. Come on, let's sort you out a bed.'

'Oh, shit man! You's really something else! How come you's got white skin?'

CHAPTER 7

'Oh, my Gawd!'

Tom rubbed his eyes, opening them to see his mother stood by the side of his bed holding a large mug of steaming coffee. She was obviously flustered about something, her face redder than normal he noticed, as she fought to place the drink on his bedside cabinet without spilling it. She was not succeeding.

'I didn't know Randy was staying over,' she spluttered, desperately trying to keep a straight face. 'I'll fetch another coffee and . . .' She lost it. Unable to keep a straight face any longer, she fled from the room laughing, '. . . and I'll leave it outside,' she blurted from the landing.

Tom blinked. Thinking his mother had gone crazy overnight, he sat up and looked around, eventually seeing the cause of her amusement. Randy was lying on top of the camp bed on the opposite side of the room, stark naked and morning proud, with his duvet a crumpled heap by his feet. Tom threw one of his pillows at him.

'Man,' he said, waking up stretching, and then reaching down to pull the cover up over him, 'what time is it?'

'Nearly eleven,' Tom answered him. Then hearing his mother returning, called out. 'You can come in, now, Ma.'

Mary peered around the door, another coffee in her hand, to see Randy pulling the duvet up from his chest, all the way up to his chin in a full modesty cover-up.

'I . . . aha, I . . . ha, ha, ha,' the tears now started to stream down her face. She looked across to Tom. 'I . . . ha, ha, ha . . .' There was no help there.

Tom too had tears in his eyes, now bursting into side-splitting laughter too. His mother could only put the cup on the floor, in the middle of the room, and flee.

'Man! What's up, man? What's you all laughing at? You lot always wake up like this, man? Shit, man, you's all crazy!'

Pulling the cover up around him, Randy wriggled down the bed until he could lean forward to reach the coffee. Tom was still laughing, although desperately trying not to, which seemed to only make matters worse.

'Man, why's she put it all the way over here?' Randy was still bewildered.

The door opened a few inches again and, having regained some composure, Mary called through the gap to tell them their clean towels were in the bathroom. Breakfast was in twenty minutes.

Ablutions completed, the two youths appeared at the table precisely on time.

'Sorry, mum. I didn't tell you last night as you'd already gone to bed by the time we came back up. I told Randy he could stay here. Mark used to put him up, so he has nowhere else to go, really. He's sort of . . . homeless. I said with all the spare rooms that we have, he could have one. I hope you don't mind.'

'No, of course I don't mind. You are very welcome, Randy. You can have the room next to Tom's. It's quite large, looks out on to the front, and it's got a Yale lock for your . . . for your . . . priva . . . aha . . . your priva . . . aha . . .' Mary, grabbing the handkerchief from her pinafore pocket, rushed out of the room, wiping her eyes.

Randy's eyes opened wide, slowly looking left to right, then back again, surveying all around him. He could hear Tom's mother in the next room, roaring in hysterics until in danger of splitting her sides. Kicking Tom's leg under the table, he gave him a long strained enquiring look.

'Forget it.' Tom said. 'We *are* all mad. I'll tell you about it sometime.'

'Something's tickled your mother,' John said, from behind a newspaper during a brief, and unusually rare, pause in the shovelling of the food into his mouth. 'I haven't seen her like that for donkey's years! Huh! Not since our honeymoon, I don't think!'

That was too much even for Tom. He immediately choked on his egg and bacon, spluttering it back on to the plate.

'Oh, man! What is you lot on?'

Breakfast over, Tom and Randy, using much of Mark's old furniture, spent the next couple of hours converting the spare room next to Tom's into a bedroom. Finally satisfied, Randy was over the moon with it, they decided to take a walk along the promenade. Tom was eager to explore the rest of the resort.

They walked slowly along the front, stopping frequently while Randy explained who owned what and for how long, and giving a brief history of each concession or venue as they passed it. It seemed he knew everything there was to know about everybody.

'Gee, it's sure hot today,' Tom exclaimed, as they came upon a Softee Ice Cream Parlour. 'Got any money? I forgot to bring any. I'll pay you back soon as we get home. I could kill for an ice cream.'

'Money? You don't need money, man. Hey, George!'

'Randy, you old son of a gun! How are you?' the ginger haired man in the blue striped apron and straw hat shouted back from behind the counter.

'Fine, man. Fine. Hey, meet Tom, he's the new main man at the Ellie,' Randy said, steering Tom up to the counter.

'Hi, Tom.' The man shook Tom's hand warmly, 'George is the name. I am pleased to meet you. What are you having? Sit down. Sit down. Now, what is it to be? Anything you like. It's all on the house, of course. How about ice cream and a milk shake? The chocolate mint is wicked today. Try it?'

'Most excellent!'

'I's forgot to mention,' Randy said, as the man started to whisk the milk. 'Anybody who owns or works in a place on the prom, they doesn't pay for anything in any of the other places on the prom. It's an old golden rule - never broken! Hope it's okay with you, man.'

'Even more, most excellent!' Tom exclaimed, then nodding towards the enormous building they could see at the far end of the promenade with its masses of lighting depicting an erupting volcano. 'Does it apply to that place too? The Inferno?'

'It does, man. But you don't want to go there. At least, not alone, man. Old Dave's all right, though. He used to own it. Yeah, he's all right, man. Bit like old Mark without the habits, he is. A genuine kinda bloke. But that Phil, he owns half of it now. Dave has to do what he's told these days. Bad news, that place is now, man. Bad news.'

'I thought perhaps we'd go there tonight, after you've finished your shift, that's if you're not doing anything else. I would like to have a look around the place. Anyway, it would strengthen our bluff that we're not afraid of them, wouldn't it?'

'Man, oh, man! After last night? You's crazy? They's would pop so much stuff in you's drink you would take off. You would never come down again, man!'

'I'm sure we could watch each drink being served. If it went out of sight, even for a moment, then we could leave that one and go and get another one. Go to another bar. How many they got in a place that size?'

'Three big ones. One on each level.'

'Go on. Please. Pretty please?'

George put two mountains of ice cream in front of them, following them with the two large chocolate mint shakes. 'You be careful if you're going in there, Tom,' the man warned, 'they're a nasty lot! You get your drinks from Denise, if you must go. Denise is okay, but not many realise it. You know her, don't you, Randy?'

'She the gorgeous dark haired one with the sick mum? Phil's bit? Ice Woman?'

'Yeah, that's her. But she is not really his, although he might think she is. It's only because she needs the money for her mother's medication that she lets him parade her around, but he's never had her you know. She isn't like that. No, Denise is okay. Stick with her if you are going to drink in there. Mind you, personally I wouldn't be seen dead in the place!'

'How's you know he's never had her, man?'

'My Maggie's great friends with her, and you know how women like to talk these things! Well, she told me, Denise reckons she wouldn't let him touch her with a barge pole, and if you can believe the rumours, that is something he definitely doesn't have! Anyway, have to go – I have punters. It looks like it's going to get busy.'

Tom and Randy fought their way through the over-generous portions then feeling extremely bloated left, giving George a friendly wave on the way out.

'Now what, man?' Randy asked. 'There's the fun fair, the Inferno, and then the marina. That's all of it on the front then. The road turns inwards at the fun fair, goes up to the cliff tops, and some camping sites, a bit like it does our end, and then on to Bristol. The other bit, the bit going past the Inferno, that stops at the harbour. Dunno about you, man, but I's don't think I's could face the fun fair, not after eating all that ice cream!'

'Me neither! It's so hot too! Let's go back and flop for an hour or so.'

Slowly, they strolled back along the promenade, their progress frequently hampered by Randy's friends stopping for a chat, or wanting to be introduced to Tom. The young Jamaican seemed to know everyone, or everyone seemed to know him. Either way he was unquestionably popular. Their progress was so slow that it was past six o'clock when they eventually arrived back at the club, walking down the side alley around to the back entrance.

'Less than two hours to blast-off, man.' Randy reminded Tom. 'Won't be time to flop now, not for me, anyway. I's better check all the lights. Do you want to help me and get to know where all the switches are?'

'Why not? Then we'll see what we've got to eat, though I'm not very hungry actually - not after the way George piled it on.'

'Right, man. Well, in this cupboard there's loads of big batteries all joined together and they's linked up to this trickle charger. Press the orange button.'

Tom pressed it.

'See, the green light came on. That means it's okay, man; they's fully charged. That's for the all the exit signs, and for all the emergency lights around the place that come on if the mains ever fails. There's a massive genny in that garage looking building out the back for if there's a power cut. Mark bought that last year after we had a power cut three nights running. It takes about five minutes to get it going. I's usually starts it up every Sunday, just to make sure it's still working. Funny though, man, we's never had to use it once since he got it. Right, now we go to the foyer. There's loads of switches in a cupboard there.'

Crossing the dance floor, and making their way towards the foyer at the front of the building, Randy explained more about the lighting systems, pointing out which parts were operated from the console and which were operated as satellites.

'Hey, man. That's strange. Real strange,' Randy said, sounding concerned, as they went through the swing doors into the foyer.

'What is?'

'That parcel, man. How did that get there?'

Tom looked at the package by the wall, a few feet inside the main doors. About the size and shape of a shoebox, wrapped in brown paper, tied with cord, addressed, stamped, franked, it looked as if the postman had left it there. Randy tried the three pairs of full glass pane double doors. One pair was unlocked.

'Oh, shit man. Shit!'

'What's wrong?'

'I's dunno, man. But something is. Postie, he don't leave no parcels at the front, man. He knows them doors is always locked in the daytime. He wouldn't even have tried them. I's don't like it, man!'

'You . . .' Tom was starting to get worried now. 'You don't think it's a parcel bomb, or something?'

'I's don't know,' Randy said. Leaning into the pay kiosk, he flicked a switch then pressed the Tannoy 'All' button. 'Mr and Mrs Patterson, and anybody else in the building. To the foyer immediately, please. This is urgent!'

'It's not ticking,' Tom assured him, after creeping up to it.

'Nor is my watch, man. It's digital. Electronic. Come away from it.'

John appeared, rushing down the stairs, with Mary following behind him loudly complaining that she hadn't turned off the potatoes.

'Randy,' he asked, 'what's the panic?'

'This parcel, Mr P. It shouldn't be there. And them doors is unlocked, man. That ain't normal. Do you know where Ian is?'

'Yes, Ian didn't feel too good earlier. We did the banking, and then he went home. Said he would be back for opening time. We didn't use the front doors at all, so they should have still been locked. They were earlier.'

'Sarah's gone, hasn't she?' Randy asked.

'Yes, she brought the cafeteria money up and left about twenty minutes ago.'

'What's the matter with the parcel? Who's it for?' Mary enquired naively.

'Them doors were locked last night. Tom knows that. They's never unlocked again until we opens at eight o'clock. Never, man. Oh, shit!'

John began to realise what Randy was thinking. 'I'll phone the police,' he said.

'They won't come, man.'

Randy disappeared into the Gents toilet, re-emerging seconds later with the long pole that was used to operate the high windows above the urinals.

'Open the door and kick the stopper down, Tom,' the deejay ordered.

'Don't be stupid!' Tom shouted at him.

'Got any better ideas, man? I's love to hear 'em!'

Tom propped the door open. Mary clung on to John, shaking while Randy carefully pushed the hook end of the pole under the wrapping cord. Slowly, very carefully, he lifted it out in front of him. Moving cautiously, he went out through the open door with it and then, waiting for a suitable break in the traffic, he crossed the road to the low sea wall before the rocks below. First checking that nobody was down on the rocks, slowly he brought the pole back over his right shoulder. Like an angler, he cast the parcel out to sea, letting the pole go with it.

Tom and his parents crossed the road, joining him as the parcel hurtled through the air. It landed hitting the rocks with some force. The pole bounced away from it, up into the air again, only to fall back and disappear into the foaming brine. They stood, watching as the waves crashed up on to the rock where the now battered parcel had landed.

After what seemed to be several minutes, it was Tom who was the first to speak. 'I bet it was a pair of shoes,' he joked, slapping Randy on the back.

Randy felt foolish and banged his fist on his head. 'Shit, man. Shit!'

'Never mind, Randy. Better to be safe than sorry,' Mary consoled him. 'I just hope my potatoes haven't burnt!'

They were waiting for a break in the traffic, to start back across the road, Mary still worrying about her potatoes, when the force from the blast, deafening even from that distance, blew them forward into the road. Seconds later they were drenched by the torrents of water that fell from above, showering down on them like a waterfall. Several cars screeched to a halt, skidding madly on the now greasy wet road. Some passers-by ran up to them to ask what had happened.

'Just an old mine got washed up, I think.' John called out to them, bundling his family to safety across the road.

'Oh, my God,' Mary started to cry. 'Oh, John, what have we got ourselves into? What are we going to do? That could have killed us all!'

John put his arm round her. 'I don't know,' he said. 'What can we do? This is all we have. Come on, let's get back inside, lock up, and have a cup of tea. Then we will talk about it. Randy, what can I say? We owe you such a lot. How can we ever repay you? You didn't have to do that, you could easily have left it there, but you didn't. I really don't know what to say. Words fail me. Really they do.'

'Don't be silly, man! You all treat me like family. I's was only looking after my family, man.'

Tom squeezed him. 'You're the best brother I never had,' he said, locking the doors behind them. 'Hope you like burnt spuds,' as he raced him up the stairs.

Mary served the dinner, while Tom made them all coffee. The potatoes had survived, but nobody ate much. Tom and Randy were still remembering the ice cream, and Mary and John were not in the mood for eating.

'It may not be for me to say, man,' Randy said guardedly, 'but you might be better off if you got rid of Ian pretty soon. Gotta be a big worry having a Phil man running round the place.'

'I know,' John said, 'but none of us know enough about the game yet to manage without him. I mean, stock control, licensing, and all that. We wouldn't have a clue what to order, what to do.'

'Mind if I's uses the phone, Mrs P?'

'This is your home, Randy. You use anything you want. Feel free. You are family. And please, call us John and Mary. Mr and Mrs P sounds like a load of old vegetables!'

Randy smiled, disappearing into the next room to use the phone.

'No probs, man!' He danced back into the room a few minutes later. 'Derek and Beryl will be here early tonight. It wasn't let on to you they's married, because lots of employers they don't like that. Upset one and you loses two. Know what I's mean, man? But Derek, he knows the business inside out. They both do. They will help you out, and bonus, man! Bonus! Derek easily qualifies to hold a full liquor licence, and an entertainments licence, so you's got no probs! He's well known, got a good reputation, he could relieve or run a nightclub pretty well anywhere with no probs, man. All you gotta do is arrange for an interim license down at the court tomorrow morning, then put in for a transfer next month. Derek, he knows how to do it all anyway, it's easy.'

'Really?' Mary was stunned. 'Derek and Beryl married? Well, I never! I like Beryl. We had a long chat last night. Oh, that would be wonderful.

But if they know the business so well, and if he is able to hold a licence so easily, why do they work here for us? Why don't they take on a place for themselves?'

'I's knows why, man, but I's shouldn't tell you. It would betray a trust. It's sorta personal to them, man. They don't like talking about it. I's expect they will tell you, though, when they get to know you better. But it's nothing wrong, man. Nothing bad. They's okay.'

'If you say they're okay, that's good enough for us,' Tom said. 'Now all we've got to do is get rid of Ian.'

'I'll do that,' John said, 'with pleasure. He can collect whatever is his and leave tonight. I'll get all the locks changed tomorrow, that might make us feel a little safer.'

'Oh, man! Look at the time. I's gotta go. I's gotta get ready. We's open in half an hour and I's haven't finished checking everything yet.'

'I'll give you a hand.' Tom followed him out of the room.

CHAPTER 8

The car skidded to a halt on the loose gravel with a cloud of dust erupting around it as Ian jumped out. Slamming the door behind him, he walked towards the house, and then throwing the double doors open with an almighty bang, he stormed into the cellar. All eyes turned towards the sudden intrusion, with Patrick's hand instinctively flying to his holster, and then resting again when he saw Ian. Ian was no threat.

'Sacked! Bloody sacked!' Ian shouted at Phil, marching up to him. 'Now what? Tell me! Now what? I shouldn't have listened to you. Leave the doors open so we can put the frighteners on, indeed! Frighteners? Frighteners? You realise, of course, if that, that supposedly harmless thing had have gone off in there it would have demolished the whole damn building?'

'Don't fuckin' blame me!' Phil slammed his hand on the desk. 'Patrick's supposed to be the bleedin' explosives expert. Some fuckin' expert!' He glared across at the man.

'Well, now what? Where do I get another job around here? One that pays as well as that one did? Are you going to take me on full time? No, I didn't think so! I'm finished here, aren't I? Finished! I don't know why I ever got involved with you lot! You're nothing but a load of ruddy cowboys! You're pathetic!' Ian turned, storming out the room, the doors straining on their hinges with the force that he used to sling them open.

'Come back here, bastard!' Phil shouted after him, but his words were lost in the noise and the cloud of dust that flew up into the room as Ian's car, wheels spinning on the gravel, sped backwards out of the yard.

Sticking two fingers up in the direction of the dust, a seemingly pointless gesture though it gave some satisfaction, Phil turned on Patrick. 'Idiot! This is all your bleedin' fault. You were supposed to frighten 'em, not try to bloody kill 'em! Now we've lost our inside man. Now we've definitely got to bleedin' go down there in force to show them just who does run this fuckin' town! That means the extra men, doesn't it? So how many extra fuckin' people have you lot managed to bleedin' drum up so far?'

'Two, I believe, Boss. I think Bob's found us two.'

'Two? Two? That's a lot of bloody good, ain't it? Two! Seems like the fuckin' poncey Ellie crowd can get help whenever they want it, but we can't! They're expecting a bleeding dozen or more to help them out. What the fuck we supposed to do when that lot turns up?'

'I could ask my brothers to come over. I'm sure they would come, if I asked them. It'd cost you though!' Patrick offered.

'Cost me? Cost me? Oh, that's fuckin' good, ain't it? Your fuckin' mistake and it costs me! How many bleedin' brothers you got?'

'Three. There's Andrew, Mickey, and then there's the eldest, Terry. They're all very handy like, and they'd be tooled up, of course.'

'Get 'em! Get 'em 'ere as quickly as possible, but I don't expect to be stung on this! And they'd better be bloody good, I'm warning you! If anybody wants me, I'll be over the club.' Phil said, stopping to check the doors for damage before he stamped out of the room.

'Strewth!' Sam emerged from the corner where he had been keeping his head down. 'I wish someone would put that man out of his misery. I mean, whoever took over the patch has got to be better than that!'

'I'll go along with that!' Patrick grinned at him. 'I'll tell you now, my brothers won't take any abuse from him. He has one hell of a shock coming to him if he starts having a go at them! Keep that under your hat, mind you. This could all turn out to be quite funny.'

Sam laughed. 'I'd like to see that. Phil meeting his match! By the way, what did go wrong with the firework? It's not like you to make a mistake with a banger, not that I've ever seen any before, but I've heard the stories. They say you're one of the best. I was on the prom when it went off. Like something out of a war film it was. Magnificent! Hell of a bang! Went twenty or thirty foot in the air it did.'

'Don't I know it! I was sat in Mario's when it went off. It was Phil's fault really. He wanted the job done straight away. Wouldn't wait a few days until I could get some new stuff in, something stable, so I had to use what was around. God only knows how old it was, I can't remember. I thought it had gone off, no good like, it was definitely very crusty, so

I put a bit extra in. Seems it hadn't gone off as much as I thought! Ah, never mind. It's just one of those things. Unless you use fresh you never know what will happen. There I was expecting a small phut, a bit of a frightener with a horrible smell, and look what I got!'

'Yeah, never mind, he'll get over it. Well, I suppose I had better make a move now or else I'll be in his bad books, too. I have to find Graham. We're both up the Ellie tonight. Mike too, I think. Looks like the three of us will be there a lot more now Bob's been barred from there. See you later.'

Patrick nodded to the lad, who went out the door smiling. Picking up the phone, he started dialling. The first number was engaged, the second connected.

'Hello?' A timid voice answered.

'Hello, Margaret. It's Patrick. Is Terry there?'

The line went quiet for a few moments, then, 'Pat?'

'Terry. How are you? Look, you know what we discussed? You know, when I was over there at Christmas? Well, I think the time has come. How quickly could you be here, with the brothers?'

'Umm . . . Tomorrow evening, I'll be guessing. That be okay?'

'Great!'

'What's expected?'

'Phil's got himself in a bit of a fix, needs some help. He wants to go in heavy with one of the locals. You get your money off him first, up front like, then we deal with him.'

'Sounds good to me, me ol' bruv.'

'Oh, and don't forget to come tooled up.'

'Now, Pat, me ol' bruvver, would we be coming any other way?'

Patrick put the phone down. He was a happy man – a very happy man. Tomorrow, he thought, tomorrow cannot come soon enough.

CHAPTER 9

'Man, I's really dunno why I's let you talk me into this,' Randy complained. Jogging up to the steps that led into the Inferno they joined the back of a short queue. 'I's only hope we don't regret it, man!'

'We'll be alright,' Tom reassured him. 'We'll be extra careful. Remember not to lose sight of our drinks. This sure is some Ritzy place, isn't it?'

Tom was impressed; stunned by the classiness of the venue. There was a 'no expense spared' feeling oozing from every corner of the building. He could see the black mottled marble of the steps under his feet continued on inside, through the smoked glass doors, gracing the expansive foyer floor before rising half way up the walls until meeting up with the chrome handrails. Above those, gigantic wall mirrors hampered only by darts of bright light sparkling, reflecting back from the huge mirror-ball in the centre, retold the story. Looking behind him, the promenade was lit up as if in daylight by the bright lights of the erupting volcano above them on the facade. Then beyond, over the low sea wall where the high tide calmly swelled with not a breaker in sight, the volcanic reflections were wriggling on the water as they trailed out to sea, until finally they met up with the moon's silver offering that was coming the other way.

Dave was in the middle of the foyer jangling his bunch of keys and dressed immaculately in an evening suit that appeared to glisten as the revolving reflecting lights of the mirror ball attacked it with regularity. Looking important, he was observing the customers entering, greeting the regulars, and giving assistance to newcomers. Glancing outside to survey the queue, he immediately recognised Randy. Stepping forward with a smile, he opened one of the next sets of doors and beckoned for him and his companion to come straight on in.

'Hello, Randy,' he said, grasping hold of the young man's hand tightly, 'I wasn't expecting to see you here. It must be months since you last paid us a visit. It is nice to see you again. And you are?' He turned towards Tom, offering out his hand.

'Tom. Tom Patterson.'

'I thought you might be. I'm pleased to meet you, Tom. Sad business. Sad. About your uncle, I mean, very sad. Old Mark and I went back a long way, you know. Had a lot of time for dear old Mark, I did. In fact, I like to think we both had a lot of time for each other. You know, we were both here long before this town took off properly. Long before. This place still resembled the fish house it once was, and yours – yours was going through its cinema days then. Oh, memories! Pioneers, you might call us, but we mustn't dwell on the past, must we? Tell me, how are you settling in? I hear the gang have started to give you trouble, already. Terrible, that episode earlier tonight, terrible! Thank God nobody got hurt!'

'Yes it was horrible, it could have been real nasty if it had gone off inside. I don't think any of us, or the building, would have survived,' Tom replied. Suddenly realising he was still holding on to the man's hand, he quickly let go. 'We're settling in okay, thanks. Although obviously we're still in a bit of a mess unpacking,' he continued. 'And yes, my uncle's death was very sad; a real shock to us. Mind you, I didn't know him all that well. Apparently, my parents thought I should be sheltered from the kind of life he led, so we rarely saw him. But here I am now, right in the middle of it all – that kind of life, I mean. Ironic, isn't it?'

'Life's a big mystery, Tom,' Dave said, putting his arm around his shoulder and steering him towards the entrance into the lower floor bar, 'a big mystery. Here, take this card and show it at the bar every time you want a drink - it's all on the house. Now, you have a good time, both of you. Oh, just a little word of warning: Phil's in there somewhere with a few of his crowd, so do stay alert, won't you?'

'Thanks!' Tom grinned at him. Dave seemed all right.

They pushed their way through the swing doors, into the thunderous sound of the music, to be hit by a wall of intense heat radiating from more than a thousand young cavorting bodies enjoying themselves. The smell, a mixture of cigarette smoke, amyl nitrate, marijuana, and spilt alcohol all blending with the intense body odour was overpowering, but homely. It reminded Tom of the Elephant's Nest.

'What you having?' Tom asked, shouting in Randy's ear when they eventually made it through the crowd to the bar.

'Safer to stick to bottles,' he shouted back. 'I's will have a Nookie.'
'A what?'
'Newcastle Brown, man. Why don't you try one?'
Sid served them. There was nobody behind the bar resembling the dark-haired Denise, who they felt would be better serving them.
'Glasses, sir?' The bar manager spat the 'sir' at Tom, as he placed the frothing bottles in front of them.
Tom signalled no, hurriedly grabbing the drinks.
'It's far too packed in here, man, and too hot by miles. Let's go up one,' Randy suggested.
Squeezing, wriggling, pushing, stepping on toes and apologising, it was an enormous effort for them to get to the doors at the far end of the bar, and then out into the cooler passageway. Passing the toilets and taking the stairs at the end, which Tom noticed were presumably rubber covered for safety but still an exact match to the black mottled marble that appeared to be everywhere, they reached the next level. Tom peered through the glass porthole in one of the doors, pulling back immediately to let an unsteady crowd spill out past them on to the landing. If it was hot downstairs, it must have been at least three degrees hotter on this equally packed floor, he guessed. Randy, signalled for them to go up another floor, to the top bar, and led the way.
Entering through the plush swing doors, Tom was pleased to find that the top floor was far less crowded. It was also much cooler. Several large chrome ceiling fans circulating the air produced a welcome breeze that played with his tousled hair. There was no dance floor, or disco lighting effects, in this sparsely lit, luxuriously furnished upper bar, but the same good music that he'd heard belting out on the middle floor was being subtly piped into this area at a level over which they could easily speak. Looking to the right of them, finding the long black marble and chrome extremely well stocked servery, he noticed it was tended by two bargirls. Both were pretty, but the one with the black hair was positively gorgeous.
'Is that . . . ?'
'That is, man. And the ugly character she's talking to is Phil,' Randy informed him, as they found some seats by a table in the far corner, diagonally across from Tom's fascination.

'That's Phil, is it? Ugh! How could she? He looks like a fat parrot! Just get a load of that nose!'

'Beauty's in the eye of the beholder, man. I's expect his mother thinks he's handsome. That's if he's ever had a mother! Anyway, don't forget, George reckons she ain't really his, she just needs the job.'

'Yeah, I suppose so. Look, Phil's going. Drink up, I'll get us another one!'

'God, man. You ain't gettin' horny over her, is you? You's dicing with death, man! Oh, man!'

Tom wasn't listening. He was at the bar the instant Phil went out through the doors. Randy started to get up, to go after him, when an enviously attractive girl, tall with shoulder length wavy blond hair, class radiating from every inch of her, spun him around forcefully. Pulling him towards her, she planted her full lips directly on his.

'Hello, big boy,' she breathed, her hand already sliding down his body, rubbing gently against his flies. 'Remember me? Caroline? We met about the same time last year. We made out in the back of your mate's car, and he went ape, remember? You do remember me, don't you?'

'Of course I's remember you, darling,' Randy lied, grinning stupidly, whilst frantically racking his brains for just some glimmer of recognition. She was class with a capital C he thought - did he really know her? Then slowly that worse for wear night flooded back to him. 'I's thought of nobody else in all this time. How could anyone forget someone like you, Caroline? Oh, man! I's been pining for you ever since you left, darling. How is you? What's you been doing with yourself?'

'Waiting, darling, waiting,' she breathed all over him again, the rubbing now becoming a feverish groping. 'I've been so desperately waiting for a return match.'

'I's can't tonight, my petal. You knows how much I's would love to, really I's would, but I's already with someone.'

'You're with the young guy over there, I saw you come in together. Oh, now don't go and hurt me. Don't tell me you bat both ways.'

'No,' he attempted a laugh, 'I's don't. He's my boss. He's new here, so I's looking out for him. He's never been to a place like this before. Led a sheltered life, he has. Oh, man, has he ever led a sheltered life!'

'Really? Oh, look. Seems like he knows what to do, doesn't it? It couldn't have been that sheltered, unless he's very quick on the uptake!'

Randy managed to pull himself away from her grasp long enough to observe Tom sitting on one of the stools at the end of the bar leaning forward, perhaps being pulled forward across the counter, with Denise's arms clinging tightly around his neck and her mouth feverishly devouring his.

'Man! The horny little so-and-so!'

'Well, looks like you haven't got to worry about him now, so let's worry about this!' She squealed, as in one move her slender hand slipped down under his belt and inside his jeans, grasping him firmly.

'Oh, man!' Randy relaxed, falling backwards in the semi-darkness onto the plush bench seat. Caroline rolled over on top of him, never letting go, her lips hungrily finding his, her tongue starting to explore.

'I've got to have it, got to have it tonight,' she panted, her body gyrating uncontrollably. Letting go of his massive pulsating erection, she slid around to straddle his lap and then began sliding up and down his jeans, the straining denim beneath her struggling to contain its aroused, volatile, prisoner. 'Where can we go?'

'Oh, oh, oh, man!' Randy grabbed her head in both hands, pulling her face forward into his, then he let his hands fall on to her well developed heaving breasts, caressing them, his thumbs and forefingers finding her erect nipples, tweaking them through the silk blouse making her squeal ever louder. 'Later,' he promised her, gasping, with sweat beginning to pour from his brow, and involuntary thrusts leaping out from deep within his pelvis. 'Later, I's promise.'

'No, now,' she demanded, as her hands crept inside again, grasping him tightly once more, playing with it, rhythmically squeezing it, so hard he thought that if the threatening orgasm wasn't soon achieved it would explode on him.

'No, not now,' he cried out with an urgency as he leapt to his feet so vigorously that the girl fell from his lap and landed sprawling in a most undignified manner across the floor.

Ignoring her protests, Randy shot across the room, rudely forcing his way to the bar through the various groups of people standing around talking. Grabbing hold of Tom he pulled him, almost had to lever him, away from the bargirl's caresses.

'Could die of thirst in here, man!' he said, signalling towards the door with his eyes. 'Where's that drink you promised me?'

'Here,' Tom replied. Leaning back, picking up the two bottles he looked across to see Phil standing a little way inside the door, talking with the smelly Bob. 'Thanks, mate. Gee, that was close! Guess I got carried away a bit there. We would be a little outnumbered if I upset Phil here on his own stamping ground, wouldn't we? God, that Denise is some gorgeous girl!'

'Yes, man. So was mine. Here, come over and meet Caroline, if she hasn't gone!'

Randy led him back to their seats where he did the introductions. Caroline was feeling a little dejected at having been so rudely deserted, but had decided to stay with it. She was determined not to let any chance of her having the virile young Jamaican that night escape her.

'Man, you must know some great chat up lines,' Randy declared, looking at Tom. 'No one's ever managed to get a response like that from Denise before. Man, she's known as the Ice Woman; she's thought to be untouchable. What the hell did you say to her, man?'

'Oh, nothing really. I just asked her what a nice girl like her was doing in a place like this. Corny, wasn't it? But it's the only chat up line I know. The only one I've heard before. Mind you, it wasn't until I offered her a job with us, that anything really took off.'

'You did what? Oh, man! Is you nuts? Phil will go berserk! Ballistic!'

'Let him. I still think our best chance is to confront him head on. Make sure he knows we're not frightened of him. Giving Denise a job with us should do that quite well, I imagine. She's going to finish tonight's shift here and then start with us tomorrow. We need more staff anyway, especially now that Derek and Beryl are managing the place, so it all works out rather well, doesn't it? Another drink anyone?'

'I'll get 'em!' Randy leapt to his feet. 'That way you might live a bit longer! Same again, everybody?'

Nods confirmed it, with Caroline explaining just how she liked her Martini.

'Randy was telling me how good you've been to him, giving him his own room and all that,' she told Tom, while his friend was away at the bar waiting to be served. 'Is he allowed to take back overnight guests, or would that be taboo, what with your parents being there?'

'Oh, he's perfectly free to do as he pleases. He is old enough and ugly

enough, as the saying goes. That's why he's got a lock on his room,'
Tom, remembering how the day had started, began to chuckle, 'for his
privacy.'

'That's good,' she sighed.

'What is?' Randy asked, returning with the drinks.

'That you have your privacy,' she said, as Tom sat grinning up at him.

'Oh, man! What is so funny? Is you ever gonna tell me?'

'One day, perhaps.'

Caroline soon returned to her task of making a meal out of Randy who,
so easily it seemed, succumbed to her plentiful charms and offered no
resistance. Tom, not wishing to intrude, and feeling quite embarrassed at
being there and having to watch all their sexual manoeuvres, decided to
return to the bar. Phil, it appeared to him, had left the room once again.
Sitting on the same stool as before at the end of the bar, he was once
again able to frequently chat with Denise.

'So, what do you do after you have finished here?' he asked her. 'I've
heard you look after your mum who's ill. I suppose you have to rush back
home.'

She smiled. 'No, I don't have to rush anywhere. Mum's sister is the one
who really looks after her. I just have to come up with the money each
week so we can all survive. Social Services won't pay for a full-time
carer for her which means Annie can't work, so what I put into the house
is all there is. It gets a bit tight at times! No, usually after work I have to
hang around here until Phil decides to drop me off home, but tonight I
shan't, of course. I shall pick up my wages and run!'

'Do you have far to go?'

'Not too far. We live around the corner from your place, in the street
right behind you. In fact, if I can't sleep of a night I pull the curtains back
so I can see your elephant bouncing up and down. Sends me off in no
time.'

'Really, that close?'

'Yes, I can see the tower from my bed.'

He clasped her hand, squeezing it gently. 'You'll have to show me
which house, so I can sneak into the tower and look down into your
bedroom of a night.'

'I'll point it out to you, sometime,' she promised.

'Tonight? From the tower?'

'Are you inviting me back, Tom? I hardly know you.' She blushed a little.

'Well, that way you'll get to know me a bit better, won't you? You can meet my parents too - I have to let them know you're starting tomorrow, anyway. And you'll be a lot safer walking along the front with us than you would be on your own, won't you?'

'Alright,' she agreed, squeezing his hand, 'you win then. I'll meet you out the front at four. But I shan't hang around if you are not there because Phil will be hopping mad, so make sure you're not late. Now, do you lot want one more drink? It's last orders any minute now.'

Tom peered across into the dimly lit corner where Randy was entertaining his amorous admirer. They were preoccupied, in a position that only the very fittest would dare undertake, but there was no drink left on the table by them, so he ordered three more, and took them over.

'Ahem,' he interrupted them politely. Randy's head emerged slowly from where it had been trying to bury itself. 'Doesn't time fly when you're having fun?' he quipped. 'These are the last drinks, I'm afraid. They're calling time. By the way, Denise is coming back with us tonight. I've got to meet her out the front at four.'

Randy looked up at him giggling, Caroline, equally as happy, copied him. Tom's eyes caught sight of the ashtray full of roll-up stubs, confirming his suspicions that they were both as high as kites. Pulling herself up, Caroline rummaged through her little black shoulder bag, producing a long silver cigarette case. Flipping it open, to show it was still more than half full of neatly rolled joints, she offered him one. Tom declined.

'Why don't you take a couple for later, man?' Randy suggested, trying to wink at him, but his co-ordination was affected, it coming across more like someone trying to forcibly expel wind. 'Especially if you's taking Denise back. It'll break the ice. Get things going, man. You will be in your room, so nobody will know. Anyway, it's only the light stuff, man. Nothing heavy.'

Tom relented, taking two. They didn't have to actually smoke them, he thought, but it would shut Randy up. Caroline replacing the case, fumbled through her bag again.

'Put those in your pocket, as well,' she insisted, pushing her hand in his jeans pocket, 'You'll have a wonderful night!'

'No, really, I can't. I mean, that stuff is not cheap, is it? No, really, I don't . . .'

'Don't be silly, Tom. Money, darling, is one commodity I am not short of. Take them. Have a bit of fun. From what I've heard tonight, you need some!'

'Don't you argue with her, man! She's used to getting her own way. Rich bitch!' Randy sarcastically drawled. She thumped him playfully on the arm. 'Daddy owns a yacht and a whole string of casinos,' he continued teasing.

'I think it's only three,' she smiled at Tom, 'but there are fourteen five-star hotels around the world, a major brewery, and one or two other things.'

'I thought you were someone out of the ordinary,' Tom said. 'I noticed earlier that those two heavy looking guys over there have been doing nothing but watch you all night. They your minders?'

Randy tried to look around him. What men? He had not noticed anyone watching them.

'Yes, you could say that. Karl and Stefan. Daddy insists I have them.' She gave them a friendly wave. 'I suppose I give them a bit of a tough time, but they're well paid, and they're happy enough. They are very good, by the way. Only the best for Daddy's little girl!' She threw her head back laughing, remembering how her father had actually said that to her once, a long time ago, when she was small enough to sit on his knee.

'Man, they ain't gonna be watching us performin' later, is they?'

Caroline laughed. 'No, they'll be waiting outside in the car, but why not? They did last year! You were so drunk you wouldn't have known if I'd sold tickets!' She cuddled him. 'Don't worry, darling. You still performed wonderfully!'

'I'd better make a move, it's nearly four o'clock. I've got to meet Denise outside. She's a bit worried in case Phil gets awkward, so I want to be there,' Tom explained, getting up.

'We'll give you a lift,' Caroline said, pushing Randy off her in order to stand up. She nodded to her minders. One of them immediately left, the other continued to watch her. 'Come on hunk, Karl's gone to get the car.'

105

Randy stood up, and swayed. 'Man, this sure is gonna be some night!'

Stefan followed them discreetly at a short distance, watching out for any threat to his charge as they went down the two flights of stairs to the foyer. Going out through the glass swing doors, the cool night air biting at them ruthlessly, Tom immediately sensed that something was wrong; that there was trouble. A large jeering crowd encircled some excitement in front of them on the promenade. Putting his hand firmly on Randy's shoulder for support, Tom leapt into the air to see over the heads of the people in front of them.

'It's Phil, he's got hold of Denise! I'll kill him!' he screamed, running forward, desperately trying to fight his way through the dense crowd.

Randy tried to stagger after him, but instead gained a threatening look by drunkenly veering into someone. Caroline turned and spoke quickly to Stefan. The minder shouted something into his lapel then, almost effortlessly, he leapt forward from the steps, into the air over several rows of heads, crashing through the swelling crowd of onlookers and belly-flopping on top of them. Flooring a whole bunch of them, and scattering them in all directions, he emerged at the centre of the melee at the same time that Karl appeared from the opposite direction.

Denise, shaking, tears streaming from her eyes, was pleading with Phil to stop tugging her hair and to let go of her. He totally ignored her desperate pleas, continuing to slap her hard on the face and swearing at her. His hand came up again, threatening to slap her once more, when Karl's uppercut caught him squarely on the chin, sending him reeling backwards to the ground amidst loud cheering from the ever-swelling crowd. Dazed, he looked up to see Stefan bringing his foot down firmly on to his forehead. Tapping his breast pocket, there was an obvious large lump beneath it, Stefan left the man in no doubt as to what it was that there lie hidden. Phil went quiet, not resisting, not daring to move.

Tom struggled out of the crowd and quickly put a comforting arm around Denise who was still sobbing heavily. 'Are you alright?' he asked her frantically.

'I, I, I think so,' she sobbed. 'He said he'd mark me for life if I left him,' she spluttered.

Stefan twisted his heel backwards and forwards on Phil's forehead. Blood began to emerge from the skin that was, bit by bit, slowly being scraped away. 'I'm sure we didn't mean that, did we?' he asked, staring down coldly at the pathetic man.

'No, no! I swear it! It was just talk! It was silly of me. I'm sorry, I didn't mean it. Really, I didn't,' Phil blurted.

'Good! Because I will be coming back here, and like a bad smell, I certainly won't forget you!'

Karl held the door of the luxurious sleek black Mercedes open as Caroline ushered them all inside, leaving Stefan to watch the crowd. Satisfied his charges were all safely inside the car with the doors closed, he gave one more twist to the thug's head with his foot before leaping into the front passenger seat. With a screech from the tyres, accompanied by one long blast from the horn, the car shot forwards, disappearing at speed along the front and into the night.

Tom directed Karl to the back door of the Elephant's Nest where the two minders elected to stay with the car, declining Tom's offer of finding somewhere for them inside for the night.

'Don't worry about them,' Caroline reassured Tom, closely following him up the stairs, 'they'll be quite happy out there. It's their job, and they are paid top rate. They do alright.'

'We's going on up,' Randy giggled when they reached the office, 'say goodnight to you's folks for me.'

Tom grinned back at them. Ringing the bell, he watched them snogging their way along the corridor to the next flight of stairs.

Mary opened the door, letting him in. 'Hello, son. Had a good time?' she asked.

'Fine, thanks. Mum, I'd like you to meet Denise. Denise this is my mum, and that's my dad, over there.'

They both greeted her warmly, offering her a seat. Mary, nothing escaped her, noticed the girl's red eyes. She immediately wanted to know what had happened. What was wrong with her? Tom explained all while his mother fussed around, comforting her, and getting the girl a stiff drink, for medicinal purposes, of course.

They were pleased she would be starting work there the next day, it had been extremely busy that night and they had struggled to cope. They really could do with more staff. Without Ian, it had been hard keeping everything covered throughout the evening.

By working normal shifts, but coming in early at weekends to help prepare the bars, Denise learned how she would be able to earn more than what Phil had been giving her. Everyone was happy with the arrangement as the job would not have to be advertised and no time would be wasted interviewing people. Immediately, the strain on the staff would be lifted.

Tom began to feel guilty. Perhaps he should have stayed there to help his parents that night instead of going out, he considered. The place was his, after all. Making a mental note not to be so inconsiderate next time, he waited impatiently whilst his mother exchanged stories with Denise, women only items, he vaguely gathered.

Some time later, sensing that cashing-up was ending, Tom yawned, telling his parents he was going to show Denise around the place first, and then he would be going to bed as he was tired. He would see them in the morning.

'So then, is it going to be coffee for one, or for two in the morning?' Mary asked, with a knowing look in her eye.

Stunned, Tom looked at Denise. They both blushed equally, and then burst out laughing.

'I think it might possibly be two,' he answered, embarrassed, hardly believing his mother would ask him such a question. How things had changed in only a few days, he contemplated, as he pushed Denise out through the door, still laughing.

Running up the stairs, passing Randy's door where the noises escaping from within left nothing to the imagination, they went straight into Tom's room, collapsing onto the bed, embracing, kissing, cuddling, hugging, with hands exploring each other.

'I'll take you up the tower in the morning, then you can show me your house,' he whispered softly in her ear.

Her hands gently slid down his body, pulling up his tee shirt, undoing his belt, then unzipping his jeans, pulling them wide open.

'I've got my own tower for tonight,' she laughed, sliding her hand into his boxers, pulling on his manhood that was fighting with the elastic top, and squealing as it won the battle, exploding out, the end slapping noisily against his stomach somewhere around his navel, 'and it's lovely. My, it is lovely!'

'Promise you won't laugh if I tell you something,' he whispered.
'I promise.'
'I'm a bit nervous. I've never been with a girl before, you'll have to tell me if I do anything wrong.'
Denise failed in her attempt to stifle the laugh.
'Bitch!' he joked, pinching her. 'You promised!'
'No, no,' she giggled, 'I'm not laughing at you. It is just that I was wondering how to say the same thing to you. I'm a virgin too.'
They both laughed, hugging each other even more tightly. Tom slowly, gently, started undressing her, undoing her blouse, releasing her brassiere, burying his head in her heaving breasts, playing with her erect nipples with his tongue, encircling them, making her squeal when he occasionally nipped them gently with his teeth. Frantically she ripped his shirt off, wrestling with his jeans that were already down around his knees, and she bit back equally on his nipples, her whole body now uncontrollably gyrating. Tom tore his jeans down the rest of the way, ripping them off, throwing them to who knows where, while she snapped open the poppers of her skirt, discarding it recklessly, before kicking her panties down her legs, until they too flew away into the darkness.
'God, you're so big,' she squealed, pulling him on top of her, 'I'm never going to take that first time.'
Exploring her, finding his target, his manhood throbbing wildly at the door of his desires, his body moving, lunging to its massive pulse, it was ready to explode, it had to be now, it had to be, he tried pushing, one desperate enormous lunge at her, forcing, forcing, it had to, it had to! She screamed out in agony!
'Oh, Tom. Oh, wait! Oh! Oh! Slowly! Oh, God, the pain! Oh! No, No! It won't go. No! No! Stop, Tom! Stop!' she pleaded, tears on her cheeks.
Frustrated, Tom pulled away, rolling over onto his back, his erect member, mountainous, dripping, oozing with the excitement would, had the light been on, have been seen to be visibly pulsating and living a life of its own.
'I'm sorry,' she said, starting to weep openly, and feeling inadequate.
There was a gentle, but firm, rap on the door. Tom looked across at the girl in the darkness with alarm, surprised, and wondering who was out

there knocking. Not his mother! Oh, God! Had she heard them? What would he say? Covering Denise with the duvet, he found the light switch then quickly slung on his dressing gown. Slowly he opened the door a few inches.

'Man, I's not one to complain, but the whole of bloody Seathorpe must know you's problem by now,' Randy whispered, his eyes glazed and his stark naked body swaying erratically, trying hard to maintain its balance. 'Here, Caroline sent this in. She says you must try the fags too, and the other things, then it'll be all right. Gotta goes back to it. G'night, man!'

Tom looked inquisitively at the blue and white tube in his hand, and then reading the instructions, smiled.

'What would I do without Randy?' he said aloud, finding his jeans and searching them for what Caroline had given him earlier.

'Toothpaste?' Denise enquired, looking up at the tube incredulously.

'Not exactly,' he laughed, turning the light off. 'The experts next door have bailed us out. By the way, do you smoke?'

'Occasionally,' she replied.

'So do I now,' he said, lighting the two cigarettes, and handing her one. 'This vase is the ashtray,' he told her, throwing the small bunch of plastic flowers on to the windowsill. Showing her the two tablets, he said, 'Caroline reckons if we take one of these it'd help. Are you game for a laugh?'

'Why not?' she giggled, taking one out of his hand, she popped it in her mouth, swallowing it down effortlessly.

Tom quickly devoured the other one. Relaxing, they lay side-by-side, naked on top of the bed, smoking, telling each other little things about themselves, exchanging confidences, and stories from their past. Tom's massive erection stood proud throughout, no longer insisting, but content now with the attention of Denise's hand continuously stroking it. Cigarettes finished, they rolled together, and started to kiss, and to cuddle again. Tom felt good now, really good. Loving, he felt so loving. Suddenly Denise's head dived downwards, Tom felt her lips envelop him, her warm wet mouth exciting him. Thrusting upwards at the back of her throat, he gasped as her teeth playfully nipped him, then he retracted as she sucked for England. Without warning, something hit them, both equally, together, a huge tidal wave surging through them, rushing in their heads, and up and down their bodies. Pulling away, Tom's hand frantically found the tube, and squeezing it he quickly lubricated his exploding manhood. Rolling Denise on to her back, he spread the remainder of the lube around the source of his yearning. Her arms reached up for him pleadingly, he came down on top of her, firmly pushing hard into her. She murmured, not squealing this time, pulling him even harder down into her, thrusting herself up towards him, she gasped, as he entered her.

'Ooooh . . . Oh, you are wonderful . . . Oh, God! Oh, so wonderful . . .' She tore at his hair.

'Mmmm . . . Oh . . . Oh . . .' He thrust his mouth down on to hers and they dissolved into being one.

CHAPTER 10

Clasping his handkerchief firmly to his bloodied forehead, and swearing profusely, Phil picked himself up from off the pavement, and forced his way through the crowd of jeering onlookers back into the club as the car sped away into the distance. Letting himself into the office, where Dave was still counting the night's takings, he went over to the small mirror to inspect the damage to his face.

'They're dead,' he shouted. 'They're all fuckin' dead! No one does that to me and gets away with it! No one! Where's that bloody Patrick? He's supposed to be here with his brothers tonight, but no fucker can find him! Where the fuck is he? He's never around when yer fuckin' want him!'

'Language!' Dave once more hopelessly insisted. 'Language! You've lost Patrick, have you? Well, the last I heard they were all going off for a reunion celebration, him and his brothers. They arrived a couple of hours ago, dying for a drink, they said. I doubt they will surface much before tomorrow afternoon, you know how they like their drink, these Irish. You'll just have to be patient.'

'Patient! Patient! I'll give them bloody patient!' Phil stormed out of the room, letting the door slam violently behind him.

Crossing the alley, after kicking out at several cars in the car park for no more reason than that they were there, he entered the yard. He was approaching the cellar door, fumbling in his pocket for his keys, still cursing away under his breath, when he became aware of the small group of people behind him staggering into the yard. Stopping to look behind him, he immediately recognised the slight shadowy form of Patrick in the group of four men. Two of them were supporting his doubtless well intoxicated, still capable of singing but incapable of walking, body.

'Out fuckin' drinkin' when I needed yer, I see!' Phil shouted at him as they approached. 'Look at me fuckin' head! Just fuckin' look at it! What the fuck do yer think I pay yer for? Bastard!'

The group stopped. Casually they guided Patrick over to the wall, propping his well-happy form up against it. Not able to support itself unaided, the drunken body slowly slid down to a sitting position, the strains of Danny Boy hardly affected, whilst the three who could still walk unaided turned, heading back towards Phil.

'Ah, now there'll be no need to be asking what your name is, will there?' The biggest one of the three spoke in the broadest of Irish accents whilst grabbing hold of Phil's lapels, lifting the man a complete foot off the ground with one hand, and then holding him out almost at arm's length.

Phil stared back, frightened. Amazed at the man's incredible strength, he was trying to look into the shadowy expressionless face before him when he heard two loud clicks from either side as his head was forced backwards until his neck was straining under the pressure of the cold metallic gun barrels that were now pushing against him, one into each of his nostrils. The smell of death wafted to the back of his throat, drying it, and closing it up. He tried to swallow, but couldn't as his throat was threatening to adhere to itself.

'I'll be t'inking we ought to be getting rid of him now, Andrew,' the one on Phil's left said.

'Now, now, Mickey me lad,' Andrew replied, 'there'll be plenty o' time for that later if we be wanting to. Remember we're here for our Patrick. We mustn't be doin' anyt'ing he wouldn't be wanting us to.'

The man lifted Phil higher, and then threw him down hard to the ground. His brothers, with simultaneous clicks, re-engaged the safety catches and pocketed their guns.

'When you talks to my brother in future, you be talking civil now,' he ordered over his shoulder, as the three of them casually sauntered back to the wall to recover their still merrily singing brother, who having finished the song once had decided he would sing it all over again.

Lifting Patrick up they carried him into the cellar, closing the doors behind them, leaving the dumbfounded Phil sitting in the yard attempting to pick the pieces of gravel out of his badly grazed palms in the darkness. Moments later, loud peels of laughter erupted from within the cellar. Convinced he was the object of their ridicule, Phil decided it would be sensible not to face any of them again tonight, certainly not now, not until at least the morning. Patrick would be sober by morning, perhaps then he would be able to control his ruffian brothers.

Humiliated, bursting with anger, he painfully pulled himself into his car, wincing each time his raw palms met with something. Finding he was only able to hold the steering wheel comfortably with his fingertips, he started the engine and pushed the selector into drive with his elbow. Speeding dangerously out of the yard, the car raced madly along the alleyway, left through the town, and up the hill into the country for about a mile, before turning left again into the narrow single track lane that doubled back towards the coast, back to the isolated prestigious house he rented on the hill overlooking the bay.

'Bay View' would be more accurately described as a mansion rather than a house. Secluded, it stood in its own grounds in excess of three acres. Sporting eleven bedrooms, most with luxury en-suite facilities, it had two heated pools, one indoor, one outside, a tennis court, and a stable block that was no longer used. It had been built in the nineteen-thirties for Norma Manton, the famous, some say infamous, British actress who later moved on to even more wealth and notoriety by pursuing her career from California. Inherited on her death by her two sons residing in America, keeping this property in the old country was considered an excellent family investment, with the six figure annual rent it accrued being considered an excellent return on their windfall. Such an amount was affordable, though perhaps sometimes not as easily as he would have liked, by the gang boss whose swindles, both past and present, allowed him to pursue the exceedingly rich lifestyle he enjoyed.

Slamming the front door, Phil stopped to inspect himself in the hall mirror. Hardly recognising the grubby, coat-torn man there staring back at him with rivulets of congealed blood marking tracks down the front of his face, he swore, thumping his fists down heavily on the Victorian hallstand, and then swore again as the wounds on his hands re-opened.

'Are you alright, Mr Blunt?'

Phil turned to see the scantily clad Maria, his young Brazilian house-girl, dressed only in her nightclothes, nervously peering at him from half way down the stairs. Directing a mouthful of obscenities at her, he sent the frightened girl hurriedly scurrying back up the stairs to her room. He waited to hear the girl's door close, before going up to his own bedroom.

Showering first in the gold plated en-suite bathroom, the shower gel biting unrelentingly at his abrasions, he dressed his wounds as best as he could, and then went to lie on his bed to think; to worry.

Phil closed his eyes. Lying there, he tried to take stock of his situation. He had lost his arm-piece, Denise. That hurt. That really hurt. She had counted for a lot, one hell of a lot, and a major part of his street-cred. To be seen around town with such a beautiful, and unobtainable young girl was impressive. Many had envied him. But now she was gone, that was going to be a great loss of face for him. Coping with that would not be easy.

Then there was his grip on the Elephant's Nest, that appeared to be gone too, he considered. His two attempts at pressurising the new owners into submission had both failed, and failed dismally. Far from becoming nervous, apparently the young lad had arranged for reinforcements to back him up, and they would probably be arriving soon. Did he even need them? He had actually had the gall to go to the Inferno that very night with no more back up than the black deejay. To his club, that night, and then steal his girl!

If all that was not enough, he realised, he could now be in danger of losing control over the gang. His gang. Patrick's brothers had left him in no doubt of what they thought of him, and he knew he was certainly no match for the four gun-toting Irishmen if they were out to challenge his leadership. From what one of those Irish brothers had said earlier, it did sound as if they wanted to take him out. That was extremely worrying. Was that what they were really here for? That eventuality was definitely beginning to look more than a possibility.

Phil thought deeply. He needed help. But who was there he could rely on? Who was left who would stand by him if the chips went down? Bob? Yes, Bob probably would stand by him. Sid, yes, he probably would too. But then, who else was there? There were the lads, Sam, Graham, and Mike - would they help? For a price they might, he thought, but how much use would they actually be? They were far removed from being hardened thugs by any stretch of the imagination. Patrick and his brothers would consider them no threat at all. There was Don and Paul, of course. Would they remain loyal? No, not them, they would more likely side with the strongest and that, increasingly, was looking like the

Irish mob. Of course, there was still Summers and Jones, but they could hardly get directly involved, could they? Though perhaps they might be useful, he thought. Yes, maybe they could be very useful! Why did he not think of that before?

Picking up the bedside phone, he rapidly dialled D.I. Summers' home number, painfully suffering the phone at the other end ringing for several long minutes before it was answered.

'Yes, yes, mmm . . . Summers here. What is it?'

'S'me, Phil. I need to talk to you.'

'You what? Phil? Do you know what time it is? It's half-past bloody five in the morning! This had better be good! I've only been in bed half an hour!'

Phil hesitated, biting his lip to hold back the abuse waiting within. This was puzzling. It was not like Summers to speak to him in that fashion.

'What the hell do you want?' the policeman demanded, rupturing the pregnant silence.

Cautiously, minding not to swear, Phil replied, 'I'm having a little problem with Patrick. Well it's not him actually, it's his brothers. I would like you to warn them off a bit. Let them know who runs this town; who the boss is. Put them in their place, for me. Be a bonus in it for you, of course. A large one.'

'It'd have to be large one to beat their offer,' Summers declared, the tone of his voice suggesting the man was now enjoying the conversation.

'What?' Phil's jaw dropped, the truth was dawning on him. 'You've met them, already? What did they offer you? I'll top it! I'll double it! No, I will treble any amount they've offered!'

'Oh yes, Phil. We all met up earlier. Me, Jonesy, and a couple of other lads from the nick, we all had a few late drinks with the Irish at old Mother O'Shea's last night. I didn't get home until way after four o'clock this morning. Nice lads, his brothers, very nice lads. No, Phil, I don't think we can do business any more. I'm afraid you'd never be able to match what they're offering.'

'What? Of course I fucking could! Do you know how much I'm really worth? I can more than match anything those bastards could ever offer you. What was it? Tell me, I'll treble it! What did they offer you?'

'Civility, old boy!' There was a loud click, and then the line went dead.

116

Phil sat down heavily on the side of the bed, aghast. He felt bad, physically ill. What should he do now? What could he do? He considered the possibility of taking out contracts on the four Irishmen, but who would do it? Anyone he knew, anyone who could do it, came from London. They would know Patrick as well. He was popular with everyone, with friends everywhere. They could easily tell Patrick of the assignment. The tables could be turned. He could become the victim himself. No, that route was dangerous. That was not the way.

Perhaps he could import some help? America? A possibility, he thought. A contract taken out there would be safe, but that would take time to arrange. A lot of time. Time was a luxury he didn't possess. It might take weeks, possibly months before he made the right contacts. The gang would be well established by then, as one with their new leader. They would all have to be taken out. The cost of that would be exorbitant, even for him, plus it would need a small army to do it. And then, what would be left afterwards?

Phil groaned out loudly, slumping forward burying his head in his hands as he considered his predicament. Patrick definitely had the upper hand. Completely. Utterly. So, the final showdown hadn't happened yet, but that seemed purely academic. It was coming. Any fool could see that, and he was no fool. Neither, obviously, was Patrick or his brothers, he realised, wondering what their next move might be. Would they simply want to take over? Merely cut him out? Doubtful, he surmised. He knew too much. That would always be considered a threat to them. Although there was not much he could do to harm them at present, the circumstances might change in time, his knowledge, his existence, could become a danger to them. They would not be likely to let that happen. So, what would they do with him? What would he do, were he in their shoes? He shivered, remembering the way he had recently dealt with Mark. They might easily dispose of him in a similar way. After all, what other options did they have?

At some time before seven o'clock Phil must have drifted off in to a troubled sleep, because it was at that time he was awoken suddenly by a noise somewhere outside his bedroom. Rolling off the bed, he had not made it to under the covers, stealthily he crawled beneath it. Hardly daring to breath, listening intently over the sound of his pounding heartbeat, he waited for what seemed an eternity. Had they come for him, already? The cistern in one of the bathrooms on the other landing flushed.

'Bitch! Cow!' he shouted at the top of his voice, feeling foolish when he realised it was only the house-girl getting up.

Crawling back out from under the bed, despising himself for being so jittery, such a coward, he slunk into the en-suite bathroom to face himself in the mirror, to shave. It was then, as he started to shave, that it came to him. There was a solution!

CHAPTER 11

'Hello, Tom, Randy. It's nice to see you both again. Now then, you must be Mr and Mrs Patterson, am I right? It is so nice to meet you at last. Come in, do come in. Sit yourselves down now. Coffee will not be a moment. Now, I don't know what all this is about, Phil's not here yet, and I'm not sure I really want to know, but if you have some business to discuss with him and you need somewhere neutral in which to do it, then I'm only too happy to oblige you at anytime. I cannot say the same for him though. He's one that's definitely not on my Christmas list.'

'Thanks, er, George isn't it?' John exchanged greetings politely, firmly shaking the man's hand.

Mary smiled pleasantly at the Ice Cream Parlour man who was ushering them inside, her eyes checking to see if the place was clean. It was scrupulously clean.

'To be quite honest,' John continued, 'we haven't got a clue what all this is about, either. Phil phoned us early this morning, very early, asking for this meeting - said it would be mutually beneficial, whatever that means. He hinted that if everything worked out okay he would happily leave us alone in the future. Well, I mean, after the bomb . . . You did hear about that, of course?'

George nodded. 'There isn't a soul on the front who hasn't heard about it,' he confirmed.

'Well, I don't mind telling you, that incident really shook us up. We have certainly had our eyes opened for us recently. We come from Brisham, you see. It is a very quiet place; an extremely respectable area. Graffiti makes newspaper headlines there. So anything that might lead to a more peaceful life here, with all its strange ways that we're not accustomed to, well, it must be explored, mustn't it? Even this meeting with Phil.'

'Too true,' the man agreed, skilfully carrying the four coffees over to the table around which they had sat. 'A small word of advice, though, if

119

you don't mind. This Phil is an extremely tricky character. Do be careful. It is not really his style to offer anyone an olive branch. There has to be an ulterior motive somewhere. I'd lay money on it.'

'Yes, that's pretty much what Randy said,' Mary agreed. 'It does seem strange, him wanting this meeting, doesn't it? I mean, he must know we're no match for him really, and that it would only be a matter of time before we succumbed to his demands. Quite obviously, when we refused to pay the extortion that first night, we had no idea he could come up with things like bombs. We knew it could get nasty, but not that nasty. If it hadn't been for young Randy here, we'd have all been blown to pieces.'

'This makes no sense, man.' Randy watched the door nervously. 'None at all. I's reckon we all ought to move to the table at the back. The one behind the screen, near the back-door might be a good idea,' he suggested. 'Man, why do I's keep thinking of the Valentine's Day massacre?'

'Oh my God!' Mary shivered. Turning distinctly pale, she picked up her coffee and clasping her handbag under her arm, she started pushing her husband out into the aisle. 'Let's do as he says John. I feel very nervous about this. Move, come on, quickly!'

The group hurriedly re-assembled around the table at the back of the café, where the small screen appeared to offer them some protection should Randy's fears prove correct. Tom tapped the screen with his knuckle as he sat down, discovering it was merely made of plastic, not a lot of protection should they need it, but he decided it best not to say anything.

George returned to refill their cups a few minutes later. 'I don't think he'd have to get you here if his intentions were to kill you,' he tried to reassure them. 'I'm sure he could find plenty of other times or places to bump you off, if that was his intention. It's hardly likely that lot would consider getting out of their beds at such an unearthly hour to do something that could be done at anytime.'

'Perhaps it's about Denise,' Tom suggested. 'Maybe this is all to get her back. Maybe, he really wants her back so badly that he is prepared to bargain for her. Well, he is not having her! No way!'

Mary leant across the table. Taking his hand in hers, she clasped it comfortingly. Tom managed a weak smile back, and then he felt her jump, violently, retracting her hand, as the steam valve on the chrome espresso coffee-maker at the end of the counter suddenly released itself, announcing that its working temperature had been achieved. Seconds later, the door opening when Phil strode in alone was an anti-climax.

'Good-morning everybody. Thank you all for agreeing to a meeting at such short notice,' he said with a smile on approaching them.

'Two whole sentences and we have not had a swear word, yet! My God! What's happened to his face?' George whispered. Wiping their table down, he collected their empty cups. 'I'll do you all a fresh coffee, then leave you to it, if that's okay,' he said aloud, returning to the counter.

'That's very good of you, George. Thanks,' Phil said with an uncharacteristic politeness. Pulling a stool up, he sat at the end of the table.

The group waited in silence while George, amidst many hissing clouds of steam, produced and delivered another round of coffees.

'I'll be out the back if you need me at all,' he said, leaving them to their business.

'Nice friends you've got,' Phil said, touching his facial wounds, and looking across to Tom and Randy on his left. 'Real handy.'

Tom over-smiled to show his pleasure. 'Few more turning up in the next day or so,' he lied.

'So I hear. How many? Are they all as good as those two?'

Tom was beginning to enjoy the conversation. 'Do you think I'd tell you?'

'No, I suppose not. But they'd better be as good!'

'Look, man. Let's stop all this bullshit. You ain't asked for this meeting to score a few points batting insults across a table,' Randy interrupted the contest. 'Something's happened, hasn't it? What's this all about, man?'

'Yes. Yes, it has. I'll come clean. Something has happened. Now we're both in deep sh . . . Sorry, we are both in deep trouble. All of us, you and me alike.'

'How do you make that out?' Tom enquired.

Mary, John, and Randy, all leaned forward. Listening intently, they waited to be enlightened.

'How can I put this?' Phil started to look desperate. 'You all know me. You three may only have been here a couple of days, but you must know quite a bit about me already. You know what I'm into. You know what I stand for - a bit of protection, a bit of, well, perhaps more of a monopoly, in the local drug market. You know all that. You've kicked against it and really rocked the boat! But it is a system that works, believe me. A system that is beneficial to everyone. The resort stays alive, everybody makes a lot of money, and everybody is happy. For over five years now that arrangement has worked here, and worked well. The place has expanded. Businesses have grown rapidly and new ones have sprung up. You ask Randy, he knows.' He stared into the Jamaican's eyes. 'I know you haven't been here as long as me, but be honest now. Who do you know who's gone bust along the front recently? There is nobody, is there? And hasn't the town benefited enormously, expanded, become more profitable, even in the time you've been here? Hasn't everybody done better? Yes, I know it may be true that as businesses have grown they have had to pay me more money - but then, aren't they making a lot more for themselves too?

'Forget that everybody hates my guts. Forget the nasty, arrogant, blaspheming Phil bit. That's just part of an image, one I have to project to keep people in line, to make it all work. Forget all that. Underneath I'm not that bad a guy. Once or twice I've had to come down really heavy on people who've challenged me, that much you know, but only because it has been necessary in order to maintain the status quo. That is all I was doing to you lot. I was coming down heavy. I was making a stand.

'The bomb at the Ellie, well - that was a terrible mistake, I apologise for that. Not my mistake, I hasten to add. That was Patrick's mistake. He was only supposed to frighten you with a small explosion, one that wouldn't do any more damage than a smelly firework. It was only supposed to be a gesture, one to make you reconsider, not to eliminate you. Believe me, that would have been pointless - there would have been no club left if that had gone off inside, so that quite obviously was not my intention. I mean, what good would it have done me? None at all. Randy, isn't what I am saying correct? You know how it is here. Does this not all make some sense to you?'

Randy fidgeted uncomfortably. 'Put like that man, I's suppose it does, in a strange kind of way. But that don't mean I's likes it, or agrees with it. Like, man, what happened to Mark? It might be okay everybody making money, expanding, an' all that, but what about him? Mark, he was a good bloke. He played by your rules, but look where it got him! Look where he is now! Dead! Man, now you ain't gonna tell me that you had nothing to do with his death, is you?'

'No, there's no point in me lying to you,' Phil now fidgeted uncomfortably, with beads of perspiration appearing on his forehead, 'but you've got to remember, Mark was no angel either. He was as much of a rogue as I am, what with all his little sidelines, but they didn't concern me. That is, not until Patrick started spreading it about that he was sure Mark was cheating the system – that he was buying his own drugs to sell in place of mine. Well, that had to be dealt with, and there is only one way you can deal with someone of Mark's calibre.'

'You killed my brother over some drugs?' John started to get up, but Mary and Tom restrained him.

'You have to understand, it's a whole different world here to what you know, Mr Patterson.' Phil leant backwards, away from the threat, as he answered. 'There's a whole different set of rules. Mark knew that, and accepted it. We all do. We have to otherwise we would get out.

'What happened to Mark was no more, no less, than what anyone would expect to happen to someone who cheated on his side of what you could call a mutual agreement, here. The trouble is, now I'm not so sure he was cheating. It all goes back to Patrick again. He was the one who pointed the finger. He was the one who convinced us all. I only did what was expected of me, what he knew I would do, I gave the orders to have him removed.

'Did you know it was Patrick who actually threw him off the cliff? He actually volunteered to do it. Patrick, Patrick, Patrick! Christ, what a fool I've been!'

Mary and John sat in deathly silence holding each other's hands, stunned at the revelations they were hearing, hardly able to comprehend the way of life that surrounded them now, a way of life that seemed a million miles from anything they knew at Brisham. Randy looked on in disbelief too, his expressions becoming increasingly more enquiring. The man sat in front of him was not the Phil he recognised. Not the hard-faced, cussing, swearing thug that everyone knew. Here was someone explaining, giving reasons, excuses even, for his actions - something that he would never have expected of the man. Why?

Tom finally broke the silence. 'You're not making a lot of sense, Phil. Surely, you have not asked to meet us here in order to apologise to us, and to soft-soap us into paying up. After all that's happened, you're not really expecting that to happen, are you?'

'No. No, I'm not here for anything like that reason, not at all. I'm here to make a bargain with you. A mutually beneficial agreement, you could call it. One, I think, you cannot refuse. At least, I hope not!'

'You's what, man?'

'You have obviously all heard the expression: "Better the devil you know . . .", haven't you?' He studied their faces closely as they each slowly nodded their response. 'Well, consider that me. I am the devil you know. The devil you don't know is out there now, waiting. He's waiting to take over. Patrick, I'm talking about. Patrick has brought his three gun-toting brothers over from Ireland to back him up. Most of the others in the clan are so frightened that they have already lined up with them. The remaining few are all sure to have to go down that road too. Join or be eliminated.

'Now, if you thought I was bad, I can promise you, you ain't seen nothing yet! Patrick and his mob will be far worse than me if they are allowed to get away with this take-over, far worse. They won't stand any nonsense from the likes of you. You will be got rid of as easily as they will get rid of me if I stay around! It will not be some arrogant, cursing, fist-thumping character like me that you will be dealing with. It will be the rule of the gun, that I can assure you! And I doubt they'll be content to stop with the ten-per-cent levy. No, they will get greedy. They'll bleed every last penny from you, killing the golden goose for sure. Are you all getting the picture I'm painting?'

'I think so,' Tom answered for all of them. 'But what on earth do you expect from us. We can't take them on to keep you in control, no matter what deal you offered us. I mean, what could we possibly do against four gunmen?'

'There's a lot you could do, actually. One hell of a lot! You know how much I'm up against it now, but then so are you, aren't you? And your troubles are about to get a whole lot worse unless we sort something out. My offer is that, should you choose to help me, I would not pursue the insurance payments from you. The ten-per-cent. That would be our little secret; nobody else would have to know you were not paying your share. Of course, I would still require the sole freedom to supply the drug market in your club, but that costs you nothing, does it? I'm sure you could turn a blind-eye to that if you wished, and anyway by now you must have realised that if you were to clean the place up, to make it a drug-free zone, you'd hardly get a soul in, haven't you?'

'Yes, that has become quite clear to all of us, I think. But I still don't see how we can help you.' Tom looked curious.

'The day after tomorrow is Tuesday,' Phil explained. 'Now, every Tuesday afternoon, Patrick, Don, and Paul travel up to London, to Hammersmith, with something like twenty grand in their pockets, to purchase enough stuff to see us through the rest of the week and over the weekend. That money, that twenty grand or however much they intend to buy this week, will not be easy for them to raise at such short notice. They will come up with it, of course, but as I say, it won't be easy for them. You see, I have always kept a very tight rein on the money. Their share, the bulk of their wages, if you want to call it that, have been the fast cars, the fabulous holidays, the good clothes, top designer wear for the youngsters, the houses – they've all got fabulous holiday homes - and the easy life-style that I have provided for them. They have wanted for nothing, but they've had precious little hard cash given them. No more than enough to easily cover their day to day expenses. That's the way I operate.'

'Man! You's mad! You's wanting us to blag this twenty grand? You must be joking! They would kill us!'

'No, I don't want you to steal the money, that would be all but impossible. No, I wasn't thinking of anything quite so crude. All I want is for you to help me swap the drugs. Swap them for a load of harmless rubbish. That way we will hit their pockets, as well as their credibility. First thing they will think is that the suppliers have cheated them. They will fall out with them, big style. Patrick will rush off, with his three hot-headed brothers, back up to the smoke to sort things out. Believe me, even they will be a long way out their depth up there. Those London boys won't stand any nonsense from the likes of them. With a bit of luck, that will be the end of Patrick and his kin. Well, what do you think of the idea? What do you say? Will you help me?'

'It all sounds extremely dangerous to me,' Mary stated.

Her husband agreed with her. Tom, still thinking about the proposal, said nothing.

'How would we do this swap?' Randy was inquisitive.

'Simple.' Phil looked relieved, he could see from their faces that they had not entirely ruled out his suggestion. 'It's a clockwork operation every week. It hasn't changed in five years, so I doubt it will now. They will leave here at four o'clock, getting there about six-fifteen, in plenty of time to meet up with the suppliers around seven-thirty in a certain pub. The sale is always at eight, in a little lock-up in the street behind the pub, only taking a few minutes. No great check is done on the goods supplied, as it's a regular weekly trade. It's such a routine operation that they probably won't even look inside the bag. They'll start the return journey straight away, then around nine-fifteen, give or take a few minutes for traffic, they'll pull into Membury Services - that's the one just before you pass by Swindon on the M4. There they'll stop for a quick coffee and the necessaries, leaving ten or fifteen minutes later in order to be back at the cellar for around half-ten. While they are in the Services, you do the swap. It's that easy!'

'You telling us they leave twenty grand's worth of drugs on the seat of a car while they go for a coffee?' Tom was unconvinced.

'In a large hold-all in the boot, yes. Whichever car they use will be alarmed of course, but don't forget I bought all their cars for them. I have duplicate keys to every single one of them, including the alarms.'

'So why do you need us? If it's that easy, why don't you do it on your own?'

'Because I'd be their first suspect. Having dealt with these same suppliers every week for nearly five years, they will look for other things first, before believing they have been ripped off. We have to convince them that they have been ripped off. Now, although I shall be trying to keep well out of their way for most of the time, I shall make a point of being seen in the club by some of the gang at the only time that the drugs were out of anybody's sight - the only time that anybody could have been tampered with them. I will be in the Inferno for all to see from nine until ten. The rest of the gang will all be working either there or at your place at that time of night so they will be able to vouch for each other.

Everybody will have cast iron alibis, making it look unmistakably as if the suppliers really have swindled them. They'll never suspect you lot, of course. I mean, how could they? How would you have known when, where, or how, the pick-up operates? Foolproof, isn't it? Now, are you with me on this, or not?'

'And if it were to work, if they did go rushing back to London getting themselves blown to bits - you'd really leave us alone?' Tom enquired.

'I would. I promise. You have my word on that. I would rather have some of the cake than none of it. Look, I'm going to visit the little boys' room. You talk it over amongst yourselves while I'm away and give me an answer when I return. Personally, I cannot see you have any alternative. Neither of us has.'

Phil disappeared through the door at the back of the milk bar, calling out to George as he closed it behind him. It was several minutes before he returned to stand at the head of the table.

'You're right,' Tom said, 'we don't appear to have any alternative. We'll go along with it. We have to. You had better sit down again. We need to go through the fine details. Like, how do we know which car . . . ?'

CHAPTER 12

It was precisely eight-thirty when John cautiously edged the old blue Sierra Estate out of the back yard of the Elephant's Nest and on to the near empty road. Turning right, heading along the promenade towards the cliff road at the other end which would take them to Bristol and then on through to the M4, he drove at a steady thirty-five miles an hour. A speed that was neither too fast nor too slow to draw any undue attention to them, he guessed.

Tom sat in the front passenger seat with Randy sprawled leisurely in the back hugging the tartan hold-all, the one that was filled mostly with scrunched up newspapers but with a few plastic bags of talcum powder, tablets made by a hole puncher and a sheet of cardboard, a few lumps of brown plasticine, and a bag of grass that really was grass on the top, in case someone should take a cursory look inside when buying the goods – they would then believe they had been fooled by the semi-darkness of the lock-up, whereas to have later found just the scrunched up newspaper would have revealed the true story.

All the way along the promenade they scanned the roadside apprehensively until, satisfied that no one who mattered had seen them leaving, they were able to sit back and relax as the elderly vehicle laboured them up the steep hill out of the town. If all went according to plan they would be back at the club sometime after ten-fifteen and, with luck, nobody should have missed them.

The three of them had made a special point of being been seen around the club shortly before they left the building secretly by the back door. They especially made sure that Sam, Graham and Mike, who were selling their wares in front of the stage, noticed them.

Randy had left a three-hour tape playing, a recording of a previous night at the club, and set the intelligent lighting system to automatic random selection. Recordings of previous nights were frequently played in the early evenings for an hour or two, especially if the night was quiet as Tuesdays often were until around eleven o'clock. Securely locking the console room door behind him as he left, he had given the key, with enough brief information, to Sarah so she could change the tape in the unlikely event that Ronnie was late and they had not returned by eleven o'clock.

Sarah could be trusted and it was fortunate that, as a result of a short fling with Ronnie, a disaster she did not want to remember, she was already quite conversant with the basic running of the console. Whilst it was true that she had never been able to successfully master the skill of mixing, she did know exactly how everything worked, and what to do if something failed. One bad changeover during the whole evening, should they be late back, would hardly arouse anyone's suspicions. Sarah would easily be able to keep the show running.

They were completely satisfied that their well-laid plans, which had been so very thoroughly thought through many times that day, were as near to foolproof as they could possibly make them. Nevertheless, all the time in the back of their minds they were painfully aware that any major catastrophe such as a road accident, a breakdown, or even something as simple as a power cut at the club, could easily foil their alibis. However those were eventualities they were forced to take chances on; things they really did not want to contemplate.

Very little was said on the journey to Membury, with both Tom and Randy making use of the time catnapping. John woke them at ten minutes past nine when, relieved that they had actually arrived in time, he swung the car up the slip road off the motorway and parked on the left just inside the motorway service's large car park.

At one point John had been worried after realising they had to travel on as far as the Hungerford junction to turn around in order to be on the correct side of the motorway. Had they allowed for that? He couldn't remember, and was fearful they might arrive too late. Of course, they could have crossed the motorway using the private staff road at Membury, but he considered that the chances of actually finding it, and of being caught, or attracting undue attention by using that route, was too much of a risk at that busy time of night.

From their vantage point in the closing darkness, lying a little way back from the entrance in the opposite direction to which the entering cars were heading, they could plainly see each one as it arrived with very little risk of themselves being seen. Nervously they waited, but not for long. Less than five minutes passed before the expected maroon coloured Jaguar swept past them at speed, although in the artificially assisted limited light of the cloudy evening it could have actually been almost any dark colour imaginable, they would never have known. However the number plate confirmed it was definitely the one for which they were waiting.

Rushing past them, the car headed directly towards the bright lights of the welcoming buildings and reversed into one of the marked bays on the right some six spaces from the end of the parking area - the area that joined with the roadway passing in front of the main doors to the foyer.

John restarted the old Sierra's engine as they continued to watch closely. Three occupants emerged from the Jaguar, and hurriedly made their way towards the building. The one who had been driving, easily identifiable as Patrick by his slight stature, suddenly stopped. Turning around, he set the car's alarm by aiming his key ring at it then waited momentarily until the hazard lights flashed twice. Satisfied the car was safely locked, he continued on to catch up with the other two, who by now had almost reached the foyer entrance.

Slowly the Sierra edged out of its hiding position and cruised down between the two rows of parked vehicles towards the Jaguar. Conveniently the adjacent space before it was vacant, so John drove straight into it.

Tom watched the thugs going through the brightly lit foyer and waited until the instant they disappeared from sight before leaping out of the car. By pressing the duplicate key fob supplied by Phil he immediately disengaged the Jaguar's alarm, cringing as the hazard lights flashed once more. Checking all around to make sure that no one was watching him, there didn't seem to be, he waited for a few more seconds to be totally sure. It all seemed quiet, so he boldly walked around to the back of the car and opened up the large boot with the supplied keys.

John waited patiently in the car with the engine still running, his right foot nervously hovering above the accelerator, occasionally flicking it, in readiness for a quick get-away should the need arise. Randy, meanwhile, was struggling with the duplicate hold-all, wrestling it out through the Sierra's back door and across into the boot of the Jaguar.

Unzipping the genuine bag, a quick look inside confirmed that Phil had made an extremely accurate guess as to what it would likely contain, and the weights of the two identical looking bags appeared indistinguishable. No adjustments to the duplicate bag's contents were going to be necessary. They could simply be exchanged.

The task was quickly completed. Tom closed the boot quietly then, resetting the alarm, he smiled confidently through the window at Randy, who was already back in the Sierra and sprawled out across the back seat hugging the genuine bag. Opening the front passenger door, Tom threw himself into the seat next to his father.

'Piece of cake,' he crowed, closing the door.

With an enormous sigh of relief his father slid the car into gear. Checking over his shoulder that all was clear, he started to slowly reverse the car out of the bay. The reversing manoeuvre was skilfully completed, and they were ready to drive off when . . .

'Oh shit, man!'

There was something in the tone of Randy's voice shouting from the rear seat that sent a bolt of ice reverberating up and down Tom's spine like an electric shock. He could feel the hairs on the back of his neck bristling, standing on end, and a cold numbness began to grow inside his head as his brain turned to ice. Looking around, mid neck-spin, to the right of his father he caught sight of a man standing by the open back door of the Jaguar. There was something the man was holding in his hand. Something he was pointing at them. Suddenly the Jaguar's lights began pulsating wildly as its horn blared out long, rhythmic blasts. The car's alarm system, detecting the opened door, was dutifully shrilling out its warning.

'Drive!' Tom screamed at his father, at the same time ducking down in his seat as low as he could, but he was too late, his voice was lost in the sound of the repetitive hammering of the bullets, the deafening explosions on the metalwork, and the noise of the shattering glass.

The old car lurched, leaping forward violently then, coughing once, it stalled. Tom looked up anxiously at his father. To his horror he discovered that all that remained next to him was an undoubtedly lifeless form slumped forward dementedly across the steering wheel. Parts from his father's head, some of it fleshy meat, some of it bloodstained matted hair and brain, were splattered across the crazed windscreen in front of him. A mass of bloody mucus was oozing down slowly, dripping into a growing pool of blood on the dashboard with sickening resounding plops, strangely each one still plainly audible to him over the near deafening sound of the Jaguar's alarm. There were a couple more shots fired and the annoying alarm trailed out into a nothingness, leaving the plopping to then become the only deafening orchestration.

Shuddering, Tom doubled forward as his cramping stomach cruelly demanded of him, his eyes now coming to focus on the eyeball suspended precariously from the rear-view mirror by a gradually elongating sinew. Dangling in front of him, gently swinging slightly back and forth like some dying pendulum, it stared at him menacingly for a few moments. Then, when the elongating thinning sinew could hold it no more, it dropped onto the gear stick beside him, bouncing off to the left, towards him, and hitting his knee before rolling down his leg to finally come to rest in the foot well, looking up at him.

Tom's brain frantically tried to question the rushing noise roaring in his ears. Like an approaching express train it was getting louder by the second. Then other sounds seemed to join in. Strange loud hollow sounds, like dried peas falling into an empty metal bucket. His brain raced madly but could make no sense of them so, choosing to ignore what it couldn't understand, it decided to concentrate on his stomach instead in an effort to stop the contents of it evacuating. It was a futile effort, and relief came swiftly.

He reached violently, vomiting up the complete contents of his stomach in one go with such a force that splashes of the sickly, gastric substances rebounded back off the windscreen, returning to smack him in the face. Gasping for air, he gagged again, but found he was unable to vomit anything more, there was nothing left, but his stomach kept trying, insisting, contracting violently, pulling his guts in ever tighter until the creasing pain became so great, so overpowering, he was sure his navel and backbone had somehow met. Then, quickly, before he could notice it coming, a deep blackness swirled in, engulfing him.

It seemed like hours later, but it could only have been seconds, gradually, very gradually, Tom became vaguely aware of some movement, of the door next to him opening, and of being dragged bodily out of the car.

Michael Knell

Still shaking uncontrollably, still involuntarily heaving but with nothing left there to throw up, he offered no resistance. Falling backwards out of the car, he crashed heavily on to the tarmac, and back into the relief of unconsciousness once more.

Randy slammed the door above them shut, then struggled with his friend's limp body, dragging it to the comparative shelter of the large silver Volvo Estate that was parked in the next row of cars. Crawling around behind it, he dragged Tom into the thin line of bushes separating that parking area from the next one, before lying down to look out through the underneath of the car. With his head down as low as he could get, he was able to see the gunman's feet approaching.

Frantically Randy's brain searched to find some solution, a way out for them. He fully appreciated any attempt to run from the assailant would be pointless; nothing more than a stupid symbolic gesture. Tom couldn't run anyway. Yet not to run seemed certain death. Randy peered under the car again. The man was almost upon them. With a few more steps he could not fail to see them. But still there was no way out for them, none that he could see. It was game over! Game, set, and match!

Closing his eyes to wait for the ending, hoping it would be painless, Randy put his arm around Tom's shoulders and, squeezing him tightly, hugging him, he whispered into his ear, 'I's loves you, man. I's wishes there'd been more.'

It might have been the squeeze, or it might been one of life's cruel jokes, but in that instant consciousness chose to return to Tom. Now he too became aware of the hopelessness of their situation. Convinced there was nothing they could do, he chose to close his eyes again. He prayed to drift back, to be taken again into the swirling darkness that took him earlier. He prayed so hard, but it would not happen. He could still hear the rush of the speeding traffic on the motorway. He could still feel the strong arms of Randy, trembling, but holding him tightly. Now he could visualise the gun pointing at his head from only a few feet away, with the finger on the trigger. He knew the inevitable was coming. It was only a matter of waiting. It wouldn't be long. The next noise would be the gun discharging. Would he actually hear the bang that would kill him, he began to wonder, and then he wondered: why had he wondered that? Did it matter, anyway?

133

Tom kept his eyes tightly closed, now feverishly clinging on to his friend's arm in the desperate belief that it wouldn't be so bad if they went together. Everyone had to die sometime. At least he would not be dying alone. Many did, but not him, he wouldn't be. He was with someone who he had grown to love, someone he trusted like a brother. No, not *like* a brother, but as a *true* brother, a *real* brother. Oh, God! Yes! Okay, then! Maybe even *more* than a brother!

There were numerous worse ways of going, he considered, as a meaningful, peaceful calm washed over him. A serenity. Tom had made his peace with the world. He was ready. He knew that whatever this experience called death was, they would be going through it together, and if there was such a thing as an on, or a hereafter, if it did exist, then they would be going there together as well. Neither of them would be alone. He was truly at peace, and in a strange way he was even happy.

Time and reality lost all meaning as Tom's brain began searching back through his lifetime, bringing forth dream-like visions from his past, all strangely mixed-up in no chronological order, but all peacefully, lovingly, happily tempered, even the bad ones like when it was his first day at school. He could see himself crying, and there . . . ? There was Randy comforting him. But, no, that couldn't be. He didn't know Randy then. But that didn't matter, it was wonderful. Many, many faces flashed across his mind. His mother. His father. Denise. Sarah. They were smiling at him. He was looking through them, out of the car's window to see the Elephant's Nest for the first time. Ben was in the way. They were on the hills. Randy was waving at them. No, he still didn't know him then. That was wrong, but never mind. Faster, even faster, the recollections came, each becoming more muddled than the last, more muddled until the entire dream became fictional. There was no reality, just dream. Happiness. Peace. Flashing lights. A noise. A wailing. A realisation, but what was it? Was it real? Was it dream? Randy was shaking him, slapping his face. He opened his eyes.

The wailing sirens were converging from the far corners of the car park, racing ever nearer. Blue lights were flashing, reflecting back brightly from whatever they found, lighting up the building, the sky, the trees, and the cars. From either end of the car park, a motorway police patrol car, awoken from its secret hideout in the darkness of the corner of the car park where unofficial coffee breaks were taken, screamed into sight. The gunman spun around, firing several shots at each of them in turn as he fled, running back through the row of parked cars, past the Jaguar, heading towards the motorway and the only escape he could see. Throwing himself head-long through the bushes of the car park's perimeter, he half rolled out, half somersaulted, out onto the service road. The road that bypasses the car park. The one intended for use by lorries to get to their parking area, or by any other vehicles that are only stopping off for fuel.

There was little, or nothing, the driver could do to miss the object that his headlights suddenly picked out no more than ten metres in front of him. He did try though, he did his best, but the wheels of the giant tanker stubbornly locked on the greasy surface, the tyres squealing mournfully as the enormous vehicle continued on, sliding forwards, on and on, barely losing any of its momentum. Then there was an abrupt bump, and a vibrating thumping as the tyres regained some traction on the crushed, mutilating body.

With one final jolt the tractor unit, finding adhesion at last, ground to a halt. The trailer behind, bluntly refusing to do likewise jack-knifed to the right, gracefully as if in slow motion, until it was precariously overhanging the steep slope down to the hard shoulder of the motorway below. The giant fuel tank, still containing more than twenty thousand litres of four-star petrol, balanced precariously for a few seconds whilst the fuel inside continued to wash forwards. Then, as the fuel returned, rushing backwards through the baffles to the rear of the tank, the trailer lunged outwards, effortlessly like some discarded toy, out over the slope, plummeting down onto the motorway deep below, throwing the cab upwards high into the night sky above it, only for it to return moments later crashing down on to the central reservation.

The inimitable sound of the twisting, grating, crushing, mangling metal, mixed with the sound of panicking horns, of skidding traffic, of squealing tyres, and of the noise of all of the resulting multiple shunts, appeared to be endless. But end it finally did, in an almost deafening eerie silence. Only a barely perceivable hiss prevailed from somewhere far below.

A seeming eternity passed before the shout. The impotent shout that preceded the almighty roar of the colossal fire-ball erupting, bellowing out its great balls of bright orange flames, suitably draped in their contrasting, almost colour co-ordinating, curtains of black smoke. Twenty, thirty, forty metres upwards and further upwards into the darkening sky they rolled, onwards, upwards into the oblivion of the night. More thick acrid clouds of the pitch black, blacker than black, smoke billowed out away from the flames, this not going upwards but preferring to spill outwards, sideways into the car park to steal the oxygen from the fresh night air, and to replace it with its own evil choking gasses. The intense heat radiating up from the inferno below began shrivelling the bushes that made up the hedge, setting them alight within seconds, whilst the tarmac of the car park began to bubble, spitting molten lumps in random directions as it melted, and forced the policemen, defensively holding their arms up in front of their faces, to retreat.

One policeman raced back towards his patrol car intending to call for assistance. He did not know the radio was already dead, a victim of the gunman's shots. He never knew. The car exploded as either the intense heat or a spark flying out from one of the burning bushes ignited the bullet ridden leaking petrol tank, with the massive force throwing the car's windscreen outwards towards the approaching officer. Slicing through the air like a guillotine, the glass effortlessly decapitated the man before continuing on its journey into oblivion.

The three remaining patrolmen, now at a safer distance, were unsuccessfully attempting to hold back the ever-growing crowd of people who had rushed out from the restaurant, or who had appeared from their parked cars. All of them now jostling for a better position in order to see, to witness the carnage, and in order to satisfy that curious human craving that loves to feed off disasters.

The bulk of the crowd now moved as if one body, surging forwards towards the burning patrol car, towards the unseen headless body hiding in the smoky darkness. Passing by the old Sierra to obtain a better view the two fat middle-aged women, arm in arm, happened to look inside. Why, with all else that was happening around them, will never be known, but their hysterical screams soon encouraged others in the all-inquisitive crowd to swarm back towards them. Once enlightened more and more people began to scream, holding on to each other, some fainting, some fleeing, and some merely standing there dazed, unable to move, unable to comprehend.

Those who had decided to continue on towards the fiery police car were now discovering their own theatre of horror. They too began screaming on seeing the head of the policeman on the ground with its eyes staring longingly towards its divorced body lying six feet away from it in an expanding pool of blood.

'Tom! Tom! Come on! Let's go, man! We's gotta get out of here!' Randy pushed him out through the other side of the bushes where they were hiding.

'Go? Go where? That's my father in there. Dead! Cold bloodedly murdered! I can't just go,' Tom protested, his eyes red and watering, but still managing to hold back from flooding. 'I can't just leave him there! That's my father!'

'Yes, man, I's know it is. But you's got to, man. You's got to leave him. He's dead all right and it's a real mean shit, man. It's the biggest shit ever, man, but us being caught here ain't gonna help him, is it? Ain't gonna help nobody. Look at you, man. All covered in blood. What's you gonna tell 'em? What's you gonna tell the police? And how's you gonna explain this little lot?' Randy offered up the drug-stuffed hold-all.

'I guess you're right,' Tom was beginning to think straight again, 'we've got to get home somehow. I have to get back. God! I have to face mother! I have to break it to her before the police do. Oh, God! Just how do I do it? What can I say to her? How can I tell her what's happened? But I have to, don't I? I have to! It will only be a matter of time before the police trace our address through the car's registration plate. I have to be there when they turn up. I have to!'

'Give us you's mobile, man.'

Tom handed it over, and watched as Randy sped through the buttons.

'You got me,' the voice shrieked.

'Ollie. Listen to me, man. We's in deep shit! When I's says deep, I's means D, E, E, P, man. Believe me, it just don't get no deeper!'

'Ran? What the fuck's you done now, boy? You is always in the shit!'

'Never mind that! I's tell you all about it later, man. Can you get your mean machine down to Bristol? Can you meet us at Junction 19 in half an hour or less, the M32 roundabout? Less would be good. Come on, man! You can, you can, you can! Say it, man! Say it!'

'Sure I can, Ran. No probs. I'm so alive I could be there in five!

'Eh?'

'I've been having a ball at the Colston Hall, where the chicks like 'em black, and the chicks like 'em tall! I'm already in Bristol, ain't I? I'll be there, but you just make sure you clean any shit off before you gets into my car, boy! I don't want no dirty footprints left on my carpets, if you knows what I mean?'

'Okay, man! Anything goes wrong we won't let you fall for it. Promise!'

'Catch you there!'

'And how the hell do we get to Bristol?' Tom asked, taking the phone from his friend's hand and pushing the aerial down.

'Easy, man! Give me those keys.'

'Keys?'

'The duplicate Jag keys.'

'But . . . But . . . The Sierra is blocking the Jag in. There are coppers and people all round it. Anyway, it's far too near to the fire, it's in the fire, we'd never survive the heat!'

'Man! You's so naive!' Randy took the keys from him, and said, 'Just follow me.'

Slinging the holdall on to his shoulder casually, Randy started to whistle and jiggle, as if listening to music. Swinging his hips madly, he walked off towards the far side of the car park, away from the crowds. Tom, confused, hurried after him.

Jangling the keys, still whistling, Randy led the way to a red Montego parked in the darkness a little way from all the other cars. He fiddled with the door lock for a few seconds, until moments later there was a mechanical clanking sound as the central locking system disengaged.

'Get in!' Randy ordered.

Tom raced around to the other side. Trying the front passenger door he found it unlocked and jumped in. Swiftly doing likewise, Randy threw the bag on to the back seat before he fiddled once more, this time under the dashboard. A few more seconds and the engine sprang into life.

'How the hell did you do that?' an astonished Tom enquired.

'You really don't want to know, man! Now buckle up. Once we get clear of here we's gonna have to shift. I's banking on everyone goggling the action long enough for us to get to Bristol because we's got to dump this heap before it's missed!'

Slowly, trying not to draw any attention to themselves, Randy eased the car out of the car park and down the long slip road to join the empty motorway. Empty, as nothing could get past the still furiously burning tanker or the multitude of shunted vehicles before it.

Behind them, somewhere back by the car park, there was another enormous explosion, an almighty one that lit up the sky like sheet lightning, the force of which travelled along the motorway buffeting the car wildly.

'Shit, man, I's wonder what the fuck that was. That sure was some motherfucker of a bang! Gotta 'ave been far bigger than the first one!' Randy declared, with a puzzled look on his face.

Sticking his foot firmly to the floor, the car rapidly picked up speed. It was exactly thirty minutes later that they were throwing the tartan hold-all into the back of Ollie's Thunderbird, and leaping in after it.

'Go, man! Go!' Randy shouted.

Effortlessly, the mean machine obeyed.

CHAPTER 13

'Hello, er . . . Is that Mrs Patterson?'

'Yes,' Mary confirmed, sitting down and putting the receiver in her other hand so she could still sip her coffee.

'It's Dave, Dave from the Inferno. Look, I was wondering if I could pop along to see you and your husband, and Tom of course. I have already met Tom. Great lad you've got there Mrs Patterson. Great lad. You must be proud.'

'Yes. Yes, we are. But, um . . . You say you want to come and see us? You mean tonight?'

'Well, if I could. Let me see, it's ten o'clock now, I could be there in, say, fifteen minutes. Would that be okay with you? It is quite important, er, what I want to see you about. Er . . . Not the sort of thing we could discuss over the phone, if you get my gist.'

Mary went silent for a moment, desperately trying to think of some plausible excuse, some way to stall the man, to delay the meeting. She knew her husband, and Tom and Randy, had not returned yet. They might possibly be back by a quarter past, she thought, but what if they were not? Anything might hold them up. It could be much later before they returned.

'Are you still there?' Dave enquired. 'Look, I'm sorry about this, but Phil's just walked in. I need to have a few words with him too. Could we now make it, er, let's say some time after half-past, then?'

'Yes. Yes, that will be fine. We'll expect you then.' Mary replaced the handset with some relief. The others ought to be back by then, she reckoned, and even if they were not they couldn't possibly be much later. She wouldn't have to stall the man for too long.

Dave put the phone down, swinging the chair around to face the ashen-faced man standing in the doorway.

'You're the last person I expected to see tonight,' he said.

140

Phil looked anxiously behind him, and then closed the door.

'Why's that? I own half this bleedin' place, don't I? I am allowed to be here!'

'Yes, of course you are. But some things seem to have changed overnight. I thought you of all people would have been aware of that.'

'Why? What have you heard? What's been said?'

'Well, quite a lot, really. I had a visit, not half-hour ago, from Patrick's three charming brothers. Laying the law down, they were; pointing their guns; threatening me. Not very nice people, I must say! They certainly left me in no doubt that they were in charge now - that they had taken over the territory. In fact, I half suspected they had already knocked you off, but apparently not. Well, not yet, anyway. Though I imagine that is a pleasure you will soon be encountering.

'It appears that we, the Inferno that is, have now lost the immunity we had while you were boss of the outfit. No longer skimming some off the profits, we now have to pay a ten per cent levy on the gross just like everybody else. Anyway, all that is changing too. Seems ten per cent is not enough for all the marvellous plans this lot's got for us. No, apparently, everyone is going to have to cough up fifteen per cent from next week. Fifteen per cent! Can you believe it? They're somewhere out there now, going along the front waving their guns around, passing on the good news to everyone. There'll be a few poor sods out there that won't be able to find that extra five per cent. Some are already on a tight margin. Strewth! And I thought you were bad! Believe me, Phil, you were just a pussycat!'

'Thanks!'

'Yes, I never thought I'd see the day I'd say it, but I'd rather you were still running things. At least everybody knew where they stood! I suppose you already know who they're bringing down from London tonight to give them a hand, don't you?'

'No. Who?'

'Jerry Cox, by all accounts. Yes, that's right, one of the Cox twins! His brother, Jimmy, is supposed to be doing a lifer for killing those three coppers in that shoot-out in Peckham last year but, if you remember, he escaped after the trial killing those two guards in the process. I wouldn't mind betting he'll turn up here as well! There goes the neighbourhood, as they say!'

'No!'

'Yes!'

'They told you all this?' Phil asked.

'Oh, yes. They were out to impress. It seems Patrick's picking Jerry up in London tonight, right after he has bought the drugs for next week. No doubt, we will be seeing him before the night's out. And maybe his brother.'

'Oh, shit!' Phil sat down heavily.

'You all right? You've turned a strange sort of green colour. Know them well, do you?'

'No, no. I've heard of them, of course. Who hasn't? They have a finger in nearly all the scams and fiddles there are in South London. Supposedly, they're strong north of the Thames now, as well. What the hell would they want with this little one-eyed hole? Nothing here is big enough to be in their league. Not even if you put it all together. Oh my God!' Phil buried his head in his hands.

'What?'

'I shouldn't be telling you this, but I've talked that lot at the Ellie into helping me out. They're only hoisting the drugs tonight, aren't they? That Tom, his old man and the black deejay have all gone to break into the car at Membury to swap the stuff for a load of rubbish. I thought we were only dealing with some half-wits who would rush back to London claiming they had been ripped off. You know what would have happened to them then! That would have been problem solved. But if they have Jerry on board that ain't likely to happen. He'll put them right. He'll know. He'll tell them that's not how the suppliers operate. Chances are it's indirectly linked to one of his operations, anyway. He'll know there must have been a switch on route. That could mean trouble with the biggest capital 'T' you've ever seen! Christ, I really hope their alibis stand up!'

'But why on earth would the Ellie lot want to help you?'

'They didn't, but I promised them immunity if they helped me regain control. I explained to them what the alternative would be like if the Irish stayed in charge. Really, they didn't have much choice.'

'I see. Well, actually that's who I was phoning when you arrived, the Elephant's Nest. No wonder Mrs Patterson was a little hesitant when I said I was going along to see them. I expect the lads hadn't returned by then, and I might have blown their alibi. Oh dear! I do hope they're all okay.'

Phil thought for a moment. 'Perhaps we ought both go down there, being as you now know the score. They will want to be shot of the drugs anyway, so I can take them off their hands. Maybe together we can think of a next move.'

'Yes, that might be a good idea. By the way, do you realise you've been here nearly ten minutes and you've hardly sworn at all? That must be a first. What's up? Taken the pledge, or something?'

'Huh? You are joking! No, it was only an act. The swearing, that is. Something I found necessary to keep the lads in line. It was becoming habitual, though. But who am I kidding now? I really am a little ol' pussycat!'

Dave grinned. 'A little ol' pussycat!' he thought, locking the door before they went down the private stairs and out through the side door to speed off along the promenade in Phil's car. Minutes later they were parking in the yard behind the Elephant's Nest.

'They haven't got back yet,' Phil stated, scanning the yard. 'Their old banger isn't here.'

'What time were they due back?' Dave waited the answer while Phil walked around the car, checking in turn that each door was locked.

'Before now, I would have thought,' said Phil, struggling to see the time on his watch in the darkness as they started to walk around to the front of the building. 'Something must have gone wrong!'

A squeal of tyres sent the two men running back around the corner to hide in the darkness behind a row of stacker rubbish bins. The large Ford Thunderbird skidded out of the side road and into the car park where its three occupants leapt out. One, the tall one, was carrying a bag. Another appeared to be consoling the third one as they made their way towards the back door.

'Tom?' Phil's voice stabbed into the night, easily heard over the muffled beat of the music penetrating through the club's walls.

The group stopped. 'Who's that?' Randy asked cautiously.

Phil and Dave emerged from behind the bin.

'Did something go wrong?' Phil enquired, speaking slowly, and then realising the obvious.

Tom sniffed, long and hard, wiping his nose on the back of his hand. 'You had better come on in,' he said, turning to open the door. 'It all went wrong.'

'My God!' Dave exclaimed when the light spilling out of the opened doorway exposed Tom's blood-sodden clothing. 'What on earth happened?'

'Randy will tell you everything. I have to take a quick shower and get rid of these clothes. Mother mustn't see me like this! You'd best all come upstairs. You can wait in my bedroom,' Tom said over his shoulder, racing away from them, and taking the stairs at a gallop.

In the office, Mary waited anxiously. On hearing the beep she looked up at the alarm panel. The blinking red light told her the back door had been opened. They were back, she guessed. With a feeling of relief she hurriedly locked the office door and started making her way along the corridor to meet them.

'Where's Tom? Where's John?' She asked with a panic in her voice as she realised they were missing from the group coming up the stairs.

Randy stepped forward to put his arms around her. 'Tom's okay,' he said as reassuringly as possible, steering her towards the next flight of stairs. 'He's got a bit dirty, so he's rushed on ahead to get changed. Come on, let's all go upstairs. Tom won't be long. He'll tell you all about it. Let's go upstairs to wait for him.'

'It's John, isn't it?' Mary had sensed something was very wrong. 'It is, isn't it? You tell me, Randy. What has happened to John? He is alright, isn't he?'

'Oh, man!' Randy's eyes started to redden.

'Oh, no! God, no!' Mary had read enough in Randy's face. Her eyes rolled upwards as her knees gave way beneath her.

Randy managed to grab hold of her before she hit the floor. Dave was at her other side in an instant. Together, with Phil's help, they managed to carry her up the next flight of stairs to the flat. Ollie, with the bag, followed them. At the door Ben faithfully greeted them with the usual wagging tail but, as they went inside, he soon realised his error. This was not a happy time. Seconds later he had his tail tucked tightly beneath him as he crouched down, whimpering.

Propping Mary up on the settee in the living room, Randy went to the drinks cabinet, returning with a very large brandy. After first stealing a sizeable sip from the glass for himself, he offered it to the vaguely reviving woman. She sat in silence, trance-like, drinking it, and then another one. Ben sat in front of her, ears down, with a reassuring paw on her knee. Nothing was said, nothing at all, until Tom, showered and re-clothed, appeared at the door.

'Mum,' he said softly, there were no tears in his eyes now, 'I'm so sorry . . .'

Mary beckoned him to sit by her. 'Tell me what happened,' she sobbed.

Cuddling up to her, hugging her, Tom related the sorry tale, or as much of it as he thought she should hear, leaving out the gory details. There was a strange coldness in his voice. Randy noticed the change but said nothing. Phil interjected at the appropriate point, explaining that the mysterious gunman must have been the unexpected Jerry Cox. He could have fallen asleep in the back of the car and the others decided not to disturb him, to leave him sleeping, when they went into the Services to answer the call of nature, or maybe have a quick coffee.

Ollie listened to the story with horrified disbelief. 'If you've no further need of me tonight, I'll make myself scarce before the police turn up,' he suggested in a rare unsung moment.

They didn't, so Tom and Randy thanked him for his invaluable assistance and promised once again that no matter what happened they wouldn't allow him to be implicated in the night's events. Phil grabbed the hold-all, suggesting that if the police were likely to arrive they may in this instance be other than Summers or Jones. It would be a good idea for him to get the drugs off the premises. All agreed that this was probably the best course of action, so he left with Ollie, saying he would return once the drugs were safely hidden.

'I'll see to the police when they arrive,' Tom said. 'They can't possibly know that Randy and I were involved as well, so I'll take them to the office to talk to them. I will tell them you are ill in bed, Mother. They'll probably insist on seeing you, but if they do, they'll have to come back tomorrow. If they saw you tonight they would know straightaway something was wrong. Tomorrow you will have an excuse for looking distraught. Somehow we have to make them believe that none of us here know anything about what has happened tonight. Now, what is the time? I'm surprised they haven't turned up already, they must have run a trace on the vehicle by now.'

'It's nearly eleven, man. Oh, shit! The music! The tape will finish soon. I's be in the box if you need me, man. Ronnie should be here any time now, so I's be back before long. Good luck!' Randy raced out of the room.

Mary wiped her eyes. 'Dave,' she said, trying to produce some kind of a smile for the man sat opposite her. 'I'm so sorry that we've had to meet like this for the first time, in these terrible circumstances. But enough of our troubles, what was it you wanted to see us about so urgently tonight? What was it that we couldn't discuss over the phone? Oh, I'm sorry, you haven't got a drink . . .'

'No, no drink thank-you Mrs Patterson. And please don't apologise about your troubles. They are all our troubles, too. Everybody's on the front, that is. We are all in the same boat.

'No, when I phoned you earlier I had no idea that all this was going on. The plan to relieve the gang of their drugs, I mean. I had no idea that you were already fighting back. That, in essence, was what I intended talking about tonight. Discussing with you what, if anything, we could do about this new turn of events; what we could do about these gun-toting Irish brothers with their new demands. Have they paid you a visit yet? They came to see me earlier tonight.'

'No,' Mary had to wipe her eyes again, 'they haven't turned up here yet, but doubtless they will. By the way, please call me Mary.'

'Mary it is.' He leant forward, grasping her hands warmly. 'But this, I feel, is not the best time to talk about such things. You will need to rest, to grieve. There will be plenty of other opportunities for us to talk, I feel sure. Now if there's anything I can do . . .'

'But talk we must,' Tom interrupted, with the strange steel-like coldness still in his voice. 'I'm going to ask Beryl to come up to sit with you, Mother. Denise can do the door. It won't hurt the punters to wait a little longer at the bar. Now don't argue. Dave and I will be in the office discussing matters, if you really need us. Randy too. He can put another tape on if Ronnie's late in.'

'Whatever you think is best.' Mary knew there would be little point in

146

arguing. 'But don't go troubling Beryl. I think I would much prefer to be on my own for a while. I have Ben here. He's good company.'

Tom gave her a big hug before leading Dave down to the office, stopping off on route at the deejay box to pick up Randy.

'Now,' he said, as he opened the top drawer of the filing cabinet and poured three large whiskeys from the bottle he had noted was kept in there when his mother had produced a drink for Denise the night she suffered Phil's abuse. Handing them one each, he asked, 'What the hell is our next move? Where do we go from here? Any ideas?'

'Well, man. They ain't got the drugs and barring a miracle they ain't got this Jerry chap no more. I's reckon he's bought it under that tanker, man. Must've done. Burnt toast, man.'

'But by now everything must have quietened down at Membury. Patrick and the other two may be learning a few truths,' Tom warned them. 'While they may or may not have heard the shots from inside the building, they definitely would have heard the exploding tanker and probably rushed out along with the crowd to see what had happened. Their first thoughts would have been for the bag, so they would have headed straight for the Jaguar. Of course, they would never have got near to it because of the fire, but they may easily have recognised our bullet-ridden car. Put that with the missing Jerry and what will they be thinking?'

'Oh, man, the shit gets deeper!'

'Or does it?' Dave was deep in thought. 'If you had a car full of drugs and the police were involved in a serious incident alongside it, what would you be doing? Would you hang around? I don't think so. I think you would be off across the fields like a scared rabbit, as far and as fast as you could go.

'With all that's happened, the gunfire especially, that place will be cordoned off for days. The police will go through everything with a fine-tooth comb. Forensics will be called in and they will search every inch, and every car, that's for sure. No one will be driving away from anywhere near the incident in their own vehicle tonight.'

'So, what you're saying is, Patrick will be thinking he's going to be arrested as soon as they trace the car full of drugs to him. That he is likely to do a runner; to disappear. Is that right?' Tom asked.

'Yes, wouldn't you in those circumstances?'

'I suppose so, but then I'm not Patrick. And anyway, the police are not going to find any drugs in the car, are they? They might be a bit puzzled at the contents of the bag, even wonder if a scam was going to be pulled, but it's hardly an arrestable offence to own a bagful of rubbish. Summers or Jones will soon let Patrick know that there's no warrant been issued for his arrest. Then he'll put two and two together.'

'Yeah, man, like two bags. One bag and another bag. He will know we got them goodies away somehow. Then he will come looking for them!'

'There's so many possibilities now, aren't there?' Tom stated, having thought of yet another scenario. 'If Jerry's body isn't found, entirely possible with that explosion and the fireball, they may even think that he's done a runner with the drugs, expecting them to believe that we have them.'

'Shit man, this is making my head hurt!'

'One thing's for sure,' Dave threw a further spanner in the works, as if there weren't enough already rattling around in there, 'the gang will want to know exactly what your father was doing there, and why Jerry decided to shoot him. You can't exactly say it wasn't really him at all – that the car was stolen, or anything like that. I mean he's not around anymore; you can't produce him. It is going to come out in the end. Then, with his alibi gone, so goes both of yours, I guess.

'But as for your Jerry theory, I can't really see them going along with that one. Twenty grand's worth of drugs might be big here, but for the likes of his crowd it's peanuts. They'll find that out soon enough. That's when, I imagine, they'll turn up here in force.

'With little money left, and their supplies running low, they will be getting desperate. They will either want the drugs back, or some big-time money to buy some more. The drugs you unfortunately no longer have. Phil has them, so you can't use them to bargain with. Do you really think Phil would give them back to you if you needed them to save your skins? I very much doubt it. I reckon he will lie low until the dust settles.

'You take it, these Irish boys have lost the money, lost the drugs, and lost all credibility if they can't get their act together. They need to produce the goods for next week. If they cannot do it, if they do lose it all, then they will go all out for revenge. I don't want to worry you unnecessarily, but I reckon they will go for a blood bath. That way they will save face back home in Ireland. Because that is where they will run to as soon as it is all over, believe me. Back to Ireland, out the way. I mean, whatever happens now, it will not be left to the local bobbies to sort out, will it? Not Summers and Jones. Not the follow up to a bullet-ridden car and a cold-bloodied murder that has happened on someone else's patch.

'Personally, I think it might be a good idea if you lot packed your bags and left tonight. Came back in a few days, when everything has quietened down. Once the police move in, the real police, you can bet the Irish won't stay around for long. They'll be off home. You'll be safe then.'

Tom was about to say he was not prepared to run away when the phone rang. One long ring, signifying it was an internal call.

'Yes,' he said, picking it up.

'Switch the television on, quickly. ITV has a news flash,' his mother was urgently shouting down the phone.

Tom reached up, pushing the button on the portable set above his head. The sound was instant, soon followed by pictures as the tube glowed into life. Randy and Tom hardly recognised the car park from the pictures being shown.

'Just to re-state, a massive car bomb has gone off in Wiltshire at the Membury Service Station on the M4 just outside of Swindon,' the commentator informed. 'Many people, including four police officers, are feared dead. Emergency services at the scene have provisionally put the number of fatalities at more than fifty. There have been many more seriously injured and the death toll is expected to rise. An emergency telephone number has been set up for those who . . .'

Tom muted the sound as the phone number was superimposed at the bottom of the screen. 'Look at that destruction!' he gasped, watching the infrared pictures from police helicopter shots that were being edited in with the ground shots. 'Look at it! There's nothing left of our car! Nothing at all! Or the Jag, that's completely gone as well! That's where it was,' he pointed to the enormous crater, 'and that, that's the car we hid behind. Christ! It doesn't even look like a car anymore! And what's that over there? That's, that's the remains of one of the police cars, isn't it?'

'Man, that must've been the massive explosion we heard behind us when we left. They must have had a load of explosives in the Jag as well as the drugs. I's bet the heat from the tanker fire set them off. Jeeesus! Were we ever lucky bunnies, man! If we had stayed hiding behind that old Volvo . . .'

'But have we been lucky enough?' Tom switched the set off. 'Get our coats, Randy. We have things to do. It'll be cold out there later.'

'Eh?' Randy was puzzled, but went to collect them anyway.

'What are you going to do?' Dave enquired.

'I want to see if Patrick and the other two actually made it out alive, or whether they got blitzed too. They weren't in sight when we left, so they may easily have survived. Who knows? They may still be trying to get back here, but either way, we do need to know who is left, and what is happening.

'We'll watch Patrick's place, until morning if necessary, to see if they made it. Think of it. With all that destruction, they won't know anything about the shooting. No one will. There's nothing left there that could be evidence. They won't know we took the drugs. We're completely off the hook - no longer implicated! They have no reason on earth to suspect anything! If they have survived they'll be more worried that the police, or the forensic chaps, might find enough of their car to incriminate them, and if they didn't survive, then all we are going to be left with here is the three paddies with no axes to grind, mourning over their poor brother's accidental death. But either way, we do need to know exactly how things stand.'

'I see,' said Dave. 'Well, I'd better let you get on. If you do find out anything I'd be grateful . . .'

'Of course. Oh, but there is one other thing . . .'

'Yes?'

'I shall be making arrangements for our takings tonight to go somewhere very safe, off the premises, somewhere where no one would think of looking. I suggest you do the same for a few days. But be careful!'

'The takings?'

'Yes. If those bastards are still in business, they have only two hopes to come up with some serious money. They will hit either your place or here, or perhaps both of us. Nobody else takes the kind of money that either of us do, except perhaps for the fun-fair and that's made up of lots of little concerns. That would be troublesome for them, especially with all the small change, so I don't think they'd go there. No, they'd go for us before them, so we do both need to stay vigilant for a while.'

Dave winked as he got up to go. 'I already have somewhere that nobody knows about. You know, I've never trusted that Phil, so very little money has ever actually been kept in the safe. Few hundred, that's all. I have been hiding it away for years. Right! Well, I will get off now. Good luck! And don't forget, tell your mother that I'm there if she needs anything; anything at all. She only has to pick up the phone.'

Leaving the office together, Tom shook his hand, thanking him, and then waited by the door. Randy appeared seconds later, clutching their two coats, and still looking puzzled.

'Hey, man. Is we doin' Sherlock Holmes, or is it Rambo tonight?'

'Don't ask, Watson. Come on, I've got to have a word with Derek or Beryl first, and then we'll have to run.'

'Run? Run, man? What gives here?'

CHAPTER 14

'Denise, have you got a minute?'

'Caroline! Of course, I have. What can I do for you?'

'I was hoping to see Randy tonight, but I can't find him anywhere. Or even Tom. I haven't seen him around either. I've been jumping up and down on the dance floor like an idiot half the night, trying to see into the deejay box, but it's been in total darkness up there. Not now though, the other guy's up there now. I've even asked the woman on the door if she knew where he was. She was extremely evasive. There's nothing wrong, is there?'

'I'm not sure. I hope not, but I was beginning to wonder that myself.' The young barmaid wiped the counter as she leant forward to divulge a confidence. 'There's been a strange sort of atmosphere about the place all evening, I don't know why. I've not even had so much as a smile out of Derek all night!

'I did actually see Randy in here once tonight, he was with Tom, but that was much earlier on. About eight-fifteen, I would guess. They were standing over there, by the doors, chatting non-stop for ages, so he must have had a tape running. They were pre-occupied, with something important on their minds I reckon, because they completely ignored me!

'Tom's been avoiding me all day. The few times I have seen him he's been sort of distant, if you know what I mean. I'm pretty sure they have been planning something together, Tom and Randy, but they've not let on to me about it, which I find annoying. I would've thought that Tom would've trusted me, but he hasn't said a word! Anyway, since eight-fifteen, I haven't clapped eyes on either of them. And, have you noticed: John is another one who seems to have gone missing? I haven't seen him in here since about the same time, which is a little unusual. Last night he was running around all over the place and helping out everywhere he could. Yes, it's all very strange. And now you tell me Beryl's being evasive with you, yet she's normally so obliging!'

'That's what I thought. She's always so helpful. That's why I particularly asked her. But really, she didn't seem to want to talk to me, so I didn't push it. I wouldn't swear to it, mind you, but I think she's a bit upset about something. You can usually tell, can't you? She may even have been crying earlier because her eyes were all puffy and bloodshot.'

'How peculiar! I think I've discovered another funny peculiar as well: Sarah has been doing the upstairs bar tonight. That is normally Louise's territory, but she's been told to help us down here tonight. I find that very peculiar! Oh damn, hang on a mo', I must see to those customers or they'll die of thirst. Don't go away - I'll tackle Derek to see if he knows anything while I'm down that end.'

Caroline waited patiently while Denise went off to help Derek serve the crowd of thirsty revellers that had gathered at the other end of the bar. Quizzing him, as they expertly weaved around each other to fetch the various drinks that were ordered, she became uneasy with the way in which he too was being evasive. She served seven people, each annoyingly wanting large orders, before a lull in the crowd gave her the opportunity to return to Caroline.

'And?' Caroline looked at her inquisitively.

'And nothing. Something's up, I'm sure of it! And I'm sure he knows what it is, but he's not letting on. Look, I have a break in a few minutes time. If you wait for me by the door, the one by the side of the stage, we can go upstairs to see what Mrs P will tell us. I reckon if anybody will, she'll tell us what Tom and Randy are up to.

'Oh, hang on a minute. That's good! Derek has given me the nod. Louise is back from her break already. We can go now.'

Struggling through the crowd, it was well after midnight and the place beginning to fill a little more at last, the two girls pushed their way out through the fire exit next to the stage, and ran up the back stairs to the flat. Denise had to ring the bell several times before the door opened and Mary's shadowy form stood silently in the darkness inside. Next to her, the Alsatian with its ears down nudged fondly at her leg.

'My God! Whatever's wrong?' Caroline screamed out, her eyes becoming accustomed to the gloom and allowing her to see the woman's face more clearly. 'Karl! Stefan! Are you there?'

The men were there. Instantly. One rushed to either side of them. Denise was noticeably shocked, visibly jumping with fright at their sudden appearance. She hadn't realised that anyone had followed them. Ben's hackles raised, he snarled fiercely at the two men who had suddenly appeared from nowhere. Mary turned, and telling him all was okay, she sent him back to the living room. Not convinced everything really was all right, the dog reluctantly obeyed, looking back at them several times.

'Look, I think we'd better come in,' Caroline insisted, 'and you can tell us what's wrong, because something obviously is. Perhaps we can help. May we?' She edged forward, not waiting for an answer.

Mary turned slowly. Leaving the door open, she shuffled towards the living room. The group followed her in. Karl closed the door.

Ben looked up from where he was lying in front of the silent television when the group walked in. He waited for Mary to be seated before sauntering over to her. Placing a large paw on her knee, he looked up at her and sighed loudly.

Patting him, trying to produce a smile for his sake, she turned to them and said, 'They know, you know - animals. They know when something's wrong,' adding, as she looked back into the dog's soulful eyes, 'don't you boy? You know that there's something wrong.'

The dog changed paws and sighed again.

'Yes, I'm sure animals do have a kind of sixth sense, Mrs Patterson, but we sure don't. What is wrong?' Denise almost demanded as she sat down on the settee next to the overwrought woman. 'Tell us everything. Please! Don't hold back! Tell us! There must be something we can do to help.'

Karl and Stefan perched on the arms at either end of the settee. Caroline heaved one of the armchairs opposite a little closer to them. Sitting directly in front of Mary, she leaned forward ready to listen intently.

It took more than an hour, with many, many breakdowns and several pots of tea being brewed, before Mary managed to divulge the full story. The others had sat there, ashen-faced for the most part, only breaking their silence occasionally to comfort the woman or to beg her to continue, until, finally, the whole story had been unravelled.

'My God! What horror! What absolute horror!' Caroline exclaimed, leaning forward further to grasp Mary's hands in her own. 'What on earth can we do to help?' she asked, slinging pleading glances upwards to both left and right, aiming them at her minders. 'There must be something we can do!'

Karl stood up and rubbed the side of his nose. It was a signal only Stefan understood. He immediately stood up too, and then swiftly followed his colleague out of the room.

The whisperings from the hallway were barely audible, certainly not decipherable above Mary's frequent sobs. Leaning to one side, the devastated woman picked up the photograph album from off the coffee table and, hugging it tightly to her bosom, she rocked slowly backwards and forwards. It was obviously some kind of comfort to her.

'It took me ages to find,' she explained, amidst the sobs. 'We hadn't unpacked it. But I had to have it.' More sobs, then, 'It's all I've got left of my John now. The memories,' she wailed, doubling forward.

Caroline leapt up, squeezing in next to her on the settee. Both girls put their arms around her now, hugging her tightly. Ben moved forward, nuzzling his nose between her legs. The comforting action moving her dress up from her knees. It was enough to temporarily compose the woman. She was forced to stroke the dog, pushing his head back so that she could unruffle her dress and pull it down to her knees again.

Opening the album for them to see, she explained, 'This is the first photo taken of us together, John and me. John's mate, Gary, took it. Don't we ever look a sight? And this one, this is at our engagement party.'

Denise and Caroline followed her through the album. It was certainly giving her some comfort. It was not, as they had first feared, upsetting her to relive the past, and surprisingly she was able to make the occasional restrained joke about the odd photo. They were just getting to the parts that Denise was waiting to see, those of Tom as a baby, perhaps the classic bath in front of the fire or the naked romp on the rug, when Karl and Stefan re-appeared.

'As we see it,' Karl spoke, 'there's not a great deal we can do at present. We're not allowed to leave you, as you know, and even if only one of us went off trying to help out there's not a lot he could do. We don't know most of these characters by sight yet, so that would be a great disadvantage. One person against we don't really know who or what, wouldn't achieve much at all in the short term. Besides, we should really have your father's blessing before we became seriously involved.

So, we suggest – now don't go and bite our heads off, Caroline, we know how much you value your independence, but – we suggest that you call your father. Tell him the whole story. See if he will arrange some kind of a back up for us. I think he probably will. Equally though, I think he will insist that we get you out of here first. But perhaps before that happens, one of us should go searching for Tom and Randy. They're quite obviously out of their depth. They ought not to be out there.'

Mary looked up at them pleadingly. Everybody knew her thoughts; she did not have to say them.

'Would you? Would you find them, please?' Denise pleaded of him. Then turning towards Caroline asked, 'Who exactly is your father? I know he is obviously someone very rich, but he sounds awfully important too. Would we all know of him? Could he really help?'

Caroline looked down, fumbling in her bag for her phone. She hated divulging who her father was, happy only to let people know that she was adequately provided for.

'Jason Harman,' she mumbled, somewhat embarrassed, 'and, yes, I know he could help.'

Denise's mouth fell open, wide. 'As in oil, film studios, music, airlines . . .?'

'As in multi-billionaire?' Mary interrupted.

'As in everything,' Caroline conceded.

'My God! Tom told me that your father owned a couple of gambling joints, but I never realised . . .'

'Hello, Daddy?' Caroline had punched the correct numbers in. 'Yes, I'm sorry. I do know what the time is. No. No, there's nothing wrong with me. No, they're fine, too. Yes, everything is all right with them. No, no. Please, Daddy. Will you ever stop asking questions and listen?'

CHAPTER 15

'Man, it sure is a cold one tonight! Perishing! I's gotta take another leak already,' Randy complained, and then made his way a few yards along the car park wall until he was a suitable distance away from Tom.

The two of them had been hiding, impatiently waiting, in the cold, half-empty car park for what had now become to be more than three hours. They had been closely watching the cellar for any sign of activity from behind the high wall, only their heads protruding over the top, not visible against the blackness of the club's rear wall, certainly not since Randy's excellently aimed stone had taken out the only floodlight. The tall building behind them, for the most part, blocked the scarce moonlight that only occasionally managed to struggle through the thin blanket of cloud covering.

Several cars had used the car park they were hiding in whilst they had been waiting there - without exception all disappointingly belonging to club-goers. Each time one had approached they had cowered down close-up behind the wall, out of sight, seeing all, but remaining unseen. The yard behind the cellar was completely empty. Strangely there were none of the gang's cars parked in there. They had seen no sign of life over there at all, not even the Irish brothers had made an appearance. All was quiet. Spookily quiet.

'How much longer we gonna wait here, man?' Randy asked. Task completed, he was zipping up his fly as he returned. 'We don't even know if they's intending to come back, do we? Not after all what's happened. They might be happy holing up somewhere for the night, making their way back here tomorrow, or even the next day. Man, come to that, they might even be dead, all of 'em, killed in the big explosion! But how do we know? We could be waiting here forever. Man, that don't bear thinking about!'

'No, I don't think we will have to wait too much longer.' Tom proclaimed, knowingly. 'The yard's empty, isn't it?' He waited for his friend to agree. 'Now, didn't Phil tell us they all had big flashy cars; real flashy ones he'd bought for them?' Another wait, another nod and grunt of confirmation. 'So, where are they?' he continued. 'You'd expect at least one or two of them to be parked up somewhere around here while the blokes were working the clubs, wouldn't you? But there's no sign of any of them. There's nothing half decent in this car park, either - nothing that you would expect any of them to have, anyway. I find that very strange!'

'Perhaps they's all gone off to Membury to collect Patrick and the other two. If they survived, man, they must have phoned someone to go pick 'em up. They ain't gonna walk back. Yeah, man. That's what's happened. They's probably gonna be gone for hours, man. I's means, the motorway will be well blocked. There'll be a tail-back stretching for miles,' Randy stated, despairingly.

'Yes, but not all of them would have gone. No way. It would only take one car to pick up three people, wouldn't it? So someone's sure to turn up here soon, even if it's not them, someone will, won't they?' Tom asked, craning his neck over the wall once more, trying to peer further into the darkness.

The reply did not come back in the time that Tom expected. There was not even the familiar confirming grunt. An icy shiver suddenly shot up Tom's spine, only to retreat all the way back down again as he realised, more instinctively knew, that something was wrong.

'Ah, I'll be betting that you're the young Tom,' a distinctly Irish voice almost touching his right ear, breathed.

Tom jumped, spinning round, almost choking on the stench of the stale, tobacco ridden, beery breath that greeted him, and was overwhelming him, to see the form of a tall man standing close to him, yet still barely distinguishable in the murky darkness. The shadowy figure moved, thrusting its head forward, even closer, until it was almost touching his face. He was able to make out the eyes easily now. They were wicked eyes. Cold eyes that had not one hint of compassion built into them, and they were drilling into his own eyes relentlessly. Shivering again, he heard the shape's involuntary belch.

The sickening gaseous fumes plainly from a long night of beer consumption, of many pints devoured, erupted into the night air enveloping them both. Immediately the stench hit Tom, invading his nostrils and sticking to the back of his throat, he felt nauseous, but he was so frozen with fear that he was unable to reach, unable to vomit and release all what was pleading to be expelled. He tried holding his breath for as long as possible to avoid inhaling any more of the fetid air, but it didn't work; neither did his attempt at shallow breathing. It was useless; there was no avoiding the stench.

The cold beads of sweat feverishly appearing on Tom's forehead began to feel the light breeze wafting in from the coast, and immediately turned into icy driblets that seemingly hung from his face. He was trying to utter something, although he didn't really know what - probably something completely stupid - when a noise to his left, more a scuffle, interrupted the attempt. He gulped, managing a painful dry swallow, when from that unknown place on his left a tortured shout stabbed menacingly into the night.

'Run, man! For fuck's sake ru . . .'

A large, rough hand slapped heavily, noisily ending the desperate plea prematurely. Spinning around towards the sound, Tom became aware of two more shadowy figures in the darkness. With sufficient moonlight suddenly breaking through the thinning clouds, bathing the area with a sparse eerie luminance, he was able to tell that they were slightly bent forward, and looking down at something. Neither of them was Randy. He was sure of that. But one of them was holding something in his hands.

Squinting, peering downwards into the gloom, Tom tried to force his eyes to see the object. It was sort of round, he could make that much out, appearing to be something like a football, maybe a rugby ball. But no, it couldn't be a ball, he concluded. That was ridiculous. These people wouldn't be carrying a ball around with them; not at that time of the night, anyway.

He squinted at the object again, this time turning his head slightly, trying to see out of the side of his eyes, vaguely remembering he had once read somewhere that this was the best way to see in the dark. Tom concentrated hard to see what it was with his side vision, and then physically jumped, choking on his breath, when he made out the two white egg shapes that suddenly appeared on the dark sphere looking up at him. They were undoubtedly eyes; eyes filled with sheer terror. They were Randy's eyes!

Tom's brain raced away feverishly. Should he run? He was reasonably confident he would be fast enough to escape the man stood next to him. The other two were farther away so they shouldn't present a problem. He guessed he was probably much younger than any of the assailants, no doubt much fitter too, and not having over-indulged in excessive amounts of alcohol like they had would surely give him an even greater advantage. He should easily be able to escape them. But then, that would mean abandoning Randy, wouldn't it? What would they do to him? Would he too be found floating in the bay a few days later? Stuffed full of heroin, like Mark? He shivered yet again, but that thought entering his mind was enough. He knew then exactly what he had to do.

Aiming at where he guessed his captor's vitals would be in the dark, Tom brought his right foot up swiftly, and with as much force as he could muster. The feel, as his foot landed, confirmed the accuracy of his guess. Spot on.

The man gasped loudly, exhaling even more of his foul-smelling gasses into the air. Doubling forward with the excruciating pain, crumpling towards the ground in writhing, sickening agony, he then discovered his chin meeting, point on, with the Tom's rapidly rising knee. The pain, already hovering on the limit of human endurance, now shot off the scale, allowing the Irishman to find his relief in the immediate unconsciousness.

Not waiting to see if the man would get up again, Tom straightaway pushed backwards with his hands against wall behind him as hard as he could. Gaining the necessary momentum, he launched himself outwards into the air with his legs astride and feet outstretched. Each foot found its target with enviable precision. The two remaining assailants both staggered, falling backwards, stunned, hitting the gravelled ground painfully hard before releasing a deluge of incoherent profanities.

Pulling Randy up from off of the ground it was Tom's turn to shout, 'Run!'

'You ain't gotta say that twice, man!' Randy exclaimed, obeying in an instant.

The two of them, still vaguely aware of the mountain of blasphemy polluting the night air behind them, sprinted out of the car park and raced along the back alley towards the safety offered by the friendly looking streetlights adorning the road ahead. Once at a safe distance, and after checking over his shoulder that they were not being chased, Tom suggested that they should walk. The adrenalin was beginning to subside. He could feel his knee that had so squarely contacted with that chin beginning to hurt him. Imagining the enormous bruise that would be there by morning, he prayed he hadn't done any serious or lasting damage to it.

'Shit, man! Where's you learn to fight like that?' Randy asked, as they slowed the pace to a fast walk.

Tom grinned back at him. He wasn't going to break the illusion now by confessing he didn't normally fight, or that in truth he didn't really know how to fight - that it was something he had never before experienced for real.

Years ago, as a young boy in Brisham, he had attended the local martial arts classes and been told he was quite good, but he had never considered that to be proper fighting. After all, everybody knew all the moves and they could anticipate exactly what was coming next. No, that wasn't fighting; that was more an arty type of thing. Almost theatre. This had been his first real fight in earnest, and he was more than pleased with his performance.

Feeling elated, re-living those last few minutes in his mind for what must have been the fifth or sixth time, Tom failed to notice that one set of headlights from the vehicles sporadically passing by on the road ahead had started to swing towards them. A car turning into the alley was driving straight at them.

Randy grabbed hold of Tom's arm, pulling him to an abrupt halt. Tom looked around at his friend momentarily, blankly, before realising they were standing in a pool of light that was fast expanding as the car rapidly approached. Quickly pressing themselves against the side wall of the narrow alley they waited for the car to pass, praying all the time that the driver was competent enough not to catch their nuts on his wing mirror.

The car slowed to a crawl, slower than they expected, something that worried them. There was plenty of room for all but an idiot to get by without going that slow. Peering into the bright headlights, trying to see beyond them, revealed nothing until the car was upon them. Then it was too late.

Coming to an abrupt halt only yards away from them, all four doors of the car seemed to open at once, each one touching one of the walls that marked the alley's boundary on either side. Tom could see there was no way past the car, and the walls at this end were far too high to be scaled with any ease. Without doubt, they would be unable to climb them quickly enough to escape if someone was out to catch them. As if one, they both turned on their heels deciding to run back the way they had come, only to then discover the three Irishmen that Tom had so efficiently dealt with in the car park had now fully recovered. They were barely twenty yards away, hurrying three abreast towards them. It became obvious to both that there was no hope of escape that way, either.

The four doors slammed shut behind them, so they spun around again to see four figures walking slowly towards them. The gun that the leading one was holding out in front of him was unmistakeable.

'That's Patrick,' Randy whispered out of the corner of his mouth. 'Man, are we in the shit!'

They moved closer to each other. Rabbits in headlights ran through Tom's mind; rabbits frozen to the spot waiting for the inevitable.

'Are you alright there, brothers?' The one with the gun shouted past them at the three.

'Ah, we be alright here, Pat. But that little arse'ole there won't be! Not when I gets me 'ands on 'im 'e won't!'

'Oh? Why's that then?'

'Sure, if me weddin' tackle could talk, it'd be tellin' ya. But that little fucker's got summit comin' to 'im alright, I'll just be tellin' ya that!'

Tom realised he was trembling. Standing so close to Randy he felt sure he must be aware of it too; it had to be noticeable. Sneaking a sideways glance, he began to feel a little better, if anyone could feel any better in such a situation. Randy was shamelessly trembling too.

'Ah, well first we shall be needing him for a while, Terry. But you are welcome to him once we have finished with him,' Patrick said. 'You can probably have the little black bastard sooner, if you want. We'll not be needing him for long, I shouldn't think.'

'As ya say, Pat, me ol' boy. You just be tellin' me when. But you remember now, I wants that other fucker! And as God's my witness, I'm gonna 'ave 'im too!'

Tom groaned, stealing a look at Randy. The situation seemed grim. There were only two of them against these seven. Patrick had a gun. His three brothers were known to have guns. The clicks he had heard behind him only moments ago suggested they were probably in their hands at that very minute. This was certainly not the time for heroics.

'Will you take them on down to the cellar for us, Terry?' Patrick called out, as he turned to walk back to the car. 'We'll follow you down.'

'It'll be me pleasure!' Terry replied, straightaway stepping forward to grab Tom's right ear with one hand and Randy's left ear with the other, then twisting them both equally.

As they were frog-marched back along the alley towards the cellar, Tom heard clicks again and presumed they were the safety catches being re-engaged on the guns of the two brothers walking a few steps behind them. It came as a small comfort to know that now at least the guns would not blow their heads off accidentally, but the pain he was in was becoming unbearable.

Tom's damaged knee made him limp awkwardly, so with each step his twisted ear was being tugged a little more severely. Each step became an agony of its own, until finally they arrived outside the cellar door and the big man let go of them. Not daring to look around, or move in any way for fear of reprisal, they waited as the big car's tyres crunched across the loose gravel of the yard, stopping only feet behind them before the engine died with one pronounced shudder.

Car doors slammed repetitively, many more slams than there were doors, reminding Tom of his father. He too had suffered from that annoying habit, a common habit of never being fully satisfied that a car door was truly shut until it had been slammed several times. Pictures of his father suddenly flashed into Tom's mind, only to be knocked out again just as speedily by Patrick pushing between them to unlock the cellar door. Reaching inside, the man switched on the lights, and hard objects, the guns they guessed, nudged their backs pushing them into the room.

'Sit there!' Patrick ordered, placing one wooden chair next to the other in front of the desk at the far end, so they would be facing into the centre of the room.

The two friends, sitting as instructed, were able to see the others who had followed them in. Terry, the big one, they now knew, and the two with him still holding their weapons, they were surely his brothers. Patrick, who had opened the door, they recognised him. Then two more came in, and Tom gave Randy a querying look.

'Don and Paul.' Randy whispered. 'But I's ain't seen the bird before.'

Bird? Tom looked back. Yes, bird. A young woman had joined them. She could only have been one of those in the car, he surmised. One of the four he had taken as all being men. Who was she?

'You haven't left the stuff out there in the car, have you?' Patrick asked, obviously annoyed and looking at the two young men standing beside the unknown female. 'Bring it in for God's sake!'

Don and Paul turned on their heels immediately, disappearing through the doorway, but soon returning with the tartan holdall which they carried over to place on the desk behind their two captives. Tom and Randy shot glances at each other in utter disbelief. What? How? They had seen the pictures of all the destruction on the news flash. The bag could not possibly have survived. The car hadn't survived. Dammit! That whole area of the car park hadn't survived. It was a crater. So, how this bag?

'Nice red glow out there.' It was Don who spoke.

'I'll bet!' Patrick laughed, and then turning to the woman said, 'Come on, love. Give us a hug. You're home now, sweetheart. Your new home. Why not pour us all a drink before we find out just what these arseholes were actually up to in our back alley. Is everybody happy with a whiskey?' he asked.

Nobody declined, so the woman poured seven glasses from one of the many bottles on the sideboard, splashing them with as much soda or whatever as each person signified. Taking Patrick's over to him, she stood at his side daintily sipping her weak one.

'Well,' Patrick tried for their attention, but had to wait whilst the noise of sirens disappeared into the distance. 'Terry, Andrew, Mickey,' he continued, pointing to each in turn with his glass, 'I'd like to introduce you to my Maria. The rest of the lads all know her as Phil's housekeeper but this, my brothers, this is the little poppet I was telling you about last night, the love of my life, the girl of my dreams, my sweetheart. Darling, say hello to my brothers.'

Don and Paul shot glances at each other. Sweethearts? Nobody knew that! That had been kept quiet! The Irish brothers moved in on her, grouping around her and Patrick, shaking their hands, asking them questions, and congratulating each of them. Don and his brother joined in, declaring what a well-kept secret it had been. Absolutely nobody had known, or even suspected. How had they managed to conceal it from Phil? Patrick laughed and went over to pour more drinks.

Tom nudged Randy, whispering, 'I'm going to hold your hand. They all seem preoccupied so I think we may have a chance. Be ready to follow me when I shout. Whatever you do, don't let go!'

'Shit, man!'

`Randy held on to his friend's hand tightly between the chairs, waiting, wondering how long before, or even if, Tom would shout, when he was violently tugged out of the chair.

'Now!' Tom's voice screamed.

Instantly the room plunged into darkness. Something shot across the room crashing out through the doors into the yard. Randy could hear the wild shouting of the Irishmen, sense the commotion, as he was yanked away into unknown darkness, and then felt Tom pushing him down, forcing him into a crouching position.

From the faint moonlight entering through a half open window above them, they discovered they were in a kitchen. In the darkness, after hitting the light switch only yards from him, Tom had thrown the bag out of one door, the one to the yard, whilst they had made their escape through another door, an internal one. Through the half open window, they could hear the desperate shouts continuing in the yard outside, and beyond in the alley.

'The bag's here, they must've dropped it getting away!' someone shouted.

'Check the car park!' another shouted.

'I'll be getting lights to the alley!' someone else, as the car started up.

Standing up slowly, Tom and Randy cautiously peered out of the kitchen window. They could barely make out the figures madly running around, searching, outside in the yard, in the alley, and in the car park. The only significant light was coming from the car circling around the car park, and shunting up and down the alley, aiming its headlamps first this way and then that in an attempt to find their hiding place.

'Man, you didn't say Rambo, when I's asked you earlier! You called me Watson! Watson is Sherlock, man! Sherlock! Not fucking Rambo! Oh, shit, man! What do we do now?'

'Follow me.'

Tom led the way out of the kitchen, passing by the door to the cellar that they had sneaked through in the darkness, along the short dark passageway to some stairs. Slowly they crept up them to find, not unexpectedly, that they emerged in the hallway of the house where a streetlight was shining through the stained glass window above the front door. With six more paces they were out into the street and quietly closing the front door behind them.

'Man, Oh, Man!' Randy exclaimed, as the two of them hurried along the street towards the centre of town. 'Life's sure got exciting since you turned up! And I's can remember saying I's would have to look after you! Wow, man!'

Tom laughed. 'That sky looks awful red up there, over on those rooftops,' he stated, looking inland. 'It looks a bit like there might be a fire. Would it be a forest fire up there on the hills? Do you get forest fires here? It has been hot lately.'

Randy started to jog on ahead. Tom tried following but his knee was paining him, so he walked. At the end of the road, he caught up with his friend who was staring up into the hills. Tom followed his gaze.

'That's Phil's house on fire,' Randy informed him. 'That's Bay View, man. Gotta be, there ain't no other houses up that part. Man, that sure is burning like a good'en. I's bet there will be nothing left of it by morning.'

'So, it's all coming together now. It's making sense,' Tom announced.

'What is?'

'All of it. Maria. The hold-all. Phil's house being on fire. It works out.'

'Eh?'

'Well, who must Patrick have phoned from the Motorway? Maria, of course. It would have been obvious to him that an explosion of that magnitude would be reported on television, so she would have been worrying in case anything had happened to him. Of all people, he had to phone her, to let her know he was all right - they are sweethearts, after all.

'She then rushed over to Membury, probably taking the back roads from Swindon, to pick them up. There was no bag. That was destroyed, quite obviously. But when they got back to drop Maria off at the house they must have met up with Phil, complete with the genuine hold-all full of drugs. You can guess what happened then! I wouldn't mind betting the remains of Phil's body are found in the ashes up there tomorrow. In fact, I'd put money on it!'

'Shit, man! We's back to Sherlock!'

'Elementary, my dear! Come on, you'd better take us home through the back streets.'

CHAPTER 16

The luxurious Betty Harman, at close on 500 feet long, was reputed to be the world's largest private yacht - although to the dilettante she could easily be mistaken for a small cruise liner. Today she ploughed laboriously through the unusually rough Mediterranean Sea. With her stabilizers fully retracted to increase her speed to maximum, she was making good headway despite the extreme conditions.

In the upper saloon, towards the rear of the second deck, Jason Harman poured over the large map spread across one of the tables. He had very little idea of where they actually were, or how much longer they would be at sea, but trying to fathom that out made him feel better. At least he was doing something.

'Latest report is no change expected in the weather conditions, Jason,' the ship's Captain informed him as he entered, grabbing hold of the bulkhead to steady himself, 'so there's absolutely no chance of using the helicopter. With these seas it would be over the side the minute we unstrapped it.

'We shall have to go all the way to Malaga. It will be a bit tricky, but if all goes well we should be able to anchor close in, just outside the docks, in about three hours or so. I'm afraid the toughest bit is going to be the launch trip in, that will be a bit hairy to start with, but once inside the harbour the conditions will distinctly improve.

'If it is too bad when we arrive there they do have a berth for us, but initially I've declined it as the launch trip in will be far quicker than us trying to go right in and get alongside.

'Anyway, the jet's on its way to Malaga now, left Gatwick a few minutes ago, so there's plenty of time for it to be all fuelled up and checked over ready to go again by the time you get there. It won't take long to make the airport once you land - there'll be a fast car waiting for you.

'And the authorities have informed customs that you're coming so you shouldn't be held up there either, that'll probably be a straight through job, but it's bad news on Bristol, I'm afraid. Apparently they've been having technical problems, gone down twice already tonight, and may still be diverting in the morning, so we've had to call in a few favours.

'If there are still problems at Bristol, they'll take you at RAF Lyneham and ferry you on to Bristol to pick up your chopper. Apparently, it's only runway traffic that's in trouble there, choppers aren't affected.'

'Thanks, Mike, you really are a star! I don't know how you do it half the time,' Jason exclaimed, abandoning the map to make his way, not without some difficulty, across to the bar. 'Do you fancy joining me in a little one to steady the old nerves?'

'Thanks, but I'd best not. Not with this sea running. I'd better get back to the bridge, just in case we hit any snags.'

'Of course.'

Without spilling too much, Jason managed to serve himself a weak gin and tonic, even making it all the way back over to the plush red leather bench seating along the port side without losing any of it. Falling into the seat heavily, he stared across the saloon at the large photographs on the other side, one between each of the panoramic windows.

Janet smiled back at him from the first photograph, Lloyd from the next one. A single tear emerged, and started to run down to his cheek. Oh, how he missed them, he realised once more. How much he truly, truly missed his wife and son. They had been his life, his whole life, and his reason for living. These last two years had been so empty without them.

Life could be so cruel, he sighed to himself, finishing the remainder of the drink in one as he re-lived the tragic skiing holiday once more in his mind. How happily he would give up all this wealth, all this luxury, just to be able to have them back again, he thought. Just to see them, to touch them, to know they were all right. If only he could.

Now there was only his daughter left to live for, his lovely Caroline. He studied her photo, the next one along in the line with the cheeky smile and the breeze that had been captured blowing gently through her long fair hair. She was all he had now. All that was left. He sniffed and wiped his eyes. What had she managed to become mixed up in now? She had always been a tearaway, alarmingly independent, and an out-and-out bossy-boots - but for her to become involved in drugs? Guns? Murder?

How dare she! How dare she do this to him! And what in hell were her minders thinking of? How dare they let her get into such a situation! She was all he had left - surely they realised that?

Sighing, he turned away from the photographs to catch sight of himself in the gold plated mirror. He looked long and hard at the sad pathetic excuse for a man who stared back out at him, and he started to take stock of himself. You don't look so bad for forty-odd, he tried telling himself. You're healthy, fit, they're still all your own teeth and you have all your hair. Some might even consider you as being handsome – well, at least good-looking. So, there's a little bit of grey coming at the sides, but so what? That only goes to make you look distinguished, not old.

You really ought to get a life, Jason, he told himself. You need to stop all this hiding, and wasting your life away on these endless trips to nowhere. You really must stop dwelling on the past. Janet wouldn't have wanted that, would she? She wouldn't have wanted you to be lonely; so desperately lonely.

Things had to change. He did need to let his hair down and to live a little. He really should get out there, socialise, and perhaps be a little bit more like Caroline. But then, how many times had he told himself all this before? Too many, he considered, far too many.

He got up to pour another drink.

#

Patrick looked up from the desk as Don and Paul, the last of those out searching for the escaped prisoners, returned. 'No luck?' he enquired, already knowing the answer.

They shook their heads and, as everybody else had, sat down.

'Never mind, they're not that important,' the new boss-man stated. 'What we . . .'

'They are to me, I be wantin' that little fucker,' Terry snarled, interrupting.

'There'll be plenty of time for that,' Patrick told him, and then continuing, 'As I was saying, what we need to do now is work out exactly where we are, what we've got, who's with us, and who ain't. Now, Phil has gone, he won't be worrying us anymore, will he? So that news needs to be spread, doesn't it?

170

'How he got hold of the drugs we still don't know. Were they really the ones we picked up earlier? They certainly do look like them, but we don't know that for sure. If they were, then how did he manage to get hold of them? Did he perhaps get someone to steal them off us at Membury, the only place where they were out of our sight, and then blow the place up, killing Jerry in the process? And if so, who did he know capable of doing a job like that? No one I can think of, and anyway it all sounds a bit too heavy for Phil!

'Perhaps they were an entirely different lot of drugs that we didn't know about - a secret cache that he had hidden somewhere in a similar looking bag. We really don't know, do we? But even if they were, we still have to wonder how he came by them? He was seen around here too many times for him to have gone any distance to fetch them, wasn't he? So, if it was a secret hoard, it must have been stashed locally. Here in Seathorpe. But where? And who with? Who would he have trusted?

'In either case, I'm beginning to wonder whether those two from the Ellie could have been involved in some way? Whilst I can't really imagine them getting into bed with Phil, especially after that episode with the bomb, I guess stranger things have happened. I mean, we also have to wonder why they were hiding in the alley and spying on this place, don't we? Is it all connected? I don't know, but somehow I can't seem to get myself to believe they would be into anything heavy like explosives.

'But, I suppose when it's all said and done, it doesn't really matter....'

'Bah!' Terry interrupted again.

'It doesn't really matter,' he emphasised, 'the important thing is, we have the drugs now and if we can hang on to them, if it's us that sells them, then we should have control over the front, over everything, shouldn't we?

'Now then, there's us four Irish here, my lovely Maria, and we're pleased to see that Don and Paul are with us. But who else have we got? How do we stand with Sid, Bob, and the lads: Sam, Graham, and Mike? Sid, we know, what with having to run the bars at the club doesn't do a lot these days, but he can be handy when needed, can't he? I wouldn't like to have him against us! Not old Sid. But Bob? How about Bob? Where's he got to, anyway? He was supposed to be selling in the Inferno, but he hasn't come back here, has he? And the lads, where are they? They were working the Ellie - why haven't they turned up either? Where's all their money?

'I've tried phoning the lads several times, but they all seem to have their mobiles switched off. Bob, we know doesn't have one; won't have one - cantankerous old sod! So we can't get in touch with him either. What's going on?

'It's pretty unlikely any of them would have known anything about what happened up the motorway tonight, not unless they were skiving off somewhere watching the news. But that's hardly their style is it? Can you imagine any of them watching news programmes? Anyway, even if they had heard about it they still wouldn't know anything about Phil's demise, would they? So why aren't they here?

'I think that until we know any better we've got to consider them not being with us, and if they're not then we will have to think long and hard what we should do about that. Either way, tomorrow we must be prepared to make up our own stock for the night, so we'd better all meet up here early. Say, four o'clock.'

CHAPTER 17

'I haven't seen this part of town before,' Tom confided in his friend, as they hurriedly made their way along the street heading for home with the first morning light beginning to grace the sky above the hills. 'You say we're two roads in from the front? I didn't realise there was so much back here. All these shops, cafés, bars and restaurants - it's amazing. Most excellent!'

'Yeah, man. And you's still got a job to find a place to eat in the summer. They gets packed, man. Packed.'

'Hey, see that place up there, on the corner, the big building? It looks like it's still open. It's still going full swing, isn't it? People are still going in. How come?' Tom glanced down at his luminous watch face, 'It's now way after four o'clock. Have they got some special kind of licence or something?'

'No, man, they ain't. They just takes a bit of a liberty. That's Dorothy's. It's a gay club, man. Always packed in there, it is - packed out solid, man. No, they just keeps it open later to let all the troublemakers from the hetty clubs get home first. But you don't have to be gay to go in there, though. Loads of people goes there, man, loads. Straights, I's mean. They says it's always a good fun night in there, and apparently it gets right raunchy at times. There's rarely any trouble there either, that's why the people likes it. Hang on a mo', man! Hang on! Clock that! Don't we sorta know that face over there?'

'Where?'

'There, man, just inside the door arch. It is, man. It is. That's Sam. You must remember Sam. He's you's new-found friend. One of those guys who got you pissed up and high on drugs Friday night!'

'No friend of mine!'

'Wait. Cool it, man. Let's wait here a minute. Watch what gives. I's wants to see what he's up to. I's means, why's he hanging around there, man?'

Randy edged Tom into the shadows of Tiffany's doorway where they waited, quietly watching for several minutes. Tom wondered why his friend was so interested in the lad. Did it matter if he was gay? He probably wasn't, anyway. He hadn't appeared to be gay the other night - in fact quite the reverse! And, as Randy had said himself, you didn't have to be gay to go in there. He was puzzled, but he decided to say nothing.

'There! I's knew it! I's knew it, man!' Randy exclaimed, elated, almost jumping up and down with the excitement.

'Knew it? Knew what?'

'Didn't you see that, man? Didn't you see it? He's just given those two blokes in the checked shirts over there a quick kiss and walked off. Now, that don't matter, man. Not the kissing. Not to me it don't. But what do matter is he's just sold them a load of stuff! And we's a talkin' a load of stuff, man! Jeees! Didn't you see the size of the packet he had hidden under his coat, man? Sam is definitely doing privates! Gotta be! He's been selling his own gear, else he's been nickin' Phil's. I's always thought he might be, but there was no concrete proof, not 'til now.'

'Is that really important? I mean, to us?'

Randy ignored him, still staring into the club opposite with eyes wide agog.

'Shit, man! This is just too good! Oh, look, man! Look! Get you's head over here, man. See? Can't you see them? It just gets better, man! Oh, shit, man! Better and better! Don't you recognise them, those two idiots? That's Graham, blue top, just inside the door. He looks blown out his tiny little mind! Snogging the hell out of Mike, he is. Christ, man, they's all at it!

'For ages, man, I's been wondering how they got on for their stuff in there because Phil wouldn't touch them. He wouldn't have anything to do with them people, man. Know what I's mean? He is homophobic. But there had to be another way for them people to get their drugs, didn't there? There had to be. I's means, has you ever heard of a gay club without drugs, man? It don't happen. No way! That would be like the Pope without a Bible, man!'

Tom grinned. It seemed the appropriate response. He didn't even know of a gay club, with or without drugs, but he decided not to mention it. Randy seemed pleased with the discovery though, that was enough.

What relevance it had to anything, he couldn't imagine. No doubt, Randy would explain it all to him at some point.

'Come on, man. We can go now. We's better get home,' Randy almost sang, skipping out from the shadows.

The few more minutes of hurrying was not helping the wounded knee, so it was with relief that Tom sighed when at last turning a corner he could finally see the silhouette of the familiar building. Against the early dawning sky, the lights of the elephant still bouncing him up and down on his nest came as a welcome sight.

Randy ushered him down the narrow alleyway cutting between two rows of the terraced buildings. They followed it, turning left along the back of the properties until, with a helpful bunk-up from his friend to get over the wall, they were safely in the rear yard of the Elephant's Nest.

Standing completely still for a few minutes, hardly daring to breath, they listened intently. All seemed quiet. Nobody appeared to be lying in wait there to re-capture them. Nevertheless they still followed the shadows of the perimeter wall as they stealthily made their way to the Stage Door where, after swiftly letting themselves inside, they closed the door noiselessly behind them.

'Shit, man. It's awful dark in here, I's can't see piss-all! Security bulb must've popped,' Randy complained loudly. 'Hang on a mo' while I's finds my key for the light switch.'

The deejay fumbled, chinking through his keys for the little one that fitted all the special light switches. Those necessarily used in the public areas to prevent the punters operating them.

'Oh, shit! These lights ain't working either, man! What gives here?'

Tom could hear the click, click, click, as Randy tried the switch repeatedly.

'Power cut?' Tom suggested.

'Hell, man, no. The Elephant was still alight, wasn't it? No, I's reckons someone's turned some of the rings off by mistake. But who would do that?'

Listening acutely, Tom could sense that his friend was moving away from him in the darkness, along the passageway. Seconds later he managed to hear a barely discernable squeak in the distance. Randy must have opened one of the double doors to the main auditorium, he guessed from the sound. Then there was another squeak. Had he gone in there, letting the door close behind him, he wondered, or was he still on this side?

'Shit, man!'

It was only a whisper, but the shock of its proximity in the total darkness caused Tom to physically leap into the air.

'Shit! Shit I nearly did!' Tom loudly whispered back his complaint. 'Don't do that! I could have died of a heart attack! Whatever's wrong now?'

'I's don't like it, man! Don't like it one bit! Seems like there's no security lights on anywhere, and you can't turn them lights off, man. They's made that way. No switches. They's always got to be on. It can't be the bulbs, man. No way. Them bulbs they wouldn't have blown, not all of them, not all at once, and I's know the batteries ain't flat. So what goes on here? I's reckons someone must have physically disconnected them. Like cut the wires. Oh, shit, man! That ain't good news! We's better get out of here, mucho pronto!'

'Don't be silly, we can't just leave. My mother's upstairs. And Beryl. She was supposed to stay behind with her after closing. She said she would, so she'll be up there too,' Tom explained. 'Ben will have looked after them. Come on, it's probably nothing to worry about at all. Only an electrical fault, main fuse gone, or something stupid like that has happened, I expect. Follow me, we'll have to grope our way upstairs.'

The darkness was complete. Total. Pitch. Tom held his hands out, waving them around in front of him at arms length, hoping to detect any obstacle in his path. Slowly he started mounting the stairs. Randy, tightly holding on to his coat from behind, followed nervously. He was a long way from being convinced that nothing was wrong.

Progress was slow as Tom tested each riser of each step with his foot before proceeding on to the next one. Each time his hands met a wall they would turn, shuffle until the next steps riser hit his exploring toe, then he would laboriously start to feel for each step and riser with his foot again. They had candles and torches in the flat, Tom knew that, but had they been unpacked yet? No, probably not, he guessed. If they had, surely there would have been some lights put downstairs. Beryl and his mother were probably trying to find them at this very moment, frantically falling around opening boxes in the dark, he imagined.

His hands touched a wall in front of him. Feeling to the left a way, then to the right a way, there was nothing either way for the second time. He whispered over his shoulder to Randy, informing him that they were now on the top landing, at last. Back to going left, a few more steps, with his hand still feverishly tracing the wall, they carried on, until there it was, finally, the door to the flat. Opening it with the second key he tried they stepped inside, closing the door behind them with a sigh of relief.

'Mum? Ben?' Tom called out.

There was no reply.

'Mum! Ben!' he called again, louder.

Nothing.

Yet again, he called out. This time very loudly, and with urgency.

The replying silence was deafening.

'Shit, man! What goes here? Mary-fucking-Celeste, or what?' Randy's voice stabbed into the creepy black silence.

'There'll be some matches in the kitchen,' Tom reckoned aloud. 'Follow me.'

Carefully feeling their way along the wall to second door, they found themselves in the long kitchen-come-diner. Tom led the way around the outside of the room, groping ahead into the darkness until he met the worktop, and then cursed loudly as with the next step the dog's water bowl somersaulted noisily, emptying its entirety over his left foot. The involuntary chuckle from behind him was far from helpful.

'Got them!' Tom declared at last, triumphantly striking one.

The match did little to light the room, the initial flare blinding them momentarily, then the small flame burning slowly down to Tom's fingertips until it got so hot it had to be extinguished. They had, however, managed to see there were two half finished cups of tea, though they could have been coffee – they wouldn't have known - and a half eaten sandwich left on the table.

'Mary-fucking-Celeste!'

Randy's voice seemed to echo creepily around in the darkness of the room, the three words having arrived far louder than he intended. Far louder than he had actually spoken them, Randy was convinced. Tom felt his friend's hold on his coat tighten.

'There's a torch in your deejay box!' Tom exclaimed excitedly with sudden enlightenment. 'I saw it there, on the back shelf. A bloody big one!'

'Oh, man. Fool! Idiot! Why didn't I's think of that? Of course there is! We got enough matches to get down there, man?'

'I think so.'

Striking the matches sparingly, they had used most of the box by the time they reached the lower circle. Wishing to save the last few matches for later, just in case – in case of what they had no idea – but nevertheless just in case, they fumbled their way past the tables in the lounge until they were inside the deejay box.

Randy groped along the shelf where the torch was normally kept, and where Tom must have seen it. Nothing. It was not there. A few old record sleeves, and a mug full of pens that he managed to knock over, but no torch.

'Shit! That's strange, it's normally kept up here but I's can't find it, man. Light another match, it's gotta be around here somewhere.'

Tom struck another match. It definitely was not on the shelf where he had seen it before or, two more matches revealed, anywhere over that side. They turned, now facing towards the lighting console and the decks with their massive amps beneath them. Tom lit another match.

'Oh, shit, man! Look!'

'What?'

'The record on the right hand deck, it's: Mighty Quinn. Remember? The emergency record? It has to be that one – it's the only seven-inch record we has, man. That there means the place was evacuated last night! They never finished the night, man! Oh, shit, man! Shit!'

Tom swore as the match burnt his fingers before it went out, plunging them into darkness again. Only this time he could see something. Two small faint, but none the less distinct against the utter blackness, red eyes glowed above the door by which they had entered. Slowly he put his arms out until he found his friend's body, then quickly following the torso up to Randy's head he placed his hands on either side and forced him to turn in the direction of the red eyes that were watching them.

'Hey, man!' Reaching upwards, Randy sounded happily relieved. 'The power's on in here!'

Tom heard the two loud clunks of the electric breakers engaging.

Immediately the disco burst into life. Lights began to flash all around the dance floor in time with a loud sish, click, sish, click, sish, click. Randy pushed past him to lift the arm off the expired record, stopping the turntable from revolving with a switch. A few more flicked switches, this time on the lighting console, and the annoying flashing stopped, leaving the whole area beneath them bathed in a soft, but plenty bright enough to see in, pinkish glow that radiated down gently from the four banks of par 56 lighting hanging high above them from the auditorium ceiling.

They leaned over the console surveying all that was below. It *was* the Mary Celeste. Looking around they could see full glasses, half-finished drinks, empty glasses, hot dogs and burgers - some only half eaten, the odd item of clothing strewn across a seat, and some girl's shoes. It looked like a snapshot that could have been taken on any night there, or every night, except that this time there were no people in it. No revellers; nobody at all.

'Man, that's creepy!'

'Let's go down and take a closer look,' Tom suggested, moving towards the door.

'Not that way, man. No lights that way, remember? Them lights don't work with this lot. They's still be off. We's better go this way; use our own emergency exit,' Randy called after him.

Tom turned to see the deejay struggling with some large cardboard boxes at the opposite end of the room. Magazines spilled out of the last one as he hurled it aside to reveal a hatch built in to the bottom half of the wall. Randy pulled off the hatch door and put it to one side exposing a void, plenty big enough to get inside, containing a shiny descending pole.

'Ever felt like a fireman?' he quipped.

'No. Not into uniforms,' Tom replied, trying to maintain the humour.

Randy went first, sliding rapidly down to the next level where he kicked open another hatch door. Tom followed him, and was surprised when he found they emerged in the foot space under one of the tills behind the bar. He had never considered that some of the walls might be false; that some had large cavities behind them. They all looked so solid. How many more routes, or other secret passages, lie behind them, he wondered?

The two lads wandered aimlessly in complete silence between the tables and stools surrounding the dance floor trying to take it all in, trying to make some sense out of the situation. But it didn't make any sense - none at all. So there may have been an emergency and the place may have had to be evacuated, they reasoned. But then, who in their right mind would stay behind running around the building switching the electric circuits off? Who would physically disconnect the back-up lighting? And, more to the point, why? There was no sense in that! None whatsoever!

'If you hold the doors to the foyer open,' Randy suggested, finally breaking their silence, 'enough light should spill out there for me to turn some more of the power on, man. The main for the flat's out there too.'

'Good thinking, Batman,' Tom nervously joked, as they swiftly retraced their steps.

Tom propped open the double doors into the foyer with tables rather than stand there holding them. There was more than enough light now to see into the lighting cupboard, besides it was getting light outside. Randy inserted his key, but found it was not locked. Opening it, he pulled some switches. The foyer lit up around them. One candle bulb immediately exploded, shooting across to hit the wall and shatter noisily at the same time that the till in the cafeteria chunked its acknowledgement it had power again.

'Shit! Them candle bulbs is always doing that, and I's still jumps, man!' Randy wiped his brow.

'If the lights are on in the flat, perhaps we ought to go up there again. Have a look round. Mother might have left a note somewhere. But, I wonder why she didn't call the mobile?'

'Okay, man. You's the boss. But if we go up the back way we can see what's happened to the back-up lighting on the way.'

Tom kicked the tables away allowing the doors to swing shut behind them. Hurrying back through the main auditorium, they made their way across the dance floor to the doors by the side of the stage, the ones Randy had crept off into the darkness to look through when they had arrived. Tom was there first, pushing hard on the left hand door, expecting it to fly open. It didn't. It moved only slightly, about an inch or so, and then it stopped abruptly.

'Fuck!' Tom uncharacteristically swore as his head collided heavily with the stubborn door.

Angrily, he pushed against it again, harder this time, but although it moved slightly, it still refused to open. Randy was alongside him by now and pushing on the right hand door. That one opened easily, with the discernable squeak that Tom had heard earlier.

Splat! A suited arm fell into their view at Randy's feet from behind the blocked door, the back of the outstretched hand slapping loudly as it landed on the tiled floor of the passageway.

'Oh, my God!'

'Fuck, man! Fuck!'

Both youths involuntarily retracted several paces, rapidly, before standing, staring with utter disbelief at the lifeless looking arm in front of them. It was several minutes before either spoke.

'Do you think we ought to see who it is? I mean, see if we know who it is?' Tom finally managed to ask.

'Hell no, man! No way, man! I's must 'as been out there in the dark with 'im earlier, man! I's was in that passage, and I's opened that door,' Randy shuddered visibly. 'Jeeesus, man! With a corpse! Imagine if I's 'ad touched 'im in the dark. Oh, Jeees man, no! No, that don't bear no thinkin' about, man! A corpse! A dead body! Urrrghh!' He shuddered again.

'We shall have to see who he is,' Tom insisted. Regaining some of his self-control, he slowly moved forward far enough to peer through the door that was being held partly open by the lifeless arm. 'It's still a bit too dark to . . .'

The left hand door now fell open, inwards, towards them, allowing the remainder of the body to fall backwards from its sitting position, its head smacking on the floor with a sickening thud to reveal a ginger receding hairline above a ruddy full bearded face. From a hole in the dead centre of the forehead, a thick dark liquid had emerged, congealing above two lifeless eyes that stared up at them.

'Shit, man! Shit! I's outta here!'

'Don't be silly! Come back – he isn't going to hurt anybody, is he?' Tom called after him. 'You wouldn't leave me here on my own, would you?'

'No, man, 'course I's wouldn't,' Randy replied, returning slowly. 'But that definitely ain't my thing, man, no way, not messing about with corpses. Not with the dead. Oh, Jeees, man. What is you doing now?'

181

'I'm trying to find his wallet. See if we can find out who he is.'

'He's known as Anton Taylor,' a voice boomed out from the darkness at the far end of the passage.

Tom leapt to his feet, only to collapse to the floor when his legs failed to hold him up. Was it fear, or merely his injured knee, that had let him down? He didn't stop to contemplate the cause. Scrambling madly across the floor, his heart now pounding heavily against his chest, his head reeling, his body nervously shaking, a feeling of an impending feint overwhelming him, he managed to make it back to his friend's side. He could hear the sound of the slowly approaching footsteps on the tiles in the passageway behind him echoing around in his head.

A massive effort, a strong helping hand from Randy, and finally he was able to stand again. Together they stood, frozen-like, side-by-side, waiting, terrified by what, more who, was approaching. Two bulky shapes gradually emerged from the dark shadows of the passageway.

CHAPTER 18

Thump . . . Thump . . . Thump . . . Thump . . . Thump . . .
Mary sat bolt upright, groaning with the excruciating pain that was erupting from somewhere deep within her head. Something inside there was rhythmically expanding, trying to crack her skull open, then receding, contracting to produce a crushing feeling, before perpetually repeating the cycle. Seeking relief, she first tried holding her head in both hands and squeezing it, but that didn't help. Then she tried to massage the back of her neck, down, across her shoulders, but that only seemed to make matters worse. There was no relief, none at all. Her head continued pounding, exploding. Her tongue, her mouth, they reminded her of the proverbial bottom of a parrot's cage, an expression she'd heard somewhere before thinking it funny at the time. Now, she realised, she truly knew what that old saying related to, and it was not funny.

She would open her eyes in a minute, she told herself, once the thumping stopped, once the pain receded a little, just a little, once the room stopped moving so much, she would. She must open them, in a minute . . .

Thump . . . Thump . . . Thump . . . Thump . . . Thump . . .

'Oh, dear. And you could have done with the sleep, couldn't you? Never mind, I'll get you some coffee now that you're awake. That'll make you feel better.'

Mary could hear the words, they reverberated in her head. Somewhere. Deep inside in some dark void they were rattling around like railway station announcements, so loud, yet so indecipherable. Concentrate, she told herself. She must concentrate. A few moments later, after a lot of effort, she had managed to piece enough of the words together in the correct order to make some kind of sense out of them. She ought to open her eyes now, she told herself, but the room was still moving too much. No, she must open them. She really must. She did.

'Caroline!' she exclaimed on seeing the face in front of her, then immediately shut her eyes again as the red hot pokers of bright morning sunlight scorched her vision, drilling into her brain through those momentary open portals. 'Oh, my God, Caroline! I feel so bad! I really do. Whatever happened to me last night? Did I have too much to drink? Oh, my head! The thumping! The room, it's moving. It's positively rolling around!'

Thump . . . Thump . . . Thump . . . Thump . . . Thump . . .

'Yes, I know. That damn helicopter isn't helping much, either, is it?' Caroline stated, sympathetically.

Helicopter? Mary forced her eyes to open again. 'Helicopter? Where on earth am I?'

'You're safe. Relax now. You're on the Lady Caroline – it's a yacht. My yacht, actually. We're about three miles out, that's why the room is moving around so much, you silly bean. It'll be a lot calmer once the helicopter moves away, I promise. The downdraft is spinning us like a top at the moment. But don't worry it will be gone soon. We have excellent stabilisers so it will be quite calm once it's gone. Oh, look, there's a friend of yours come to see you. I'll leave you with him while I go to get you some coffee and an aspirin.'

Ben leapt on to the bed from the doorway in one move, fully spread-eagling himself across Mary as he licked at her face, furiously at first, then relaxing some he pulled back to lie on her legs, staring up into her eyes, panting contentedly as he licked her hand which was trying to stroke him.

'Ben, my boy. My, don't you look the happy one? Oh, do stop licking me! Your mum's feeling a bit queasy today, come on now you'd better get down. There now, be a good boy. Sit!'

'He should be happy, he's just devoured two enormous steaks, not to mention the half a loaf of toast. They don't keep dog food on board.'

'Beryl!'

'How you feeling now, Mrs P?'

'Er . . . I seem to be suffering from a bit of a hangover, I think. I don't seem to remember much, I mean . . . What are we doing here? How did we get here? I don't remember us getting on a boat last night. Why would we? Was I, er . . .' she started to whisper, 'a little bit sloshed?'

'No, of course not, but . . . Really? You really can't remember last night. What nothing? Nothing at all?'

Mary thought hard for a while, holding her hand up to shade her eyes from the bright sunlight still stabbing at her through the porthole. 'No, I can't seem to remember anything from last night. Not a thing. That is strange, isn't it? I should be able to, shouldn't I? How peculiar. Why, what happened last night? What have I missed?'

Beryl didn't know how to answer her. What she should tell her. She didn't remember anything? Nothing? That was incredible. Not the well-laid plans that had gone so fatally wrong last night? Not her husband? Not the story of his horrific death? What could she say? She was about to splutter something out, she wasn't sure exactly what, perhaps something vague but comforting, when Caroline returned with the coffee and two tablets.

'There we go,' she said sweetly, carefully placing the steaming drink on the small bedside cabinet, 'one lovely hot cup of coffee and two strong pills. You get that down you. You'll soon feel a lot better then. The doctor will be down to see you before long, perhaps once he's been you'll be able to come topside with the rest of us. By the way, have you noticed how much calmer it is now? They have Daddy on board and the helicopter has gone. You would hardly know we were at sea, would you? Anyway, don't worry, we're already heading back in towards the shore. We shall be anchored outside the harbour within the hour.'

'You have a doctor on board? Just how big is this boat?' Mary was bemused; still fighting to follow the conversation; still a few lines behind.

'Oh, it's quite a size, too big to get into the harbour, in fact. And yes, we do have a doctor on board. He's actually a full blown surgeon, but we all call him Doc, he doesn't seem to mind,' Caroline replied. 'It's not my idea, but Daddy insists. Fathers are like that, aren't they? Overprotective of their daughters to the extreme. Anyway, here he is now. The Doc. We'll leave you with him for now and see you later on. Just be a good girl and do as he says or I'll set Daddy on to you. Now, there's a threat!'

Caroline smiled back over her shoulder as she led Beryl out of the cabin past the patiently waiting physician.

'She doesn't remember anything,' Beryl whispered sideways to Caroline, 'but she knows who we are!'

'Don't worry,' Caroline reassured her, 'it's probably only the drugs working that the Doc put her on last night. Those others that I have given her this morning are not aspirins at all. They are to bring her back slowly. The antidote, if you like. The Doc said she needed the rest from reality last night, otherwise anything could have happened to her. She was in such a bad way. Come on, quickly. Follow me up the stairs. We all have to meet up with Daddy in the lounge, that's if he's managed to get out of his Biggles outfit by now.'

Beryl grabbed hold of the pristine brass handrail and began to follow her up the equally unblemished brass stairs, feeling embarrassed at the way her handprint was being left behind every time she grasped the shining metal to haul herself up another step. She wished she could climb them as easily as Caroline was managing, unassisted by the rail, but she was having trouble even with its assistance. Guiltily glancing behind her at the damage being caused by her sweaty hand, she was relieved to see that the palm prints were slowly evaporating away, leaving the rail looking untouched. She was so impressed by the effect that she had to pause at the top to look back down, watching them patiently until they had all disappeared. Satisfied they had, she turned around.

Apart from when they had all boarded the yacht in darkness, during the night amidst a torrent of confusion, this was Beryl's first look topside. Then it had been too dark to see much at all, but now, in broad daylight, it was a world the likes of which she had never before seen. Riveted to the spot, mesmerised, and standing in awe for a full minute before she could move, she surveyed all that was around her, hardly able to believe any of what she beheld. Her brain questioned the reality of it all. People actually live like this?

She had already appreciated from what she had experienced below that she was on an exceedingly luxurious craft, but this, this was truly unbelievable, and it exceeded anything her imagination could have ever suggested. The panoramic tinted windows, the gold plated edging to everything, the highly polished walnut wood, the mirrors, the crystal, and the well-stocked bar across the corner at the other end. All glistening like icicles caught in the sun. To Beryl, it was a fairyland.

'For God's sake woman, close your mouth. Come and sit down. You'll show us up,' Derek called over, breaking the spell in an instant.

'Yes, please do come and join us,' said the undeniably distinguished looking yet casually dressed man sitting next to her husband, whilst getting up from his seat as a politeness to pull back a chair for her at the long table, 'breakfast is on its way. It's such a beautiful day that I thought we could take it in here. The views are marvellous, aren't they?

'I'm Jason, by the way, Caroline's father. It's so lovely to meet you.' He held out his hand, taking hers, guiding her into the chair, and waiting there to make sure she was completely comfortable before returning to his own seat.

Beryl smiled politely. Sitting down, she surveyed the table. Pure best Irish linen she guessed, expertly testing the feel of the starched tablecloth secretly between her thumb and forefinger under the table. She also noticed how the silver cutlery and condiments were so highly polished that minute sparkling stars with halos radiated from them every time the ship moved a certain way allowing the sun's rays to kiss them. She wanted to pick them up, to see the hallmarks she knew would be on them, but resisted the temptation.

'Hello, Beryl. Alright?' Denise greeted her, adjusting an earring as she sauntered in to the room from the doorway between Jason and the bar. 'Just had to take a pee,' she confided, before sitting down next to her.

Beryl scowled disapprovingly at such blatantly inappropriate commonness, giving her a look as only she could, but it went almost unnoticed. Caroline, at the head of the table, inwardly chuckled at Beryl's embarrassment - she had noticed it. Then, looking across at the young man who had appeared in the same doorway moments later, she nodded to him signifying they were ready to be served with their breakfast.

'I wish Tom was here with us,' Denise sighed. 'I do hope he's alright, and that nothing's happened to him.' Then, remembering Caroline, quickly added, 'And Randy too, of course, we mustn't forget Randy. I wonder what they are doing, where they are right now? I'm so worried about them.

CHAPTER 19

The voice from the passageway severely shocked both Tom and Randy, cementing them to the spot and temporarily paralysing them. It came so unexpected. They had already convinced themselves that they were alone in the building; completely alone. That this was their own personal Mary Celeste.

'Sorry if we frightened you,' Stefan laughed.

Now they both felt foolish, becoming annoyed at the two men who emerged from the darkness, and annoyed at themselves too for being so jumpy.

'Stefan! Karl! Jeeeesus fuck, man! Did you ever shit us up!' Randy managed.

'What the hell are you doing here?' Tom asked, mopping the sweat from his brow, and realising he was still trembling, trying desperately not to show it. 'And where is everyone? Where's Mum? Denise? Beryl? And all the others? What the hell happened here last night?'

'Caroline?' Randy added quickly. 'Aren't you supposed to be looking after Caroline? Where is she? Nothing's happened to her, has it?'

'Whoa. Whoa. Slow up,' it was Karl's turn to speak. 'One thing at a time.'

'Everybody's okay,' Stefan told them, 'they're all safely on Caroline's yacht at the moment, heading off out to sea with a crew of twenty-odd on board to look after them. They're enjoying a life of pure luxury, so there's nothing to worry about. Nothing at all. They will all be perfectly safe. We've just returned from seeing them off, so we know that for a fact.'

Tom sighed with relief, the trembling receding rapidly.

'Yacht, man?' Randy queried. 'I's knows her old man's got a bit of money, and supposedly he has his own yacht, but Caroline's never mentioned that she's got no flippin' yacht, man! Not one of her own, she ain't!'

'Yes, man. She's got a yacht, man. She's got a yacht all of her own. And, man! It's a real biggun!' laughed Stefan. Momentarily, he couldn't resist the take-off, but then continued more naturally, 'So you don't need to be worrying about any of them. They will all be perfectly okay. No doubt they'll be back sometime later this morning, after Jason has boarded. Jason is Caroline's father, if you didn't already know that. Jason Harman.' He lifted an enquiring eyebrow.

'Man!' Randy's jaw dropped. He had not known that.

Tom was speechless, although the well worn 'Most excellent!' did fleetingly shoot through his mind in ten foot high letters.

Jason Harman was somebody you only read about in newspapers or occasionally saw in the news on television. He was someone who no doubt really did exist, but seemingly existed in a completely different world. Not his world. And now he knew this man's daughter! He knew her as a friend. More than that, his best mate was actually bedding her!

'We were hoping to have arrived back here long before the two of you returned, then if you weren't here Karl was going to go out looking for you, in case you were in trouble. I was going to stay behind here, to cover the eventuality he should miss you, keeping myself amused by switching all the lights back on,' Stefan explained, breaking into Tom's realisation, then nodding towards the corpse, 'and tidying up a bit, too.'

'Well, what did happen here? And who is this bloke, Anton what's it?' Tom, snapping out of it, asked.

'Taylor. Anton Taylor. Used to be a big time hit man, one of the best. But he got too old for the game, started to get a bit careless and had his knee blown away on a job that went tits up in Paris. Now walks stiff-legged, or rather, used to. He took up with a guy called Chance, a strange character. Nobody ever knew his real name. Huh, he took one chance too many last night though, the stupid idiot! He's out there on the stairs. First landing. Similar state. Talking of Chance, any chance of a coke?' Karl asked, heading towards the bar.

'Sure, if the equipment's still working. Help yourself to anything,' Tom replied as they all followed him over to the bar, with Randy shuddering at the thought that earlier he had passed yet another corpse somewhere out there in the darkness.

'He was with a couple of young lads who were selling drugs in here last night, so we guessed he was part of the gang.' Karl continued. 'Bit of a come down for him, this. I expect he needed the money though. He had a gambling habit, big time. Spent it quicker than he could make it, always did, and believe me he could really make it a few years back,'

Stefan took the story along further: 'He must've recognised Caroline in here earlier tonight when she came down to have a word with Beryl and Derek. He probably thought she was on her own because I was upstairs with your mother at the time, and Karl was working at a distance. I'll bet he couldn't have believed his luck. I mean, can you imagine just how much he could have asked for as a ransom? Do you know how much her old man's worth? The sky is the limit. Literally. He could have asked for just about anything. Certainly more than enough to have kept him and his habit going for the rest of his life, five star!

'Anyway, putting it in a nutshell, it all got a bit hairy in here for a while earlier on. He grabbed hold of Caroline, and then panicked when he saw Karl moving in. She struggled with him, and then as he was trying to get his gun out she managed to pull away from him, running off into the crowd. That's when the bullets started flying around the place. Theirs, not ours, I hasten to add. We held back until the place was empty. But with all the panic, people screaming, and rushing for the exits and that, it was only minutes before everyone was out of here.

'By the way, Tom, you might need to compliment your security blokes and the staff. They were pretty damn good and really held their cool. The second the deejay played some crappy old record, one that I guess you play in an emergency, and had put the lights on they were at the doors ushering everybody out and calling for a calm, orderly evacuation. There's many that would have been first out, believe me!

'Anyway, once the place had emptied we were only left with the crap to deal with - Anton and Chance. They were holed up in the wings of the stage, hiding behind a load of stacked up tables and stools.'

'By that time your security blokes had managed to get everyone else, including your mother and the rest of the staff, out of here safely,' Karl interrupted. 'Caroline, your mother, Denise, a couple of the others, oh, and the dog, were all bundled into the Mercedes to wait for us in the car park. The rest of your staff were then all sent home and told to phone in later today.'

'Man, it looks like we weren't the only ones having one hell of a night, then,' Randy muttered with a shocked look on his face.

'Why did they have to wait in the car park? Wouldn't they have been far safer driving off?' Tom protested, wondering what would have happened had Anton and Chance got the better of the two minders.

'No, they were quite safe. That car is a lot more than just bullet proof. With all its concealed armour plating and defences it weighs several tons more than a normal Mercedes. It was specially made to withstand an attack. Of course, a mortar wouldn't do it a lot of good, but even then the occupants are expected to survive. Caroline knew that. They were quite safe once they'd locked themselves in,' Karl reassured him.

Stefan continued, 'Well, after we'd found all the light switches and managed to disconnect the security lights it was a bit of cat and mouse game for a while, but it was only a matter of time before we'd successfully dealt with Anton and his sidekick. We carry night-vision glasses, they obviously didn't, so that's why we needed the black-out, to give us the advantage

'Once we'd terminated them, we drove everyone down to the marina, and then Caroline ferried them out to the yacht in the launch. We waited on the jetty until she called us on her mobile to tell us they were all safely on board and under way heading out to sea, before coming back here.'

'And then on arriving back, there you were frisking the corpse like an old pro,' Karl explained light-heartedly, grinning in Tom's direction.

'Well, that's our story. Now let's hear yours. How did you two get on? Spying on the gang's headquarters, we were told. Why was that necessary? Did you, in actual fact, find out what it was you wanted to know?' Stefan was curious.

Tom and Randy, interrupting each other frequently, related the sad tale of their whole night's events, from the beginning right up to the present time. They had to fill in all the gory parts at the Membury Service Station, parts that Karl and Stefan couldn't have known fully about as they had not thought it fitting to disclose some of the finer details of that bloody episode to anyone earlier. So it was some time later that, once updated with all that had happened, the two minders disappeared for half an hour to dispose of the 'rubbish'. They didn't mention what they had done with the bodies when they returned, but that didn't matter to Tom who wouldn't have cared, or to Randy who was simply happy know the corpses had been removed.

With hours still to go before the yacht was expected back, they spent the time usefully employed. Karl skilfully re-connected the back-up lighting – it had merely been disconnected without any need to cut the wiring - whilst Tom and Randy emptied the tills, locking the money in the office safe to be counted later.

At one point during the long wait Randy performed miracles on the hotplate in the cafeteria, producing succulent cheeseburgers all round with frequent cups of fresh coffee.

Later, Tom collected all the discarded articles of clothing that littered the building, storing them in the still full cloakroom. No doubt, he realised, there would be hundreds of people creeping back some time later that day to retrieve their belongings, with few of them still having their cloakroom tickets, and all of them asking awkward questions. They would need to come up with a plausible story before then!

By nine o'clock, they were satisfied the venue was respectably tidy again, or at least in the state the contract cleaners would be expecting. They, a crew of eight, normally arrived around eleven, taking about an hour or so to clean the public areas – everything else, like the cafeteria and the bars were cleaned by the staff. Randy had expertly repaired all the bullet holes and scars in the plaster with the quick drying filler and paint that was specially kept for accidental damage. It was a familiar job, damage was a frequent occurrence, although never before had it been attributed to gunfire, normally it was the result of a flying stool or a bottle.

It was ten-fifteen on Tom's watch when the unmistakeable thumping noise of a helicopter passing low overhead woke him from the short sleep. He had tried hard to fight off the tiredness, but it beat him in the end and he had slumped forward awkwardly into his folded arms whilst still sitting on a stool at the bar. A position, he realised, which undoubtedly accounted for the painful crick in his neck. Looking around, rotating his shoulders to try to ease the ache, he found Randy was in similar discomfort. He too had succumbed.

'That'll be Jason,' Stefan informed them.

Neither of the two minders had dozed off, yet outwardly neither of them appeared to be tired.

'I don't envy him being winched down on to the Lady Caroline at sea,' he continued. 'She's a big craft, but not *that* big. Being lowered on to her would be no picnic for anyone who's an expert and used to doing that kind of thing; people like the air-sea rescue wallahs. Still, no one argues with Jason, do they? Well, that is except for Caroline, of course. Let's hope he makes it safely!'

'He will,' Karl stated with confidence. 'I suppose we'd all better make our way down to the marina soon, to meet them. Once he's on board it won't take them long to sail back here. Although, as they'll probably leave us waiting on the dockside for hours, I'm sure there's more than enough time for another one of those delicious cups of coffee before we go.' He grinned across at Randy.

CHAPTER 20

Mike gazed across the table at Graham. They were both giggling, but neither really knew for what reason. It was nearly eleven o'clock and he was still high from last night; as high as the proverbial kite. Not as high as he had been though, as high as they both had been during their night of ecstatic drug-crazed sex, but still very high. The glazed eyes and the stupid grins said it all. There was no hiding it.

'You know, if Phil could see us now he'd go absolutely ape,' Graham stated, laughing aloud as he reached over to squeeze his partner's hand.

'He'd be giving out more fucks than even Doris has had in her lifetime, and that's saying something!' Mike quipped back, making sure he had said it just loud enough for the tall middle-aged man to hear – the one who was struggling two enormous cooked breakfasts over to their table.

'Now, now. That's enough of your cheek, you little tarts,' the unshaven Doris retorted in her usual unashamed but undeniably camp way, with all the evidence of the previous night's drag make-up still noticeably apparent, but now severely cracking under a new day's growth of facial stubble. 'I shouldn't think anyone could get it together as many times as you two over-sexed faggots did last night, anyway. Noisy little sods! Rod and I didn't get a wink of sleep! Not a wink, darlings!

'That is definitely the last time you pair of randy buggers get the room next to ours, I'm telling you! If you crash out in here again my little chickadees, you're going in the attic!' She carefully placed the still sizzling meals in front of them and then blowing an emphatic kiss into the air at each of them, she breathed, 'Enjoy!'

Both Mike and Graham were suffering with a severe case of the munchies - the craving for food often experienced when the effects of certain illegal substances begin to wear off - so they made short work of the generous breakfasts. After the third cup of coffee, several cigarettes and a lot of mindless chatter, each one saying their piece and with neither actually listening to the other one, Graham went quiet.

194

Now content, having eaten well, and extremely tired, he desperately wanted to crash, he needed to, but knew he had better not do it there. They hadn't had any sleep the previous night, none at all, but he wasn't going to let Doris know - that would be just too much ammunition for her act that evening! So instead he began to stare about the place they were in.

Through a veil, a dreamy mist, he began studying the Greek scenes on the extensive murals that ran the full length of the walls on either side. Then his eyes were drawn towards the clashing stark yellow brick road that emerged from the main doors, the brick tiles winding through the tables, running past where they were sitting, to finish up at the wall to the rear of the cabaret stage, right by the entrance to a magnificently painted-on-the-wall fairyland castle. The straw man. The tin man. The lion. They were there too, gracing the wall. Even Toto had his place. He was painted on the flowery grass outside the castle. But with the house lights on they all looked so harsh; so hostile. Dorothy came across as positively minacious, someone far removed from the innocent little girl she was supposed to be, and Toto the dog, well he didn't resemble anything at all canine in the cruel naked lights. He looked more like an overgrown furry caterpillar. Or was that the drugs still working?

The Wizard of Oz theme was such a contradiction to the life-sized artistically nude statues of David, Apollo, the Wrestlers, the Discus Thrower, and the various other Greek styled 'art' figures that were mounted on low pedestals in front of the murals that repeatedly adorned the perimeter. Statements have to be made he supposed, easily dismissing the outrageousness of it all, as he observed that without the club's normally subdued lighting subtly complimented by the warm ever-changing coloured spotlights that normally bathed the statues, even they appeared old, haggard and noticeably smoke-stained.

Looking across, through the fake stone archway built to the side of the long bar, Graham could see into the 'dungeon' area where a multitude of whips, handcuffs, chains, and other alarmingly fetish articles hanging tauntingly, adorned the artificial stone walls. This was the dark place where the leather queens, and others, nightly paraded their wares and did their thing. The young man chuckled openly, remembering how it was only two short years since, sexually confused, he'd bravely gone in there one night as an experiment, as a way, he had hoped, of putting to rest some of the strange abnormal feelings he'd been experiencing about some men – or more accurately, many men. Feelings that aroused him sexually, and all he knew telling him that should not happen.

The doltish smile spread into an all-encompassing open-mouthed grin, as he recalled how that cure never happened. How, far from being repulsed, as he hoped to be, even expected to be, he immediately enjoyed the inviting atmosphere of the place and all the friendly attention the regulars gave him. The drinks were flowing easily on that first night, and there was a plenitude of drugs of which he enjoyed taking his full share.

Somehow the grin now incredibly expanded even further across the lad's face as more of the happy memories flooded back to him. Memories like those of the earth-shattering surprise of discovering the person who he landed up snogging with, and frantically groping with that first night in the darkness of the dungeon, on a joint trip to the more lit bar area to replenish their drinks turned out to be none other than his workmate, Mike - the guy he sold drugs with at the other clubs every evening, and probably the last guy on earth that he would have ever suspected as being gay.

Mike was one of those people who particularly aroused Graham's secret feelings, and that had frightened him. He was afraid that one day the guy would notice the strong infatuation he had with him. So he was one of the very reasons, if not the main reason, for that first night's quest; that search for a cure.

The doorbell shrilled long and loudly, somehow managing to relate a perceivable sense of urgency in its tone. It was enough to force Mike and Graham to break off from the induced pathetic grins they had been giving each other for several hazy minutes, whilst they had both been away daydreaming in their own little worlds. They turned and watched as Doris clattered to the door in her flip-flops. On opening it, she revealed a sweaty, and breathless Sam.

Sam had known all about Mike's sexuality a long time before Graham had found out, but the secret had been safely kept. Although he was not gay himself, Sam was one of those people who could be totally at ease with gay people. He had never found a problem with any differences there might have been, and he truly enjoyed their company. They were fun. Happily, and frequently, he would now visit Dorothy's with his two gay colleagues where, as an obvious spare part alongside his two devoted mates, he would often attract the attention of many a recently arrived newcomer to the establishment. He would get an enormous kick out of leading on any amorous guy, before giving him a peck on the cheek only to confess in his ear, 'Sorry darling, I'm straight.' - but never before he'd been bought at least a couple of drinks by the unsuspecting loser.

'Phil's dead!' Sam exploded at them as he rushed in gasping, frantically trying to catch his breath. 'Bumped off last night! Apparently, Patrick's had him killed so he and his brothers can run things. They've even burnt his house down an' all! Everybody is full of it on the front! And it seems like the Irish are far worse than Phil ever was - they've been pointing their guns at everyone and telling them they'll have to cough up more money now!'

He paused, bending over for a second to gulp in some air before continuing: 'And I've found out where Patrick, Don and Paul got to last night. Their car blew up in Membury Services. Apparently they were bringing some explosives and another gunman back with them to join the clan. Seems like he bought it, though.'

'My God!' Doris exclaimed. Visibly shocked, she hastily bolted the door behind their distressed visitor before ushering him over to his friends' table. 'That's certainly not good news, is it? Not good news at all. I'd better get Rod up, he'll want to hear all about this.'

Doris's partner, the butch one of the two, obviously wasn't called Rod for no reason, as his prompt response to her ear-piercing shriek through the door behind the bar revealed when he emerged dressed only in his boxer shorts. Rugged, six foot three at least, heavily tattooed – almost totally - and built like the proverbial, it was plain for all to see that this man was big in every way.

'Luv?' he questioned, more grunted, over the resounding long drawn out rasp of his breaking wind. 'Whassup?'

'You filthy thing,' Doris screamed at him, 'you should get your arse into order before you make an appearance! How disgusting! What will people think? Really! And why aren't you ready yet? We open in less than an hour and you know I still have to get ready. My makeup doesn't put itself on, you know!'

A grin spread across the mammoth's face, one that said, 'I don't give a monkey's . . .' Lifting a leg he repeated the gesture as an encore.

Choosing to ignore his coarseness this time, Doris informed him of Sam's urgent news concerning Phil's demise.

'Nothing more than the tyke deserves,' Rod proclaimed. 'Tell me where they bury him and I'll go and dance on his grave. Homophobic bastard!'

'He might have been homophobic, but at least that meant he left us alone!' Doris explained. 'We may not be so lucky with this new set-up. You know, old Singh at the curry house pays them a fortune every night - a lot of them around here do.

'And what about all the happy stuff that goes through here? Are they going to want to get in on that too? Is this going to go like the Elephant did? You only own it in name? Every penny you make going to the likes of them?

'Sam, and his mates here, they have done us proud over the last couple of years. Best stuff; cheapest prices. What's going to happen to all that now?'

'It was only because Phil was such an idiot, not noticing how much we were ripping him off each week, that we could do those prices,' Sam explained. 'By mixing that lot in with the stuff that Auntie gets us from Bristol, we were able to keep the prices down.'

'Urrrgh. Bloody drugs. Drugs, drugs, drugs, that's all you seem to hear around this place,' Rod growled.

'Bloody drugs they may be to you, dear. But they're nectar to some of us queens,' Doris spat back. 'Besides, you'd be the first to scream if you didn't have your bottle of poppers! What do think they are, if they're not drugs?'

'They're legal,' the mountain threw back as he disappeared out through the door to get ready.

'They're only legal if you use them as room odourisers,' she screamed after him. 'Still, you're getting as big as a room, aren't you?' Then, flicking her head back as if she was wearing one of her long wigs, 'Fat git!'

Sam sat down next to Mike at the table. The three lads thought nothing of the apparent animosity between their hosts. It was normal, an everyday occurrence. They knew that they were thoroughly devoted to each other, and totally inseparable. Being bitchy is a drag queen's trade, something that cannot be turned off and on easily. The bitchiness and mannerisms become a way of life for them that is simply accepted by others and rarely taken as a real offence.

'Don't forget you two didn't cash-in last night,' Sam reminded his colleagues. 'I've already been down to see Patrick this morning, to pay my lot in, that's how I know some of the lesser known details about Phil, and everything else that's happened. It seems Patrick knew nothing at all about the gunfight the two new blokes started at the Ellie last night, and he's no idea what's happened to them either. Nobody has seen them since. They're missing, presumed dead, as they say.

'I told him that was the reason why we didn't cash in last night, we thought it better to lie low in case those other blokes were police, or worse, from outside. He accepted the story anyway, but Patrick's definitely not a happy chappie at the moment. He wasn't even told the two casual hired hands that Bob found for Phil were guns. He thought they were just heavy. Well, we all did, didn't we? So, I think he's really hoping that they did get taken out, in case they should become a threat.

'And that's another thing: Bob. He hasn't paid his money in either, which is unusual for him. It turns out he's another one that no one has seen for a while, or has any idea what's happened to him. Anyway, the orders are, we all have to meet up down there today at four o'clock sharp. At the cellar. Patrick wants to talk to us all.'

'Great!' Graham groaned.

'I don't think so,' Mike added quickly, having somehow miraculously managed to clear his head. 'We all know none of us paid in last night, what with all the trouble at the Ellie and the rumours that Patrick, Don and Paul had gone missing - everybody thinking it best to keep a low profile. But now the shit's really hit the fan, hasn't it?'

'Why?' Graham was finding it hard to keep up in his condition. The time was fast approaching when he would have to close his eyes, to leave the world and its troubles for a few hours, and to drift away and dream those sweet dreams. He yawned. He was a little annoyed that his partner was more with it than he was that morning. Mike took a lot more than he did last night.

'Don't you see?' Mike continued, 'Things have changed dramatically. It's now a whole new ballpark. I mean we all knew Phil's nose was out of joint recently, didn't we? But did any of us really think he was going to lose it - for real?

'A few days ago we had Phil, the grumpy old bastard that he was, running things. We had Patrick as our so-called explosives expert, our one gunman, and our final resort if things got sticky. We all knew exactly where we stood, what we could do, what we could get away with, and what we could not. But since then, in just a couple of short days, we've landed up with likes four Patricks. Four mad Irishmen toting guns, not to mention the other two guns, that pair of idiots who started blowing holes in the Ellie last night, though they're probably dead now. Then there was the other one you just mentioned, the one they were bringing in from London, the dead before arrival bloke, yet another gun. I mean, how many more guns are coming? How bad is it going to get here?'

'It is getting a bit Chicago,' Sam agreed.

'What worries me most,' Mike went on, 'is I can't see they need us any more - certainly not all of us. One gun is worth a dozen men. Probably more. They might want to keep Bob on, to do the cutting and all that shit. But all of us? I don't think so.

'But if we are pushed out, how do we continue making a living here? How do we maintain the lifestyle we are used to? Don't forget, once we are on the outside all the little "on the side" scams we've been doing, like supplying the market here, will stop as well. Income nil; prospects zilch!'

'Bob knows all our scams, as well.' Sam added. 'That could be bad for us if he's in and we're out, or if it turns into a competition about who stays. And anyway, who's to say they would just let us go? They might think it's not safe merely to sack us – they might feel safer terminating us!'

'Time for bed, said Zebedee.' Graham was not getting any better.

CHAPTER 21

'Come in, come in,' Jason said, walking over to shake their hands warmly. 'Tom. Randy. It is so nice to meet you at last. Caroline has told me such a lot about you already this morning. Your mother too, Tom. She's such a nice lady, your mother. And your father, I think I would have liked him too. It's all so tragic; so sad. You have my deepest sympathies. Your mum's all right now, isn't she? I know you've been below to see her. She does seem a lot better now, I think.

'Apparently she was in such a bad state last night that the Doc had to give her something quite severe to calm her down, but she's been back to normal for the last couple of hours. I've spent some considerable time with her since I came aboard. To me she seems to be coping very well considering her enormous loss, and all that she's been through what with those gunmen running loose in the club. Here, do grab a seat and make yourselves comfortable - don't stand around on ceremony. There'll be some coffee along in a minute.'

'Thank you, sir,' Tom and Randy replied almost in unison, each one opting for a leather armchair so sizeable it threatened to devour them, whilst their host chose to sprawl along a matching settee.

'Sir? Sir? You don't have to call me sir. I'm not a sir. Not by a long way. That's me,' he said, laughingly pointing over his shoulder to the large gold-framed black and white poster on the wall behind him of a teenage boy swinging a guitar above his head, 'I'm Jason. Everybody still calls me Jason, so you must too. That picture was taken back at a time when I had less than £100 in the bank and holes in my underpants. Yes, the underpants I was wearing the day they took that photograph truly had holes in them, I swear it. The socks too! Caroline keeps that photo there lest we should ever forget who we really are.'

'Really?' Tom was amazed at the revelation.

'Yes, really. Believe it or not, I was a poor spotty teenager once, just like millions of others.'

'That photo must have been taken about the time you did Sweaty Betty, I's suppose, man,' Randy said, still studying the poster, his extensive knowledge of pop music not failing him. 'That was number one for ten weeks, wasn't it? Wow, man! Jason! The follow up only made sixteen though, didn't it?'

'Don't remind me,' Jason laughed out loudly. 'I try not to remember that bit! Yes, Jason, the one hit wonder. Original claim to fame: I scored with Sweaty Betty! Hah! But it did open all the right doors for me. It enabled me to start my first recording company, and record label, etcetera, etcetera. And it's from those that everything else has grown. All that you see today I really do owe to Sweaty Betty. God forbid she really exists! Since those long gone days there's been a few other Sweaty Betty songs made by various artists, so if she does in fact exist she has all my sympathy – unlike mine, some of them have been quite crude.

'But enough of my past, what about your future? Your mother has told me some pretty horrific tales about Seathorpe.'

'It's certainly different from Brisham, where we come from,' Tom said. 'I never realised there were places like Seathorpe. At times it's like something out of an old American gangster movie here. A place where Al Capone would have felt at home.'

'It doesn't have to be like that, it could be cleaned up quite easily,' Jason said. 'The authorities obviously have no idea of what is happening here. It would only take a word in the right quarters to have those crooked cops removed overnight, and replaced with some real law and order. However Caroline insists that no one would thank us for that. She says it's not what the people would want. I find that strange, but there you go, there's nowt as strange as folk, is there?'

'I think everyone would enjoy some kind of law and order,' Tom said, 'but not the kind supplied by the normal authorities. That would kill the place overnight, putting many of the business people here into bankruptcy, and they don't deserve that – on the whole they are good people, merely caught up in bad circumstances.

'Overall, they seem quite happy to suffer the criminal element and having to pay some protection money, so long as they can afford it. I don't think they really mind if they still make enough money for themselves, and above all know exactly where they stand. Phil, for all his faults, apparently did provide that for most of the time. Stability. That is until we turned up and rocked the boat.'

'No, man. It weren't you's fault,' Randy insisted, 'it was gonna happen one day soon. Patrick would have brought his brothers over to sort Phil out one day. Perhaps you brought that day a little bit closer, but it definitely ain't you's fault, man.'

'Well, none of that matters much now, does it? It's what's out there at this moment that matters, and what we can do about it,' Jason said. 'Law and order, the correct way, I could arrange for you quite easily. No probs, as you modern people like to say. It would only take one phone call. Being infamously rich is not without its perquisites, a major one being people listen to you. They act on what you say. But hiring mercenaries and importing a small army in to Seathorpe to deal with these Irish, what Caroline expects me to do, is really not on. She will hate me for not doing it, but hopefully one day she will realise that a person in my position really cannot get involved in that type of action. The truth would out one day - with incalculable consequences.

'No, what I intend,' he continued, in a tone that was engraving it on stone tablets, 'is to leave Caroline's two minders here with you as some protection for you. They will be protection for you and the club for the next few months. I think they should be able to accomplish that without too much trouble, and hopefully without actually becoming personally involved in your little war. After all, they are professionals.

'We shall not be here because Caroline has to be in Milan in a little under a fortnight for a big fashion show. Anyway, it's soon coming up to the party season over there for her crowd, and she definitely won't want to miss out on all that!

'Her not having her minders gives me an excuse to spend some quality time with her. We don't seem to spend enough time together normally. We both have our commitments to contend with and rarely are they in the same places, but we've decided to rectify all that by taking a break and spending the next few months together.'

Jason cleared his throat and sat up before continuing, 'I was thinking of asking your mother if she would like to accompany us, Tom. She could obviously do with the rest, and I think it would do her the world of good to get away from this place for a while. Personally, I think she'll jump at the idea. I hope so, anyway. Really, I do.

'We have a lot in common, your mother and I. We have both suffered terrible losses, granted hers more recent than mine, but I think even in this short time there is already an understanding between us - something mutual. We could be a prop for each other in their times of need. God knows there are plenty of them!

'Hopefully, things will settle down here once the Irish have found their feet. Perhaps that stability you talk of will have returned by the time we come back. Either way, you'll be much safer with the boys looking after you, and then if nothing has changed by the time we return . . . Well, in that case, we shall have to chew the cud again, won't we?'

Tom thought, how do you argue with a man like this? Then he realised, why should he? Everything the man had said was sensible. So, he would miss his mother if she was to go on this trip, but it would be pure selfishness for him to ask her to stay if she wanted to go. She would be better off away from all the trouble, anyway - far safer too. Of course, the decision had to be hers, he concluded, and hers alone. Although, it was slowly dawning on him that she may have already agreed to go. Maybe she hadn't wanted to mention it earlier in case it hurt him.

'Like, when's Caroline leaving, man?' Randy asked, not overjoyed to hear she was deserting him.

'We thought tonight would be a good time,' their host replied, then turning towards Tom, 'early evening, after your mum's picked up her passport. You have the club to run, so you'll be kept occupied. I'll give you a number that you can ring at any time to talk to your mother direct. You'll only be a phone call apart, so there's no need to worry about her.'

'Fine,' Tom said, his suspicions now confirmed. His mother *had* made her mind up already. The arrangements were already in place - right down to picking up the passport. 'I'd better go back down and say goodbye to her then, before we go,' he said.

'Yes, of course, but there's still plenty of time for all that. And we should see you all briefly at the club before we leave, anyway. The car has been booked to pick us up about seven. Then we shall drive to a little place I know in Bristol and have a meal before flying out,' he explained. 'So there'll be plenty of time to say your goodbyes. I expect you'll want to spend some time with Caroline before you go ashore as well, won't you Randy?'

Randy smiled, indicating that he would.

'I hope she hasn't stolen your heart, lad. She is a bit of a good time girl is our Caroline. She loves her fun. Here today, somewhere else tomorrow. The world is her oyster. I'm not saying she doesn't care for you, I know she does. But I do know her track record. Don't take it all too seriously, will you? She'll only break your heart if you do.'

'No, of course not, man. Not too seriously,' Randy replied smiling, but inwardly feeling let down; hurt.

'Ah, here's that coffee at last,' Jason said, noticing the steward with the tray passing the window, 'I was beginning to think they'd forgotten us.'

CHAPTER 22

Tom, with the faithful Ben by his side, watched from the front steps of the Elephant's Nest, waving to his mother, and forcing a carefree smile at her as the hired limousine pulled away heading towards the cliff top road. He walked slowly after it, to the end of the building, his eyes not leaving it for a moment, waving all the time, until it went around the bend out of sight, hidden by the bushes and the trees of the hedgerow. He continued to wait patiently on the corner, knowing he would catch one last glimpse of it as it passed by Jumper's Point.

The fresh sea breeze was feeling cold to his skin causing goose pimples to appear on his uncovered arms, but he chose to ignore them. He suspected they were just a product of his tiredness, the result of so much lost sleep lately. It was not cold, he told himself, it couldn't be. It was still summer. Wondering if she could see him, whether she was actually looking back at him, he vigorously waved again as the car became visible again for a few seconds as it skilfully negotiated the dangerous hairpin bends at the top, and then it was gone.

With an empty feeling, a sense of inner loneliness, of loss, he sauntered back to the entrance where Ben was still obediently waiting. Sighing deeply, he went inside. The dog followed him in, and then lying down by the glass doors, looking out through them with his ears down, he too sighed. He didn't need telling she wouldn't be back for a long while; he knew.

Tom was already missing her dreadfully, and he knew he would miss her a whole lot more before she returned. Three months was a long time, but he had to accept she needed this holiday; she deserved it. She had looked so ill, so mentally and physically wrecked when they had said their goodbyes. It was all there, deep inside her eyes. She had been unable to hide any of the heartache and the suffering she was enduring. He had seen it all. The soul windows had revealed it. Those encouraging smiles, the warm hugs, and the countless motherly kisses of the emotional farewell were all meant, he was sure of that, but they were forced. He could tell she did not want to be doing them; they were not what she was at that time.

There was a lot of heart-wrenching in coming to terms with there not being a funeral held for Tom's father. Tom and his mother had soul-searched and in the end decided it would be best not to publicly acknowledge John's death. Not yet, anyway. Not until it was safe to admit it. There was no body. That would have been cremated in the fire at Membury; his ashes scattered to the wind. So for now they would pay their respects privately in their own hearts and minds. In time they would be able to do something fitting.

They doubted the story to be put around that John had rushed off to nurse his sick mother in Scotland would hold water for long. With her being dead the past ten years that could easily be disproved, but for now it should work. It would take the heat off Tom and Randy for a while.

Nothing would ever replace the loss of his father, Tom knew that, he felt the loss terribly, but he realised his mother would be suffering even more than him. John had been her chosen life-long companion. They had been a married couple that had struggled through all life's torments and survived them, laughing at their triumphs and crying at their failures, and doing it together for so many years. Her loss must be far greater than his own, and that was a seemingly endless void. It was an enormous chasm that he knew would always be there. It would be there for both of them, but to his mother it would always be that much greater.

Nothing could change any of that now. It had all been written. It couldn't be undone. So if his mother had to suffer, and he knew she had to, it must be far better for her to do it somewhere anew, in a place away from memories that might hurt. Somewhere exciting like a foreign country in the sun where she would want for nothing materialistically, and would be with someone with whom she had an obvious empathy.

But as much as Tom appreciated all of this, it did not ease his great feeling of loss - a loss that had now become a double loss - not by one iota.

Caroline's last few moments with Randy can only be described as being far from passionate. They too had been forced and unreal, with theirs being little more than a necessary politeness between them. There were a couple of theatrical embraces, a few friendly kisses that were nothing more than mere pecks, expected gestures, and then that compulsory promise everybody makes on leaving someone - the one to keep in touch. That, no doubt made with each of them remembering the many times they had made the promise before to someone, and never had done.

Randy had pondered on Jason's earlier advice. Normally he wasn't a great thinker, he usually accepted what was without question, but Jason's words had bothered him, they had made him think this time. On the trip back from the yacht he had given the relationship, if it could ever be called that, a great deal of thought. Perhaps he *had* been taking it too seriously, and hoping for too much, he admitted to himself.

There never was a relationship there, not really, not in the sense that there could ever have been a future to it, he realised. Relationships needed equality, or something near, an equal giving and taking. What had he to offer her? Absolutely nothing. He could give her nothing at all, except perhaps for a good time in bed. With her money and lifestyle that kind of action she could acquire anywhere, and obviously did. Besides, he would never be able to fit in with her way of life. The high social circles she bobbed around in - the Hoorah Henry crowd of which she was a fully paid up member. That was not his style, he knew nothing of it, and would never be happy being so out of place. There was no hope of him ever attaining her social level no matter how hard he tried, and she would never be able to sustain his social level for long - she would miss out on too much.

No, he finally conceded, he was merely a toy to her, a plaything. Nothing more than an enjoyable holiday fling. They had absolutely nothing in common. She had taken her pleasure, probably living out some wild fantasy of a young virile black man, of a big black dick, and he had enjoyed all the attention, the drink and the drugs, and, he guessed for he couldn't remember it too well again, he had enjoyed screwing the arse off one of the richest bitches in the world; a damn pretty one at that! That was all there was to it! It had been mutual gratification, nothing more or nothing less. Now it was merely something they could both laugh about, even boast about - her in some highfaluting social conversation, and him with his mates over a pint at some seedy bar.

Yes, they would both laugh about it someday, he guessed. But at that particular moment, as much as he had convinced himself, he didn't feel a bit like laughing. All that he had hoped for, all that he had needed from her, was gone; and he knew it was forever.

With Caroline gone he knew there was nothing to help him with that which had raised its ugly head again in the last few days. The thing he thought he had put to bed all those years ago, but which had now come back with a vengeance to haunt him again. It was stronger than ever this time and it demanded an answer from him. It worried him deeply. He never had found the answer before, and that is why it had been buried. But Caroline might have held that answer for him. Recently he had hoped so, desperately hoped so, for without it he was knew he was lost - and he feared all the hurt that would undoubtedly be coming.

'Cheer up,' Tom said, on entering the foyer and seeing his miserable looking friend tending to the lights. 'She'll be back.'

'I's don't think so, man.'

'Of course she will. She sorted you out again this time, didn't she? She still remembered you from last year, so you must have made a good impression the first time round!'

'Yeah, man, but . . . Once a year, man . . .'

'Don't tell me you were actually getting serious! Wanting to settle down with her? I thought casual sex was your thing, the way you liked it, a bit of a laugh and a joke; a good time. I never imagined you of all people getting serious. Not yet, anyway.'

'No, I's don't normally, man, but . . . I's dunno what I's does want. I's awful confused.'

Tom watched Randy slink out of the foyer with heavy shoulders and go into the main disco area - to tend to more lighting, he presumed. They would be opening soon and no doubt there was still much for him to do. Then it suddenly dawned on him that he had never seen his chum so unhappy before. Sure, there were times when he had seen him frightened, terrified even when they had been up against it, but apart from those times he couldn't remember ever seeing the guy unhappy. Unhappiness was not his style. Randy was a person very much like himself – one who always wore a cheeky grin on his face. He was a person who could instantly make you feel good, just by seeing him. He most definitely had that effect on him – he was like a tonic. No, this young man was not the Randy he had come to know, and to love as a brother.

Concerned, and completely forgetting about his own bout of depression for a while, the empty lost something special feeling he was suffering, he decided he should follow Randy to offer him some support. The guy was distraught. He obviously needed cheering up.

Tom was about to go after him when he was distracted by the front doors noisily bursting open, and Ben threateningly growling.

'There yer be, yer little fucker,' said a voice that Tom recognised with horror and disbelief, 'I got yer, at last.'

Tom spun around, a sinking feeling in his stomach. 'Heel!' he immediately shouted to the dog who, hackles raised and still growling, reluctantly, but nevertheless obediently backed up to that position.

The four Irishmen had spread themselves in a straight line across the foyer, each of them with a firearm aimed directly at Tom's head. The smile of satisfaction spread across the older one's face - Terry, on the left of the group - made the vulnerable youth swallow hard. He could see this man was serious, out to kill, he knew he meant it, and he realised Patrick would not be able to stop him this time. He looked far too determined. There was no way was he going to listen to reason.

'What do you want?' Tom forced himself to ask, saying it quickly in the hope that no nervousness could be detected in his voice that way.

'You, yer little fucker,' Terry exploded, ignoring the steely side-ways look slung at him from Patrick.

Tom could see the finger tightening on the trigger as the man spoke. His face was as black as thunderclouds. Evil was stamped all over him, and positively radiating. The man was almost shaking with his rage, unable to contain himself. This was the moment he had for so long been waiting - this was payback time!

He knew the man would not be hanging around. That was plainly written on his face. Another second or two and it would all be over, and he would be dead, for he knew it would be pointless him trying to run. He would never outrun a bullet. But there was no point in Ben being killed too, as he surely would be if stayed there, he considered. With a look and a pointed finger, Tom sent the dog upstairs before taking a deep breath, which he guessed would probably be his last. He stood upright, proud, and he waited, with his only concession to the fear being choosing to close his eyes. He didn't want to see the gun go off. His imagination would suffice.

The wait was short. There was a loud explosion as the sound of the gunshot echoed around the foyer and Tom fell to the floor.

'Bastard! Bastard! Bastard!'

Tom heard the words agonizingly screamed. He was not dead? He couldn't be - he could still hear! Surely, you couldn't hear anything if you were dead? Besides he hadn't felt anything. And then he wondered: did you actually feel anything when you died? Perhaps this was it. Perhaps this *was* after death. Opening his eyes, he saw the tall Irishman nursing his hand with blood steadily dripping from it. His gun was lying on the floor a few feet away from him.

'The rest of you, drop 'em, too!' Stefan snapped the order from half way down the stairs, with the gun in his right hand still smouldering, and the dog stood by his side somehow knowing that was where he should be. Slowly, the man continued the rest of the journey down the stairs with authority, all the time watching them closely for the slightest movement, and ready to react instantly. The dog followed him, and then went over to check on his master lying on the floor.

'Not a chance,' sneered Patrick, who was not one to be so easily beaten. 'There are still three of us left. You couldn't possibly kill all three, not before one of us got you. You might get one, you might not, but we'd sure finish you off, and that bloody dog, long before you had a chance of a second shot, that's for sure. Now,' he continued, a confident smile spreading across the sinister bony face as he shifted his aim across to Stefan. 'How lucky do you feel? You going to go for it, or are you going to see sense and throw your gun down?'

Tom's fingers crept forward. He stared up at the Irishmen, watching them closely lest one of them should sense his movement. Inch by inch his hand stealthily edged across the floor, creeping slowly forward until his forefinger was able to wrap itself around the trigger guard. Gradually he pulled Terry's dropped gun back towards him. Nobody had noticed. He wondered, as he drew the weapon closer, would he be able to do it? Would he be able to aim the gun at one of them and pull the trigger? Could he actually kill someone? Then he remembered his father with his head splattered across the windscreen, and the eyeball that had so menacingly dangled in front of him. Yes, he knew he could.

Randy charged in through the door. 'Man! What the bloody hell was that . . .'

The voice faded out as the young man grasped the situation. Stopping abruptly he stood there feeling foolish, impotent, and wondering what would happen next. Who had the advantage?

Tom profited from the sudden diversion. In one swift movement he jumped to his feet, confidently waving the gun in front of him at the Irishmen. Aiming at them each in turn, not able to make his mind up which one he should settle for, he smiled overtly and wondered which one of them he would mostly like to shoot. He was so engrossed in taunting them, enjoying having the upper hand, that he missed seeing the downstairs door to the flat open slightly.

'Careful, Tom. That could quite easily go off,' Stefan warned him from behind.

'Good!' Tom said, with enough venom to convince the Irish not to be foolish; that they would be stupid to try anything - he really meant it!

Karl cursed inwardly on seeing Tom through the crack in the door. He had the three gunmen loosely covered. The tall one on the far end he could see was damaged, nursing his wound. He was no threat now. If anything started, of the remainder he knew that Stefan would go for the middle one first. That was Patrick. He was confident he could definitely take out one of the other two with the gun in his right hand, but he knew he could only accurately aim one gun at a time. The gun in his left hand might take out the other one if let off in the general direction. But if it didn't it could easily hit Tom instead. The standoff was no good like this, he decided. He would have to come out behind them and show himself. That way, he hoped, Tom should have the sense to move out of his line of fire.

'Drop your weapons,' Karl ordered, stepping out of the doorway. 'I think you'll find we have the advantage now.'

Tom, whose main concern was with threatening the thugs in front of him, enjoying the power over them that the possession of the firearm offered, was startled by the demanding voice, and at Karl's sudden appearance. The slight flinching movement of his surprise was enough:

the gun involuntarily discharged twice, rapidly. With deafening sound in the confined foyer, the first shot hit Patrick's leg somewhere above his knee, the second, where the gun had violently recoiled, buried itself in the ceiling. Patrick screamed out in agony, falling to one knee as the scorching metal passed through his leg. The pain causing him to momentarily lose his concentration too so that now his gun discharged, the bullet whizzing slightly upwards and passing by Tom's ear with an evil zinging sound. There was a sickening thud as it found a home in Stefan's chest. The minder staggered, falling backwards on to the bottom stairs; the force expelling the last of the life sustaining air from his lungs with one loud gasp.

Seizing opportunity out of the chaos, Randy bolted out of the foyer and back into the comparative safety of the disco area, tightly gripping the door handles together so no one could come in. Karl moved quickly. Stepping forward he brought his two gun barrels down hard on the backs of the necks of the remaining two Irishmen. Neither of them had time to fire a shot. Both slumped forwards crumbling into dazed heaps on the floor on either side of Patrick, who now dared not move. The Alsatian's teeth were already well sunken into the back of his neck.

'Oh, shit!' Tom exclaimed, the tell-tale whispers of smoke still wafting from the barrel of his gun, and the strange cordite smell fascinating his nose.

'Oh, man!' Randy, sensing that no further gunfire might mean it was safe for him to return, peered through the slightly opened door.

Ashen-faced, Tom rushed across to check on Stefan, kneeling down beside the lifeless body. 'Oh, God. He's dead! It was all my fault!' he shouted, turning towards Karl who had by now disarmed the gunmen and was keeping watch on them carefully, and covering them with his gun.

The minder looked back at him, shocked. Tom stared up into the man's eyes, his own starting to water. He didn't know what more he should say; what he could say. The man's colleague, his close friend, had been shot dead, killed, and all because of his stupidity.

Then, strangely, Tom thought he noticed a change creep across Karl's face, one he couldn't understand. It was only a hint, a mere fleeting shadow, a minute change in the expression, but it was definitely there. Was that the start of a poorly concealed grin he could see? Was the man fighting to hold back something? Laughter? It looked like it. No! What? Tom looked back at Stefan's motionless body, staring at it, his eyes watering so much he had to wipe them to see properly. Perhaps, that was a professional's way of dealing with death, he thought. Maybe that was how they coped - they were trained to laugh at it.

Sensing everything was under control, Ben released his grip on the Irishman's neck and bounded over to inspect Stefan. Pawing the man, he started licking his face furiously. The minder opened his left eye, and then both eyes. Spluttering, pushing the saliva-slopping dog away from him, he looked up at Tom strangely, and then sat bolt upright with a humongous grin on his face. Tom jumped, falling backwards onto the floor. Both minders now exploded into fits of laughter. Tears started to roll down Stefan's cheeks and he had to double forward to try to stop the mirthful pain that was threatening to destroy him, whilst still fighting off the dog's over-zealous licking attentions.

'But, but, you're dead!' Tom blurted out, the foolishness of the statement only increasing the poor man's laughter pain further as he erupted once more.

'Ah, by fuckin' Jeeesus!' Terry blasphemed, devastated at seeing the man not only alive, but joking around. It was a sentiment echoed by his brothers.

'But why ain't you dead, man?' Randy demanded, cautiously creeping all the way in, his eyes open unnaturally wide; agog. He was fearful in case he should hear something he didn't want to hear; something supernatural.

'I reckon he must've taken his proMAX this morning,' Karl managed to say, amidst more hysteria.

The Irishmen looked at each other, cussing loudly. They knew exactly what he meant. Randy and Tom were stupidly amazed, each wondering how taking a tablet in the morning could stop someone from being shot dead. Bewildered, Randy lifted an enquiring eyebrow.

'This is proMAX,' explained Stefan, still manically laughing whilst, fumbling, unbuttoning his shirt to reveal the famous brand of body armour underneath.

'Man, that's good news,' Randy stated. 'I's thought for a minute you might be aliens or ghosts or something weird!'

Tom felt beyond foolish. Trying to deflect everyone's attention away from his naivety, his utter stupidity, he asked, 'So, what are we going to do with these?' He pointed at their prisoners.

'Throw them out, I suppose. We don't want them in here making the place look untidy, do we? Maybe by now they've learnt their lesson - to leave you alone. If not, we'll kill them next time,' Karl said, smiling at them. Holding one of the main doors open he gestured for them to get out.

'I hope you know when you're outclassed,' Stefan said, looking into the eyes of each of the walking wounded as pathetically they staggered out: Patrick limping badly on his blood soaked leg, Terry still nursing his bullet grazed hand, and the other two rubbing the backs of their necks.

Ben joined them at the door to watch, and insisted on dutifully barking at each of them in turn as they departed.

'Perhaps that's the last we shall see of them,' Tom said, hopefully.

'I's doubts it, man,' Randy stated, 'Patrick don't ever give in. That's why Phil kept him. They will be back - they's just be more careful next time. Shit, man!' he swore on noticing the small group congregating outside. 'We's open in fifteen minutes and I's ain't nowhere near ready. Ain't nobody else here yet?'

CHAPTER 23

It was nearly a month before either the injured Patrick or Terry were to be seen around the town again, both of them preferring to lie low and lick their wounds. Business carried on pretty much as normal for the gang throughout this time, with a few minor but necessary modifications. The two Italian brothers carried out the London run, to buy the drugs, competently every week without Patrick's assistance. They, with the help of the three youths, covered the supplying of the clubs each night, whilst the remaining two Irishmen collected the imposed dues from all the other venues and vendors. The extra five percent they were demanding was making life hard for more than a few and 'For Sale' signs started to appear on several of the buildings. Some of the vendors were already finding they were eating into their savings to meet the new charges, and the season wasn't yet over. There would be harder times to come.

Bob still remained missing. Patrick guessed he had deserted them when things became hot on the night of the Membury incident, although how he would have known very much about all that was beyond him.

A sense of normality prevailed at the Elephant's Nest. With the legal formalities over the inheritance completed, everything now belonged to Tom. He was his own master, at last. Derek and Beryl still competently managed the nightclub, but now by being the actual top dog, Tom discovered there was a whole lot of work for him to do too.

There were no further threats from the Irishmen. No attempt to collect any levy by them. Those who supplied the drugs at the club each night never mentioned anything about the gang's fortunes. They, now it seemed always to be the three young lads, had been well behaved and courteous to the point of becoming friendly. And business had been extremely good those few weeks with the place heaving, and literally packed to its very limits nearly every night.

Time had healed things somewhat for Randy who had forgotten all about Caroline - dismissed her from his thoughts entirely. He was back to being his normal everyday happy-go-lucky self again. And Tom's affections towards Denise had rapidly cooled too. That may have been due to the extra responsibility of being in overall charge, with all the additional work involved leaving little time for recreation. Tom didn't know, or perhaps didn't want to admit the reason, but it had certainly cooled between them and that made him happy - more than that, he was relieved to feel free again. He remained good friends with Denise and she still worked at the club, a situation that continued to be beneficial to both of them, but she was no longer any kind of a sexual attraction.

Putting the relationship on the back burner was a mutual decision, both of them realising that anything there was between them would have only been sexual and of the moment - their hormones demanding they did something to satisfy them. It wasn't true love, not by a long way. So they had broken up with no tears, and no animosity - just a smile and a few encouraging words.

Tom knew he would always remember Denise with affection. She had been his first, and that alone made her memorable. He guessed she would probably remember him likewise. But after all the excitement of doing it for the first time, and the relief of finally losing his virginity, he had found there was no longer a want, a need, to have sex with her. There was very little that seemed to turn him on these days, and whatever did, he dismissed. He was far too busy.

In the routine of things, every morning Tom would phone his mother to see how she was, and every early evening before opening time she would invariably phone him. It had become almost a ritual. She appeared to be happy enough these days, coping with everything well, and apparently even enjoying herself on some days - perhaps most days. It seemed that she was meeting someone new almost every day now, someone important, or famous, or else they were all going out to some fantastic 'do' - one that it would be 'simply unforgivable' to miss.

Of course, Mary hadn't forgotten her husband. She thought about him every day. But Mary was the realist type - she knew there was no point in throwing the rest of her life away in some eternal grieving. That would achieve nothing. She had, it seemed, almost miraculously been given the opportunity to experience the kind of life that most people would give their right arm for – and she wasn't silly enough to let it pass her by. John was John. He was an enormous and a wonderful part of her life – but a part that she, with her methodical ways, had managed to file away in a very special place where, from time to time, she could revisit it and spend tender moments again. It was all still there – but not now.

Life at the Elephant's Nest had become so much of a boring routine that Karl and Stefan decided it was safe enough for them to relax a little. They started to spend considerable time 'only a phone call away, if we're needed'. Tom didn't mind. It was beginning to annoy him knowing they were always around; always watching. He was, in a way, pleased when they weren't there. After all, it looked as if the gang had given up on pressuring them after the incident in the foyer. They didn't appear to be a threat anymore.

It was around lunchtime on that hot Wednesday when Randy burst into the office with a large wad of assorted envelopes in his hand. 'Hey, man, you's loads of post,' he told Tom.

'Great! I've only this minute finished going through yesterday's little lot! What I need is a secretary!' Tom stated, looking up at the wall clock to discover it was already one o'clock.

'No you don't, man. What you need is a break. Man, you ain't taken five minutes off in a month. How's about you and I's spending a few hours away from here today? You's been here all this time and you still ain't seen half the town yet, man. Not proper. I's know where we can get a wicked all day breakfast!'

Tom's taste buds did the deciding for him. Since his mother had left, meals were something neither him nor Randy had prioritised correctly, most days surviving on toast in the mornings, supplemented only by burgers or hot dogs from the club's cafeteria later. The thought of fresh sizzling bacon, sausages, baked beans, fried tomatoes, mushrooms, runny eggs . . .

Ten minutes later they were sat at the table in the window of Tiffany's sipping their hot coffees, and contentedly watching the world go by whilst waiting for the breakfasts to be freshly cooked.

Tom's mobile rang. 'Hello,' he said.

'I thought we agreed you'd tell us if you were going out,' the voice said.

'Karl! Oh, shit! Sorry. Totally forgot,' Tom lied, adding, 'Randy and I have only popped out for a bite to eat. We're in Tiffany's. That's only around . . .'

'I know where it is,' Karl butted in, 'we saw you go in there.'

Tom spun around on his seat, nearly knocking the two enormous breakfasts that were then arriving at the table out of the poor woman's hands. Peering out of the window he scanned up and down the street looking for the minders. There were lots of people out there busying around, all going about their business, but no sign of Karl or Stefan.

'Where are you?' Tom asked, holding his 'wait a mo' finger up in reply to Randy's enquiring expression.

'Almost directly opposite, and waving at you like some demented moron,' came the reply. 'Come over and join us when you've finished your meal.' There was a click as the line went dead.

'Karl's over the road. Wants us to join him in minute. Damned if I can see him, though!' Tom explained to Randy, who then started to look as well.

'There they are, man. Both of them,' Randy exclaimed, 'sitting just inside Dorothy's at the first table.'

'What on earth are they doing in there?' Tom queried.

'Oh,' Randy looked a bit sheepish, suddenly remembering an omission. 'I's only found out a couple of days ago myself, man. I's meant to tell you, but I's forgot all about it. That's where they go, man, when they goes out. They's both gay. They's an item. Dorothy's is now their local, man. Yeah, man, it turns out that Jason always hires gay blokes to look after Caroline – did the same for his wife when she was alive. There's no complications then.'

'No!'

'Not a problem, is it, man?'

'No, of course it isn't. It's . . . I . . . But . . . But, they're such hard nuts! Fighters! Gunmen! Killers, even! They're gay? They're really gay? I would never have guessed!'

'Don't all have handbags and high heels, darling!' Randy quipped, pursing his lips.

Tom grinned, thumping him teasingly, before they both started tucking in to the immense breakfasts in front of them. Fifteen minutes later, thoroughly satisfied with the meal and suitably bloated, they quickly paid the bill and left. Crossing the busy street they went into the obviously very popular - judging by the numbers there - gay club. Tom was thinking how fortunate they were that their place didn't open in the afternoons as well as the evenings, and was about to whisper that into Randy's ear, when he noticed some familiar faces. More than a few. Before he could question his friend on what they would all be doing in there, a shrill voice screamed into a microphone from the stage at the far end. Tom's head shot around so that he could see who it was, and what was happening. Was that a woman on the stage?

'Oh, my God!' Doris exclaimed from her vantage point. 'Look everybody, look by the door! Oh, my chickadees! It's Prince Charming. My Prince has come! Ooh! Don't you wish? He could come over me any day, I'll tell yer!' She flicked the hair of her long blonde wig back over her shoulder in an outrageously camp fashion as her audience roared their appreciation. 'Every day would be better,' she added, to even greater appreciation. Falling to her knees she started to reverently worship Tom, 'We are not worthy. We are not worthy.'

Tom felt himself go bright red. By now, Randy, Karl, Stefan, in fact everybody there, were creasing themselves.

'Blow her a big kiss, man,' Randy only just managed to get out.

Tom, at a loss what else to do, did.

'Ooh! Did you see that? I've scored! Me luck's in! I'll see you later, lovey, after the show,' Doris announced, before totally ignoring him and resuming her normal repertoire.

Tom apprehensively sat down at the table, facing Karl. Randy was about to go to the bar when Stefan pushed him into the seat next to Tom, saying, 'I'll get them. What are you having?'

They both ordered a vodka and coke before Tom asked, 'What's everybody doing in here? I know quite a few of these people. Are they all gay? There's Dave from the Inferno - surely not? Sam, Mike and Graham. We saw them here before, but Doug, our security bloke? George? George from the ice cream parlour? He's married, isn't he? He said he was. And isn't that Ollie over there? And there's . . .'

'All right! All right! You sound like a talking Who's Who,' Karl laughed. 'No, they're not all gay. Not all of them, anyway.

'There's a bit of a meeting going on here later. All those who are struggling to pay the new levies or are opposed to them are having a get together here at three o'clock. It's one of the few places that's big enough. They couldn't hold it at the Inferno, for obvious reasons, and you aren't actually paying at the moment so they thought it unfair to ask you to put it on. Some have just come a bit early to watch the show and have a laugh first. Doris is good, isn't she?'

'It's okay.' Stefan, returning, joined in the conversation as he placed the drinks on the table. 'You could bring your grandmother here in the afternoons. There are lots of straight people who come here just to see the matinee. They've got a pop group on later, and then a comedian after that, I think. Or is it the other way round?'

It was the pop group first - a well-known band from yesteryear who had the whole audience singing their old hits along with them. By that time the club was heaving; packed solid - partly because the dungeon area was always politely curtained off in the afternoons, considerably cutting down the available space. The group were so well received they had to do two encores before the audience would let them go, and then only reluctantly. The comedian who followed was brilliant too, with the crowd demanding more each time he tried to finish, so it was as late as three-twenty before Doris could get the stage again to tell everybody that the place was closing until six o'clock. Those not staying for the meeting should drink up and leave.

The meeting proper started nearer to four o'clock with self-elected chairperson, Doris, minus the drag but still heavily made up, on stage trying to keep order. Tom, who by then even after pacing himself was on his fourth drink, looked about him trying to count how many people had stayed behind for the meeting. Finding it difficult, though he guessed about a hundred, he decided he ought not have any more. Randy, who was two drinks ahead of him, he noticed, seemed unaffected by the drink.

'Order! Order!' Doris shouted. Her partner, Rod, standing below the stage in front of her with his arms folded as if in some sign of authority pulled himself up to his full stature and sniffed long and hard as he glared into the gathering. It went quiet.

'Now, we all know why we're here,' she continued. 'It's the fifteen percent levy. Some, like ourselves, simply can't afford to pay that much.

Others, the few who can afford it, simply don't want to pay that much. And who can blame them? It's an exorbitant tax!

'Most of you know, or will have gathered by now, that this establishment was fortunate when Phil was running things. We didn't pay anything then. He avoided us like the plague! But now, out of the blue, we are having to find that fifteen percent just like all of you. And like most of you, it's an amount that isn't there - one that we can't budget for.

'These stupid Irishmen don't seem to realise that a fifteen percent tax on gross doesn't simply mean we only have to raise our prices by fifteen percent to maintain the status quo. We all know that isn't so. Massive price increases would be needed to find that extra five per cent. Prices that people wouldn't pay! Who would come here if we had to charge nearly three pounds a pint? Not many, I'm sure! But the Irish are so thick that they haven't got enough brains to see that! So most of us are now working for nothing, and some are losing money.

'Phil's ten percent, even though some thought that was ambitious, never put anybody out of business. Phil, the arsehole that he was, made this place what it is today – and dare I say it? - made most people here what they are today. Most are a damn sight more successful today than they ever would have been if he hadn't come here, that's for sure! Yes, he took that ten percent off all of you. But he knew that was the limit he could go to. He was clever. That amount did turn out to be affordable – by everybody.

'Yes, I know he lived like a Lord. The Lord of the Manor living off of your backs and off all your hard work - and his gang did too. You only have to take a look at these three lads,' Doris pointed out Sam, Mike and Graham, 'sat there spilling their beers all over what must be at least three grand's worth of clothing, to see what I mean.

'Nevertheless, Phil also invested heavily in this place. I mean God only knows what it cost him to have the harbour dredged, or laying that new bit of road leading up to it. We should all remember that he had that started within three months of him arriving here - long before he'd made very much money out of any of us. He invested in all of us - even those who paid him nothing at all like ourselves. We all benefited considerably.

'Now, I know many of you found the drug scene hard to accept at first - but you're all pretty liberal minded about it now, aren't you? The lack of proper policing, that worried you all once - but now nobody even thinks about it. Would all the clubs, bars and restaurants be staying open as late as they are, and making all that money, were we to be properly policed? You know they wouldn't, not here, not in the West of England - this ain't London or Manchester! But it's the things like these, the things that we get away with that make this place so successful - things that have only come about because of Phil. They are what bring the people here. Take them away, have a level playing field with all the other resorts, and in no time at all we'd land up with next to nothing.

'What I'm trying to say in my own stupid way is, were it to be possible: come back Phil, all is forgiven. Because although we have to find a way of getting rid of these Irish idiots - and that's why we're all here now, they have got to go - we still have to find someone to take their place. A person who could keep this town prosperous, and one that we could all accept. Now, how do we go about this? How do we get rid of the Irish? And who could, or would, be their successor? Has anybody got ideas - any suggestions?'

Heads turned in all directions, with everyone looking at everyone else to see who would have something to say. After some time it was Sam who stood up.

'Doris, darling, thank-you so much for mentioning our clothes,' he said.

She smiled down at him, giving him a camp, over-the-top, bow.

He waited for the loud cheer to subside before continuing, 'And thank-you everybody else for not ripping them off our backs!' Another cheer, louder, and more laughter. 'How to get rid of the Irish? That we don't know any more than you do. But we do have the perfect person in mind to replace them.

'I promise you that should you be able to get rid of the Irish there is someone who would be prepared to take over, and I guarantee it wouldn't be anything like fifteen percent they wanted. They have already categorically stated - watch my lips - five percent!'

A unified gasp went around the club.

'Who is it?' Doris asked. Several others too, but she had the microphone. 'Do we know them?'

'That we don't really want to say at the moment unless we have to. Not while Patrick and his brothers are still at large. But I promise everybody he'll be okay for the job.'

Stefan stood up. 'Would anybody mind if a comparative outsider put his oar into the water?' he asked.

Doris waited. There were no dissents. 'No, nobody minds. Say your piece, lovey,' she said.

'I'm not a greatly religious person, but I do know that of the thirteen present at the Last Supper, one turned traitor for a few pieces of silver. Here we number over a hundred. With no disrespect to anyone intended, if these Irish were to get wind of what your intentions are, and were they then to offer enough silver, how many of those here might feel tempted to become a Judas? Secret information that's held by a hundred people is hardly secret at all.

'I think it would be prudent to establish a goal today, one that everyone could sign their agreement to, and then to elect a small working committee of no more than say nine or ten people to plan and organise things. This committee alone should be privy to all the finer details such as who's who, who will be doing what, and when. That way you're less likely to be betrayed.'

'Sounds good to me,' Doris said, 'I'll put it to the vote. Hands up all those in favour of electing a small working committee.' A sea of hands flew into the air. 'And those against this?' No hands. 'Then it's unanimous. We shall elect a committee. So, now I suppose it's: hands up all those who would like to stand for election to this committee.'

No hands. Not one. The drag queen waited patiently. A whole minute passed and there were still no hands. Doris began to look flustered. What now?

Sam, who no one had noticed was using his mobile phone throughout the whole time, walked over and leapt up onto the stage. Grabbing the microphone from out of Doris' hand, he put the phone's earpiece up to it.

'You fucking load of lily-livered bastards! What are you? You're nothing more than bunch of pissin' wankers! I don't know why I ever fuckin' bothered with any of you! You stick some fucking hands up there, you fucking load of shites, or you'll all be sorry!'

There was utter silence. Shocked, nobody moved for a moment. Then all at once a multitude of hands shot into the air.

CHAPTER 24

With hindsight, it is doubtful if the trader's meeting would have been held at Dorothy's, especially on such an easily liquor-laden afternoon as they always were on Wednesdays. The relaxing atmosphere, the good entertainment, fun and merriment, had meant that all present had somewhat succumbed to the demon drink by the time the meeting started. So much so that nobody realised Odd-Socks was still present, sitting quietly in the corner supping his pint - one that he would no doubt have bummed off someone earlier. Sitting, supping, and taking it all in.

It would have been far better, with hindsight, to have asked to use the Elephant's Nest where with no afternoon bar staff it would have been a much more sober affair, or perhaps to have even found an accommodating venue a few miles up the road in Weston-Super-Mare. Driving to the latter would have meant that many would have had to abstain from drinking alcohol, so in either of those places enough people would have been sober. Odd-Socks would have been noticed. But, it was far too late for that now, the meeting had been held.

The whole idea of having a meeting at all, something never before considered by the traders, belonged to Dave, Doris and Rod. Or so they thought. But they were wrong. They may have arranged it, thinking it was their baby, but unknown to them the original idea had been Phil's. Sam, Mike and Graham had for more than a week skilfully planted the seeds in their minds. Seeds that grew.

It was exactly a week after Bay View had been burnt to the ground with, as everybody believed, Phil inside it, that Sam received a strange phone call. A male nurse from the Frenchay Hospital in Bristol informed him that someone, on whom they had performed emergency surgery and who was still quite poorly, was being transferred to a certain BUPA hospital in Bristol to recover. This person, who he said didn't want to be named, and especially didn't want anybody else to know where he was, urgently wanted Sam to visit him.

Sam couldn't think who it could be. Who did he know that would be taken to a hospital in Bristol for treatment? Not family, they were hundreds of miles away, and anyway they didn't have a clue where he was living. It was better that way. Friends? Perhaps. But friends that would be close enough to ask for him would have been local, and he would have known if any of them had suffered an accident. And anyway, why all the subterfuge? It didn't sound right. Suspecting a possible hoax, a wind-up by one of his mates, he half-mindedly thought of ignoring it. However, in the end curiosity got the better of him. On the pretext of going shopping for clothes, he decided to get up early and go to the hospital the very next day.

Early for Sam was nine o'clock, extremely early, but he had still shaved, showered, and had taken breakfast quickly enough for him to arrive at the hospital in Durdham Down before ten. Feeling a pudding head at having to ask if he could visit he didn't know who except that they'd been transferred there recently and wanted to see him, he was relieved when, instead of bursting into fits of laughter, as he'd half expected should it have been a joke, he was led down the corridor and shown into a private room. There, he discovered most of the head of the occupant, the person lying in the bed, was covered in bandages, so too were their arms.

'Hello,' he said, tentatively walking up to the bed, 'I'm Sam. I believe you wanted to see me. Do I know you?'

With difficulty the patient wriggled himself up in the bed, turning until he was sitting on the side of it and able to reach the keyboard on the bedside table. The bandaged fingers made many errors, often hitting two keys at once, as they typed away frantically.

'Yes, you know me well. Tell no-one. Bandages come off day after tomorrow. Will be able to talk then. Please come back and see me then. Important you don't tell anyone,' Sam managed to decipher from the disaster that was actually written on the monitor screen.

Saying he would come back, now more curious than ever, Sam wished him well and left. His clever sideways glance at the chart on the bottom of the bed as he departed revealed nothing. Strangely, the section titled: Patient's Name was filled in with only a long number. Stopping off in the city centre before driving back to Seathorpe, Sam bought a leather jacket deliberately one size too large. Having to exchange this would suffice as an excuse to cover his next visit.

The two days of waiting dragged. Sam's mind often wandered in that time, visualising the patient in the hospital. Who was it? What did he want with him? This unusual preoccupation had not passed unnoticed by Mike and Graham. Suspecting he was possibly getting serious over a girl, or worse, had received the bad news – the test was blue – she was pregnant, they teased him ruthlessly. Sam wished he could tell them, but he knew he mustn't. Not yet, anyway.

The day came at last. Sam arrived at the private room around two-thirty. He had waited until the afternoon before visiting in case the bandages hadn't been removed earlier and he may have had to wait around. Taking a deep breath, he opened the door and walked in. The man in the bed turned towards him.

'Hello, Sam. Come in and sit down.' the hoarse, croaky voice said, 'Over here by the bed. I can't talk too well, yet. They say the voice will be all right in a few days, so you'll have to bear with me.'

Sam gulped. Moving up to the bed, he quickly manoeuvred the chair around before sitting, so he could face the man. He was not a pretty sight: his hair was gone, his scalp burnt a painfully sore scabby red colour with patches of dried yellow puss. There were obvious burns to his face too, with two massive plasters, X fashion, across the bridge of his nose. Slowly, a realisation dawned on him.

'Phil?' he queried.

'Hard to believe, isn't it?'

'But, it said in the paper that the remains of your body were found in the ashes of Bay View. Everybody thinks you're dead! The body was even identified as you!'

'I know. I want it to stay that way for now.'

'It's a job to tell if it's really you. You certainly look a bit like the Phil we all knew, but you sure as hell don't sound like him,' Sam remarked.

'Oh, don't make me shout, swear and crash around to prove who I am, the pain would be too much! I told Dave it was only an act. He didn't believe me either. I'm not really like that, I only did all that to keep people in order.'

'Certainly used to work! Something's still bothering me, though. Two things, really.'

'What?'

'Firstly, who's body did they find after the fire and why did they say it was yours? Secondly, why did you ask for me to come and see you? Why me? Why not Dave, or Sid, or one of the others that you go back a lot further with? Why me?'

'The body was Bob. They thought it was me because I put my watch and rings on him before I got away. Seems that Patrick and his brothers weren't the only ones who wanted me out the way. You see, that night I'd arranged with someone to steal the drugs from Membury. I think everybody must know by now it was the lot from the Ellie who did it - the old man getting killed in the bargain.'

Sam grunted, 'Everybody thinks that, but nobody's admitted it. Go on.'

'Well, it all went tits up that night, resulting in Membury Services being blown up, big style. A gun that Patrick was bringing down here, he bought it there as well. It all got very hairy. Nobody really knew at the time who was alive and who was dead. But the drugs did get back to the Ellie. I picked them up from there, and had just got back to Bay View with them when Patrick and the Italians turned up. I only managed to get away by throwing the bag of goodies at them.

'Running indoors I caught sight of someone in the darkness. Someone who was carrying a two gallon can. I can only guess why. Anyway, ignoring him I rushed straight through the house and out the back door, hiding behind one of the bushes. Patrick and the other two chased in after me a few seconds later and in the darkness they mistook this person for me and shot him full of holes. Then they either set light to the place, or the can this person was carrying was hit by a bullet and exploded. Who knows? But the place erupted in flames.

'Hearing them drive off, I went back inside to discover that the unknown person they'd mistakenly killed in the darkness thinking it was me, was actually Bob. Seizing the opportunity, I put my watch and rings on him so anyone would think it was really me. All this time the fire was getting worse, and getting closer to another petrol can he'd placed near the door. Unfortunately, before I could get out safely, the sheer heat in there ignited it and there was a massive explosion, a fireball that sent me flying, and badly burning me as you can see. But obviously I did manage to get away. I don't know how I did it, but I walked all the way to the village half a mile up the road and stole a car which I somehow drove to Bristol. That should cover your first question. As for the second question, why you, well . . .

'When you think you're done for, that your time has finally come and you're facing death head on, you suddenly realise how many things you've left undone in your life. Things that you should have put right, things for which you forever find excuses to put off doing. There's one big thing I need to put right, right now.'

'What's that?'

Phil paused for quite some time, then said, 'There's no easy way of saying it, son, so I'll come straight out with it. Sam, I'm your father. Your real father.'

'What? Rubbish! Crap!' Sam stood up.

'It's true. I used to go out with your mother, Jean, the same time as Reggie did. She couldn't make her mind up which of us she wanted. First me, then him, then back to me. She finally picked him. They arranged a rush wedding, so she couldn't change her mind again, and then a month later she discovered she was two months pregnant. It had to be mine, she hadn't done it with Reggie before the wedding. You know how religious he is, he wouldn't go all the way until after they were married. He was always the goody, goody and I was the baddy.

'Of course, I offered to pay for everything, to cover all the expenses, buy clothes, pay for your schooling and all that, but she'd have none of it. She wouldn't take a penny in case Reggie found out. He still thinks you're his to this day.'

Sam sat back down, his face ashen.

Phil continued, 'I moved away, it was thought best at the time, and for sixteen years, until you upped and ran off, all I ever knew of you was what your mother would secretly put in a Christmas card once a year. A few photos. There are about twenty photos of you growing up, and I still have them all. I've even kept the lock of your hair she sent me from your first haircut. Thankfully, they were too secret to leave at home so they are kept in a bank deposit box, or else they would have been destroyed along with everything else in the fire.

'The only other time she ever made contact with me was the week you had that really big row and ran away. She knew you and Reggie could never get on, and she was so frightened that one of those fights you frequently had would lead to the death of one of you. She didn't want that, so she didn't want you back. She pleaded for me to find you and to watch out for you. How much can I trust you, Sam?'

'I might be a shit at times, but I can be trusted. Why?'

'Remember when you had that pathetic job at Burger King in the West End? I forced Graham to pal up with you, to get you drunk that Friday night so you would miss work and be sacked. When he told you not to worry, that he could find you top paying work at the seaside it was pretty obvious you'd take it.'

'The little shit!'

'Would you rather still be clearing those tables in London for peanuts?'

'No, of course not. Christ! I just thought I was lucky meeting him! Lucky to get the job. You know, it's always puzzled me why I could get away with so much more than all the others. Why you rarely bawled me out. Now I know. God! You really don't want to know some of the strokes I've pulled!'

'What, like holding back and selling some of my stuff at Dorothy's? I'm not stupid. I knew. As for Graham, you mustn't have a go at him. He couldn't have told you for fear of what I'd do to him, although it's surprising he didn't mention something once he thought I was dead. Little crack-head's probably been too busy getting his arse banged by Mike, I suppose!'

'You know about that too?' Sam was shocked.

'Known a long time.'

'But you're so anti-gay!'

'Not really, it's just had to look that way. There are reasons, but I can't tell you about them now. Not until I've cleared it with someone else. Someone special who knows you too. Oh, God! What a tangled web we weave . . . I certainly have!' Phil said, the tears painfully welling up in his eyes.

Sam wanted to squeeze Phil's hand affectionately but daren't, the bandages suggesting the tenderness there would be beneath, so he placed his hand on his shoulder instead. 'It's okay, Dad,' he said, with wet eyes, 'Its okay.'

CHAPTER 25

Odd-Socks was a strange character – odd! One who it would be difficult to put an age to, but if you had to you would probably say very much the wrong side of sixty, and then be shocked when you saw him leaping down the road like a stick insect on speed. Nobody knew where he lived, or seemed to know much about him at all, not even his proper name. To everyone he was always just Odd-Socks. He had acquired that label for the obvious reason that he was never to be seen wearing a matching pair. Probably, he didn't possess such a luxury.

There were rumours that the old man was the last of the fishermen, one who had stayed behind, but no one seemed to really know for sure. Many pitied the man who would be seen pushing his banana coloured bicycle with a trailer at the back and a basket on the front through the town looking for scrap iron, thrown out old clothes, or anything that might make him a pound or two. Others held him in contempt for his persistent begging. But either way, Odd-Socks was an integral part of Seathorpe.

That day he had done well around the town, picking up nearly ten pounds by his persistence. Feeling like a drink, as he often did mid-afternoon, he decided to pop into Dorothy's to see if he could cadge a pint off of somebody. Should he be unlucky in his quest it didn't really matter, he had plenty of money with which to buy one for himself, although that was an option he tried not to consider. Dorothy's had long been one of odd-Socks favourite haunts when he fancied a drink for it was a place where they never got violent, and they never threw him out like so many other places often did.

Poor, and getting old the man may have been, but with poverty often comes a sharpness. When, at around three-thirty on that day, Doris had asked all those not connected with the meeting to leave, Odd-Socks had a feeling, a hunch that he was about to discover a juicy bone. One with more than a morsel of fat left on it. He edged himself into the corner and waited quietly. Such a regular sight was Odd-Socks, such an insignificance, that no-one noticed him. He could probably have sat anywhere amongst the crowd and not been seen, but he chose the corner and listened intently.

Abandoning his push-bike, for that was all it was - a push bike, it went far too slow and was too laborious to be ridden with the attached trailer - the old man all but sprinted down the road when the meeting broke up. Hardly slowing to catch his breath, and with his long gangly arms and legs going like comical pistons, he made it to the back door in Bridlington Street in a few short minutes. What he knew would be worth a fortune!

Opening the door, Andrew let the man in. Patrick, behind the desk, withdrew his hand from where it had hovered over the Colt 45, and asked, 'What do you want?'

'Oh, I don't want anything,' Odd-Socks replied in an astonishing posh Oxford accent. 'It is you who may be wanting something. I know of a secret; some knowledge that is of great importance to you!'

'A secret, eh? What's the secret?'

'That, Patrick, my dear boy, will cost you!'

'Will it now? How much?'

'Oh, let me think. Yes. It has to be worth at least five hundred pounds to you, I would imagine.'

'Ah, by Jeeesus!' Andrew exclaimed. 'Let's rough the bastard up. He'll soon be tellin' us his bloody secret then!'

Patrick waved a hand for his brother to be quiet. Up until then he had suffered the old man with humour, but the moment he'd mentioned the five hundred pounds a seriousness took over. Such a sum wasn't in Odd-Socks life. It might have been once, but not now. Now it was beyond a fortune; beyond wild dreams to the man. Whatever he knew, for the vagrant to ask for such an amount it had to have significant importance.

'Now, I am only asking for five hundred pounds, Patrick,' Odd-Socks reminded him. 'I imagine it is worth a lot more than that to you, but I do know you, don't I? I shall not be greedy.'

Patrick put his hand in the drawer and took out a wad of notes. Counting off twenty-five twenties, he said, 'Right, let's hear this secret.'

Andrew looked across at his brother as if he had gone mad.

'Well, I imagine from what I have heard that you are totally unaware of the meeting that took place at Dorothy's this afternoon. The meeting of all the traders who pay you to look after them, and a lot of their friends who support them.'

Patrick didn't know anything about the meeting. If he had, he would have stopped it. 'What kind of meeting was it?' he asked.

'It would appear that its sole purpose was for these traders to rid themselves of you,' the man answered. 'And there was something else . . .'

There was a long pause so Patrick was forced to ask, 'What?'

'Something to which you appear oblivious. Phil, the previous man in charge here is not dead. You may have all thought that he was, but apparently that is not the case.'

'You drunk Odd-Socks? Phil has been dead for a month or more now. Of course he's dead. Everybody knows he's dead. The body has been identified, too - and buried, what was left of it. You're pushing your luck, old man. I'm not paying you for bloody fairy tales. Piss off!'

'It's Gospel, Patrick, it's Gospel.' The old man's eyes were convincing. 'I would swear to it!'

'You've seen Phil then, have you?'

'Oh, no. I have not seen him, but I have heard him. There was no doubt about it. It was he. Cussing and swearing he was; absolutely foul language. We were all subjected to it. He was on that youngster's mobile telephone. He put it right up to the microphone so there was no escaping it. You know the youngster I mean, Sam. One of your people, I always thought. Obviously incorrectly. Cussing and swearing the man was. It was terrible! Everybody heard him. And there's something else I find most peculiar. Everybody there appeared to be wanting him back in charge of things again. Don't you find that amusing? It was only a few weeks ago that they couldn't stand the man!'

'Sam was at this meeting?'

'Oh, yes. His two friends as well, the one's that he's always seen around with, they were there too. It seemed that everyone who mattered was there - numbering well over a hundred, I would hesitate a guess.'

'Really? Well, here's your five hundred, Odd-Socks. Well earned. Now then, you keep your eyes open for me and you might get some more. Understand me?'

'Oh, yes, Patrick. Thank-you. I shall keep my eyes peeled for you. You are a good man with whom to do business. You are very generous and you have a kind heart. I shall look forward to seeing you again.' With that Odd-Socks departed.

'Yer not be believin' him are you me ol' bruv?' Andrew asked, flabbergasted. 'He's either takin' you for a ride, or he's a bleedin' nutter! My money's on a nutter!'

'That man may be many things,' Patrick said, 'but a nutter isn't one of them. We have trouble on our hands! It needs nipping in the bud, before it gets out of hand.'

'What we gonna do then, bruv?'

'Tonight we keep quiet. Carry on as normal. Observe. The lads will be here soon so not a word! Don't let them know we're on to them. They won't have got much organised yet, that's for sure. Tomorrow, we shall make a few enquiries. Shake down a few of the traders - they won't feel so strong on their own. There's nothing so brave, or so stupid, as a crowd of people. Each one on their own will be putty in our hands. We should easily be able to find out exactly what is going on. And with luck we may even find out Phil's whereabouts. If we do, then we'll make double sure that we finish him off next time. That'll quieten things down a bit then!'

Twenty minutes later the three young lads bowled in to the cellar to prepare their stuff ready for the evening's trading. Cheerful as ever, laughing and joking around, it was hard for Andrew to believe that his brother hadn't been conned with the story from the strange character earlier, but he said nothing. Don and Paul rolled in a little later to prepare their wares, soon followed by the other two Irish brothers. By seven o'clock everything was ready and there was nothing more to do but to sit around and talk whilst waiting for eight o'clock when the clubs opened.

'Same as usual tonight, Patrick?' Sam asked. 'Us three covering the Ellie and Dorothy's between us? Don and Paul over the road, with Andrew and Mickey dropping off at the pubs?'

'I suppose so. Seems to work, doesn't it? Although, Terry and I may start doing a bit now we're fit again. If it gets heavy, give us a call. We could do a bit at Dorothy's to lighten the load. Yes, in fact, that might be a good idea. I'm sure we're not getting as much out of that place as we should. Perhaps we should do Dorothy's tonight. Leave enough stuff on the side for us to take. You just see to the Ellie.'

'Right, boss.' Sam said, unpacking some of his cache and placing it on the coffee table. Mike and Graham each shed some of theirs to add to it. 'We'll get off now and take a slow walk. See you all later.'

'Left a tad early tonight, ain't they, bruv?' Terry half asked, half stated, when they had gone.

'Yes, maybe I upset them by saying we'd do Dorothy's.' Patrick said, picking up the phone and dialling a number. 'I think maybe we've ruined some little scam they had. I'd already noticed that since they started doing Dorothy's their take has hardly increased, yet there should have been a dramatic increase. That's what I'd expected, anyway. But I'm not surprised, not now. There, I thought so! Sam's mobile's engaged. He's probably on to Dorothy's right now,' he said, replacing the receiver. 'Let me fill the rest of you in on something Andrew and I learned today . . .'

#

The three lads left the cellar casually, strolling leisurely out of the yard into the alley as they normally would, but once they rounded the corner where the wall hid them from anyone watching from the house Sam rapidly punched numbers into his phone. Patrick was mistaken, it wasn't Dorothy's that he had dialled, at least not first.

'It plain to see that you got me,' the shrill singing voice replied.

'Auntie, we've got a problem tonight. We can't do Dorothy's. Patrick and his brother are covering it. We haven't got any spare now, either. Have you got enough? Can you get any more? Will you be able to keep them happy with the Irish hovering around?'

'Man, oh, Man. The shit's hit the fan. I got no stuff, least not enough. Anyway, I ain't gonna sell for a trip to Hell. If they caught me puttin' it around, they'd find a hole for me in the ground. This little Auntie's havin' a fright. This little Auntie's stayin' home tonight!' he screamed, cutting off the call.

Sam pressed the cancel button, then punched in more numbers. 'Doris,' he said when at length it was answered, 'I've got a feeling we've been rumbled. Patrick has decided to look after you himself tonight. Him and his brother. Auntie hasn't got much and won't come near the place tonight anyway. All in all, it's a complete fuck-up. Somebody's sure to say, "Auntie don't charge that much. Where is she?" to Patrick. What then?'

'Oh, my God, that is bad news! And we shall be packed solid tonight, as well. There's a famous raunchy double strip act on at ten. Never mind, we'll manage somehow - they'll just have to pay the full price for a while. I'll try and get everyone put wise on the door as they come in, but there's no guarantee that the punters will remember anything once they're pissed. Chances are it'll all come out. If it does come out then it's you we have to worry about. Once you leave the Ellie tonight, it's not going to be safe for any of you three, is it? I wouldn't even recommend you come here to hide. This could be one of the first places they'd come looking for you.'

'Don't worry about us, we'll be alright. I think Tom at the Ellie will look after us. After all we are on the same side now, and he's been quite friendly recently. We'll be safe there. The Irish won't go anywhere near there - they're too frightened of his minders after the last hiding they got.'

'Well, you all look after yourselves, and keep in touch. Kisses!' The phone cut off.

Graham, not usually the brightest spark, had a sudden brain flare. 'What will the Ellie do for drugs tomorrow night?' he asked.

Sam stopped dead in his tracks. 'Damn! That's something we never thought of, isn't it? Tom won't be a happy chappie if the place empties through lack of supply. Of course, Patrick might send Don and Paul down to cover it, but I doubt it. Who would cover them at the Inferno? The Inferno has to be covered first - it's bigger.

'Come on, step it out, we need to talk to Tom before the Ellie opens. I'll give him a ring to let him know we're coming early.'

CHAPTER 26

The day started early that Thursday morning at the Elephant's Nest, albeit this early wasn't at such a time that would have been early for the rest of the world - only for them. Away from this place of unreal reality the rest of the world had already performed their monotonous morning endurances hours ago.

People had fought for their bathroom space, and cursed whatever it was they ate last night, the essence of which now contaminated their small area seemingly sticking to the tiles and hanging there as it removed all traces of any other breathing material. They had already regretted that second 'one for the road' they had 'forced' themselves to drink at some God-forsaken hostelry the night before, and vowed never to do it again - but then, that would have been again. Lunch-boxes had long ago been filled and kids packed off or taken to school. Busses had been caught, busses missed, and heels caught in drains chasing them. Cars had been stuck in traffic jams, and cars broken down, threatened, kicked and sworn at.

Yes, it had all happened before now for the rest of the world that morning. By now all those people were fully absorbed in the routine of their daily employment that was possibly just as mundane, but hardly as tempestuous as the start of day. A time that was now forgotten about until the morrow, when they would suffer it all over again. However for those rising at the nightclub who had known none of this, it was still early - very.

Tom okayed it for the lads to stay over once Sam had told him the full story. They had all guessed he would - he was a good lad, was Tom. Besides, Sam was a pretty good storyteller, a professional in his field who usually got what he wanted. He knew how to sport the kind of face, the honest expression, the one that would make you feel guilty if you weren't to believe him. He was an expert at it. Even though somewhere inside you the warning bells might be working overtime you had to believe him, or feel bad.

Any animosity there had been between Tom and the three lads over the drink-spiking and the drugs on that first night had long since passed. Now they were quite friendly - in fact, one might even say chummy, as they very often shared a joke together. Tom had never been one to harbour a grudge for long. It was something his inbuilt good nature and happy go lucky attitude would not allow, although that was noticeably often put under strain when coping with life in Seathorpe.

Limited for space, with Karl and Stefan staying there too and having taken the only spare room, the three gang lads found that somehow they had to share Tom's mother's double bed. There was no other available room - not comfortable, anyway.

The situation did raise a few smiles at the time, but nobody pushed it too far, and they certainly weren't forthcoming the next morning on how well they managed with the forced share: two gay guys - an item, and a straight guy all crammed in the one bed together, but manage it they must have done unless one of them suffered the floor. Possibly there would be some humorous anecdotes to emerge in the fullness of time, Tom considered, amidst the morning oblivion. It was then that his mind took advantage of him and wandered off down a path of its own to impishly query: what type of gays were the two lads? What were they into? Were they the type to have spent the entire night trying out his mother's wardrobe? Perhaps tottering around in her high heels and dresses in front of the mirror? A stupid grin found a home and stayed there for a while, but nobody noticed. Nobody would - it was far too early in the day to notice a grin.

Nine o'clock chimed somewhere in the flat, but nobody noticed that either. The seven guys in varying degrees of dress, or more accurately undress, blearily wandered the kitchen-come-diner, each independently trying to make themselves toast and coffee, or something that didn't require too much effort. Each trying to stay in their own little world where life was still sufferable, where they were at home, and where they could remain unaware of the presence of the others in case that should require something resembling an intelligent communication between them. At such an unearthly hour, that would be unthinkable.

Ben sat by the table watching them, taking it all in. It was an amusing scenario even to a canine patiently waiting for the opportunity to seize an unguarded piece of toast. Several opportunities did arise, none of them missed, and but for cocking a deaf ear, an art he held to perfection, the dog would have more than doubled his understanding of the profane that morning.

A short time after eleven, with the scars of suffering only a couple of hours sleep temporarily concealed by the swift piping-hot showers, rapid shaves, and excessive splashes of the flesh-eating acid laughingly called after-shave, the group began to make their way out to the street for the short walk to Dorothy's and the first meeting of the committee.

They were running late, but they weren't worried. There were far more important things to worry about - the sun for one. That was surely out for vengeance, fiercely burning their stinging faces as they left the shade of the building to meet it full on. Hanging high above them it defied them to look upwards, towards it, as it gloated that there wasn't a solitary cloud anywhere to come to their rescue. The heat was stifling as the golden orb cruelly blazoned down its fiery scorching message from its vantage point, now almost directly overhead.

Tom guessed the temperature was well into the nineties. His loose fitting tee shirt was already sticking to his body and ripping into his damp under-arms, whilst with every footstep his boxers threatened to creep ever deeper into a sweaty crevice to glue themselves there forever, never to be seen again. Reliving the television advertisement for his chosen brand of anti-perspirant in his mind for the third time, the one where a man trekking across the desert bumps into a bimbo - an unlikely event in itself - and they bonk away under the midday sun with not a bead of perspiration showing, he found he wanted to shout out: 'Bollocks!' at the manufacturer. He had only walked little more than twenty yards in the sun to become thoroughly sopping wet – and that, he considered, was without the desert or the bimbo!

With feelings of 'better the devil you know' firmly embedded in people's minds the previous day, once they learned that Phil was still alive so many of them volunteered to stand for the committee that the time scale involved in actually electing one would have been unthinkable, and a far too complex affair. In the end, after a hesitant suggestion from Tom

- he'd been wary in case Doris should put him down in her quick-witted way, but she hadn't - it was unanimously decided to let Phil choose the committee himself. That way would at least produce one made up of the people he felt best happy to work with and able to trust. However, Phil's selection was not entirely as many of those present had expected.

For the line-up he chose Dave, his business partner from the Inferno - that was no real surprise to anyone; Tom and Randy - some had considered they might be in; Sam, Mike, and Graham - well, yes, everybody guessed they would be in – skivvies were always handy; but surprisingly to most people and unbelievably to some, he had chosen Doris and Rod. Eight people who, as Phil put it, should possess more than enough brain-power to find a way of removing four obnoxious Irishmen. He would be the ninth member himself on his discharge from hospital should the task not be completed by then, but he was full of confidence it would be. Full of confidence.

Karl and Stefan, who were unable to become involved in the local warfare any further than to protect Tom and his, were to be around merely for security reasons: to look after Tom and Randy. Phil had remembered his treatment by them on the night that he lost Denise, so he wasn't too happy about that, but in the end he considered it was unavoidable and he would have to live with it. Besides, their presence would doubtless make the rest of the committee feel much safer about the meetings.

Doris let them in as they arrived. She had been anxiously watching out for them from the window. Everybody politely exchanged greetings, commented on the exceptionally hot weather, the usual nervous stuff, before she invited them to flop wherever they felt comfortable. Dave wouldn't be coming, she explained. He was under the impression he was being watched by the four Irishmen who had turned up at the club remarkably early that day, so had decided it wiser to miss the first meeting rather than attempt to shake them off – but he was happy to go along with anything they decided.

With a flamboyant gesture, Doris explained she had considered pushing some tables together to make it a formal type of meeting - a long-table job - but seeing no advantage in it hadn't bothered. Nobody objected so, first offering everyone a drink - without exception everybody chose a long, cool, soft one - she then called through for Rod to join them.

The welcome shade, and the noticeable coolness of the air-conditioning inside the club, was being appreciated to the full by all those who had suffered the attack of the sun on the short trek from the Ellie. The stale smell of alcohol, cigarette smoke, and the one or two other commodities that frequent a nightclub were considered insignificant - a small price to pay.

The big guy finally sauntered in. He was looking very unhappy. Walking over and sitting down heavily next to Doris, he complained, 'You know, I never thought I'd see the day I'd be sitting down somewhere trying to help that Phil. Homophobic bastard that he is! God, it's a bloody strange old world!'

With his new found feelings for Phil, Sam couldn't let that go. 'Phil's not homophobic at all,' he protested, loudly. 'If he was, do you think he would have picked you and Doris to be on the committee? Remember, you were his choice. He didn't have to pick you, did he?'

'That's right, Sam, you put him right. You tell him,' Doris said, before turning to glare at her partner. 'Ignorant git! Now you just sit there, be quiet and behave yourself. Remember who's the boss around here. You know the rules: if I say it's Easter, you lay an egg! That way everybody's happy!'

'Bah! If he ain't homophobic, then I don't know who is! Tell me why he never had nothing to do with us here, then! Why did he leave us alone all that time! He was frightened he might catch something, I'll bet!'

'It was good he left us alone, wasn't it? Would you rather all these years we'd been paying out ten percent like all the other poor sods?' Doris screamed at him. 'If you really must know, he left us alone because I asked him to, not because he was frightened of us, or of catching anything!'

'Huh! You asked him, and just like that, he left us alone? That's a likely story! Do you think I've just come down from the trees?'

'Sometimes I wish you'd go back up 'em!'

Rod got up and started to stomp out of the room. He didn't want to be there in the first place.

'Rod! You come back here now! How dare you show me up! Come back here and sit down!'

'Not until I know what's been going on. Why it is, all of a sudden, you're standing up for that arsehole? Why?'

'Do you really want to know? Do you really want to know?' Doris screamed at the top of her voice, standing up to face him, her face colouring up. 'Because that arsehole's my brother! Do you think I really wanted anyone to know that? But now you know! Now they know! And soon now every fucker will know! Are you happy now?'

If shock could be harvested and sold, there would have been fortunes made there that morning. Stunned, shocked into silence, everybody glanced at everybody else looking for a reaction. It might have passed on a polite pretext of being unnoticed - but it didn't stop there.

'Auntie Doris!' Sam blurted out. 'If Phil's your brother that makes you my aunt, or rather my uncle, I suppose. Phil confessed to me that he was my real father. He told me so. I had no idea until then that he even knew my family. But if you two are brothers, I guess you would have known all about it, wouldn't you?'

Doris nodded her affirmation. This, by now, had become all too much for Randy. Whilst the others were with difficulty, but nevertheless competently, managing to hide their amazement, and had sat quietly taking everything in, all the time politely hardly seeming to notice, Randy found he could not. To him the whole situation had become so farcical, so side-splitting, that it was much more than he could handle. Unable to hold it back any longer he exploded, so that when Rod stopped dead in his tracks with the shock of Doris' revelation, involuntarily breaking wind at the same time, the poor deejay collapsed in a limp heap on the floor, rolling about uncontrollably with tears of mirth gushing from his eyes, whilst all the time holding himself and desperately praying not to wet himself. Rod turned around, open-mouthed, and just stared at his partner.

'Well, you wanted to know. You made me tell you.' Doris retorted, sitting down again and composing herself after the outburst. 'It's all out now, all the dirty linen for everyone to see! Phil's my brother, and Sam's his boy. We're all related. Now, unless somebody else wants to claim a relationship, I suggest you get your arse back down here and we all get started!'

Randy managed to pull himself back up onto his seat. 'Oh, man, oh, man, oh, man! Oh, I's so sorry Doris. Sorry Rod. Oh, it was so funny! Sorry! Oh, man!' he said, wiping his eyes again, with his shoulders still involuntarily lurching and a snigger having to be stifled each time he thought back to it, or dared to look across at Doris.

Ignoring Randy, Rod sat back down with a dumbfounded look on his face. He opened his mouth to say something, then noticing the sharp sideways look Doris slung in his direction, a look that could cut a diamond, he thought better of it. Doris coughed, clearing her throat - a gesture to bring everyone to order.

'Do you think we should be formal at all?' she asked, looking around for an answer. 'You know, elect a Chairman, a Secretary, keep records, have minutes, and all that kind of crap? Or shall we stay informal and just chew things over between us, deciding what to do as a group and only acting on what the majority agree on?'

She didn't get her answer. Karl interrupted the proceedings by shouting for his colleague to join him where he was standing by the front window observing what was happening outside. All eyes watched as Stefan ran to the window. Some rapid exchange of information was whispered between them. Information that annoyingly no-one else could hear. Everyone else sat up attentively, watching them and waiting in complete silence, impatiently, to learn what it was that so concerned the minders.

'What's wrong?' Doris stood up and asked finally, her face draining to an off-white the second the two men took out their guns, checking them.

'Not sure, but something is!' Karl said. 'Two cars parked farther up the road a few moments ago. The Irish are in the first one, and the Italians, with that bar manager from the Inferno, were in the other. The second lot has just run past us and around the corner out of sight. They're probably going to watch the back door, I guess. But it's strange they haven't bothered to hide themselves, yet they've deliberately kept the cars well away. Hmm, I don't like that. That could be bad news. Real bad. I think we need to get out of here as quickly as possible. Front or back is not a good idea unless we have to. Are there any other ways out?'

'No,' Doris said.

'Yes,' shouted Rod, 'follow me!'

Rod led them through the door behind the bar, then sharply turning left took them up a flight of stairs. On the landing he opened what would easily have passed for an airing-cupboard door to reveal a narrow wooden staircase that led up to the attic.

'Of course, the flat roof and the fire escape!' Doris exclaimed. 'Why didn't I think of that?'

'Maybe because I'm the one who has to produce the bloody eggs!' Rod quipped, scowling satisfyingly at his partner. 'And it ain't even Easter!'

Both the minders pushed past Rod, rushing up the stairs to the small but by no means pokey room above. The remainder closely followed them. Sparsely furnished as a bedroom, it was intended only as a back-up room for occasional guests. No-one would want to live in it permanently as it had severe sloping ceilings that stole much of the space towards the front gable window, and it somewhat resembled a hut placed on top of the mostly flat-roofed building as an afterthought. The dank smell of disuse was prominent.

Speedily crossing the room, the minders looked out of the window. Large enough to climb out through easily, for that was the intended purpose of it in an emergency, it laid back a little way from the edge of the building and provided access to the main flat roof which itself was about a foot below the top of the building's perimeter walls. The exposed one foot of perimeter wall was topped with a two foot high, once black but now noticeably extremely rusty, iron railing that offered some protection against falling over the edge.

Carefully opening the window to its full extent, Stefan signalled for the rest of them to wait inside, before he crawled out. Keeping low, he wriggled on his stomach the short distance to the railing and then peered down at the street below, studying it for a few moments before wriggling back to them.

'Everybody crawl out like I did,' he said, 'and make your way to the centre of the roof. Don't get lost. It's quite a way behind this attic by the large chimney stack. Stay low, very low while you're near the edge or else someone may see you if they look up from the street.'

One by one the group obeyed, nervously crawling out through the window on their hands and knees, turning left, and heading back on themselves until behind the attic, far enough in, they could stand up without any risk of being seen from the road and run the last few yards to the chimney stack. Once all were safely assembled there, Karl and Stefan told them to stay put, and left them - each moving off in a different direction to explore. Up above the sun bore down ruthlessly as the group attempted to remove some of the grit and tar from the heat-moistened bitumen covered roof that had adhered to them whilst crawling over it.

Cowering down as they neared the edges of the roof, the two minders surveyed the perimeter, searching for the best escape route. They quickly discovered the intended route in case of fire was by an iron rung ladder which descended to the side street below from half way along the side wall. The bottom section of the ladder was held up some fifteen feet from the pavement by a rusty looking spring mechanism which was presumably supposed to release itself once some weight was placed on it. The mechanism looked doubtful, too rusted to work, but that was purely academic. This route was of little use to them with one group of their suspected assailants hanging around watching the building from a little way farther up that road.

From either end of this length of roof above the side street, the two men started to crawl towards each other, to debate their next move, when there was a loud muffled explosion somewhere below. A 'thud' sound of enormous proportions. The group by the chimney felt the building rock, physically moving several inches they were sure. Gasping, holding on to each other, they watched in horror, helpless, as the side wall, the complete section with the iron railings on top, slowly began to part company with the rest of the building. Slowly, so slowly, as if in a time-stretched dimension, it moved outwards.

Strange creaking and straining noises, wrenching sounds, could be heard. They were the desperate moans from the dying building as its joists were being agonizingly twisted and pulled apart. Farther and farther away from them the wall moved, precariously leaning over the side street, taking along with it a large section of the roof, a section that now projected upwards at an alarming angle. It was the section on which Karl was crawling!

Stefan jumped to his feet and ran forward, desperately hoping to be able to grab hold of his partner before the section of roof moved too far away for him to be reached, and before it collapsed into the street below as it surely would now that the whole wall was precariously untied from the building. It was swaying, as if deciding which way it should fall, inwards or outwards, and rocking to and fro in its indecision. Stefan made it to his partner. Grabbing hold of Karl's wrist he tried hard to pull the man towards him, but he found he was leaning too far over the precipice. To exert any more force would have toppled him over the edge, and there was nothing around him to hold on to for anchorage. Karl tried to stand, to scramble up so he could run forward a step and jump the ever expanding gap between them, but the wall's momentum coupled with the acute angle that section of roof had adopted, prevented him. There was no way that he could balance upright.

The wall falling away, parting from the rest of the structure, had been purely the result of an enormous shockwave that ran through the entire building, literally rocking it on its foundations. It was not the actual pressure of the explosion itself that had caused it; not directly. No, that had happened further inside the building, somewhere deep inside where strangely the walls had contained the blast. It was somewhere that only Patrick knew. Somewhere where he had secretly planted the deadly parcel the night before, and somewhere where it had laid in hiding, waiting patiently for the signal to carry out its one and only purpose. It was also somewhere where now the sudden and enormous build up of pressure was urgently seeking a way out; looking for a weak point. It soon found one.

The giant aluminium cowling on the roof ripped off its mounting effortlessly, with no warning, no straining sounds, and no discernable moans from the ripping bolts heard, as the pressure below escaped through the ventilation system with the roar of a mighty jet engine. Looking like some Chinese man's oversized hat, a coolie hat, the cowling lifted and spun madly, manically, sideways, outwards towards the tottering wall with an eerie whistling sound. Seemingly not affected one iota by any effort that may have been required for it to decapitate Stefan as he knelt by the expanding chasm fighting to save his partner, it continued on its journey until, across the road, the opposite building's tall end wall curtailed its mindless spree abruptly with a rasping sound like that of a circular saw finding a nail in its path. A sickening sound, followed by the noise of scraping as it slid down the wall, finalised in a loud clattering as it came to rest in the street below.

The minder's head had followed the homicidal metal disc, the executioner, outwards for a split second or so before apparently stopping, hovering motionless for a mere moment to stare at the horrified group with its blank unknowing eyes. It stared at them through the fountain of bright red blood gushing, rhythmically pumping, from its decapitated remains, before it seemed to glance downwards, longingly, at its rightful place where its disassociated body's arms remained outstretched with hands that were still firmly grasping hold of Karl's wrist.

As if as one, as if a signal had been given, the lonely head, the spurting body - now only dribbling, the pump had given up - and the helpless Karl all moved at the same time, plummeting downwards, down amidst tons and tons of falling masonry as the wall and the roof section, having at last decided which way it should fall, finally gave way completely, collapsing, and spiralling down to become nothing more than a mountainous pile of rubble in the street below.

Seconds later, in return, a large mushroom of dirt and dust flew up from the rubble slowly, ever so slowly, rolling over into itself and billowing like some atomic cloud bringing up with it, onwards, upwards, the screams from the crowd of terrified witnesses below; those who had run out from the nearby bars, cafés and shops on hearing the sound of the explosion.

For those remaining on the roof, the people's screams of horror were soon frightened into an inaudible submission when they met up with the more pronounced, longer enduring, and totally hysterical shrieking noises that emanated from the violently shaking Doris, as she unavoidably watched the whole evil episode through to its conclusion.

Tom for most of the morning had been somewhat subdued, in a trance-like state and feeling low, something to do with the heat or maybe lack of sleep he presumed. He had not said much to anybody so far that morning, being content to just go along with everything. But now he was suddenly jolted back into life, back into all the truth of reality, and with a vengeance. No more, it hit him with the force of a sledgehammer, no more could he enjoy the freedom that he had enjoyed recently; the freedom of not having to worry about the gang. No more would Stefan and Karl be there to protect him, or any of them. It was a frightening realism, and it came at a frightening time.

In the blazing heat of the near mid-day sun, Tom suddenly realised he'd turned quite cold with the fear. There were goose bumps appearing on his bare arms and he was shivering. Looking at the six around him, he guessed everyone there was equally as frightened. They certainly all looked it, and probably like him, they too were trying hard to put on a brave face. Everyone, that is, except for Doris who, shamelessly distraught, continued to wail and scream whilst shaking like a wind-up toy soldier. But then, like him too, Tom realised, the others were just standing there in shock and not knowing what to do next. Someone needed to do something.

Walking over to Doris, Tom slapped her hard across her face. Harder perhaps than he should have done, or maybe intended to do, but it worked. The result was immediate, she went much quieter, now staring at him with indignation, and hurt, as she continued to weep less noisily. Rod put a comforting arm around her, pulling her in close to him and stroked the back of her head as she sobbed onto his shoulder. Standing back from them, Tom scrutinised the big guy's face with quite some relief. Thankfully he hadn't misconstrued the intention of the slap - that *would* have proved unpleasant!

Randy, who was still staring expressionless at the open expanse where once there was a wall and a roof, exclaimed, 'Shit, man!' for perhaps the ninth or tenth time. Nobody was counting.

Sam, Mike and Graham, like three bodies sharing but one mind, were staring at Tom, looking questioningly into his face, looking there for some inspiration, some sign of leadership to emerge, as they appeared to be nervously waiting to be told what to do. Making decisions was not their forte. They were minions, and as much as they didn't want to be there, a solution to their predicament was way beyond them. To them Tom seemed to be their only hope of salvation. They were convinced that he alone would be the only one there who might be able to take charge and get them to safety. Nobody else appeared capable.

'Quickly everybody, follow me!' Tom ordered, at the same time tugging at Randy's tee shirt to break the spell. Rightly or wrongly he had to try something. The rest of the roof, or the whole building, might easily collapse with them on it if they stayed there much longer. He had no idea whether his quick-fired plan would work, or even could work, but he knew it was their only hope, and it had to be tried.

Without question, everyone followed Tom as he ran to the edge of the roof directly opposite to the departed section. This edge had a wall that ran down to meet up with the roof of the much smaller, fisherman cottage-sized, premises next door. In turn this provided access to all the rest of the roofs in that row of about a dozen terraced buildings. However, none of these roofs were flat - not until the last one along the line where there stood another large building; a mirror image structure to Dorothy's.

Peering over the railing, it was as Tom had hoped. The apex of the adjoining roof was little more than a few feet below them; not inaccessible with care. 'Watch how I do this,' he ordered them, trying to sound confident and as if he did this kind of thing on a regular basis, 'then you all follow me one at a time.'

Swinging himself over the rusty railing that despite its appearance remained strong, he clung to it as his legs dangled down to within inches of the apex of the roof below. Carefully adjusting his position sideways, moving along the railing left a little until he was satisfied his feet were aimed equally either side of the ridge tiles, he lowered himself further by moving his hands down the railings until, when he was only hanging on to the top of the wall by his fingertips, he let go.

In a line above, the others watched how at the last minute Tom managed to pull his feet towards each other in order to gain friction, to slow his descent as he slid down astride the rooftop until he was sitting upright on the apex. Randy cringed, visualising the result of too fast a descent, but still volunteered to go next.

Once Randy too had successfully made the descent, Tom wriggled back a few feet along the roof, away from the wall, and then lifting his right leg over the top he swung his body around until he was dangling down the back slope of the roof. Still tightly holding on to the ridge tiles, he pushed into the roof with his toes to find enough grip to help support his weight.

The blistering hot roof, with a heat haze wriggling up from it that distorted everything in his vision, burnt his hands and was fiery on his chest but, with concentration and frequent movement, Tom discovered it was bearable. It had to be anyway, he knew there was no alternative. There was no other way down; no other means of escape. To try to find a way down through the building would be extremely unwise. Doubtless there was little left of the inside and to even look could be to enter a death trap. The whole place might fall on top of them at any moment.

One by one, perilously, with a few sharp intakes of breath but with no disasters, they each in turn managed to follow Tom's example until all, like him, were precariously clinging on to the rooftop and dangling down its back slope.

Dorothy had needed a lot of coaxing to get that far. A born fatalist, she was convinced her time was nigh, that she would be going down with her club, and that her next audience would be celestial. Trying to escape the inevitable, to attempt to crawl along rooftops to safety at her age, she considered to be nothing but a complete waste of effort and a quite futile exercise. No drag queen in her right mind would ever consider such an exit. Where was the style? Besides, it was something she would never be able to do - she wasn't butch. She was incapable of such an escapade. But do it she did. She was forced to, and once she had achieved it she felt proud. Oh, so proud. If she could do that she could do anything!

Slowly, hand over scorching hand, the group ever so carefully made their way along to the next building, and the next, and the next, and so on. With the sun blistering down on to their backs, and sweat pouring from them, they were forced to stop frequently to rest, so it took the group a good twenty minutes and many sharp intakes of breath when someone's feet or hands occasionally lost their grip, usually happening when negotiating the chimney stacks between the properties, before they all made their way to the other end of the terrace, to where the building that was a mirror image of Dorothy's loomed above them.

In the distance, approaching at speed, they could hear the sirens of at least two fire engines coming in from Weston-Super-Mare. Looking back along the rooftops, through the wriggling heat haze to the remains of Dorothy's, they soon realised the reason for them. Seriously large flames were now furiously licking the air high above the building, doubtless coming from the side and the hole where the roof was missing. Flames, frequently hidden by gusts of thick black bellowing smoke that fought with them, and raced with them, to reach skywards.

'It's gone,' Dorothy sobbed, 'it's all gone! Our life! Everything! Gone!'

Rod wanted so hard to comfort her at that despairing moment, but found he was unable to. His excessive weight demanded that he clung on to the roof with both hands. A sympathetic smile was all he could offer her, but to Doris it was enough; it was everything. She knew she

would be okay now. She knew she would survive. The song immediately exploded in her head. There on the rooftop she could visualize the dance floor, the lights, the sounds, and all the appreciative queens screaming their tits off to the music, strutting their stuff to Gloria Gaynor, to those immortal realms of 'I Will Survive'. She wanted to sing it out aloud; she wanted to be herself again; she wanted to command her audience. She shed a tear, instead.

'Well, Rambo, you's got us this far, man. But how's you gonna get us up there?' Randy asked, nodding to the railings of the roof towering above their heads.

'Easy. One of us will pull themselves up and sit on the top, like we did the other end, but this time leaning back against the wall for support. The rest of us will scramble up onto his shoulders one at a time. From there the railings are easily reached. The hairy bit is that we can be seen once we move from here, so it's a "do it as quick as you can" job. Mind you, I don't think many will be looking this way; there's too much excitement at the other end. I hope not, anyway.'

And, it was that easy. Nobody noticed them. The only minor hiccup to the clockwork exercise being Rod. His massive form had needed an extra shove on his jacksie by two others to launch him skywards - two others who fervently prayed that the big guy's recurring flatulence wouldn't re-surface at that time. They were fortunate, or God had listened, for it didn't resurface, and now they were all safely on the flat roof. Now it was just a matter of climbing down the fire escape ladder on the opposite side of the building; down to the street below and safety.

Stooping low, they swiftly crossed the roof to where they could see the top of the iron ladder hooped over the wall between a gap in the railings. Looking down, their hearts suddenly fell. The ladder descended less than eight feet, and then there was nothing. All the other sections were missing; long gone it seemed by the look of the wall.

'Damn! We shall have to break in through the gable window, and then find our way out through the building,' Tom stated, moving off in that direction. 'Of course, the owner may not be too happy about that, but never mind. It is an emergency, isn't it? Whose place is it, anyway?' he asked as they all jogged towards the gable.

'Mother O'Shea's,' Sam answered.

It was only a name, quite a short one at that, but there was something in Sam's voice, the tone, and the manner in which he had said it, that suggested to Tom that was not good news.

CHAPTER 27

The window was slightly ajar, too distorted by weather and age to ever again close properly. Tom's hands grasped hold of the old wooden frame and pulled at it apprehensively. The hinges corroded by years of salt air creaked and moaned, protesting loudly at the demand, but finally they relented and allowed him to struggle it open wide enough for them to climb through. Peering inside he was not surprised to discover the room was almost empty. It was certainly devoid of any normal furniture or carpeting one might have expected had the room been lived-in. There were just some wooden crates, about half-a-dozen he guessed, untidily stacked on the bare floorboards in the far corner from them.

An unusual odour to the room fascinated Tom's nose. Not an unpleasant one, but one he couldn't quite place, although there was a kind of familiarity to it. He had met it before somewhere, and he was sure it must have been quite recently. But where? He appreciated that smells normally had a good historical memory and would usually bring an association back to mind in an instant. That it was the way of things - animal. But for some reason this one didn't, and that annoyed him.

Deciding to work on the smell later, it was hardly that important he guessed, he carefully lifted his foot over the windowsill and began to slowly venture inside. Heading towards the door at the end of the wall to his left, all the time hoping upon hope that it wouldn't be locked from the other side, he could hear the others behind him struggling through the window.

Sam, bringing up the rear, sniffed the air as soon as he made it inside. 'Phew! I know that smell,' he exclaimed in a shouted whisper. 'Patrick often smells like that. It's the oily stuff he uses to clean his guns. The stuff he pours on a rag and pulls down the barrel with a bit of string. I think it's some kind of light machine oil. I know he stinks the cellar out when he uses it. It's a bit strong in 'ere, isn't it?'

That was it! Tom instantly recalled where he had before encountered the odour. It was on the night that they had been frog-marched to the cellar. It was the fragrance of Patrick and the cellar.

Although his hand was already holding the doorknob, grasping it firmly ready to turn it to see if the door would open, curiosity made Tom delay the attempt and instead he walked over to the other corner of the room to begin inspecting the wooden crates.

'Christ Almighty!' he exclaimed, looking into the first one; one that didn't possess a lid. 'It looks like a bloody arsenal! Come and have a look at this lot! There's a load of guns and rifles all packed in straw. At least half a dozen that I can see and there might be some more underneath. And what about the box below it? That one has got a picture of a grenade stamped on the side of it, and arrows saying, 'This way up'. Yes, I guess that's about right. If one of them were to go off we would definitely all be going that way up! Jesus, this really is an arsenal!'

'Man! Sure is a pity Karl and Stefan ain't around no more. I's bet they could have made some good use of this lot!'

'All this stuff must belong to Patrick and his brothers,' Sam informed them. 'This is their boozer; their local. It's the only Irish pub there is, so they spend a lot of their spare time here. I know for a fact Patrick is a close friend of old Mother O'Shea. Anyway, he don't keep nothing back at the cellar; none of his guns or explosives, that is. If he wants anything he disappears for a while and then comes back with it. This must be where goes; where he's been keeping everything. This must be his secret hidey-hole.'

'Yeah, man. And I's bets you they's not up the road no more, them Irish. They's not still watching them firemen. No way, man. They's thinking we's all been killed and they's downstairs here celebrating what a good job they's done. Downstairs here getting pissed! Ain't that good news, man!'

'You're probably right,' Tom agreed. 'Which means we can't get out this way, doesn't it? We can't exactly go waltzing down there and apologising for breaking in, can we? "Sorry, just passing through," kind of thing. We'd get our heads blown off. So how the hell are we going to get out of here?' His mind went into deep thought, whilst his hands continued to explore, rummaging through the remaining crates.

'Any bombs amongst that lot?' Doris asked, sarcastically. 'So I can blow their fucking place up before we leave, like they have mine!'

'Yes, I think there are, believe it or not,' Tom answered, to everyone's amazement. 'This box contains two disc-shaped things, each one with what looks like a remote control, although I guess they are really more short-lived powerful radio transmitters than remote controls because on them it says the maximum range is half a mile. They seem to be colour coded, so you can tell which one goes with which bomb. And, if you look here, you can see there's a space at the end where a third one obviously used to live. Probably the one that's blown your place up, Doris.

'I reckon one of them must've planted it in there last night. Probably Patrick. He's the so-called explosives expert, isn't he? Then today, when they thought they could kill all of us, the whole committee in one go, they detonated it with the remote control. I mean, them all turning up there together today wasn't to take us on in some kind of gunfight at the OK Coral type of thing, as we might first have thought, was it? No, they were only there to witness the carnage; to enjoy seeing the place blown up - with all of us inside it!'

'My God! If only we could sneak one out, I'd do it! I swear I would!' Doris stated, the anger making her head jerk haughtily. 'I'd do exactly the same to them as they've done to us!'

'First, we gotta get out of here,' Rod reminded them all.

'I think I might have worked that one out,' Tom replied. Then, looking in turn at both Rod and Doris, he asked, 'Is there anyone along here, in this row, that you could really trust? And I mean, really trust.'

'Most of them, I should think. I would hope so, anyway.' Doris told him. 'But definitely old Bill Johnson, two along from here, the newsagent. He's a very close mate of ours. You could trust him with your life. Real steady old boy, he is. He's one of us, and one of our regulars.'

'Good. Well, we'll see just how matey he is about having half his roof ripped off. You wouldn't happen to know his number by any chance, would you?' Tom asked, pulling his mobile phone off its belt clip.

'What? Oh, yes I do.' It was the big man who replied and, intrigued, recited the number as easily as if it was his own.

Tom punched it in. 'Hello, are you Bill? A good friend of Rod and Doris?' he enquired down the handset moments later.

'Yes, I am, but who wants to know? Who is this?'

Tom explained only as much as he thought the man needed to know at that time and was delighted to hear back how relieved, how overjoyed, the man was that the blast at the club hadn't killed his two friends after all. Apparently the horror stories were already circulating and had all of them listed as dead; blown to kingdom come!

Bill explained he didn't have many friends - not close friends. Because of the shop he knew everyone, of course, but none were what he considered to be really close friends except for Doris and Rod who were sort of special to him. So when Tom told him of his plan, and what he required of him, the man was only too happy to oblige. He was prepared to help them in any way he could; any way at all. Rip a part of his roof up? Of course they could. As far as he was concerned, if it was to save his friends they could rip the whole damn place to pieces!

Minutes later, perhaps ten, having all safely retraced their steps back as far as the second roof along the terrace, Tom carefully proceeded to remove some of the roof tiles just below the top on the side away from the street where they couldn't be seen. Only about a dozen or so, gently sliding them down the roof one at a time to Randy, who had become as one with the roof, finding he could stoop-walk around on it without fear. He expertly caught the tiles and placed each one singly along the guttering so it couldn't fall.

Once he was satisfied the whole was large enough for them to pass through, Tom punched a hole in the exposed felt lining. Ripping it apart and looking inside, he was pleasantly surprised to find Bill waiting for them on the boarded walkway below. The man was struggling with a step ladder and attempting to manoeuvre it into place directly beneath the hole.

It was not long then before they were all safely inside and downstairs in the newsagent's living room behind the shop, planning their next move over cups of hot tea - a disgustingly stewed brew that Bill poured from a large metal teapot they imagined simmered on the hotplate all day. Not wishing to offend the guy, they had after all just ripped the man's roof to pieces, they all drank it and lied about how it was a real good cuppa. All, that is to say, except for Randy who, fortunate in having taken the seat next to a giant cheese plant, at the first opportunity, when Bill had to leave them to tend to some customers, quickly poured his into the leafy monster's giant pot.

Swallowing his down in one so it could hardly have time to hit his taste buds, Tom rang Derek and Beryl to explain what had happened. Bad news always travelling the fastest they too had already heard the stories and believing that everybody attending the meeting had been killed were, at the very time when he rang them, debating whether or not they should open the club that night. Would it be appropriate in the circumstances? They had considered it might appear disrespectful.

Tom told them they must open. They were to carry on as normal and to tell anyone who questioned them about opening in such tragic circumstances that that's entertainment. The show must always go on. However, he explained, they would need to have Ronnie in early that night, or find someone else to deejay for the early evening, because the presumed dead were going to stay that way for a while. They were going to lie low until under the cover of darkness, if all went according to plan, they would sneak back in to the club.

There had been no debate about the plan. No discussion at all. Tom had undoubtedly taken charge of the whole situation. He was making all the decisions, and giving all the orders, and nobody was objecting. Some kind of leadership quality, one which over the last few weeks had maybe occasionally surfaced momentarily, emerging only to hide again almost immediately, had come out fully and taken him over; completely engulfing him. It was now his style. Leadership was now him, and so naturally so that everyone else took it for granted, as if it had always been that way. Nobody appeared to have noticed this change of character, not even Tom. He was equally as oblivious.

Nobody, it has to be said, except for Doris. Nothing ever got past Doris. She alone had noticed the change. And she knew exactly the moment it had happened too. It was when Tom had slapped her across the face, that's when it happened. She knew he had changed then, and for that she was grateful. Extremely grateful. After all, who else could have safely got them this far? There was no-one, especially not her, she knew that for certain. Command an audience, yes, that she could do. Have them eating out of her hand, yes, that too - and God help anyone who was silly enough to heckle her. She could make mince-meat out of hecklers, and often would, so she wasn't without her own inner strengths. But all those strengths were in her own world, and that world was a trillion miles from the one they were now inhabiting - the world where Tom had been crowned king, and somehow everyone else had missed the coronation.

For the remainder of that afternoon and right through into the early evening, until eight o'clock when Bill closed the shop, the group spent the time in desperate boredom. Desperate. Nothing on the television satisfied them. With Bill only having four channels the choice was far from good. It started off with: golf; a discussion on women's problems; the sexual life of a wood-louse; or more golf, and it became no better with time.

None of that was for them, and any attempts at starting conversation were usually short-lived, until finally they dried-up completely. Even Doris, who was never usually short for a word - was short for a word. Dozing seemed to be the preferred option and they all tried it, but with little or no success. Randy's frequent, 'Oh, man!' would interrupt them as he'd shift around in his seat as once more he tried to find comfort. Maybe comfort is an impossibility for some on a cottage chair with wooden arms and thin cushions, but had Randy only opened his eyes, just momentarily, he would have noticed how the cheese plant was faring from his force-feeding it his tea, and perhaps he would have counted his blessings. The plant too was suffering extreme discomfort.

Ron's flatulence, immediately followed by a scolding retort, or an accentuated 'tut' from Doris, regularly shattered the silence, as did the harsh bell on the shop door - that seemed to go off every few minutes! The boredom, the waiting, and the eternity of it all was gut-wrenching. Not even Sam's expertly timed, 'More tea with that, vicar?' in reply to one of Ron's massive expulsions, one a bull elephant would have been proud of, did anything to relieve it. It seemed to them that several lifetimes passed before eight o'clock finally arrived and Bill, having shut the shop for the night, threatened them with more tea.

Then later many more lifetimes could have passed, lifetimes of back-breaking exertion, of blood and sweat, of curses, cuts and broken fingernails, before Bill's delivery van, over-laden with the wooden crates that they had so laboriously, and so dangerously, gone back for and hauled across the rooftops, finally pulled up outside the back door of the

Elephant's Nest. It was then just a mere fifteen fleeting minutes more before, with Randy's expertise at operating the hoist, and with the noise of the disco camouflaging their efforts, they had successfully hauled their deadly cargo all the way up to the top landing un-noticed, and stowed it away safely in the upper circle.

CHAPTER 28

It was during that night, the one that followed the destruction of Dorothy's, that Fate decided to intervene. As can happen all too often, the hot and beautiful summer day of blistering uninterrupted sun and of record-breaking temperatures came to an end with billowing dark clouds rolling in from the sea. A greenish tinge embellished the sky that evening, as behind those clouds the sun sank into the sea beyond the horizon. The humidity must have gone off the scale as the unbearable stickiness and the lack of any refreshing air to breath screamed out that the Mother of all thunderstorms was on its way.

Tom, Randy, and the rest of the committee, with the exception of Dave who hadn't joined them that day and who was now under the impression they had all perished, were pleased when four o'clock next morning finally arrived and the last punter had left the nightclub. It had been an eventful and strenuous day for them all, but for much of it they had been trapped like prisoners, first in the eternity of the newsagent's living room and then later in Tom's flat, so the Tannoy message from Derek informing them that everyone had left the building, the place was secure, and they could now safely come down, was greeted with sighs of relief. They were still prisoners, of course, but their cell had immediately become so much less confining.

Since stowing the cache of arms in the upper circle, and bidding a fond farewell to Bill, thanking him for his invaluable assistance with a promise they would see his roof was repaired, the group had spent another three hours cooped up in Tom's flat. That too had been an eternity for them, albeit a far more comfortable and bearable one. With all that satellite television offered there were passable programmes to watch through their long wait, and then there was some relief found when they all got stuck-in to clean up the mess made and left behind earlier that day in the kitchen-come-diner. Even the cleaning up had been preferable to more sitting around, and so they spent a lot of time at it, doing it meticulously.

Arriving down in the auditorium and sitting around a couple of tables by the cafeteria, the group related the day's events to an engrossed Derek and Beryl over several long cool soft drinks. Each of Doris's frequent interruptions to elaborately re-enact a scene from the day would receive another, 'Ooh, I say!' from Beryl, as she attentively leaned even further forward on her seat in order not to miss any part of the next revelation.

Tom, however, was only there in body. Allowing them the pleasure of re-living the day for the benefit of his managers, his mind was already elsewhere wrestling with the problem of what they should do next.

So they had stolen the Irishmen's arsenal, but with none of them being thugs, or being anywhere in that league, the weapons were of little use to them. Perhaps the only benefit of having the boxes was that they were depriving the Irish of making any further use of them – there would be no more buildings blown up for a while - but he doubted it would take people of that calibre too long to replace them.

The thought that the next time it could be the Elephant's Nest that would be targeted crossed Tom's mind and he shuddered. He realised that but for the expertise and the alertness of Karl and Stefan none of them would be alive now - they would all have died at the meeting. But who was there to protect them in the future, now those two were gone? It was obvious they couldn't all remain hidden in the club, forever pretending to be dead. Cooped up those past few hours had been hell for them; even a day or two more was totally out of the question.

Tom knew that he needed to come up with a plan, or a way out, or something by next morning - the others would be expecting it of him. But what?

#

Several thousand miles away in Rome, in a luxury hotel a short distance off the Via Veneto and overlooking the Medici and Borghese Gardens, Mary couldn't sleep. She kept going over the telephone conversation with Tom the previous evening. It had been distinctly short; even abrupt. Unable to get hold of him at the club, strange in itself immediately before opening time, she had found him on his mobile. He had assured her everything was hunky-dory, they were his words, but that he was very busy. Exactly what he was busy doing he hadn't said, but it seemed he couldn't get her off the line quick enough. She had received an almost identical reply from Beryl on telephoning her a couple of hours later. It was most worrying.

Jason hadn't seemed at all bothered when she mentioned it to him later that she was worried. He had merely told her to stop being a mother hen and that Tom was old enough to look after himself. Besides, he had the minders to look out for him and the club, so there was nothing to worry about. The lad probably had a hot date and she needed to accept that hormones took precedence over a mother at his age.

It was a sensible way to look at it, she told herself. Jason was always sensible. But Jason had never been a mother. Mothers instinctively know when something is wrong; mothers have presentiments.

Unknown to Mary, in the next room Jason too was unable to sleep. The news that the minders were still unreachable concerned him. Not one to dismiss Mary's worries that easily, he had earlier tried to phone the two men hoping for some news that would reassure the woman. Unable to contact either of them, he had arranged for someone to try their numbers at fifteen-minute intervals. For several hours now both numbers had repeatedly been 'unavailable'. He would give it until morning, he told himself, and then if nothing was heard by then he would himself phone Tom.

\#

Outside the cellar the rain started to bucket down. A stormy wind had sprung up from nowhere forcing the dark, heavily-laden, low clouds to rush by overhead to the raptures of distant thunder claps, whilst impressive sheet-lightning flashes filled the sky with regularity to back-light the menacing warriors. It was a hell of a night out there, evil, but inside the cellar where the celebration was going full swing again, it all went unnoticed.

The day had been a very rewarding one for the gangsters. Patrick had become the man of the moment since his bomb had so excellently accounted for the fall of Dorothy's and the demise of all opposition. That more than made up for all the extra work they had suffered that night through no longer having the three lads to cover the Ellie, and the losses they must surely have sustained by employing a couple of tourists to help them out with selling the drugs. They knew the young guys would rip them off, it was obvious they would, but it didn't seem to matter that night. With Dorothy's gone both the Ellie and the Inferno had been extra busy, and after their full afternoon celebrating at Mother O'Shea's they couldn't possibly have managed to cover everything without the extra help. In the circumstances the few quid or the small amount of drugs that might have been stolen was of little consequence.

Both Don and Paul had recently left the land of the knowing and were slumped together in front of the sideboard with pathetic grins left on their faces. They could drink, but they could not drink like the Irish brothers. Of the four of them it was Terry who could get the most pints down his neck - and in the fastest time. Slamming his glass heavily on the coffee table, to make the point it was empty again, he flashed his besotted grin towards Patrick.

Maria didn't wait to be asked, she crossed the room to collect his glass for refilling, but that was all it took for Andrew and Mickey to immediately down theirs and slur almost as one, 'Ah, while yer there, lass.'

Patrick knew this was going to turn into a heavy night, a don't dare look at the sunrise session, and so he did likewise.

#

By five o'clock in the morning the storm was at its worst. Now directly overhead, and with gale force winds, the thunder and lightning mercilessly crashed through Seathorpe. Heavy seas, with waves whipped into a frenzy, claimed the promenade as theirs as they challenged the steps up into both of the nightclubs, one at either end of the resort, and washed up the streets in-between them. In the marina the richest of last night's revellers fought desperately to save their crafts as they dragged their anchors and threatened to be lifted out on to the promenade, or at the very least be wrecked by smashing into each other. Several were.

Up on the cliff tops, and on the hills behind the town, tents took off and sailed away into the near blackness of the exceptionally darkened early morning. Many caravans were blown over, with two amazingly flipping against the wind to topple from the cliff top by Jumper's Point down on to the rocks below, only to be eaten there by the ferocious waves. And unseen from the town below, through the rods of driving rain, a long line of vehicles began to crawl away, bumper to bumper, being buffeted along the road inland in their attempt to seek shelter.

In the town, huge gusts of wind, gusts with the force of a million raging devils, raped the streets leading off the promenade. Tiles were lifted, ripped up from many roofs and slung into other buildings, whilst some were embedding themselves in the sheet metal of the parked cars to make them resemble dinosaurs with plates, fins, erected along their backs.

Somewhere near the electricity sub-station behind the fun fair there was the enormous flash of a bolt of lightning, one that came with a spitting sound that could be heard over the howling wind. The crack of the deafening thunder was immediate, if not simultaneous, and likely happened low down, almost in the streets, for the pressure took out several windows and rocked many of the buildings. The spectacle, although it is doubtful anybody was actually out there watching it, was followed by total darkness throughout the whole of the resort as every line out of the sub-station over-loaded and tripped.

Above the front bar at Mother O'Shea's, in her bedroom, Sheila O'Shea the landlady, better known throughout the town by those, the many, who disliked her as Fat Sheila, awoke with a start. The wind was battering the building, but it was the bedroom door, along with some others, rattling against the doorposts that worried her. She wondered if she had left a window open somewhere, or could it be that somebody had broken in and left an outside door open to the elements? It needed investigating. Her hand found the bedside lamp and flicked the switch. Nothing.

Now, once down Fat Sheila doesn't get up too easily, so it was with profanities strong enough to crack the blarney-stone on her gasping-with-the-exertion breaths that she rolled off the bed, and then struggled into a kneeling position, before heaving her twenty-something-high stone frame upwards into a standing position. Once that had been achieved she waited for a moment to catch her breath before shuffling over to the main light switch. When that produced no results either she was forced to feel her way along the wall to the wardrobe, on top of which she knew there was the big torch. It wasn't supposed to be there, it should have been replaced next to the bed, and she cursed her daughter for putting it up there after borrowing it on one of her rare visits.

With arms incapable of visiting any space above her head, Sheila's only hope of reaching the torch was by standing on the footstool. This she somehow managed to do successfully, although with great difficulty, and had only just managed to grab hold of the torch when the stool gave way under her weight. The resounding thud of her hitting the floor would, at the very least, have frightened any burglars away, she considered, after spitting more obscenities at the world as once more she had to pull herself up.

On subsequently checking the three other rooms on that level for open windows and finding them all securely closed, she cursed again, now believing the wind to be entering the building from somewhere downstairs. To have to go all the way downstairs made her very unhappy. Very unhappy indeed.

Being so heavily challenged by mass, Sheila negotiated stairs with difficulty. She had to take them one step at a time, and not in the normal way of one, two, three, four. With her it had to be one, one, two, two, three, three, and so forth as both feet had to meet up on the same step to prevent her centre of gravity becoming unsustainable. For this reason she normally made a point of only going up and down the stairs once a day, so this extra excursion in the dark, and only aided by torchlight, was most unwelcome. It was more than that when she finally arrived downstairs only to discover that there everything was perfectly still, with all the doors and windows securely bolted.

Only now did it enter her head that the wind would be coming in through the attic window. Although she hadn't been all the way up there for years, she remembered that even that long ago the window had never closed fully enough to allow the latch to secure it. It had probably blown wide open. Convinced now that the world was playing mean tricks on her, she poured herself a large brandy, and then another, before attempting the mountainous climb.

By the time the poor woman reached the top of the building to discover the wide-open window - and nothing in the room - the storm had departed, the clouds gone too, and the risen sun was providing adequate daylight.

She had little idea of exactly what should have been up there in the room, only that something should be. There should at least have been the two boxes she saw struggled up there by Patrick only last week, and probably a whole lot more, she guessed.

It was eight-thirty before Fat Sheila's persistent ringing was finally answered by an almost incoherent Patrick, and then only another ten minutes before the wrecks of six men: four Irish and two of dubious Italian descent, were banging hell out of her pub door.

'Alright! Alright! I'm coming,' she screamed from the bedroom window, 'I'll be there in a minute!'

Fat Sheila was, quite obviously, only speaking metaphorically.

CHAPTER 29

Tom received the call on his mobile phone some time shortly after nine. The rest of them had found somewhere in the building to get their heads down hours ago, soon after Derek and Beryl left, taking with them the not-wanting-to-go Ben to keep up the pretence, but not before Randy and Sam had braved the elements to start the back-up generator. Tom felt guilty in having the only apparent premises with electricity for as far as the eye could see, and so asked Randy to turn off as much of the outside lighting as he possibly could without putting anything too expensive at risk. Nevertheless, except for the few minutes it took to start the genny, the elephant had continued to bravely defy the storm throughout the whole of that tempest night, jumping up and down on its nest as usual, and about that he felt proud.

Still looking out of one of the small windows in the tower, the place where he had gone to think once everybody else had turned in, and without even looking to see who it was calling, Tom pressed the phone's OK button and said, 'Yes?'

It was a difficult conversation, one that wasn't easy for either of them. Jason was horrified to learn about the tragic deaths of Karl and Stefan, and dreaded having to tell Caroline the terrible news. He knew what she would demand of him, and equally he knew he couldn't do what she would want, least of all for revenge. She had been through a shed load of minders in her time, finding faults with all of them and demanding they were sacked. They had all been too interfering, too imposing, too invasive, too this, too that, or too something or the other until those two came along. With them something immediately gelled. He never understood why, but they could do no wrong. She thought the world of them, they were almost like brothers to her, yet they were more invasive and more on the ball than any of the others. Caroline was going to be devastated, and he prayed she wouldn't run off and try to seek revenge on her own.

What he should tell Mary was a problem for him too. He didn't want to lie to her, but he wondered: how do you tell someone, a person you care for, and feel for, that her son is in what is tantamount to a war zone? Or that he'd only escaped death by the skin of his teeth the previous day, and that the people they were up against were no longer out to persuade them to pay the protection money - now they actually wanted him and several of his friends dead? She would immediately want to rush to him, to try to help him as any decent mother would, but he didn't want that to happen. Was he being selfish - or simply being sensible? Maybe both, he considered - but how could stop her if she was determined?

In the back of his mind Jason knew what he must do. No matter how much Caroline, Tom, or any of their friends, or the people of that God-forsaken resort objected, he would have to notify the authorities so the place could be properly cleaned up and policed. He knew just the right person to have a word with to get that into action, and fast, although first he would need to get Tom and those who were closest to him out of there. But then, there was that cache of arms now stowed in the club. That would have to be moved, to be got rid of, and before any investigation started otherwise it could easily incriminate some of those at the Elephant's Nest - especially Tom.

Mary wouldn't thank him if through his actions her son was imprisoned for being thought a terrorist, and that couldn't be ruled out. Who could foretell what conclusions might be arrived at by any investigatory team? It could all go horribly wrong. Some kind of a clean up was definitely called for *before* the authorities carried out their cleaning up.

The deeply concerned billionaire was about to bounce some of his thoughts off Tom, firstly the idea of cleaning all traces of fingerprints off the boxes and then, under the cover of darkness, throwing them off the top of one of the cliffs, when he heard a disturbance at the other end . . .

'Tom! Shit man! You's gotta come quick!' Randy burst into the tower breathless, and looking as white as a black guy can go. 'It's Doris and Rod, man! They's gone - and so's the fuckin' bombs!'

'What?'

'Yes, man. I's got up early to make everyone a morning drink, but them two wasn't in the living room where we left them to sleep last night, so I's goes looking for them. They's nowhere, man. And when I's looks in the upper circle for them case they's there, I's sees the box with the bombs is gone too!

'I's couldn't find you either, man! Not until now, so I's thought you might all have gone off together to do something without me. I's was real worried, man! Oh, man! I's was so worried!'

'I shall have to call you back, Jason.' Tom said urgently before immediately ending the call.

It was then that he realised Randy was holding him. He was trembling, and looking deeply at him, into him, and he was sure there were tears hidden behind those eyes.

Randy let go, and looking ashamed said softly, 'I's sorry, man. I's woke up and couldn't find you. It hurt, man. It hurt right here.' He tapped his stomach. 'It was like a big empty hole was there. Man, it hit me like an express train. It was the first time since we's known each other that I's not know where you is, and it frightened me. I's just don't know what I's would do if anything ever happened to you, man.'

Tom grabbed him, pulling him in tightly, intimately, and hugged him. 'Nothing's going to happen to me, you stupid thing. We've been in this together from the start, haven't we? Since that first night it's always been you and me against the world, you know that. Look at all what we've been through together. I wouldn't do anything without you, or without at least telling you what I was going to do. We're brothers, remember? In fact, sometimes I think we're a lot more than brothers.'

The deejay squeezed him back tightly and rested his head on Tom's shoulder. 'I's never had any one in the world who's cared about me 'cept you. I's never known anyone like you, man. Never, man. You's something else. You's a lot more than a brother to me. I's sorry, but you is.'

Tom didn't know why he did it, it just felt right at the time, and somehow there was a desperate need, an undeniable want to do it - he kissed Randy tenderly on the cheek which, because of the way his head was resting on his shoulder, was only inches from his mouth. He'd intended it to only be a quick peck and then to pull away, something that, pushing it, could be excused as an emotional but nevertheless a brotherly kind of love thing. However the second his lips touched the guy's skin he knew it would be impossible to pull away, and a million questions suddenly exploded in his brain - all of them demanding an answer. And although he knew that answer, he didn't want to give it.

Randy was surprised, more shocked by the kiss, and waited for it to end. He knew he didn't want it to end. It felt like nothing he had ever experienced before and he craved more of it. It felt so good, so natural, and as if it was so long overdue. He wanted to turn his head and to kiss him back, but he was frightened. There was something somewhere in the back of his mind suggesting Tom might only be doing what he thought a good brother should be doing in the circumstances. It might only be his way of trying to reassure him how important he was to him - as a brother. But for whatever reason it was happening he knew he liked it, and that he would never forget it for as long as he lived. He prayed for Tom to keep on doing it; for it to never end – not ever. It was magical. It was the best day of his life. The best thing of his life. It was beyond anything of which he could ever have dreamed.

For Tom, suddenly there was no other world around him, there was absolutely nothing anywhere of importance anymore, nothing at all apart from what he was now holding - and having hold of it at last, he didn't want to lose it. It was too precious to be lost. It was the most precious thing in the world. Slowly, he licked his tongue up the black guy's face, up until it met with his ear where he allowed it to tease the inside of it for a while until he nudged his face down a little in order to nibble tenderly at guy's earlobe for a few moments before he softly whispered, 'I love you, Randy. Hell! You've made me say it now!'

Randy pulled his head away and spun around to look Tom in the eyes. He was more than half-expecting him to be grinning back at him; laughing; winding him up. He was ready to feel embarrassed, foolish for going along with it, and wondering what on earth he could say, when he saw Tom's face. He wasn't grinning at him or laughing, he was serious, and his eyes were deadly serious. They were frightened, yet they were asking, inviting, and pleading - and were everything that he wanted. For a split second they hesitated, staring at each other to be sure, to be absolutely certain that there was no mistake, and then slowly, very slowly, they pulled in tighter to each other until their lips met full on.

Their passionate moment would probably have gone the full ten rounds, but for Graham appearing at the door. 'Oh, my God!' he exclaimed loudly, unable to help himself.

The passionately interlocked pair jumped back from each other at the outburst to see Graham standing in the doorway. It appeared the lad had lost the ability to close his mouth, and was completely baffled as to what he should do next.

Unashamedly, Tom pulled Randy back in close to him. Hugging the deejay tightly, he informed the intruder, 'No, Graham, he's not your God. You already have one. This one is my God!'

'Oh, right. Yes. I meant . . . Yes, I know . . . I mean . . . I didn't mean . . . I didn't know . . .' he spluttered.

'No, we didn't know, either,' Tom said. 'Now, did you want something?'

'Randy told us we ought to get up straightaway. That something important had happened. Er . . . We're all up now.'

'I's didn't tell them what was wrong yet,' Randy whispered across to Tom, 'in case they turned up, or I's find them.'

'Right, well we'll see you in the kitchen in a few minutes. Make us all a coffee, and make sure Sam's there.'

'Okay,' the lad replied, and then flew off down the stairs at the speed of light. Oh, boy! Did he have news for the other two!

The moment the lad disappeared from sight, Tom turned to Randy and after giving him another kiss, it was only a peck this time, he joked, 'I guess that's what they call: "coming out of the closet", isn't it?'

Randy couldn't hold back his emotions. 'Oh, man, I's so happy! I's always known I's was gay, deep down inside I's did, but I's would never admit it, not to myself. Not to anyone. I's didn't want to be that way, so I's fought it, I's never had nothing to do with it.

'And then one day you turned up here and I's could have died. Oh, man. You made me hurt so much inside. I's loves you from the first time I's sees you, but I's could never let you know. You's might have been upset and I's wouldn't have seen so much of you.'

'Me too. I've been exactly the same. I've loved you too right from that first time we met, and like you I've fought it, denied it, and done everything possible for it not to show. I've refused to believe I was gay too, even going with Denise to prove it, but all the time I knew I was, deep down I did, because I couldn't stop thinking of you. I couldn't get you out of my mind. In the end you were too much. Too much to deny. Too much to let go, and to miss.

'That kiss just now, the first one, I had to do it. I just had to. You could have killed me for doing it and it wouldn't have mattered. Not one bit. It would still have been worth it because I love you so much. I didn't have the slightest idea that you might feel the same way. I mean . . . I . . . Oh, God! Randy, I do love you so much!'

They grabbed hold of each other, and the two of them stood there hugging tightly for several minutes, relishing the moment, hugging and holding, both happy beyond belief, and both with tears flooding in their eyes. Tears of relief, and of happiness.

Finally it was Tom who broke away, and said, 'Come on, we have the rest of our lives together for all this if you want, and I desperately hope you do. But for now we have to go down and face the others. And don't you go worrying any more about Doris and Rod, they won't be blowing themselves up, I promise you.'

'Oh, man. Of course I's does. I's wants nothing else. And I's the happiest little bunny ever. I's really is. But Doris and Rod, they's mad, man. They will blow themselves up for sure. They's going to get killed.'

'No they won't, there's something I've got to tell you. You were all asleep earlier, and I didn't want to wake any of you. We all had a hell of a day yesterday and you deserved the rest. It would have been pointless waking you, anyway. It wouldn't have changed anything. You see, up here, on my own and with no distractions, I thought of something . . .'

272

CHAPTER 30

The four Irishmen stared down at the line of wrecked roofs that led along to the burnt out remains of Dorothy's. All around them they could see the devastation caused by the overnight storm. Many streets had been affected, there were numerous roofs with gaping holes, and looking up to the cliffs and the hills behind them they could see caravan after caravan turned over, mangled and wrecked, and not one tent left to be seen anywhere. Below them, in the back alley, Don and Paul scurried around looking for clues.

'I'll be thinking Seathorpe won't be open for business for a good few months,' remarked Mickey. 'No, not at all, at all, at all.'

'Fuck Seathorpe!' Patrick shouted at him, and then regretted it as his hangover protested by thumping him inside his head. 'I just want to know where all our stuff has gone! It was here yesterday, and now it isn't! It can't just vanish into thin air! But it fucking has!'

'Ah, I wouldn't be listening to that old Mother O'Shea,' Terry advised him, 'the only way that stuff could have left 'ere is through the pub, and she be knowing about it.'

'I heard that! Are you calling me a fucking liar?' Sheila screamed at him from the open window, through which, although attempting it, she had no hope of passing. 'Well, fuck you!' And with that she pulled the window closed as much as it would allow, and then left the attic room, locking the door behind her.

'Ah, by Jesus!' Terry moaned, struggling the window open again for them to all climb back through.

All back inside, they soon discovered the locked door and shouted for Sheila to open it. Sheila chose to ignore them, and so in desperation Patrick's three brothers emptied their guns into the door around the lock. The door immediately fell open inwards, swiftly followed by Sheila's massive form. She lay there at their feet holding her enormous blood-soaked stomach, looking back up them with disbelief, and then gurgled, choking momentarily on a mouthful of blood, before her eyes glazed and she was gone forever; gone to wherever all dead Fat Sheilas go.

'Oh, Mother of God!' Patrick cried out. 'What else? What else? What else? What else can go wrong? Yesterday we had it all. We'd destroyed the opposition, and the town was ours, it was all ours - but now look at it! Overnight the town has been wrecked, it'll be months before it recovers, our store of arms has mysteriously disappeared, and now to cap it all you've gone and killed our Sheila! I don't believe it! How could it all go so wrong?'

From the rooftop outside the window, from where he had returned for some fresh air, Andrew shouted back at them. 'It'll be a lot to do with the fairies, I be thinkin'. Yer ought to come and get an eyeful this little lot afore yer start yer crying.'

Led by Patrick they scrambled back through the window onto the rooftop and gazed down to where Andrew was looking. Two men could be seen, although that might have been debatable considering the manner in which the nearest one was screaming abuse at the other one as they were struggling down the street trying to carry a box between them. A familiar looking box.

'Ain't that the two poofs who own Dorothy's, and with one of our boxes?' Andrew enquired. 'They don't be looking anywhere near as dead as your Sheila does, that's for sure!'

'What?' Patrick was dumbfounded. How? His head hurt and he could hardly think, but he knew that no-one, positively no-one, could have survived the blast that brought down Dorothy's, and yet equally he knew those two, along with others, were definitely inside that building. The place had been surrounded. No-one had got out. So how?

'Ah, by Jesus! Don't no fucker die in this town for long? We shot that Phil fella stone dead. We riddled him with bullets, and the place burnt down on top of him, but everybody keeps telling us he's still alive. And now these two? After blowing 'em sky high? I'll be betting none of 'em is dead if those two ain't. Just what yer gotta do to kill some fucker in this 'ere town?' Terry asked despairingly.

Dazed, and with no answer to Terry's question, Patrick was only able to say, or more accurately to almost sigh, 'Go and get them. Bring them inside.'

Once his brothers had left, he knelt down and closed Sheila's eyes. Not being one to say anything over a dead body, he did this time think the words. He knew she of all people wouldn't have betrayed them; he knew her better than his brothers. With a mournful sigh and a last look back over his shoulder, he left her and went down to the bar.

The two captives were huddled together on the bench seat under the window, with the box being left in the middle of the room in front of them. Doris was panicking, frightened, and shaking madly, but Rod was only nervous because of the guns that were aimed at them. Had it not been for those he would have fought back, and been a formidable opponent.

Striding up to Rod, Patrick withdrew his gun from its shoulder holster and, cocking it, pushed the barrel squarely into the centre of the big man's forehead before maliciously looking across at Doris and asking, 'Where's the other boxes?'

She just continued shaking, and said nothing.

'I'll give you to three. One . . . Two . . .'

'They're in the Ellie!' she screamed.

Doris was no hero, but she was clever. It took the Irish only a few minutes to learn everything they thought they needed to know from her – and nothing that she thought they didn't need to know.

Terry was all for immediately rushing around to the nightclub to reclaim their boxes of guns and ammunition, and shooting everyone in there in the process. That is until Patrick reminded him that since he and his brothers had emptied their guns into the door upstairs, killing Sheila in the process, their ammunition was very limited. Tom, however, now had an arsenal, and from what they had encountered once before in the foyer of the Ellie, he would not be frightened to use it on them.

No, Patrick had a better plan. They had hostages, didn't they? They had bargaining power. They could get their boxes back with no risk to themselves at all. Once they had them back - well, that's when they could kill Tom and his colleagues.

With a smile on his face, the plan forming more and more to their advantage every time he went over it in his mind, Patrick walked across to the phone behind the bar and dialled the nightclub's number. The call wasn't answered, but that was something he had expected. He waited for the answerphone to kick in.

'You've got the Elephant's Nest,' a recorded voice informed him. 'I'm sorry, we can't answer the phone right now, but if you leave your name and number, we shall get back to you as soon as possible. Please leave a message after the tone. . . . Beep!'

'This is a message for Tom,' Patrick said. 'You have some boxes of ours, and we've got two of your friends. We need to trade. Ring me on 254582 as soon as you get this message.' He nodded across to Mickey who at that appropriate moment twisted the drag queen's ear, making her scream out loudly in her own inimitable way, before replacing the receiver. 'And now we wait,' he told them.

It was a long wait; more than an hour. Doubts were beginning to creep into Patrick's mind. What if they didn't check the answerphone? But with a little more thinking, he dismissed them. Even if they didn't check it, he realised someone would at some point. The staff would be turning up at sometime during the day, and even if nobody else bothered, that Beryl certainly wouldn't miss checking it. It was annoying, but they just had to wait.

Waiting around was not one of his brothers' strongest points. As time passed they became more and more irritable. Terry and Andrew had already started knocking back copious amounts of the freely available nectar, when finally the phone rang.

'Hello?' It was Tom, and his voice couldn't conceal his anxiety. He was obviously nervous.

'I've got your two friends here, Doris and Rod, and they tell me our boxes are stacked up in the Ellie. We haven't harmed them, and we won't – that's providing you do as your told.'

'How do I know that? You might have already killed them. Can I speak to them?'

Patrick was annoyed, but realised it was a reasonable request in the circumstances and signalled for Doris to come and speak on the phone.

'Tom! Tom!' Doris squealed. 'Please give them what they want! Please! I know they'll kill us if you don't do as . . .'

Grabbing the phone off her, and pushing her back towards Terry, the Irishman said, 'There! They are alive! Now, are we going to trade?'

'What do you want me to do?'

CHAPTER 31

It was midday. As arranged the boxes were stacked neatly in front of the stage, and the Stage Door was unlocked. The cleaners had been sent home, and all the staff telephoned and told not to report to work today, whilst on the front doors a prominent sign proclaimed the nightclub was closed until further notice.

Everything was as Tom had been instructed. However although they were being held over a barrel, he had managed to negotiate a small concession to Patrick's demands. Having pointed out to the man that there was no insurance against them merely coming into the building and shooting everybody dead, he did convince him to allow two of his group, saying it would be himself and Randy, to have use of a gun each from one of the boxes. That would ensure a more equal stand-off where, with a little respect on both sides, a successful trade could be carried out.

Tom and Randy, with the three lads, stood in a straight line across the dance floor a good ten feet back from the boxes and waited. The Irish were late, but Tom guessed that was intentional and in order to make them feel more nervous. At five-past twelve the four Irishmen, each with a gun ready in their hands, filed in through the door next to the stage, safely hidden behind the gagged and hands-bound Doris and Rod, with Don and Paul arriving behind them a minute or so later. They formed a straight line across the other side of the boxes, with the guns of Terry and Andrew firmly pushed into each captive's head.

'What now?' Tom asked nervously. The gun in his hand was pointing outwards at Patrick, and it was noticeably shaking.

'We all lower our guns before someone has an accident.' Patrick quickly suggested, lowering his gun at the same time.

Slowly, watching each other, everybody likewise lowered their guns, but kept them handy by their sides.

'Don and Paul will load the boxes into the car and deliver them somewhere. It will take them several trips, we've only got a car, so meanwhile the rest of us will wait here and not do anything silly. Once they've delivered all the boxes, these two will walk slowly towards you as we make our way out through the door. The deal will be done.'

'Okay,' said Tom.

'What's to stop you shooting them in the back as you goes through the door, man?' Randy sensibly asked.

Behind her gag, there was still no mistaking Doris' squeal of terror.

'Ah, by Jesus!' Terry was heard to swear.

'All right!' Patrick snapped. 'Before we go they can climb up on the stage, where we can't get at them.'

It was little more than fifteen minutes, but it had seemed like hours, before the two Italians returned from their last box-moving run. Not a word was spoken between the opposing sides during that time. Sam, Graham, and Mike, like mice in a field with an owl circling overhead, didn't flinch a muscle. They stood motionless, like statues, without even a change of facial expression between them.

Randy, often the pessimist, whilst suffering the wait couldn't stop thinking back to the wonderful time in the attic that morning. The time when he and Tom had discovered truly how much they meant to each other. On the one hand he was happy, more happier than he had been at any other time in his struggle through life, but on the other hand he was fraught with fear. He remembered back to his earlier days, to his childhood and the so many times before that life had dealt him an evil blow. He was frightened, plagued by the fear that he had only been given something in order for it to be cruelly taken away from him, and with that premise he was more than half-expecting the trade-off to go wrong - for Tom, or for him, or perhaps for both of them, to be killed before there was any chance of them enjoying all that love and happiness that was there waiting.

The deejay had never properly thought of his future before, or ever made plans for it. Convinced life would offer him little of value he only lived for today, and he would get through that with a grin, and a laugh, and a forced 'fuck you' attitude. But now, for the first time in his life there was a promise of a future, of a time to be planned for, and to be looked forward to, and to be enjoyed. It was all there, and it was his - but for how long? His stomach kept feeling empty, a hurting void as if the worst had already happened, and to reassure himself it hadn't he frequently stole sideways glances at his new-found lover and would move, swaying slightly, so their bare arms touched and he could feel all the fire that was Tom.

That fire Randy yearned was equally as happy, but without all those fears. Tom also took life as it came, and he too would lead his life on a day to day basis, but that was only through a habit forced on him by his family's unfortunate financial predicament in the not too distant past. Yes, there were times when, like Randy, he couldn't see anything for him in the future, but the difference was he always expected better times to come - they were anticipated, and he was quite happy to wait for them.

So whilst Tom too spent the time waiting in deep thought, he wasn't blaming life for ever being cruel to him. Life was life, and something like happiness depended a lot on what you did with what you were given – and what he had now been given with Randy was still amazing him. It was so incredible. He knew the guy had been out with girls before, and had frequently bedded girls – there was Caroline as proof. So the fact that he was gay came as a total surprise. There was no way he would ever have suspected. How could he? By all accounts Randy had a very long line of female conquests - or had he?

Randy had boasted about his conquests when they first met, people do boast, but how many did he actually know of apart from Caroline? There were none, he realised. The guy never went out, and that is hardly the lifestyle of a womaniser! There was only the one time it happened, and that was instigated by Caroline. She talked of the previous year and of the romp in the back of the car with him, but on that night he was apparently drunk and high on drugs. So much so that he could hardly remember it. And it was the same this year too.

Neither of those conquests were Randy's, they were most definitely Caroline's, and both times they were of someone debilitated by drink and drugs. Someone incapable of saying no, and who having got into that situation wouldn't anyway for the fear of not appearing normal. Like himself, Randy had been forcing himself to live as the world expected him to, and that meant living a lie.

The million questions stacked in Tom's mind waiting answers had fallen like nine-pins. He remembered the night at the Inferno, the time when he went to get their drinks, and how whilst waiting to be served he had watched as Caroline moved in on Randy; exciting him with all her groping. He didn't want to admit it to himself, not until today, that getting off with Denise was only to prove himself a man. It was what men did; what was expected. It was what they were brought up to believe was their role. So he too had been living his lie that night. More than that, he had been lying to himself!

Few young men enjoy the stigma of being a virgin, and so on seeing Randy getting off with Caroline, and with the added benefit of alcohol, he had felt he should push his luck with Denise – it would be expected - and surprisingly it had happened. It had been fun, she was a nice girl, and the sex was pleasurable. But, since kissing Randy, he now realised that would have only been because there was no other experience for comparison at the time. If it came down to measuring anything, Denise couldn't even appear on the same scale as Randy. Everything about him was superior to her; immeasurably so. Would he have pushed it so much with her, to get as far sex, without the alcohol? Or without Caroline moving in on Randy? He knew the answer.

He was gay – he was totally gay, and inside him he had always known it. He may never have followed it through with anyone before, he may have always denied it, and pushed it away, refusing to accept it, but there had been too many strange fascinations that had worried him going right back to his schooldays for it not to be true, with the most recent, before Randy, being Kenny the postman back in Brisham. What was all that about?

Kenny was attractive, but he was ultra-straight. He knew that – he went to school with the guy. Now married with three kids, he'd made his girlfriend pregnant whilst still at school – at fourteen – stuck with her and knocked out two more. There was no real attraction there for him, no love, no want of love, no real yearning, but the fascination and the morning teases of getting the mail in his undies had been the fodder for many a gratifying fantasy!

There had been several other teases too, all similar with none of them serious or with anybody he felt desperate about, and he had always passed them off in his mind as merely having a joke because he kept convincing himself he was straight.

But with Randy it was different. Entirely different. Of all of them, none had ever conquered his determination that he was straight, or managed to expose the real truth, the real him, except for Randy. He, of all of them, could not be denied. He was everything. If God ever created anyone better, then He must have kept them for Himself. There *was* no better person than Randy, and now he was actually *his* lover, and it was all so absolutely, fantastically, incredibly, mind-blowingly wonderful!

Tom remembered that first meeting when, surprised, Randy jumped and turned around and they saw each other for the first time, their palms touching in that funny handshake, and the chummy hug that followed. He had known it then, simply melting on seeing the guy, and finding his touch ecstatic; pure electricity. Hadn't he wished and hoped and prayed, and then afterwards forced himself not to think about it by fighting with himself when taking Ben across the road to the rock pools?

Yes, he'd been turned on by girls in the past, but he was young, and that would only have been his hormones working. By doing their thing they had confused him; led him to believe that perhaps he could be straight. Hormones will do anything for relief. Sex is only a relief. Denise had proved that to him.

Okay, he had done it with her, and thought it was good at the time, and yes, the equipment had worked well for him, it was being satisfied, but throughout it all his mind had been telling him something was lacking. It was not right. Not for him. It had a completely unnatural feel to it. He'd hit the board, three treble twenties, but nothing had shouted out: one-hundred-and-eighty! He may have been in bed with her and physically acting out all the emotions, but his mind was trying to be elsewhere; imagining another. Who had he been thinking about, and fantasising over in his mind? Who did he always think about? Since he first met the guy, Randy had been the fantasy for every single self-gratification under the bedcovers or in the shower – and at his age there had been plenty of them. So why had he stupidly tried to pretend, to convince himself, that he was straight? Was being gay that bad? Or just the fear of it?

Randy was the best, the biggest and strongest attraction of his lifetime, the only real one, that he now knew for sure! He was the one he truly wanted, the one waited so long for, and the one for whom he ached. Even before knowing him he was the one, the imagination with neither face nor form that spurred him on. And now he was actually there! He existed, and he was his to love, and to be loved by. A love that only yesterday seemed unattainable, a million miles away, was really only three words away from him all the time, and now he had said those three words, and accepted them. I am gay.

Those few tender moments with Randy had shown him an undeniable truth. Sex you can do with anyone when the sap is rising, but love - love is only possible with someone you do love, and whoever that may be isn't exactly down to choice.

That first kiss he had given Randy had been unavoidable. Totally. With him so close, touching, holding him, there was no way he could have stopped himself from doing it. Then, when his lips had actually touched that cheek, felt the warmth of it, and the life of it for the first time, there had been an ecstasy, an experience the likes of which nothing before had ever come close. There had been no alcohol or drugs to enhance his feelings, yet that one kiss remained solidly as the most pleasurable experience of his lifetime, and now he positively ached for more. If that was being gay, and it obviously was, then from now on he would be openly and undeniably gay to the world – because it was bloody great!

With hindsight Tom realised how stupid it was for either of them not to realise it was not only themself in denial. They spent all their spare time together, they did everything together, they were never apart, and neither of them ever questioned it. It was as they both wanted it to be. They had been lovers from first sight with a love so pure, so strong and meaningful, it was able to survive without acknowledgement, or sex – and it had done so, very successfully, during all the time each had hidden his own truth in case it should be discovered by the other and affect their closeness.

No wonder Randy was upset that morning, and fearful when he couldn't be found. Wouldn't he have felt exactly the same? He knew he would, and now it hurt him deeply to even imagine his life without the wonderful guy. He desperately needed to tell him that, and he needed to tell him now, so despite the tenseness of their situation he turned his head to smile and wink at his partner, with eyes that said it for him.

'We's got so much to catch up on, man.' Randy returned in a whisper. 'I's loves you billions.'

Tom was going to come back with 'trillions', when they were interrupted by the return of Don and Paul signalling the task of re-locating the boxes was complete. Now, he told himself, if it's going to get at all hairy, it will be anytime soon.

Patrick slowly walked over to Doris and Rod and nodded for them to clamber up onto the stage. Leaning over on it, and by gaining purchase with her elbows, Doris was able to pull herself up and roll over onto the stage with a little effort, but nothing requiring that much agility was possible for Rod whose attempts were pitiful.

'Give him a shove up.' Patrick ordered the two Italians.

It required a lot of effort, for Rod was a big man, and as he did at last manage the ascent, it was a big and noisy load of gaseous air that he expelled into the heaving-him-up guy's faces. They leapt backwards, Terry blasphemed again, and the first movement from the three lads became apparent with the uncontrollable snigger from Sam.

'Right! The deal is done.' Patrick told Tom. 'We will back out that door, and you will do nothing. You won't move until after we're gone.'

'You have my word,' Tom replied.

With that the gang slowly backed out through the doorway, and were gone.

Randy carefully placed his gun on the floor and straightaway turned to openly kiss and embrace his partner, who likewise eagerly responded, hugging him tightly. The deejay was relieved it was all over, and that it hadn't gone wrong as he had feared it might. The prospects of there being a future with Tom once more looked good for him. Life was wonderful.

Sam and his two mates wasted no time in leaping up onto the stage to remove Doris and Rod's gags, and then untied their hands.

Doris couldn't resist immediately proclaiming from the front of the stage, with all the theatrical gestures she could muster, 'Wasn't I right? Wasn't I right? Didn't I say those two are, and that they're made for each other?' Turning to Tom and Randy, she went on, 'Congratulations, you daft pair of buggers! It's lovely to see you've got it together and come out at last! Did you know someone's actually been running a book on when you two would get it together?'

Tom and Randy both blushed, and held hands, grinning.

'Now what?' Sam asked, looking down from the stage at Tom; his two friends aside him looking equally as inquisitive.

'We wait,' Tom said.

'We wait? Wait for what?'

'You'll see!'

'Eh?'

'We've got time. How about you three make us all a coffee? I think we need one. The hot water thingy in the cafeteria is bubbling, it won't take you moment. Oh, and make an extra one with no sugar.'

'Sure,' Sam replied, 'but I wish I knew what was going on. Aren't you frightened that now they've got those boxes back they'll try to blow us all up with one of those bombs? They may have planted one somewhere here already. Shouldn't we get out of here?'

'Try to blow us up?' Tom grinned. 'I'm counting on it! But I hope they don't do it too soon! That would be annoying!'

'What?'

'Make the coffee, and don't forget that extra one.'

Puzzled, the three lads soon produced a coffee for everyone.

'Whose is this one?' Sam asked, holding the extra cup.

'That'll probably be mine, I guess,' the voice of the man who was coming in from the Stage Door passageway said.

'Dave?' the three lads turned and exclaimed in unison.

'You were right, Tom.' Dave said. 'I watched them being carried inside, and then I toddled around here and waited until I saw the gang depart, driving away in the direction of where the boxes are stored.'

'Will somebody please tell me what is going on?' Sam pleaded.

Tom grinned and signalled for everyone to follow him. Carefully carrying their cups of coffee, the group filed along the passageway and out through the Stage Door until into the centre of the car park.

'About now, do you think?' Tom asked Rod.

'Any second now, I should think,' Rod replied.

Tom lifted his finger for the lads to be quiet, and they all waited in silence. The explosion didn't rock the building, it was too far away to do that, but the 'thud' was unmistakeable.

Tom, Randy, Doris, Rod, and even Dave, put their cups on the ground and began to dance about each other with glee, whooping and cheering like infants at play.

The three lads could not believe their eyes. What the hell was happening here? What were they on? Undoubtedly they had gone mad! Completely stark, raving, bonkers!

'Oh, Randy,' Tom finally said, the tears in his eyes were for joy. 'Will you put them out their misery, please. I know I should wet myself if I tried.'

Randy gathered them into a circle, and heads forward they listened attentively whilst he explained, 'Once upon a time there was a very nasty crook man who, with his evil brothers, they's takes over a town. Man, they's real rotten and nobody did like them, but then one day they makes everybody happy.'

'Eh? How?'

'They's so evil that they blows themselves up for everybody.'

'Patrick's quite an expert when it comes to explosives, so how would he manage to do that?' Sam asked, still not understanding any of it.

'Oh, my chickadees,' Doris interrupted, the tears of mirth still running down her face, 'it's because we swapped-over the little colour stickers on the radio controls for the two bombs that were left. You just heard one of those bombs go off – the one that was still in Mother O'Shea's place.

'They would have gone back there to detonate the bomb that they will have planted somewhere here in the Ellie, before spending the rest of the day celebrating and getting drunk. But because of the swap they've let off the bomb they were sitting on, instead of the one that's here!'

'Oh! My, that was clever!' Sam exclaimed, and then after a moment's thought, 'But suppose they had brought both bombs round here, that wouldn't have been so clever, would it?'

'They could only use one bomb,' Tom explained. 'We sabotaged the other radio control so it couldn't work. Patrick wouldn't have brought a bomb all the way over here unless he knew that the handset for it would switch on and go into prime mode. He would have tested them both before coming here, and with only one working, it was obvious he would only bring the one bomb – the one that can't go off because the controller is blown, but nevertheless the one he thought would explode with the working handset.'

'Phew! Thankfully, it looks like you thought of everything.'

'Yes, except for where they would hide the bomb in here. The Italian two, who if you remember came in after the others, would have spent that time in hiding it somewhere. They weren't too far behind the others, so my guess is it's somewhere like the first landing, or at a push the quiet bar.'

'But what was to stop them letting off the bomb as soon as they'd gone out the door?' Graham had been thinking. 'It might have blown up Mother O'Shea's place instead of here, but it wouldn't have got rid of the Irish, would it?'

'And how did you know they were going to attempt to bomb you, anyway?' Mike asked. 'They may have just left and picked us off one by one at some other time.'

'Well, that much I'll admit was a bit of a gamble,' Tom confessed, 'but not much of one. You only have to look at Seathorpe today to realise it would take months for it to return to how it was before last night's thunderstorm - probably many months. There's a lot of work to be done, expensive work, and I'll bet many traders have let their insurances lapse in order to pay their dues to the gang whilst trying to maintain a reasonable lifestyle. Many, perhaps most, will have lost everything. They will have no hope of picking themselves up, or of starting all over again. Even here, only the building is insured, and there's the third party liability cover, of course – but nothing material inside is insured.

'Patrick, and the rest of them, would have realised it was all over the minute they hit the streets this morning. There's no more money to be made out of Seathorpe. There's nothing at all left for them to stay here for – except revenge. They would have wanted the satisfaction of killing all those who stood against them, and as soon as possible, before running, I'm guessing now, back to Ireland. As long as we were dead, then they could go home and hold their heads up high. So bombing us was pretty much a certainty after Tom and Doris did their street cabaret act, ensuring they were caught and the bombs landed up back in the gang's hands. We must never forget their braveness, for nobody else but them would have been credible enough to have pulled it off so successfully.

'As to why they didn't just go out the door and press the button, well, that's down to a lot of reasons. Firstly, if a wall were come down like it did at Dorothy's, and were it to be the back one here, they would have risked being killed themselves – our walls are twice the height of Dorothy's. Secondly, if the side wall fell, then they wouldn't be able to get out of the car park. But thirdly, and most importantly, they would have noticed, as I did this morning from the tower window, those men working, sieving through the debris of Dorothy's club and milling around over there, they are not all local guys. There's a big army truck parked up there and two army landrovers, so without doubt that'll be the bomb squad – and if they are here then you can bet everybody else will be here, including the proper police. There will be reporters out there from all the national newspapers who follow the bomb squads everywhere they go and, if they are not here already, the television crews will be arriving soon.

'Someone has blown the whistle, it's all over, and whoever has done it will make a fortune from selling their story. So no, Patrick wouldn't have pushed that button until he was safely back inside Mother O'Shea's. The last thing he would risk is being stopped in the immediate vicinity of another explosion.

'Really, it was all quite elementary. Don't you agree, Watson?' He grinned at Randy, who teasingly thumped his arm.

CHAPTER 32

It was an hour later, a respectable amount of time to leave it they thought, before all those at the Elephant's Nest that afternoon strolled along the front to the second street and then, turning right into it, followed it up to the corner where once stood Mother O'Shea's but now little more than a pile of rubble. The street was cordoned off at the junction, and a crowd were pushing against the tapes trying to see as much as they could of the disaster.

As Tom and his group arrived behind the crowd it started to part, and to make a way through for them to the front. People murmured, and jostled each other, and said things like, 'Look, they're still alive!' and, 'Look who's here. It's incredible, they are not dead, after all!' There were many happy faces that greeted them that day.

Nobody had any idea what had happened to the building in front of them, except that it had blown up, and with people inside. Bodies, and bits of bodies, were being brought out. But once Tom and the rest of the committee were seen to be alive, and were seen to have come there to watch, then everybody guessed who was responsible, and guessed whose bodies were coming out of the building.

'How many bodies have they found?' Tom asked George, as the man jostled his way through the crowd towards them to shake all their hands.

'Rumour is they think they've got six from inside,' he replied, 'when they put all the bits together. There's lots of bits that have come out of there – it's been a real messy job for those poor army blokes. And then there was Fat Sheila – they had to climb up to get her off the next door's roof. Apparently she was in one piece, but had been riddled with bullets. They think she's been dead a lot longer than the others.'

'Thanks,' Tom said. 'You are a mine of information. How on earth did you find all that out?'

'Oh, easy. Odd-Socks is keeping me updated. I get on alright with old Odd-Socks. Everyday I give him some milk, and a lot of the stuff I wouldn't use the next day, because I feel sorry for him. He's such a nice chap - polite and grateful, but very shrewd. Did you know it was him who alerted the press after Dorothy's was destroyed? Upset him, that did. Now he's feeding them bits of stories in return for what they know, and no doubt for a considerable sum of money as well. I said he was shrewd, didn't I? He's very well educated too. Not many know this, but he used to be the headmaster of the local school here when this was nothing more than a fishing village. He stayed behind when just about everybody else left. I must go over now and tell him that you lot are still alive. He'll be so pleased; so happy to see Doris and Rod again.'

'Right,' Tom said, to the back of George's head as the man turned and again fought with the crowd.

'Man, it's all over. It really is all over. No more threats or worries for any of us from the gang. Oh, Man!' Randy secretly squeezed Tom's leg affectionately. 'But what's we and everybody else going to do now, I's wonder?'

'Well, man. We's is going to go home,' Tom aped with a wink and a cheeky grin, as he deliberately allowed his hand to brush heavily against his lover's crotch on turning around. 'We's has lots of things to catch up on.'

Randy giggled. 'Most excellent!' he joked back.

EPILOGUE

Seathorpe prospers again today, but in a much different vein. The money from the blockbuster movie made of this story by Jason's film company, mostly taken from Tom's computer diary of events, and mostly shot on location, with the pooled resources of the business people of the town and an extremely generous anonymous donation, gave this once simple fishing village yet another chance of a successful life. This one a far more sober and upmarket one than the last.

Jason married Tom's mother little more than a year later, and they now enjoy a quieter lifestyle with him taking more of a back seat in the running of his companies. They spend a great deal of their time casually exploring different parts of the world.

Caroline is happy with her new minders, and the world still remains her oyster. She has never re-visited Seathorpe.

Sadly, Denise's mother died of her illness, but the once bargirl has since found happiness. She now lives in Florida with her boyfriend, an executive from the company that supplied the lenses for the movie. They are expecting their second child. The first, a boy, they named: Tom.

The Inferno is again solely owned by Dave, and it now operates as a prosperous and upmarket waterfront casino nightclub. Sid still works there.

Doris and Rod were adequately insured, allowing them to rebuild Dorothy's in its original and much loved theme. Graham and Mike now live and work there with them. It is as popular as ever.

Phil bought the ground off the brewery, and where once stood Mother O'Shea's, he has built a successful fun pub. He and Sam live above it and run it together. It is aptly called: Bangers!

The Elephant's Nest has become the resort's only youthful straight nightclub, and as such it is invariably full. It is still managed by Derek and Beryl, and the upstairs bar has been renamed: Sydney's, after the son they lost to alcohol poisoning.

A memorial service to John Patterson was held at the Elephant's Nest six month's after the end of this story. The venue was packed out. A plaque has been attached to the sea wall directly opposite the nightclub, aside the section of road now affectionately known locally as: Patterson's Prom.

Drugs may still be obtained quite easily in Seathorpe – you ask for Auntie, but mum's the word!

There are no protection rackets operating, and the resort once again enjoys proper policing. Summers and Jones left the police force. They were last heard of working as seasonal security personnel at a holiday camp in Bognor Regis.

Tom and Randy now live happily together near Marlborough in a large house in its own grounds where, in his twilight years, Ben enjoys the freedom. As well as the Elephant's Nest, they now own a major recording company and have become notably wealthy in their own right. Frequently to be seen visiting their many friends in Seathorpe, the two young men have not survived without encountering other adventures. However they are different stories.

Printed in the United Kingdom
by Lightning Source UK Ltd.
112464UKS00001B/130-147

9 781897 312179